# SPEARCREST KNIGHT

─── ◆ ───

*Audentes*
*Fortuna*
*Iuvat*

Copyright © 2022 by Aurora Reed

*All rights reserved.*

*No portion of this book may be reproduced, copied, distributed or adapted in any way, with the exception of certain activities permitted by applicable copyright laws, such as brief quotations in the context of a review or academic work.*

*For permission to publish, distribute or otherwise reproduce this work, please contact the author at dearest@aurorareed.com.*

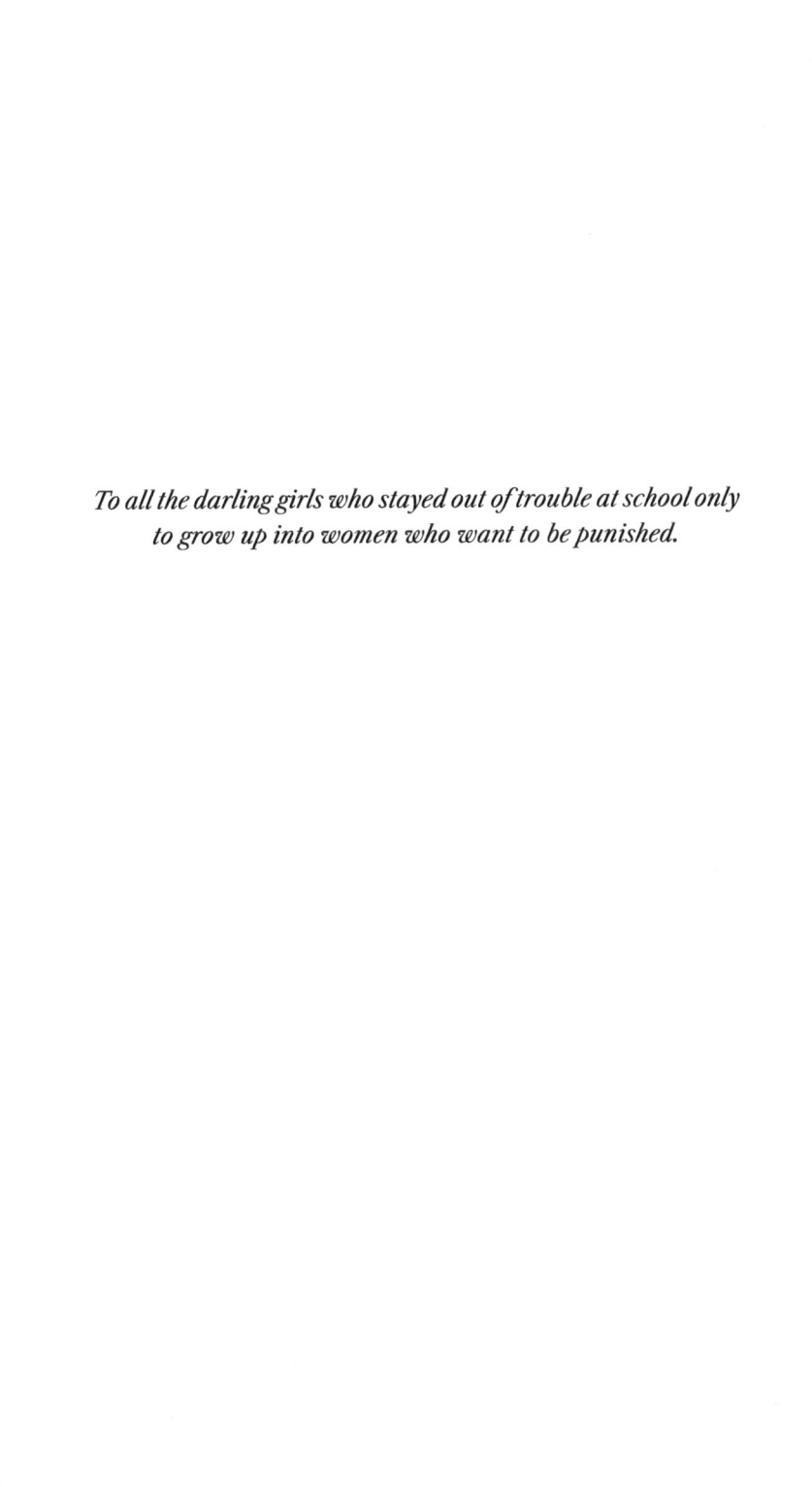

*To all the darling girls who stayed out of trouble at school only to grow up into women who want to be punished.*

# CONTENTS

| | |
|---|---|
| Playlist | X |
| Author Note | XII |
| AUTUMN | 1 |
| 1. Clipboard | 2 |
| 2. Tutoring Programme | 9 |
| 3. Illicit Shindig | 21 |
| 4. Zero Tolerance | 30 |
| 5. Bootlicking | 37 |
| 6. Freddy | 46 |
| 7. Burn | 52 |
| 8. Secret Boyfriend | 61 |
| 9. Bullet | 71 |
| 10. Capitulation | 82 |
| 11. Aggression | 91 |
| 12. Honey | 98 |
| 13. Cursed Star | 107 |
| 14. Treachery | 117 |
| 15. Deadly Serious | 124 |
| 16. Dragon | 131 |
| 17. Despicable Cinderella | 142 |

| | | |
|---|---|---|
| 18. | Cookies | 153 |
| 19. | American Dream | 165 |
| 20. | Intoxication | 174 |
| 21. | Obliteration | 182 |
| WINTER | | 191 |
| 22. | Networking | 192 |
| 23. | Coward | 201 |
| 24. | Nobody | 212 |
| 25. | Royal Subject | 219 |
| 26. | Blow for Blow | 227 |
| 27. | Scathed | 234 |
| 28. | Apology | 241 |
| 29. | Whisperer | 250 |
| 30. | Victory | 257 |
| 31. | Dirty Liar | 266 |
| 32. | Greek Tragedy | 275 |
| 33. | Persuasion | 284 |
| 34. | Interception | 296 |
| 35. | Fishnets | 308 |
| SPRING | | 319 |
| 36. | Paralysis | 320 |
| 37. | Complicated | 329 |
| 38. | Compensation | 336 |
| 39. | Wentworth | 346 |
| 40. | One Day | 354 |
| THE END | | 361 |

| | |
|---|---|
| Dear Reader | 362 |
| Further Reading | 363 |
| Annotation & Study Guide | 364 |
| Acknowledgements | 366 |
| Also By Aurora Reed | 367 |
| About Aurora | 370 |

# PLAYLIST

**You're Mine** - Phantogram
**Animal** - Caroline Rose
**Journal of Ardency** - Class Actress
**Hurts Like Hell** - Fleurie
**So Good** - Warpaint
**Mad About You** – Hooverphonic
**Daft Pretty Boys** – Bad Suns
**Blue Obsession** – Geographer
**Fight or Flight Club** – Madge
**Bending Back** – Art School Girlfriend
**Fall In Love** – Phantogram
**Golden Boy** – Bryce Fox
**American Money** – BØRNS
**Want You So Bad** – The Vaccines
**Swoon** – Beach Weather

**The Love Club** – Lorde
**Affection** – BETWEEN FRIENDS
**striptease** – carwash
**Guilty Pleasures** – Georgi Kay
**Mistakes Like This** – Prelow
**Electric Love** – BØRNS
**The Fool You Need** – Son Lux
**iloveyou** – BETWEEN FRIENDS

# Author Note

Dear reader,

This book takes place at the fictional private boarding school **Spearcrest Academy** and is set in the **United Kingdom**.

Speacrest Academy is a **High School and Sixth Form**, so students are aged **12** to **18**. If you are a US reader, I've included a little comparison guide of US and UK school years for reference.

**UK High School (also known as Lower School) Years**
**Year 7** = 6th Grade
**Year 8** = 7th Grade
**Year 9** = 8th Grade
**Year 10** = 9th Grade (Freshman Year)
**Year 11** = 10th Grade (Sophomore Year)

**UK Sixth Form/College (also known as Upper School) Years**
**Year 12** (Lower Sixth) = 11th Grade (Junior Year)
**Year 13** (Upper Sixth) = 12th Grade (Senior Year)

**The main characters in Spearcrest Knight are all in <u>UK Year 13 (US Senior Year)</u> and <u>18 years of age</u>.**

I hope this guide makes sense and helps you during your time within the hallowed halls of Spearcrest Academy.

# AUTUMN

*"This is the very ecstasy of love.
Whose violent property foredoes itself,
And leads the will to desperate undertakings."*

**Hamlet**, William Shakespeare

# 1

# CLIPBOARD

## Sophie

I STAND OUTSIDE THE assembly hall and take a long, deep breath. The smell of fresh-cut grass and honeysuckle fills my lungs. It's the first day of the autumn term, but it still smells like summer.

This is my last year at Spearcrest. Even though I started here halfway through high school, it still feels as if I've spent a lifetime here. When my parents got jobs in the admin team and managed to get me a place here, they'd considered it a blessing. Never would I otherwise have had the opportunity to attend one of the most prestigious academic institutions in Europe. Never would I have been able to rub elbows with the sons and daughters of millionaires and aristocrats.

Except it hasn't turned out to be quite the dream I was sold. The campus is something straight out of a fairy tale, the education is world-class, the teachers exceptional.

Everything else... not so much.

Still. This is my last year.

I've made it this far—the finishing line is finally in sight. All I have to do now is keep my head down, focus on my exams and university applications, and then I'm free.

Free to leave Spearcrest, get as far away as possible from its claustrophobic world of elitism, nepotism and narcissism.

Loud noises interrupt my thoughts and I close my eyes, bracing myself for impact.

Walking up the path towards the assembly hall with their shirts untucked and their carefully curated nonchalance are the so-called Young Kings of Spearcrest. Luca Fletcher-Lowe, Iakov Kavinski, Séverin Montcroix, Zachary Blackwood and Evan Knight.

Combined, their five families are wealthier than the rest of England put together. And that's something they don't let you forget. Their straight postures and easy manners are only this relaxed because they know they'll never have to face consequences for anything they do as long as they live. Their sleeves are only rolled back to show off their obscenely expensive watches.

Every careless little thing they do is calculated to project wealth and power.

I glance at the tower clock. They're fifteen minutes late to assembly. Although I make a quick note of it, I say nothing as they approach. I might be a prefect, and I might hate the way they think rules don't apply to them, but I'm not about to draw their attention or their displeasure.

I know better.

Instead, I keep my head down, eyes glued to the clipboard propped against my legs. I stand utterly still, like a trapped rabbit playing dead while it waits for prowling wolves to pass it by.

If only things were that easy.

"Mr Fletcher-Lowe!" roars a stony voice from behind my shoulder. "Mr Kavinski, Mr Montcroix, Mr Blackwood and Mr Knight!"

Shit. I push myself back against the red brick wall, hoping and praying that the headmaster, Mr Ambrose, doesn't drag me into this skirmish.

"This is the first assembly of your final year here upon the hallowed grounds of Spearcrest. Is this how you want to begin such an important year?"

The self-titled Young Kings might run Spearcrest all they like, but even they have no choice but to bend the knee in front of Mr Ambrose. An alumnus of the school and its headmaster for the past fifteen years, Mr Ambrose rules with an iron fist. Unlike all the teachers at Spearcrest, Mr Ambrose isn't one bit scared of the Kings' parents.

And that makes him untouchable.

Unlike me.

"Mr Kavinski, tuck your shirt in—and try not to get into any fights this year. Mr Montcroix, that tie is not a fashion accessory, and those fanciful rings are in direct violation of the dress code policy. Mr Knight, must you forever look as though you've just emerged from some brawl in a village pub?"

With great reluctance, the boys obey Mr Ambrose and grudgingly fix their uniforms. I hardly dare breathe. So far, it seems my presence has been completely forgotten.

I can only pray and hope it remains so.

If only my luck was that good.

"Miss Sutton," Mr Ambrose booms, "you have the lateness register. Write down all their names, and log an hour's detention for every late-comer. Now, let us hurry inside, gentlemen. Welcome to your final year at Spearcrest."

He pivots on his heels and disappears through the entrance. I keep my eyes down, waiting for the boys to follow him inside.

Another prayer that goes completely ignored.

"Sophie, Sophie, Sophie," Luca says, looming over me. "Put that pen down."

I hold both the pen and the clipboard up as a sign of capitulation. "Right, right, okay. Just go on in."

"You better hope my name doesn't end up on the detention register," Luca continues, leaning down so his face is right in front of mine. "Or we're going to be very upset with you."

I hate having my personal space invaded. I hate it more than anything else. I try to suppress my anger, though, because I'm not stupid. I know he's waiting for me to slip up.

"Okay, Luca," I say, looking down.

He pats my head.

"Good girl, good girl."

"Come on, Luca," Evan Knight calls. He's leaning against the doorway, hands in his pockets. His loose sandy curls fall over his forehead, his blue eyes fixed on me. "She's not worth your time."

This time, I look up. I meet his gaze, hatred burning through me.

Because no matter how much I hate the Young Kings of Spearcrest, it's Evan Knight I hate the most. He might have everyone fooled with his crooked grin, his natural athleticism and his care-free laughter.

In reality, it's all a facade, a perfect illusion. I should know.

I used to be his friend.

---

# Evan

IT'S BEEN TWO WHOLE months since I've last seen Sophie, and she looks completely different than I remember. For some reason, in my memories, she always looks like she did when we first met in Year 9. Brown hair in pigtails, spotty cheeks, feet slightly too big for her body.

Back then, she used to stick out like a sore thumb. It was so easy to tell she wasn't from money, that she was... normal. Common as they come.

Now, she looks more Spearcrest than she would care to admit. With her impeccable uniform, those shiny badges on her blazer lapel. Her long, straight hair parted in the middle, her thick-framed glasses. She's not so spotty anymore, and she grew from the feet up. She's one of the tallest girls in our year.

That's probably why I can't stop staring at her.

I don't even hear a word Mr Ambrose says. I just stare at Sophie in a mixture of fascination and curiosity.

She's holding her clipboard propped against her long legs, her eyes stuck firmly to it. I remember when she used to glare in the face of anybody who dared look down on her, how she used to pick fights with anyone that made her feel small.

Now, she's tall and striking, but she never looks anybody in the eyes. She just keeps her head down and glides in the background of Spearcrest like a ghost.

When Mr Ambrose tells her to put our names down, there's a tiny flash of panic on her face. She knows the consequences of Mr Ambrose's words will be hers to face. Unlike Mr Ambrose, she has no authority to keep her safe from us.

In fact, the moment Mr Ambrose goes inside, she assures Luca she's not going to write our names down.

For some reason, my stomach churns. It's not like I didn't work hard over the years to put out the fight in her. So now she's so easily defeated, where is the sense of triumph I've been waiting for?

Then Luca's face is right against Sophie's, and the churning in my stomach turns to spikes of ice, almost painful. A brutal instinct roars through me, makes me want to grab Luca by the neck and yank him away from her. I can't stand him getting close to Sophie.

I can't stand anybody getting close to her.

"Come on, Luca. She's not worth your time."

She looks up then, for the first time. Her eyes are so dark they look black, but they are actually a soft, hazelnut brown. In sunlight, they are almost limpid, like dark honey.

But right now they are just dark. Dark and hard and full of hate.

A hot flame of triumph leaps in my chest. My blood pumps through my veins when her gaze collides with mine. The sharp, defiant look in her eyes makes me want to go toe-to-toe with her, to fight her to the death.

It makes me want to rip everything that separates us just so I can rip into her.

"You're right," Luca guffaws, turning his back on Sophie. "Wouldn't want to give her the attention she so clearly craves."

Her eyes leave mine and pierce the back of Luca's head. Oh, she hates him too, she can't even hide it. But the thought of her hating Luca more than me fills me with fury.

I don't want her looking at him like that. I don't want her looking at him at all. I want her to look at *me*, to focus all her hatred on *me*. I can't get enough of her hatred, and I'm not about to share it with Luca.

"It's not like she's ever going to get anything better than attention though, is it?" I say lightly. "Guess most guys don't wanna fuck desperate little social climbers."

My friends reward me with bellows of laughter.

Her eyes meet mine. There are no tears in them, not even pain.

There's nothing in them but pure, raw, delicious *hatred*.

I turn and follow the others inside the assembly hall. This is not the first, or the only, or the last heinous thing I've said to her or about her. But I can't stop myself. I can't get enough of her hatred—it's like I'm addicted to it.

And I've only got one more year of getting my fill before I'm cut off forever.

Might as well make it count.

# 2

# TUTORING PROGRAMME

## Sophie

Evan's words sear through me, burning like a brand for hours. It's not even like it's the first cruel thing he's said to me—it's just that my thick skin always softens over the holidays, leaving me weak and exposed to his barbs.

The first blow of the year is always the hardest to take, but I'll toughen quickly.

Because only the tough survive Spearcrest.

I'm distracted for the first half of the day, but I immediately cheer up at lunch when I spot Araminta Wilson-Sing and Audrey Malone. They are sitting in our patch of grass west of the campus, by the big oak trees near the old Greenhouse. They wave me over and I hurry towards them, my heart suddenly lifted.

They are my only friends in Spearcrest—they are the ones who picked up the pieces of me after Evan destroyed our friendship.

The two people who make life here bearable.

"Sophie, how did you ever manage to get this tall?" Araminta exclaims when I reach them.

Araminta is short and curvy and full of this super feminine energy. Her parents are both in politics, and they probably hope she'll follow in their footsteps, but if I'm honest she's too good for politics. Too beautiful, too lively, too sincere.

"I told you milk was good for you," I tell her, sitting at her side.

She pulls a face, but before she can lecture me on how disgusting cow milk is, Audrey wraps us both in her arms and squeezes, knocking our heads together.

"I have missed you girls. So. Bloody. Much!"

Audrey is probably one of the smartest students in the school. She's wiser than most adults I know. If I ever need advice, she is my go-to.

We eat lunch in the grass near the sixth form dormitories, doing our best to catch up. After I finish eating, I lie back in the grass with my head on Araminta's lap, listening to Audrey. She's telling us about some exotic older guy she'd met on holiday.

"An older man, Audrey?" Araminta asks salaciously. "You have to be careful with those. You know they only want one thing."

"And boys our age don't?" Audrey retorts, rolling her eyes. "At least older guys are more subtle about it. They know how to woo a girl."

"*Woo?*" Araminta cackles. "Who are you, Jane Austen?"

I melt into easy laughter. When they're not around, I always get this horrible sense of urgency, like I'm running out of time. Like everything is going to go wrong.

But around the girls, all the worry fades. It's still there, just out of focus. Mum and Dad are always reminding me of how hard I'm going to have to work for even a fraction of the opportunities Spearcrest kids are going to have, but Araminta and Audrey make me feel like I'm one of those Spearcrest kids.

It's only an illusion, but a lovely illusion. The illusion of belonging.

"How about you, Sophe?" Araminta asks.

I shrug. "Same as usual. Went to visit Mum's family in Yorkshire. Saw some old castles. Read books. Researched universities. Nothing quite as exciting as Audrey's scandalous affair."

"I'm sure there'll be plenty of opportunity for scandal this year," Araminta says, waggling her eyebrows. "The Young Kings are running out of time on their bet to shag every girl in the year group before final exams."

I prop myself up on my elbows, my good mood suddenly evaporated. "God! I forgot they said that!"

"At the end of Year 11, remember?" Araminta cackles. "Such a power move."

"Such a dick move, more like," Audrey says, shaking her head. "You couldn't pay me to go near one of them. I'm done dating little boys."

"They're not so little anymore," I mutter. I used to be taller than most boys in my year, now the Young Kings are all taller and bigger than me.

"Alright, between us girls," Araminta says, whispering loudly, "if you had to have sex with one of the Young Kings, who would it be?" She doesn't wait before continuing. "I'll go first. Luca. He's the biggest arsehole of them all, but that's because I reckon he's the most insecure. He wouldn't want anybody to spread the rumour he's shit in bed, so I think he would make an extra effort to make me come."

I choke on my own breath.

"Araminta!" I stare at her in horror.

Audrey is laughing so hard she's making my head bounce on her lap. "You really came prepared with that analysis, Minty," she says. "I can tell you've given this some thought."

"Well, I'd rather be prepared," Araminta says with a shrug. "Besides, it's our last year at Spearcrest, and my last year in the UK. I can't waste it."

She has a point. I nod reluctantly, even though sex with Luca sounds like the most disgusting thing I can imagine.

"I mean we're all going to fuck some arseholes at some point in our lives," Araminta adds. "I might as well get mine out of the way. Set myself up for success."

This time, even I have to laugh.

"Audrey," Araminta continues, "who would you pick?"

Audrey thinks carefully, tapping her manicured fingers against her lips, and ends up answering, "Sev Montcroix."

We all groan.

"He's so... pretentious and moody," Araminta winces. "So... I don't know, full of himself."

I nod. "Not to mention a total fuckboy."

"The word you're looking for is *French*!" Audrey exclaims. "That's what you guys are trying to say. That's what the problem is. He's so *French*."

"Yeah, *too* French," Araminta says, "besides, I heard a rumour he's engaged now."

"Engaged?" I cover my mouth. "Imagine being the poor girl who's going to have to put up with his pissy attitude and fuckboy behaviour for the rest of her life."

The bell rings, drowning out the girls' giggles. I reluctantly leave the comfort of Araminta's lap, grabbing my bag as I get to my feet.

Araminta grabs my wrist.

"Not so fast, Sophe! You owe us an answer."

"I would tell you," I say, "but I genuinely have to go!"

"Liar!" Araminta exclaims, pointing an accusing finger at me. "You just don't want to tell us."

I pull a letter from my backpack and brandish it in her face.

"I'm not lying. See? I have to report to Miss Bailey for the academic mentor programme!"

Araminta reads the letter with narrowed eyes and sighs. "Shit."

With a smug grin, I take my letter and stomp away, waving at them over my shoulder.

"Whatever!" Araminta yells, pulling out her tongue at me. "We all know who you'd pick anyway! Ev—"

The rest is muffled by Audrey's hand, but it's too late. I turn to throw a thunderous glare at Araminta. She gives me a thumbs up.

"We love you, Sophie!" Audrey says warmly.

I pull a face at them and hurry away. Based on how warm my cheeks feel, it's a good thing they didn't get to see how red my face probably is.

Not that Araminta is right. She's just saying it to wind me up because she knows how much I hate him. Still, the disgusting thought of sleeping with Evan Knight follows me like a shadow all the way to Miss Bailey's office.

Miss Bailey is one of the younger teachers at Spearcrest, and she used to be my English teacher back in lower school. I miss having her because she has this incredible calming influence on everyone around her.

The kind of calming influence I need right now.

When I walk into her office, she's watering her little collection of ferns and succulents. She's wearing a cream satin shirt and loose trousers. Her heels are lying abandoned under her desk, and her dark bob is pinned back by tortoiseshell hair clips.

She gives me this huge grin when I come in, and even makes me a cup of green tea when she makes herself one.

"I can't believe this is your last year," she says. "I'm never going to be able to replace you in this programme."

I can't help blushing a little bit, even though she probably doesn't really mean that.

The truth is that no matter how hard I work, I'm nowhere near the smartest student in Spearcrest. Still, I've done everything in my power to be the best mentor I could be to every student Miss Bailey has ever entrusted me with.

After a quick catch-up chat, Miss Bailey turns towards her computer.

"Right, down to business, then. This year is going to be a little bit different. Normally, I have Year 12s mentor students in the lower schools, and Year 13s mentor Year 12s, but I've had some special requests from the governors this year. So..." she looks up at me, widening her eyes, "how would you feel about mentoring another Year 13?"

"Someone from *my* year?" I say, unable to stop the surprise seeping into my voice.

She nods.

That definitely doesn't fit well into my plan of keeping myself to myself this year. I don't feel good about it at all, but Miss Bailey is looking at me with her big hazel eyes, waiting expectantly.

"Alright..." I say. "I suppose I could."

"Oh, Sophie, that's wonderful! I know it might be a little awkward for you, but I've been put under some pressure to make sure certain students get their target grades."

"It's okay, Miss Bailey," I say.

I can see how hard Miss Bailey works, and I can only imagine the pressure she must be under. Besides, this is my last year. So it might be a bit awkward tutoring a kid from my year, but how bad can it be?

"You're a superstar, Sophie," Miss Bailey says, sounding genuinely relieved. "Since you're doing exceptionally well in your Literature class I've paired you with a student who is currently failing Literature."

"Failing?" I wince.

How can someone fail English Lit? I'm pretty sure all you have to do to pass is just read the books.

Miss Bailey sighs. "Unfortunately, yes. Except that failing is not an option this student's parents are willing to accept."

"I can imagine."

"I've scheduled your sessions for Tuesdays and Thursdays, six in the afternoon. How do you feel about that?"

I check my planner. In between chess club, my study timetable, and the lower school book club I run, my time is already slipping away from me. Still, it's too late to turn back now, and I have every intention of getting into every university I apply for, and this is my ticket.

"Alright, Miss Bailey, that's fine, I've made a note."

"You absolute angel!" Miss Bailey exclaims, typing into her computer. "You're quite possibly saving my life! Alright, I've booked you in. You won't start until half-term, so you get to have those afternoons for yourself now."

I nod and make a note of that too. Miss Bailey beams at me. "You remind me so much of me when I was your age, you know."

I try to hide how much it pleases me to hear this. I tuck my hair behind my ears, a little self-consciously, then put my planner away and stand.

"If I grow up to be like you, Miss Bailey, I would be pretty proud."

She laughs.

"What! A boring old English teacher! No, you've got a much more impressive future ahead of you, I can tell. Well, have a good term, my darling."

"Thanks, Miss Bailey."

I stop at the door.

"Who will it be, by the way?"

"Your lucky tutee?"

I laugh.

"Yes, my lucky tutee."

"Mm," she checks her computer. "Evan Knight."

My entire body becomes entombed in ice.

"Who?" I ask even though I heard perfectly well.

"Evan Knight," she looks up from her computer. "Do you know him?"

The ice of which I am now made cracks and shatters into splinters. I can barely move.

"No," I say weakly. "See you later, Miss Bailey."

And then I run away, trying to keep the bits of me together long enough that Miss Bailey doesn't see me fall apart.

And then all the pain from Evan's words this morning, from every cruel thing he's ever said to me, and the oldest pain of all, the pain of betrayal, all come rushing back like a blow.

## The First Time Sophie Met Evan

*It's my third week at Spearcrest and it's been raining the entire time. I know because I spend almost every lesson with my gaze out of the window. I stare at the looming tree line, the dull wall of shapeless clouds, the mist clinging to the corners of the building like a tepid breath on a cold day.*

*A voice pulls me back to reality. It repeats a question for the third time.*

*I sigh and turn. "No, my parents aren't cleaners."*

*"Oh."*

*The girl next to me has long, perfectly curled hair, thick eyelashes, and clear skin. She doesn't look like the Year 9s in my old school used to look. She definitely doesn't look like me. Her manners are polished and she speaks with a sort of thoughtful confusion which I'm sure allows her to get away with a lot.*

*"But they do work for the school, right?" she asks.*

*When my parents finally convinced me to go to Spearcrest (well, not so much convinced me as forced me) they promised me nobody would ever find out they work for the school.*

*"Won't the kids there wonder why a normal person is going to their school?" I'd asked as a naive Year 8.*

*"They are normal kids," my parents said, "their parents are just wealthier than other people's. That's all."*

*Of course, they were lying.*

*Spearcrest kids are so far from normal I don't even count them as kids at all. Most of them don't even look like teenagers. They look polished and synthetic, like robots created to look like teenager but with every setting turned to a hundred. They are tall and lithe and athletic, eerily beautiful. Blinding white teeth, glassy skin, doll-like eyes.*

*Not just the girls, but the boys, too. Even in Year 9, they are already showing the outlines of muscles, and they walk with a cocky strut that indicates their place in the world, somewhere above everybody else.*

*When I look at the Spearcrest kids, I don't see teenagers, or peers.*

*I don't even see people.*

*So, most of the time, I don't look.*

*I sit with my elbow on my desk and my chin propped in my palm. I gaze outside, dreaming about what my life will be like when I get to leave this place. I've only been here for three weeks, and I already can't wait to be gone.*

*All I have to do, I keep reminding myself, is to be patient and bide my time.*

*Of course, that's easier said than done.*

*"If your parents aren't cleaners," the girl next to me continues. "Then what do they do exactly?"*

*I weigh my options. Answer, or keep ignoring her?*

*If I ignore her, she might eventually leave me alone. Or she might keep pestering me, which is what she's doing right now.*

*If I answer her, she'll have to leave me alone.*

*I turn to give her a look. "They are administrators."*

*She gives me an innocent look, wide doll eyes and mouth open in a pink O.*

*"So... like secretaries?"*

*I sigh. "Sure."*

*She leaves me alone after that, but by the end of the week, everybody at school thinks my parents are cleaners.*

*Of course by that point, I have bigger things to worry about.*

*Like my mattress being soaking wet every night when I go to bed, handfuls of mud and leaves smearing the blankets.*

*Or my school books getting ritualistically defaced, my pencils snapped and my notes torn to shreds.*

*Or having my breakfast dashed into the bin and my drinks knocked over every time I refuse to butter the bread of the upper school girls.*

*Telling my parents isn't an option: they already know. They even warned me about this. "They will expect you to prove yourself to them, Sophie. You mustn't crack. You must show them how strong you are."*

*So I do my best not to crack, but something's got to give.*

*For me, stress comes in the form of a horrific acne breakout, my inner distress destroying me from the inside out. Add to that the fact I'm the tallest girl in our year group, and there's literally no hiding.*

*One day, a Year 11 girl spots me when I'm standing outside a classroom waiting for my lesson. She's tall, as beautiful as a model, her face picture perfect. She stops, her features twisted with disgust, and says to me, "You have got to be by far the ugliest thing I've ever seen in my life. Spearcrest must really be letting just anybody in nowadays."*

*I don't cry at that, but I do cry that weekend, when my parents tell me I'll be spending every weekend until half term break in school to "make friends and build connections."*

*I do end up spending every weekend in school, but each day is spent hiding in dark corners of the library, the study hall, empty classrooms. Anywhere I can find where I don't have to speak to anybody.*

*It works, for a while.*

*Until Period 5 on a glum Wednesday afternoon.*

*Our English teacher, Miss Willard, pairs everybody up to read a scene from the Shakespeare play we are studying. I close my eyes and wish with my entire soul that I could disappear from Spearcrest, disappear from this world.*

*But Miss Willard, relentless as a machine, calls out, "Miss Sutton and Mr Knight."*

*I might spend all my time avoiding the other students, but even I know exactly who Evan Knight is. He's one of the most popular boys in our year group: rich, sporty, flashy.*

*The golden boy of Spearcrest, he draws attention to him wherever he goes.*

*He's hard to ignore because he's one of the only boys who is as tall as I am. His head is a shiny cloud of golden curls. But I keep my eyes firmly fixed out of the window, forcing him to come and sit next to me. I only look at him when it can no longer be avoided.*

*He's looking at me with a smile. His bright blue eyes meet mine, and then drop, sweeping over my ravaged cheeks. Students are prohibited from wearing make-up, and even though this seems to be a rule everyone ignores, my parents took it seriously. I wasn't even allowed to bring a concealer or half a tub of cheap foundation.*

*So my spots are raw and red and exposed for all to see, and Evan isn't exactly trying his hardest to pretend he doesn't see.*

*"You have got to be by far the ugliest thing I've seen in my life," I think to myself, imagining his thoughts.*

*But he doesn't say this. Instead, he passes me a copy of the scene we have to read together and says, "What are we doing, then? I have no idea what any of this says."*

*I raise an eyebrow. "Did you not read the teacher's notes?"*

*His blue eyes widen. Because of his curly blond hair and his boyish face, he looks like a cupid painting on a Valentine's Day card. "What notes?"*

*Reaching into my bag, I pull out my English folder. "Those notes. The ones Miss Willard said to study before we start the play."*

*He peers at them with an expression of confusion which tells me he has never seen those notes before in his life.*

*"Um, I don't think I got those," he says, brushing his hand through his hair.*

*He definitely got them. I'm tempted to say as much to him, but I make a tactical choice not to. So far, Evan Knight hasn't said a single cruel, unkind or hurtful thing to me, and I'd like to keep it that way as long as possible.*

*"Well," I say, my stomach clenching uncomfortably. "I can, uh... I can explain it to you, if you want. Before we start with the reading. Then we'll both know what we're doing."*

*And Evan Knight does something totally unexpected.*

*He looks right into my eyes, gives me a bright, genuine smile, and says, "Yeah, that'd be awesome. Thanks, Sophie."*

# 3

# ILLICIT SHINDIG

## Sophie

OVER THE NEXT FEW weeks, I fall into my routine. While the other students are stressed out about catching up and applying to the best universities, I'm prepared. All my hard work over the years, all the colour-coded notes and timetables I meticulously mapped out at my desk while I ignored the elusive British summer, are finally paying off. I'm organised and ready to take on the work the teachers are already piling on us. I don't dread the challenge—I embrace it. Besides, keeping myself busy also has another advantage: it stops me from thinking about Evan.

Because if I *do* start thinking about him, the wave of anxiety will inevitably flood in.

The thing is that I could have dealt with Evan if he was like any other boy at Spearcrest: disgustingly wealthy, vapid and arrogant. But Evan is more than just another Young King, more than just another rich arsehole who would never matter to my life.

Evan was my first friend at Spearcrest, there for me when things were the most difficult. He was my closest friend in Year 9, someone I grew to trust and love.

How things ended up the way they are now, I still don't know.

I'll never understand how things could go so wrong between two people that got on so well.

In any case, I have far more important things I need to think about. This year, I'm lucky enough to not share any classes with any of the Young Kings. If I play my cards right, I can stay out of their way for the majority of the year.

My luck runs out on a Friday night.

I'm sitting in a corner of the study hall, annotating my copy of Othello when the doors slam open. The study room is suddenly flooded with the sound of voices and laughter. I stay low and peek around my table lamp.

The Young Kings, their female counterparts, their friends and sycophants are all pouring into the study hall, holding bottles of Dom Perignon and boxes of pizza.

Their parties are notorious throughout campus, but their smaller gatherings are what people really care about. They are intimate little affairs held in some unlikely part of the school where they won't be caught. Rumour has it all sorts of debauchery go down at these events. Everyone in the school secretly longs to be invited, to be chosen to spend time with the elite amongst the elite.

Even *I* used to be curious about those scandalous get-togethers.

But certainly not curious enough to stay now. Unlike the Spearcrest elite, if *I* get caught, there *will* be consequences. Both from the school and my furious parents.

And I'm not about to get in trouble in my final year at Spearcrest. Not when I'm applying to the kind of university I don't have the wealth or influence I need to get into.

I cringe behind the little ledge of my desk, hoping to go unnoticed. With quick, quiet movements, I close my books and shove them into my backpack. I can hear them talking and laughing as they settle themselves around the room, filling the air with the pounding of music and the clinking of bottles and glasses.

Hopefully, their heads are too far up each other's arses for them to notice me. I finish packing my stuff and shoulder my backpack.

Then a lazy voice crawls like ice up my spine.

"Leaving so soon, Sutton?"

I look up.

Evan Knight out of his uniform is a perfect cliche of the all-American boy. In his plain white t-shirt and jeans, he looks like a Calvin Klein model. Tall and athletic, he has broad shoulders and big, sun-kissed arms.

He always returns from summers in the US like he's been dipped in sunlight: his sandy curls bleached almost silver in places, his skin polished gold. His clear blue eyes, set in that handsome tan face, are bright as gemstones.

As beautiful as he is, it means nothing to me.

Because behind his lazy drawl, his easy laughter, his golden skin and cerulean eyes, I know how ugly Evan Knight really is.

"I wasn't invited," I say, dropping my eyes to avoid his amused gaze.

"No, something tells me you don't get invited to many parties," he says lightly. "That's what happens when you're a total buzzkill. But it looks like the party's found you. Don't you wanna see what the fuss is all about?"

I glance over his shoulder. The other "kings" are busy pouring glasses of champagne for beautiful girls. I spot Seraphina Rosenthal—the Rose of Spearcrest—and suppress a shudder. She hates my guts and will never miss an opportunity to make me feel like shit if she can.

So far, none of them seem to have noticed me, which is probably the only reason Evan is alone.

Normally, he's always surrounded by his little gang, their sneers and snickers. I can't remember the last time we spoke alone. I don't *want* to remember the last time we spoke alone.

"I'm alright," I say as politely as I can manage given how much my skin is crawling with alternating ice and fire right now. "I'm pretty sure the last thing this party needs is a prefect in attendance."

"What are you going to do, Sutton?" His voice depends as he lowers it, the curl of his lip is mocking. "Tattle on us? Write our names down on your little clipboard?"

"No clipboard."

I tuck my chair in and try to make a beeline for the door, but Evan is fast. He's hopped off the desk in the time it takes me to go around it. Now he's standing right in my way, close enough to touch.

Close enough that I can smell his expensive cologne—cedarwood and frost—and feel the heat exuding from his skin.

"No clipboard," I repeat, showing him my palms. "No pen. Nobody's going to find out about your little illicit shindig, so you can relax. I'm just heading back to my dorm."

But he stays in my way, looking down at me.

In Year 9, we used to be identical heights, chin to chin. Now, he's annoyingly taller than me. Meeting his gaze from this close requires tilting my head back. Something I have no intention of doing.

So I keep my eyes firmly fixed on his trainers, which are much too scruffy for the amount of money he's doubtlessly spent on them.

Then he raises his hand, placing a finger under my chin. He tilts my face up towards his, forcing me to look up.

"Stay," he says, his voice more like a caress than a sound.

A dangerous caress.

His blue gaze pierces me, unflinchingly direct and yet indecipherable. Tiny waves of shivers skitter across my arms and back. His finger drops from my chin, scrapes down the length of my neck.

I narrow my eyes at him. "Are you ordering me, or asking me?"

As soon as the words leave my mouth, they immediately sound like a challenge. The corner of Evan's mouth rises in a slight, crooked grin, full of charm and danger.

"Whichever you prefer, Sutton. Or maybe you'd rather I beg?"

There is a dark suggestion in his tone, but before I can think of something non-committal and safe to reply with, a girl calls out, "Evan, are you coming? You've got the cards!"

His eyes stay fixed on mine as he turns his head slightly to respond, "I'm coming!"

Then, lowering his voice again, he says, "Are you sure you don't want to stay? We're going to play Strip Kings. You might get to see me naked."

"I'll pass, thanks," I say quickly, pushing past him and hoping my cheeks don't look as red as they feel.

"You're going to regret it," he calls after me. "Might be the only action you get this year."

"Then I'd rather get no action."

Then I practically run out of the study hall, my heart beating so hard I can taste my pulse in my mouth.

# Evan

"Evan! You coming, or what?" Giselle calls.

I take the pack of cards from my pocket and saunter over to the others. Luca is reclining on a desk, his arm wrapped lazily around Giselle, who sits on the bench next to him.

He raises a pale eyebrow at me in question, but I toss him the cards instead of giving him an answer. Then I take two glasses of champagne and down them, trying to swallow back the sudden anger welling up in my chest.

I dated Giselle last year, so of course, Luca has to make a point of flashing her on his arm like he flashes his watches. I don't hate him for it—the privilege of being one of the Young Kings of Spearcrest comes at the cost of never having anything truly for yourself. That's fine.

But he doesn't need to know my every thought and emotion.

Especially not when it comes to Sophie.

A perfumed arm wraps around my waist, and a pretty voice reaches my ear. "Why so gloomy, Evan?"

Seraphina "Rose" Rosenthal appears at my side. If I had to pick someone to be the polar opposite of Sophie, it would really be her. Where Sophie is tall, Rose is petite, where Sophie is dark-haired and olive-skinned, Rose is fair, with long blond hair that makes her look like a Disney princess.

Where Sophie is serious and austere, Rose is as light-hearted and frivolous as a cupcake.

Of course, I'm not an idiot. I know Rose wants me—she's wanted us to be a couple for a long time. She knows what I deep-down also know: that we would make the picture-perfect Spearcrest couple. We are both good-looking, both American, both fun-loving and rich as the day is long.

But Rose, for all her beauty and outrageous outfits and airy laughter, doesn't excite me like Sophie does.

She doesn't captivate me, she doesn't draw me in. She doesn't fill me with adrenaline, with the urge to dominate and defeat.

If I had to choose, I would pick fighting Sophie over fucking Rose.

Every time.

"I'm not gloomy," I say, plastering a grin on my face and handing her one of my glasses of champagne. "Why would I be gloomy?"

"I saw you talking to Sophie Sutton." Her tone is light, but Sophie's name in her mouth makes my skin crawl. "She's always so fucking stuck-up and miserable. Just looking at her face sends me into a depressive episode."

Her arm is still around my waist and for a second I have the urge to throw her away from me. But Luca's eyes are on me, and at his side, Giselle is watching me closely. Giselle, who spent much of our time together asking me why I'm so obsessed with Sophie. Even Iakov and Sev, who are in a corner talking, have looked up.

They all look at me, waiting for my reaction.

I shrug and squeeze Rose's waist, drawing her closer even though I would have rather pushed her away.

"No matter what she thinks," I say lightly, "a prefect badge isn't going to make her one of us. She's just desperate for us to forget she's just a Spearcrest charity case. She's not worth the depressive episode—come on—let's dance."

She smiles in quiet triumph. I swallow back a lump of fury. Luca's cocky smirk, Iakov and Sev's shrugs, Giselle's little satisfied smile—I do my best to ignore them all.

In reality, they love this. They love that I can't approach Sophie any more than she can approach us.

The Young Kings can have anybody or anything they like in Spearcrest—but no matter what, Sophie is out of bounds.

And even though I spend the rest of the night dancing with girls and laughing with my friends because that's my role, in the privacy of my mind, I can do what I want. I can think about nothing but Sophie, for as much and as long as I like—however I like.

I picture her, with her long dark hair and her serious mouth and her brown eyes. She's probably gone back to her dorm.

What is her dorm room like? What pictures and posters does she have on her wall? Probably revision timetables and terminology lists. She probably has a tidy desk and impeccably organised stationery. Paperbacks lining her windowsill.

She's probably going to take a shower, brush her hair until it's so straight and smooth it falls like silk around her head. What does she look like, stripped of the armour of her school uniform? Stripped off her badges and glasses? What does Sophie Sutton look like, naked with her wet hair gleaming on her shoulders?

What does she wear to bed? She's so serious all the time, I bet she wears matching pyjama sets, trousers and long-sleeved tops with contrast piping along the collar and sleeves.

Or maybe she wears nothing at all when she gets in bed.

And when I picture her getting in bed, it's my bed I imagine her crawling into. I don't know why, and I can't explain it. But I picture Sophie, with her long hair falling forward, climbing into *my* bed, her long limbs sliding against *my* sheets.

If Sophie Sutton were in my bed, there would be no cuddling, no tenderness.

I'd have her by her throat, on my cock, taking me. Her arrogant face twisted in pleasure and pain. Her hands clutching my chest, fingernails digging into my muscles.

Sophie's a prideful, stubborn little thing. How hard would I need to fuck her to get her to beg, to break, to scream?

The thought of it brings a smile to my mouth. Breaking Sophie Sutton is a game I never get tired of playing. Imagining all the ways in which I could break her brings me so much satisfaction, it's almost better than sex.

But breaking Sophie hasn't been easy—and this is my last year to do it.

Guess I'm going to have to get real creative with it.

# 4

# ZERO TOLERANCE

## Sophie

I USUALLY STAY AT school over half-term while everybody goes home because my parents work on campus and don't have a holiday until Christmas. Most of the time, I end up spending most of my time curled on my bed reading a book. But this year, it's different. A lot of students, under the pressure of university applications, are staying on campus too.

Araminta and Audrey are both staying for half-term. It's a rare and precious opportunity because we're all usually split up over holidays.

Sixth-formers are allowed to go into town during the half-term breaks, so we take the opportunity to go out for strolls, or to shop and catch films. It's a much-needed break, and, crucially, a much-needed distraction.

Between my weird encounter with Evan in the study hall and the mentoring programme approaching fast, my anxiety is ramping up.

Unfortunately, having to mentor Evan is not my only source of anxiety. Aside from worrying about my grades and university applications, I've also started to worry about money.

At Spearcrest, my living costs are absorbed by the school. I live on campus and spend most of my holidays here too. My parents give me a small allowance for food, clothes and books, and that's more than enough to get by on.

But now, the reality of money is settling in. Even if I can get loans or scholarships for my tuition, I'm going to need money. Money for travelling, for rent, for food, for bills. Money for everything—more money than my parents will ever be able to afford.

Especially if I get into Harvard Law School, where my parents don't even know I'm applying.

Getting a job wouldn't be a problem, and it's not like I'm afraid of hard work. But Spearcrest has a rule forbidding students from getting part-time jobs. And doing so isn't even an option, because unless it's a holiday, we're not typically allowed off-campus.

Money is an issue which constantly weighs on my mind even when I'm with the girls. Audrey, of course, doesn't fail to notice this.

"What's on your mind, frowny-face?"

It's almost the end of half-term. We're sitting in a little café in Fernwell, the local town, sipping sugary hot drinks while we watch the sun slowly set outside. The café is a cosy place full of leather seats and plants. There's a sign stuck to the window reading "Hiring Now."

I've been staring at it without realising.

"I wish Spearcrest would allow us to get jobs," I said, turning back to Audrey.

She laughs. "I doubt it's an issue many students worry about."

Araminta scoops a spoonful of whipped cream from the top of her hot chocolate, raising her eyebrows, "You want to get a job? Would you even have the time?"

"In between chess club, book club, study club, student club and club club?" Audrey says a little wickedly.

"Maybe I could drop a club," I say.

"Drop a club?" Audrey exclaims. "Who are you and what have you done with Sophie?"

"What club would you drop?" Araminta asks.

"The mentor programme."

Now Audrey is truly aghast. "Miss Bailey's academic mentor programme? You've been doing it since Year 10! You love that shit! Why on earth would you drop it?"

I hesitate. "This year she wants me to mentor someone in our year."

"What? Who would need a mentor in our year?"

"Apparently a few people in our year are failing some of their subjects. Their posh mamas and papas are displeased, so Miss Bailey is using the mentoring programme to help those students."

"Anybody failing at this point just doesn't *want* to do well," Audrey says, a little scornfully.

"Or doesn't *need* to do well," I say.

"I bet it's one of the Young Kings," Araminta pipes up. "They've made it pretty obvious they're too rich and powerful to care about grades. I always thought it was just the image they were trying to project, but maybe they've been pretending to be useless for so long they've *actually* become useless."

Audrey is watching me with her shrewd eyes as Araminta talks. She leans forward in her comfy seat.

"Oh my god, Sophie. It totally is, isn't it? One of the Young Kings."

I nod.

"Ugh!" Araminta exclaims in disgust. "One of them is failing? What a turn off! I bet it's Iakov, I swear all that guy does is smoke and drink and fight."

But Audrey is still watching me with those eyes that seem to see a lot more than they should.

"It's Evan Knight," she says. "Isn't it?"

I nod again and drop my head back against the wings of the big chesterfield I'm nestled into. Both girls give me looks of sympathy. Audrey reaches over to rub my arm.

"I mean, let's look on the positive side," Araminta says. "It might put you at an advantage to be his mentor. I'm sure he won't want people to know he's failing. He might try to act nice in exchange for your silence."

"Nice or not," I say. "The programme is two hours a week, twice a week. Four hours of Evan. *A week*."

"God..." Audrey mutters, shaking her head. "What are you going to do?"

"I'm going to tell Miss Bailey I can't tutor him."

"Are you going to tell Miss Bailey the truth?" Araminta asks, wide-eyed.

"What truth? I hate Evan Knight because he's horrible and fake and a complete loser? I can't say that to Miss Bailey, it would sound so pathetic."

"Just tell her he's a bully," Audrey says.

Now it's my turn to raise my eyebrows at her. "Because reporting bullying in Spearcrest has a history of going well and not at all having negative consequences..."

The truth is that Spearcrest as a school *does* have a zero tolerance for bullying.

So reporting bullying does mean the school will challenge and punish the bully. But that bully will be back at one point or another, and they will have the full force of very angry, very wealthy, very powerful parents behind them.

And that's when your life can become a living hell.

Not something I would risk, especially not this year. I've done my suffering here. Now it's time to stay under the radar and plan my escape.

When I go to her office on the first Monday of the new half-term, I stay as vague as possible and do my best to simply dodge the situation.

"Miss Bailey, if it's not too much trouble, I was wondering if it would be possible for me to get a different tutee."

Today, Miss Bailey is wearing a green silk blouse and black velvet culottes. She looks radiant in the pearl-grey morning light drifting through her windows, but as soon as she hears my request, her face drops.

"Oh, no Sophie, can you not tutor Evan anymore?"

"I..." Luckily, I've prepared an array of excuses. "I'm nowhere near the best student in Literature. I think another student who is achieving better grades might be better suited to tutoring him."

Miss Bailey shakes her head.

"Sophie, you're one of the only mentors in the programme also taking English Literature. You're also an Oxbridge and Ivy Leagues candidate, which is going to go down well with the parents. Not that it's at all your responsibility to worry about that, of course!"

She looks at me with an expression of worry bordering on panic.

"It's just that..." I mumble, feeling completely ashamed.

"Of course, you shouldn't need to worry about any of that," Miss Bailey repeats, holding up her hands. "I'll just have to find someone to replace you, that's fine—that's fine." She's half mumbling as she scrambles between her computer and her planner, making notes, talking distractedly. "Okay, I will sort this out." Then she looks up beseechingly. "Any chance you would mind just doing the mentoring sessions while I look for somebody else to replace you? One or two weeks, that's it."

The terror of having to mentor Evan for even a single session makes war with the devouring guilt of the stress I'm causing Miss Bailey, each trying to overcome the other.

In the end, I say, "Of course, Miss Bailey, no problem."

The words spill from my mouth before I even have the time to shove them back behind my teeth. Already, a sunray of hope is lighting up Miss Bailey's face.

"Oh, thank you so much, Sophie! I genuinely appreciate this, I hope you know I don't take your work and kindness for granted," she points her pen at her computer. "I promise you I will sort this out as soon as possible." She grabs a thick manila folder and passes it to me. "Here are all the details for the session tomorrow. Thank you a thousand times, Sophie."

She is beaming with such genuine gratitude I can't regret giving in to her. I leave her office feeling like I did the right thing, and simultaneously so sick with nerves I'm nauseous.

I slump against the wall next to her door. The corridors of Spearcrest, with their chessboard tiles, tall windows and arched ceilings, normally feel cavernous, but right now they seem to be closing in on me.

I shut my eyes and take deep breaths, reminding myself this is the last year. The last year of having to endure the whims and caprices of rich kids.

The last year of trying to survive Evan Knight.

---

That evening, when I'm back in my dorm room after a very long, very hot shower, I climb into bed and finally open the manila folder Miss Bailey gave me. There are photocopies of some of Evan's essays (tragic), notes from his Literature teacher about the topics and skills he needs to focus on and some textbooks.

There is also a printed map with an address written on a post-it. I frown, looking closer, then scramble for a note. Sure enough, I find instructions in Miss Bailey's elegant handwriting on the back of the map.

*"Out of respect for Evan's privacy, his parents wish him to be tutored at their home near the school. Taxis are already*

*booked and paid for, so don't worry about getting there. I've attached the address and a map just in case."*

I toss the map away from me and drop back into my pillows, scrunching my eyes close. His house? I have to go to his *house*? Why? Because his parents don't want anybody to find out their precious golden boy isn't capable of reading a book without having his hand held?

It's so typical of these rich arseholes to do something like this. I don't even know why I'm surprised.

So once more, I force deep, long breaths down my constricted throat. My frustration is almost suffocating, but there's nothing I can do for now. I'm sure Miss Bailey won't let me down.

All I need to do now is make it through the next couple of weeks, and then I never have to speak to or think about Evan Knight ever again.

To comfort myself, I open my heavily annotated copy of Jane Eyre. Normally, it's a comfort read, but today, Jane's story hits too close to home. She, too, fell for someone's sweet lies only to end up betrayed and hurt.

I can only hope to one day leave Spearcrest with as much pride and dignity as she left Thornfield.

# 5

# BOOTLICKING

## Evan

When my parents told me I would be getting tutoring and had no choice in the matter, I was more than a little pissed off. But as soon as I found out I was allowed off campus to receive the lessons, I felt a whole lot better.

Two afternoons a week, I could leave school and chill in our big, empty house. My parents spend their time divided between the US and their international offices. They only ever really stay in this house when they want to get the whole family together.

The rest of the time, it's gloriously empty. The cleaners and gardeners only visit once a week to maintain the property. It would be ideal if I wasn't stuck at Spearcrest. Now though, all I have to do is placate whichever sucker signed up to be my mentor and I have two afternoons a week just for myself.

I'm in the middle of checking out the wine cellar for stuff I think my dad's not going to notice has gone missing when I hear the intercom. Frowning, I check my watch.

Six o'clock exactly. Almost rudely punctual.

I tuck a bottle under my arm and make my way back upstairs to open the door. I know everyone in the year group, and I'm not about to ruin my reputation as a loveable party boy.

When I open the front door, I freeze for a second.

Spikes of adrenaline stab through my skin.

Saying I haven't fantasised about having Sophie Sutton to myself in the comfort and privacy of my own home would be a complete lie. Still, I never imagined she would come of her own volition, a lamb leading itself to the slaughter.

I stand in the doorway and take in the sight of her from head to toe.

I don't even care that I'm being shamelessly obvious.

She's still wearing her uniform, of course. So am I, except I've loosened my tie, untucked my shirt and thrown my blazer over the back of an easy chair in the lounge. But Sophie wouldn't be caught dead with her uniform looking anything less than impeccable.

So she's wearing her tie straight, tucked into her sweater vest, and her skirt is the appropriate mid-thigh length over her black tights. Her blazer is spotless, those pretentious pins shining over one lapel. Her hair is tied back in a low ponytail and her face is free of makeup. The picture-perfect image of the Spearcrest student.

It's immediately clear that she doesn't want to be here. She can't even bring herself to glare at me. Her shoulders slump in downward slopes, her cheeks and lips are pale.

She looks fucking miserable.

And yet I can't stop the pure elation surging through me. I greet her with a shit-eating grin plastered across my face.

"Well *hi*, Sutton. What brings you here today?"

A flash of anger crosses her face and is quickly stifled. She answers tightly, "You failing English Lit."

"And you're the best Spearcrest could come up with?"

It's a harmless jab, but it doesn't have the intended effect. A new expression passes over Sophie's face. Not hurt or anger, something else. Something like hope.

"Then complain," she says. "Or better yet, get your parents to complain."

I stare at her with some surprise. "What, get you fired as my mentor?"

"Exactly." She points her chin over her shoulder. "I can turn and leave right now and you could have a new mentor in no time if your parents throw a fit."

I shake my head. Obviously, she doesn't want to be here. I guess I just didn't realise quite how much she wants to be rid of me. Getting rid of my mentor was exactly my intention, so why do I feel an itch of irritation deep under my skin?

Sophie doesn't get rid of *me*. *I* get rid of Sophie.

"Well, you've come all the way here," I say, standing aside to free the doorway. "It'd be rude of me not to invite you in for a drink."

She hesitates and looks over her shoulder at the big open courtyard where the taxi must have dropped her off. Her reluctance is palpable. I roll my eyes. "Come in already. I'm not going to bite you." I hold up the bottle of wine in my fist and shake it. "Let's negotiate over a drink."

That gets her attention, and she finally follows me inside. I swing the door shut after her and lead her into the big open-plan kitchen. She stands stiffly by the marble-top kitchen island and watches me as I grab two wine glasses from a cupboard and pour us drinks.

I've never particularly liked wine, but I'm more nervous than I want to be, and I could do it with some liquid courage.

I gesture at a stool. "Don't be so fucking awkward. Sit. Drink."

I slide one of the glasses across the kitchen island

"I'm not going to drink," she snaps, throwing a scornful look at the glass.

Sophie might look down on all the posh rich kids at our school, but the truth is that she's the most stuck-up person I know in Spearcrest.

"I should have known you don't drink," I say with a sneer. "Perfect prefect Sutton. Too scared of losing control to ever let loose."

She perches on a stool, her back straight, her chin stuck out. "I don't drink around people I don't trust."

I can't tell whether she's implying that she doesn't trust me, or that she doesn't trust anyone. The only thing I can tell is that I suddenly find the prospect of getting Sophie tipsy has become my most urgent goal in life. She's so tightly wound, so rigidly in control of herself.

The thought of pulling on a loose string and unravelling her sounds delicious.

But she sticks to her guns and never even glances at the wine. I don't let her judgemental expression bother me. I hop onto the counter, sitting cross-legged in front of her, letting her crane her head back to look up at me.

She leans back, putting distance between us, and frowns imperiously. "I thought I was here to negotiate?"

"Let's."

"Then I'm going to just go ahead and be honest," she says, crossing her arms. "I don't think you care at all whether or not you pass English Literature, and I don't want to be tutoring you. So you should tell your parents I'm a bad tutor, or that you don't like me, or literally whatever you want to tell them, I don't care. Then I don't have to come here anymore, and you can do whatever you want."

I stare at her as she speaks. In Year 9 she used to be so animated, with a big goofy grin and chaotic hand gestures.

But now, she is poised and still and almost expressionless. Robotic.

I watched this change happen over the years, and I always expected her to change so much she would be a completely different person. Maybe then I could be indifferent towards her.

But if anything, this change is having the reverse effect. The more she retreats inwards, the more I want to chase her down. The more walls she builds between herself and everyone else, the more I want to tear them apart.

I covet every emotion she swallows back, every truth she hides deep within herself.

Everything she covers up, I want to strip bare.

"Well? What do you think?" she asks, voice pinched with impatience.

"I don't think it's a good idea," I finally answer, taking a sip of wine. "If I complain about you and they send me someone else, then I'll still be in the same situation. As things stand, we both have a common goal: to get away from these stupid tutoring sessions. So let's work together and both get what we want."

"What is it you want?" she asks warily.

Her distrust is tangible but unsurprising.

"You're right, Sutton: I don't give a shit about passing Lit or getting tutored, but I do want to get away from the school. You could come over, pretend to tutor me, but we just don't do the work."

"That sounds like a good bargain for *you*," she says. "What do *I* get out of it?"

"Well," I lean down, closing some of the space between us, "what is it *you* want, Sutton? A wire transfer? Money in a suitcase?"

She throws me a look of pure disdain. Then she looks away, thinking in silence. Her fingers tap her arm, her teeth tug at her bottom lip. I watch her, alcohol and excitement burning in the pit of my stomach.

It's so easy to dislike her when she's so fucking stuck-up, so fucking serious. A total buzzkill. It's so easy to fantasise about bringing her low, making a mess out of her.

She speaks up finally, interrupting my thoughts.

"Alright, I think we could do something like that. The taxi drops me off at yours so the school thinks I'm here, but I'm going to leave. Then you get your time to yourself, and we both win, just like you said."

I frown. "Where are you going to go?"

"Town."

"Why? Where?"

She lifts an eyebrow. "It's none of your business."

"Won't it be weird if we go back to the school separately?"

She shrugs. "I doubt anybody will notice."

"The taxi is going to come here, so what if I come to pick you up on the way back?"

She hesitates. "I might stay longer in town."

"How long?"

"I'm not sure yet."

I hop off the kitchen island, standing right in front of her to peer into her face. "Such secrecy, Sutton. What are you up to?"

Colour rises in her cheeks but she holds my gaze. "It's none. Of your. Business."

"You're not scared I'm going to rat you out?"

She narrows her eyes. "*Are* you going to rat me out?"

"What's my incentive not to?" I say lightly, more to wind her up than anything else.

"Are you really trying to blackmail me?" she asks witheringly. "What are you going to do, shake me down for my lunch money? Force me to carry your school books? Make me lick your boots?"

She looks pretty confident given I'm standing so close to her. None of the cowering I'm so used to, the darting escapes away from me. It makes the heat in my stomach flare, flames rising in my chest.

I've never ever had the urge to get physical with Sophie before—I don't hurt women and I can hurt her plenty with my words. But right now I have the urge to touch her, grab her, make her realise I'm the one with the power.

I'm *always* the one with the power.

"It's not your lunch money I want," I say, taking her chin gently in my hand.

My voice comes out rougher than I expected, but I'm past caring. I have the irresistible urge to bend her to my will. To make her do what I want.

To make her mine.

It's not like I'm *into* Sophie. I've worked hard to ensure I never would be.

No, this is more like the obsession a fighter might have over a formidable opponent. The desire to defeat, to conquer.

It probably feels different today because we're alone, and the wine is clouding my brain and my senses are filled with the sweet smell of her, like warm vanilla or molten sugar. And her cheeks are smeared pink and her big brown eyes are wide as they stare up at me.

I have her at my mercy. Isn't this what I wanted?

Anything past this would be sheer indulgence.

Time to get a hold of myself.

"I don't want you to lick my boots, Sutton, or anything else you're thinking of," I say with a smirk, letting go of her face. "I want you to do my Lit assignments for me."

She looks furious, and her fury is more satisfying than if I'd grabbed her and kissed her full on the mouth. Blood instantly rushes to my cock.

"You want to blackmail me into doing your homework for you?" she says, voice shaking with anger.

I shrug and lean back against the kitchen island.

"It's in your interest to do so. Otherwise, everybody's going to realise pretty quickly we're lying about the tutoring."

She glares at me but doesn't say anything.

"Fine," she finally grinds out. "I'll write your essays."

"Good girl." I pat her head, her hair soft as silk under my fingers. "Make sure they don't sound too much like you wrote them, alright? We'd both get in trouble if we got caught."

She smiles mirthlessly, pulling away from my hand. "Don't worry. I'll make sure they are still underwhelming, lacking in perception and riddled with errors."

"Why must you try to hurt my feelings?" I ask, tilting my head. "Play nice, Sutton. We're making a deal and helping each other out, after all. Let's shake on it."

She hesitates but sticks out her hand in a comically formal gesture. I take it in mine. It's surprisingly cold, but I'm more surprised at how strong her grip is.

"You have my back, and I'll have yours," I say, peering deep into her eyes and seeing nothing even close to trust there. "Alright?"

"Right," she says, a slight curl of derision on her mouth. She tries to pull her hand from mine, but I keep holding on, pulling her closer.

"Allies?" I ask sweetly.

As if. Being allies with Sophie Sutton is like trying to pet the wolf you've kept caged and starving for years.

"Sure," she snaps.

My mind scrambles for an excuse to keep holding on to her hand, to keep her close, to keep her in my house. But she gives me nothing, she just watches me blankly as she waits for me to release her.

"Anything else you want?" she snaps.

"Mm, no, Sutton—why? What are you offering?"

She rolls her eyes, but doesn't take the bait. "If you don't want anything, then can you let me go, please?"

I don't need Sophie knowing how much I like keeping her close. She's already unbearable enough as is, she doesn't need any sort of ammunition against me.

So I let her go, follow her to the front door, and watch her leave. As soon as she's disappeared down the long drive, I slip my hand down the front of my pants. I'm not as hard as I was before, but I'm semi-hard.

I shrug. Maybe I'll spend this precious alone time jerking off.

Jerking off to the thought of Sophie Sutton on her knees on my kitchen floor, licking something other than my boots.

# 6

# FREDDY

## Sophie

I LEAVE EVAN'S HOUSE jittering with a mixture of fear and triumph. All in all, I handled myself as well as I could have. I entered the enemy's lair and got out not only unscathed but with something I wanted.

Getting two afternoons away from school a week is exactly the chance I needed. Evan's house is on the outskirts of Fernwell. If I manage to find a job there, I could begin saving money.

A complete win-win for me: getting away from Evan and getting a job. Two birds, one stone.

My instinct leads me to the café where I saw the *Now Hiring* sign during the holidays. It's very quiet now half-term is over. Inside, it's warm and cosy, with big felt armchairs and lots of plants. Soft jazz and the smell of coffee and pastries mingle in the warm air.

A girl about my age is standing behind the counter, a cup of tea in one hand, her phone in the other. She has brown hair dyed purple at the ends, and delicate piercings all along her ears.

When I approach the counter, she looks up with a polite smile.

"Oh, hi! What can I get you?"

"I'm here because of the sign?" I point, a little awkwardly, to the sign still stuck to the window.

"Oh!" she says again. "One sec." She walks to the door behind the counter and pops her head in to call out, "Freddy!"

A boy a couple of years older than me appears, carrying a box of coffee filters. He looks like the male version of the girl, with soft brown hair and grey eyes, piercings in his ears and a big woolly jumper. I can't remember the last time I met a boy who doesn't go to Spearcrest, a boy who's normal and nice, and my heart skips a beat when he looks up with a smile.

"Hi! How can I help?"

"She's here about the job," the girl says, hopping up to perch herself on the counter behind her.

"Oh, right," Freddy puts the box down and pulls a notepad out of his back pocket, a pen stuck in the coil. "The job you'd be applying for is actually Jess's job," he points at the girl. "She needs to drop her hours to focus on her studies, so we just need someone to fill in for her."

"I can only do Tuesday and Thursday afternoons, and maybe school holidays," I say with a wince.

It feels rude to be applying for a job and already making demands, but I don't have a choice. Freddy doesn't seem fazed at all though, just casts a questioning look towards the girl—Jess. She shrugs. "Sure, whatever, I could make that work."

"Do you have any work experience?" Freddy asks me.

"No," I admit. I hesitate, but something about his friendly smile and soft grey eyes feels trustworthy. "I'm not really allowed to apply for a job."

Freddy frowns. "How old are you?"

"Almost eighteen!" I say quickly. "But I go to... the school I go to doesn't allow students to get jobs."

Jess narrows her eyes. "You go to Spearcrest?"

"Only because my parents work there" I hurry to explain. "I'm not... uh, I definitely could do with a job."

For some reason, I am completely embarrassed: embarrassed I go to Spearcrest, embarrassed I'm not rich, embarrassed I've never had a job.

"Well, it's not like this job is rocket science," Jess says to Freddy. She turns back to me. "I could teach you how to make coffee and work the till, but apart from that, there's nothing much to it."

"I'm a fast learner," I say quickly.

Freddy is smiling—not smirking or sneering. He's genuinely, openly smiling—something the boys at Spearcrest are far too cool to do.

"We could give it a go, couldn't we?" I can't tell whether he's speaking to me or Jess, but we both nod. "Why don't we start Thursday? Come in and Jess will show you the ropes, then you can see how you feel about the job."

I nod, flooded with relief. It's hard to believe my mission is going so well, that things are going so smoothly for me.

"I would love that," I say, smiling back at him. "Thank you so much."

"Don't be so quick to thank us," Jess says. "The pay is shit."

"Jess!" Freddy exclaims, more amused than scandalised. "She's not wrong," he says to me. "We're not exactly raking it in over here, so we're all pretty much on minimum wage."

"That's more than I'm earning right now," I say.

They both laugh, and Freddy passes me his notepad and pen. "Here, write down your name and number and we'll stay in touch. Are you sure it's going to be ok with your school?"

"I'm just going to try and make sure they don't find out."

"So long as I'm not signing up for something illegal," Freddy says.

"No, no, of course not." I quickly write down my name and phone number and hand him his notepad back.

He glances down at it and looks up at me. "Nice to meet you, Sophie. I'm Freddy, and this is Jess, my little sister."

She gives a little wave and I can't help the big goofy smile on my face. They feel so welcoming and... normal. Just nice people who don't live in massive villas and travel around in Bentleys and private jets.

People like me.

"Nice to meet you both."

After I leave, I make my way back to the school, walking on clouds. Each footstep is lighter, the weight on my shoulders suddenly lifted. I left school crushed by anxiety, but I'm returning and I don't have to worry about Evan (for now) or about finding a job (for now), and that's a victory.

That night, I treat myself to a rare evening off and cuddle up on the common room couches with Audrey and Araminta. I am extra careful to check nobody is around when I tell them about the events of the day and my new job at the café.

"A café job!" Audrey laughs. "Could you be any more wholesome?"

"I'm sure it won't be as cute as the movies make it out to be," I say. "But it beats having to tutor Evan."

"I still can't believe you made a deal with him," Audrey says. "Like making a deal with the devil. You sure you know what you're doing, Sophie?"

"I think it's kind of hot," Araminta says. "Two deadly enemies turned reluctant allies. You know what's next, don't you?"

"I wouldn't call us allies," I interrupt quickly. "I'm just lucky my plans happen to fit in with his laziness."

"Still, though," Audrey says. "Best be careful. I wouldn't be surprised if he tried to lock you up in his house and torment you or something. You know, torture you for his own amusement or whatever gets him off."

I wince. "Well, he's making me do his Lit work for him, so it's not like he's doing any of this out of the kindness of his heart."

"I'll never understand it," Araminta says. She's in her satin pyjamas, absent-mindedly pulling on strands of her long black hair. "It's like he hates you, but he's obsessed with you at the same time."

"Hardly." I try to shake my head, but Audrey forces me to stay still. I am sitting at the foot of her armchair while she pulls my hair into two French braids. Despite her firmness, it's strangely soothing, so I don't mind her manhandling me a little. "He wouldn't give me half as much shit if I was rich."

"I don't know..." Audrey says dubiously.

"You're wrong," Araminta curtails the conversation. "Evan Knight would find a way to crawl his way under your skin even if you were the bloody queen of England."

"I'd have him thrown in the Tower of London," I mutter darkly.

"You won't need to anymore," Audrey says lightly from behind me. "You've got sexy Freddy to protect you now."

Heat rises to my cheeks and I turn to glare at her. "Don't be childish, Audrey. He's not even sexy."

"Did she," Audrey says to Araminta as she pushes my head away to continue braiding my hair, "or did she not spend at least half an hour describing how 'stylish' and 'kind' and 'sweet' Freddy seems?"

"A crush on your boss, Sophe?" Araminta says with a suggestive waggle of her eyebrows. "My my, such scandalous behaviour."

"I blame myself," Audrey sighs dramatically. "I didn't think my summer fling would have such a profound influence on the poor girl."

"You're all a right pair of idiots!" I say, my cheeks ablaze. "So immature."

"Alright, alright, we'll stop teasing if you answer one question," Audrey says, and her evil grin already tells me she's looking for trouble. "Who's hotter? Freddy or Evan? You have to be honest, though."

I think about it. Evan's height and gold skin and broad shoulders. His dangerous grin and summer sky eyes. Those big arms, that mop of loosely-curled fair hair. His long strides, easy laughter and pretty teeth. Evan is gorgeous like he's from a movie, gorgeous like he knows it and feels no shame, with a sort of laid-back arrogance.

Where Evan is like the ultimate American rich kid cliche, Freddy is comfortingly British. Brown hair, grey eyes, big jumper. A kind, open smile. Not good-looking in the captivating, electrifying way Evan is, but... normal. Warm.

Safe.

If I had to be honest, I know whose name I would have to say to Audrey. But I don't want to be honest. So I don't give an honest answer.

Instead, I give the answer that feels right.

"It's Freddy."

7

# BURN

## Evan

ON THURSDAY AFTERNOON I'M in the hallway getting ready for a run when I hear the taxi pull up outside. I wrench the door open. Sophie is out of uniform today, and it completely throws me off.

It's not even like she's dressed particularly provocatively. If anything, it's the opposite.

She's wearing a big, ugly, baggy jumper, like someone's grandad would wear, a short black skirt, black tights, old black boots. Her hair is loose around her shoulders and a little wind-ruffled.

When she sees me, her face immediately scrunches into a frown.

"I like your jumper," I call out from the doorway against which I'm leaning. "The boomer vibe is a good look on you. Really suits your miserable personality."

"I'm not here to get fashion commentary from a guy wearing shorts in this weather," she says.

I glance down at myself. I'm wearing a long-sleeved top and loose shorts. It's not so much an outfit designed to be stylish—I'm only wearing what's comfortable for running. In reality, I could go running in a tank top and hot pants and still not be cold. I spent a big portion of my childhood winters in Cape Cod; British autumn doesn't even come close.

"Don't know why you're complaining," I say. "You get to check out my legs."

"A gift I never hoped for," she deadpans. "You might even say a gift I never wished for."

"Please, Sutton, everyone in Spearcrest knows you want me."

She rolls her eyes. "A rumour invented by you and spread by you. Bit embarrassing, if you ask me."

"Don't they say there's an atom of truth to every rumour?"

"Not this one. But well done for knowing what an atom is. You're not as dumb as you look."

I give her my most charming grin. "I never said you wanted me for my brain, Sutton."

She sighs, walks up to stand at the foot of the steps leading up the door, stretching her hand out.

"Talking of things I don't want, do you know what else I *don't* want?" she says. "Your homework. But here I am."

If I'm honest with myself, I completely forgot about asking her to do my homework. My mind got a little sidetracked after she left.

I definitely expected a lot more of a fight on that issue, and I'm not about to pass up the opportunity to get Sophie Sutton to do my schoolwork for me.

"Alright, come in!" I call, then run inside to go grab my backpack where I dropped it in the atrium, by the 17th century Greek statue my dad won last year at Sotheby's.

"It's in here somewhere," I call over my shoulder when I hear Sophie approach.

She doesn't reply, and I end up pulling out every notebook, booklet and handout I stuffed into my bag throughout the week. I hand them over to Sophie, who looks at the messy pile with open disgust.

"What on earth am I looking at?"

"My Lit homework."

"That's not homework," she snaps. "That's just a big pile of... stuff!"

"Well, I don't fucking know!" I say, dumping the pile on the floor where I'm kneeling. "Mr Houghton is always giving us stuff. I have no idea what half this shit is. You sort it out, since you're so fucking smart."

Sophie gives me a look of barely repressed exasperation but kneels next to me, setting her bag aside.

Now she's so close, I can smell her, that warm vanilla scent that makes me think she must taste sweet as caramel. She tucks her hair behind her ears and pushes her glasses up on her nose, leaning down to sift through the pile. With that serious look and those thick black frames, she looks almost like a teacher.

The kind of young, hot teacher you want to bend over your desk and fuck from behind.

"Right." Her tone is crisp and business-like, startling me back to reality as surely as a slap to the face. "I've roughly sorted it into three piles: the poetry comparison material, the Shakespeare material and your research project. Have you picked a topic for that yet?"

I already know she's going to be mad, so there's no point in delaying the inevitable. "No. I don't even know what I have to do for it."

She rolls her eyes and sighs. "Right, right. Well, the deadline for that isn't until Spring Term, so let's leave it for now. What essay do you have due first?"

"An essay on Hamlet in a couple of weeks."

"You guys are doing Hamlet for your Shakespeare?" she asks with a frown.

"Uh... aren't we meant to?"

"Of course you are, don't be stupid. Your teacher's probably selected a different text from our teacher. I'm doing Othello, which means I can't even use my notes. Do you have any notes on the Hamlet lectures?"

I hand her a notebook, knowing full well she's going to be displeased by its contents. As expected, she flicks through the pages with the tips of her fingers and her face twists into a grimace of disgust. "Most of this is doodles."

"Not just doodles," I say, grabbing the notebook and flipping proudly to one of the last pages. "I also got Grace's number, look. She even drew a heart."

Sophie gives me a withering look but doesn't comment.

"So you have a Hamlet essay and no notes. That's all I have to go off?"

"I have those handouts," I say, pointing at the essay booklet Mr Houghton gave us.

She sighs and picks it up. "Well, actually that's probably going to be of some help." She puts the Shakespeare pile she made into her bag, making sure none of the papers bend and then looks back up at me. "How on earth can you be failing Lit with Mr Houghton as your teacher? He's incredible."

I shrug. "Sure, but he's pretty boring."

"He's not—" she interrupts herself and takes a deep breath. "I suppose everything is boring to someone like you," she ends up saying, voice dripping with disdain.

She stands and I quickly follow suit. "And I suppose everything must be interesting to someone as boring as you."

Even though I said it to get a reaction out of her, it's a bare-faced lie. I've never found Sophie boring. I don't find her boring when she's nagging, or judgemental, or doing some impossibly snooty prefect stuff.

She wasn't even boring when she was going through my Lit stuff, and I find Lit *depressingly* boring.

But she completely ignores the insult and instead, she gestures at the piles still on the floor. "Keep all this somewhere safe and tidy for when we get to the next assignment. I'll take the Shakespeare stuff and sort out the essay."

Then she turns around and strides away. I scramble to catch up with her and all but throw myself against the door when she reaches for the door handle, stopping her exit.

"You're leaving?"

"I got what I came for," she says. "Now I'm off. That's our deal, remember?"

"You're going into town?"

She sighs. "Yes. I am. And you're in my way."

"Want me to drop you off?"

"You drive?" she asks with a frown.

I grin. "Of course. And all my dad's cars are here."

"Oh my god, a joyride with the cutest boy in the year?" she says, her voice and expression completely blank. "What more could I ever want?"

I stand a little closer to her, and that familiar heat in the pit of my stomach is back. She's not giving me a lot, but she's giving me enough for the excitement and adrenaline to rush through me.

"The cutest boy in the year, Sutton?" I ask, watching her face closely for the smallest reaction. "Is that so?"

She nods. "Totally. My only dream is that you'll take me to prom."

Her words unleash a flood of images through my mind.

Sophie in a prom dress, probably something edgy and black because she's too cool for jewel tones and crystals.

Sophie in the passenger's seat of my car, filling the air with the sweet vanilla perfume of her. My hand resting on her thigh as I drive, slowly moving up, her skirt gathering in the crook of my elbow.

Walking into the party with Sophie on my arm, fetching her cups of spiked punch, dancing tipsily with her under the glittering lights of cheesy disco balls.

Kissing Sophie, hard and breathlessly, outside against the hood of my car. Pushing her into the backseat to kiss my way up her legs, to taste her pretty pussy and take her, hard and rough in the darkness.

Not because I like her and she likes me.

But because Sophie is so closed in on herself that touching her is an act of conquest, of victory.

"Really?" I breathe, my throat suddenly tight.

"No," she snaps. "Obviously not. Spearcrest doesn't even have a prom. Nor do I want you to drive me anywhere. I want you to honour our deal and get out of my way."

I move away from the door and let her through.

She doesn't bother to say goodbye. She simply stomps away like the uptight, cocky little fucker she is, disappearing around the bend in the drive. I remain standing in the doorway for a long time, the adrenaline ebbing and fading.

And when it's gone, all that's left is the aching, hungry thought of touching Sophie Sutton.

## The First Time Evan Touched Sophie

*I DIDN'T EVEN REALISE I was becoming friends with Sophie while it happened. I didn't realise until one day when Sophie and I were walking from our English classroom to the Science building, talking about our plans for the weekend.*

*"My parents are away but my sister is flying in from New York, so we're going to spend the weekend in London. She'll probably make me carry all her shopping bags around like she normally does."* I turn to Sophie. *"What about you?"*

*She shrugs. "Stuck here again. My parents are refusing to let me come home from Spearcrest until I make friends."*

*I grin at her. "Well, can't you tell them you're made a friend? I count, don't I?"*

*She stops in her tracks and looks at me. I really like the way Sophie looks at me: direct and serious. Often, looking at Sophie feels like looking at an adult, a young woman who is already miles ahead of me. It's a little intimidating, and totally captivating.*

*But today, she is more serious than usual.*

*Her voice comes out low and earnest. "Are we friends, then?"*

*My heart is a little too light in my chest, like the flutter of nerves before a rugby match. I bite the inside of my cheek, then shrug.*

*"Yeah—right?"*

*She looks at me, and I can't read her expression at all. Then she gives a slow nod. "Yes."*

*After that, it was like I had blurry eyesight and was now wearing glasses. Everything came into focus. Our friendship was very different from my friendship with Zach, with the other boys in the circle, Luca, Iakov and Sev.*

*And it was different from my friendship with girls, too. Every girl at school appeared to me in the form of a potential girlfriend.*

*But not Sophie.*

*Our friendship existed in a sort of in-between state. I didn't view her the way I viewed my friends, but I didn't view her the way I viewed girls, either. Our friendship filled the gaps, then grew.*

*We would sit together in English at first, then in our other classes too. At the time, Sophie had just arrived, and she had been placed in all middle sets. I knew she would soon outgrow me and end up in all the top sets where the Spearcrest geniuses, like Zachary and Theodora, ended up.*

*But in the meantime, I wanted to enjoy sitting with her, listening to her explain things to me. We'd walk together from one lesson to the next, even when we didn't share lessons or classrooms.*

*Bit by bit, we started hanging out outside of lessons. Sometimes, I'd spot her alone in the quad and I'd go sit with her. After school, if I didn't have rugby practice, I'd sometimes trail her to chess club and watch her while she played. Looking at her serious eyes, her frown, her spotty face, all still like undisturbed water, no expression rippling the surface.*

*Then, everything changed.*

*It was a late October afternoon. Sophie was doing homework in the study and I was sitting at her side, pretty much copying her answers. After we finished, she sat back and gave me a disapproving look that belonged more on the face of a sixty-year-old librarian than a fourteen-year-old girl.*

*"You can't keep doing this. At some point, you're going to need to start studying."*

*"If you help me with my homework this year, then I'll work so hard for my GCSEs I'll be in all top sets with Zachary."*

*She gave a little laugh—a Sophie laugh. Dry and low and with a mocking edge to it. "Hah, is that a promise?"*

*And then I extended my hand to her. "It's a promise."*

*And then she put her hand in mine and we shook.*

*It was my first time touching Sophie, skin on skin.*

*The warmth of her seeped from her skin into mine, and shot right into my veins. In that moment, something strange and irreversible happened. Everything seemed to dull and darken and soften around us, until there was nothing else but Sophie in the dim lights of the desk lamps.*

*Sophie, and her dark eyes, and thick eyelashes, and the dark curtains of her hair parting around her face. Sophie's acne-ridden cheeks and the way the corners of her lips lifted in a slight smirk.*

*Sophie's hand in mine, and the warmth of her skin against mine.*

*And that was the first time I touched Sophie. When I did, her presence burst into flames in my life. She has been a burning beacon ever since, drawing me to her like a moth to a flame.*

*But I have no intention of being the one to burn.*

8

# SECRET BOYFRIEND

## Sophie

OVER THE NEXT FEW weeks, the café becomes the most comforting part of my day. At first, it's stressful learning the pricing of things, how to make coffee, working the till. But Jess is so relaxed, and Freddy, who's technically speaking our supervisor, is so sweet my nerves soon fade away.

The more time I spend on the job, the better I get at it. On my sixth shift, Jess even leaves to go to the library to work on some assignments, and I work most of the shift alone.

Freddy is never gone, though. He tends to be in the office managing the place or baking the treats we sell in the shiny window displays. Still, I'm never lonely, and Freddy even encourages me to bring a book with me so I don't get bored.

Compared to the slowly mounting pressure at school, the café is a much-needed sanctuary.

As for Evan, since entering into this alliance, he's been a lot more bearable. Of course, it helps that I never have to see him at school and that he's clearly trying to stay on my nice side for the sake of his assignments.

He keeps asking me where I'm going every Tuesday and Thursday, but since there isn't much he can do to force me to answer, I just ignore his questions. I can tell he still says things to try and get a rise out of me, but it's getting easier and easier to brush him away.

Maybe part of it is due to spending time with Freddy and getting to know him more.

Freddy's parents own the café, and Freddy handles it while they are busy running another café they own in London. His actual dream is to be an artist, so in his spare time he paints and sketches. A few of his paintings—moody landscapes and soulful animal portraits—hang in the café. His brushstrokes are exactly like him: gentle and expressive.

The more I get to know Freddy, the more I despise the boys at Spearcrest. Even though they have every opportunity at their fingertips, they do nothing with them. Apart from finding newer and more obnoxious ways of displaying their wealth, they don't *spend* so much as *waste* their time.

But Freddy... Freddy is *into* things. He has hopes and dreams. A personality instead of an expensive watch.

And he's actually interested in me. We discuss movies we like and books we've read. Instead of constantly being on edge like I am around Evan, I can relax around Freddy, be a softer version of myself.

Things go smoothly until the British autumn sets in for good.

Clouds stack on top of clouds throughout the week. Daylight becomes as dark as dusk. By Wednesday, rain is inevitable. And on Thursday, while I sit in the taxi on the way out of Spearcrest, a booming crack startles both the driver and me.

By the time I reach Evan's house, the clouds are gutting themselves.

Rain falls so thick and fast I don't even know how the driver sees anything through the windshield. I thank him, get out of the car, and run over to Evan's doorway just for the shelter of his porch.

The best I can hope for is that the rain stops eventually. I have a little umbrella, but in this wind it's useless. Freddy is expecting me, so if the rain doesn't stop I'm just going to brave the deluge and hope for the best.

I wait a whole fifteen minutes, but the rain shows no sign of relenting. My coat doesn't have a hood but I have a woolly hat on, and my trusty old boots. Although both will only be able to protect me for so long, what choice do I have?

Time to brave the flood.

## Evan

I WAS JUST COMING out of the shower when I heard the taxi pull up outside fifteen minutes earlier. Since I had to cut my run short due to the pelting rain, I expected to hear a knock on the door any minute.

Obviously, I should have known better.

Taking a seat in my mom's reading nook, I peer through the curtains. This vantage point gives me a perfect view of the porch. There, Sophie Sutton sits like the prideful, stubborn little thing she is.

She's wearing a big grey coat, a hat and her big old boots, her legs tucked against her. Of course, she's too proud to ask me to come in. Or afraid. It's hard to tell with Sophie.

I'm not wearing my watch, but I glance around the corner at my dad's ugly vintage Patek Philippe clock, which dominates the wall above the mantelpiece. Fifteen minutes. For fifteen minutes, she's been sitting on the cold steps, hugging herself and waiting.

When she finally stands up, a sharp blade of triumph cuts right through me. Watching her pride shatter as she knocks on my door is going to be so sweet, and I'm already anticipating the taste of it.

Except that, of course, Sophie pulls her woolly hat deep over her head and ears, and sets off down the porch steps straight in the direction of the pouring rain.

"For fuck's sake," I grit out, jumping to my feet.

I'm at the door before she's reached the end of the steps. She starts when I call out, "Sutton!"

She turns, startled. Her eyes dart down my body, then back up, almost too quickly to notice. But it reminds me that I'm only wearing boxers, a towel wrapped around my shoulders.

A flush colours her cheeks, sending a tendril of dark pleasure unfurling through my chest. I want to tell her that she can look all she likes. I've been playing sports my whole life, I work out on a strict schedule and I was a part of Spearcrest's rugby team up until last year, when I had to stop due to injuries.

I know what my body looks like. I've worked hard to make it look that way.

So if Sophie wants to look at it, she can look her fill. I *want* her to look.

But her eyes are firmly pinned to mine when she belligerently snaps, "What?"

I jab my head up towards the sky. "You're not going to walk to town in this?"

She raises an eyebrow. "No? What am I going to do, fly?"

I roll my eyes. For someone so smart and well-read, she can be so stupid when she wants to be. I hold the door open. "Don't be so fucking stubborn. Come in already."

"While you're prancing around naked? No thanks."

"What are you afraid of, Sutton?" I ask with a smirk. "Never seen a naked guy before?"

She looks totally unimpressed. "Not one I didn't want to see."

I narrow my eyes at her. She's not implying she's seen a guy naked? Uptight, stuck-up Sophie? No chance.

"But as charmed as I am by all this," she continues witheringly, "I have somewhere to be."

"Fine, don't come in. Just wait here, okay?"

She narrows her eyes and hesitates.

"Sutton, I mean it. Wait."

Sophie gives me a long look and doesn't say anything, but she's not going anywhere either. So I close the door and sprint up the stairs and to my room. I throw on the first clean clothes I can get my hands on: black sweatpants and a white t-shirt, socks and my old white sneakers I mostly wear when I'm driving somewhere.

I keep the towel around my shoulders, because my hair is still wet, and grab the first set of keys I find in my dad's office desk. By the time I pull around in the Porsche Boxster, I half expect Sophie to be gone.

But she's still there, and she actually gets in the car. Her posture screams her discomfort and mistrust. She sits with her back straight and her legs crossed, hugging her backpack to her chest.

Low music plays in the car, the bass pounding like a pulse. I can smell the metallic heat of the car, my shampoo, the warm vanilla of Sophie. My heartbeat quickens, even though there's no reason for it to.

Her proximity is tantalising. I desperately want her to say something, to give me anything to hold on to and pull on. Every interaction between Sophie and me is always a confrontation, a battle, but this far away from Spearcrest, in the small cabin of the sports car, it's like the rules have changed.

How do I approach her when she's this close? Without the Young Kings around us to make sure I never close the distance between us? Without Spearcrest to remind us we belong in different worlds?

The silence stretches on. Sophie says nothing—doesn't even look my way. In the end, I'm the first one to speak.

"Well? Are you going to tell me where to drop you off?"

"The high street."

I wait, but she says nothing else.

"Anywhere in particular on the high street?"

"No."

Since it's clear she's not going to give me anything more to go on, I drive on. It's been a while since I've driven stick, but it comes back to me quickly. There's something grounding about the gear stick, the responsive pedals under my feet. Something comforting about the control I have over the car—the kind of control I could only ever wish to have over Sophie.

She stares out of her window and says nothing.

For weeks, I've been wondering where she's been going—for weeks she's given me absolutely nothing.

But there can only be one thing Sophie is doing away from school.

Sophie has never dated anyone at Spearcrest. Even if she had done so in secret, I would have known. I would have destroyed anyone who dared go near her. But I've never had to, because I worked very hard to ensure everyone would know about the special attention I pay Sophie.

Special attention which keeps her alienated and untouchable at all times.

Not that I've needed to work *that* hard—Sophie keeps herself isolated quite well on her own. Her open disdain for the kids of Spearcrest and her arrogant self-reliance have done well to keep others at bay.

It's a miracle she has any friends.

But I'm not naive. Just because Sophie hasn't been dating Spearcrest boys doesn't mean she's not dating at all. She might not have the polished sheen and picture-perfect good looks of the prettiest girls in the school, but she's not bad-looking by any stretch of the imagination.

Her looks are particular: with her thick, dark eyebrows, her heavy-lidded eyes, that austere centre parting and her thick, shiny brown hair. With her long limbs and broad shoulders, she looks almost athletic, but she has the rigid posture of an old-timey schoolmistress. Her strides are long and authoritative. She stands out even when she's trying to blend in with that sort of awkward arrogance she exudes.

Everything about her is hard and unyielding, but it's part of what makes her so intriguing.

She makes me want to test her strength, to see how far she can bend before she snaps. But just because I feel this way doesn't mean the prettiness of her dark eyes, her pouty lips and her smooth skin have gone unnoticed by other guys.

And Sophie's used to being either mocked or ignored by the boys at Spearcrest, so I bet some guy could slip right past her defences if he was sweet enough to her.

The thought is both electrifying and infuriating.

I sneak a glance at her. She's leaning against the window, her chin propped in her palm. I know this pose well—she always sits like this when she's deep in thought. What is she thinking about? Her secret boyfriend?

If Sophie had a secret boyfriend, what would he look like? Knowing Sophie, he'd probably be older. Smart, polite, well-read. He'd study something pretentious, like Classics or Philosophy. He'd probably fascinate her and make her smile.

I turn my eyes back to the road, the row of glowing red brake lights ahead. Traffic into town is slow because of the almost-blinding rain, and my mind wanders, lured down a slippery path of questions. What must it be like to be this guy, to have Sophie's attention and affection? To take her on dates and hold her hands and talk to her without every conversation being laced with insults? To spend time with her doing nothing, just listening to music or idly touching her long hair while she reads a book?

When I imagine it, my mind plays the film of a relationship with Sophie with me starring as the boyfriend.

We're in my bedroom, and it's my bed she's lying on while she's annotating some boring copy of whatever she's studying. It's my hand stroking the glossy length of her brown hair. I'd try to play a game on my phone but I'd be too distracted by her slight frown of concentration.

Not because I'd want to be her boyfriend, but because I can't ever picture someone else being at the centre of her life.

She'd look up at me, and I'd notice how soft and kissable her lips are. My hand would brush her cheek, wrap around her neck, pull her slowly towards me. She'd melt into me, her mouth would open under mine, my tongue would glide against hers. Then I'd pull her to me, slide my hands under her shirt, my finger searching for—

"Stop."

Sophie's voice startles me so much I pull a muscle in my neck turning my head.

For a terrifying second, I'm scared I've been thinking aloud and that Sophie is trying to stop me from expressing some deep and disturbing desire. But she's unbuckling her seatbelt—we've arrived on the high street.

Besides, if she'd heard what I was thinking, she'd probably have thrown herself out of the moving car. I know I would have.

I pull the car to a stop in a parking bay outside a florist. Sophie shoulders her backpack and pulls on her door handle but hesitates.

"Hey, uh... thanks for the lift."

Her gratitude is unexpected and throws me off a little. I shrug.

"Anytime, Sutton."

She doesn't say anything else. She gets out of the car, slams the door shut and runs off in the rain. Her big boots splash into puddles as she darts across the street and disappears through the doorway of a shop. I look up at the sign, peering through the thick grey blur of the relentless rain.

Gold letters on a green sign read "The Little Garden". The vintage style painting of a cup of coffee tells me this is a café.

I stay parked for a while, but Sophie doesn't come back out. Nobody else walks in apart from some old ladies. If Sophie is meeting her secret boyfriend, then he's already inside. The rain is falling too thickly to be able to see anything through the window apart from the vague glow of golden lights and the outline of plants.

For a truly stupid second, I have the impulse to get out of my car and walk into the café.

I'd know for sure then. I'd be able to see what it looks like to be someone worthy of Sophie's affections. But if I go in, there's no chance she won't see me. And if she knows I followed her she'll be understandably furious, and I'll look pathetic. I can't even think of a good excuse to give her.

So I turn the key in the ignition and set off home.

Even though I'm driving away feeling like I've just turned my back on a battle, I know better.

Because I'm not going to cede Sophie to some other guy—some insignificant nobody from some shitty British village. I've worked too hard to make Sophie untouchable, to ensure nobody could ever approach her on my watch.

I'm the one that fucked up this time, though.

Because I had the perfect excuse to keep Sophie close to me, and I gave it up like a fucking idiot. I didn't realise what was at stake when I first made that deal with Sophie. It never occurred to me Sophie would seek the things she'd never get within Spearcrest *outside* of it.

Clearly, I underestimated her.

Now, all I have to do is find a way of bringing her back to me. She won't get away as easily this time.

# 9

# BULLET

## Evan

KEEPING SOPHIE AND HER secret boyfriend out of my head is a struggle, but it's a little easier in Spearcrest, especially now I don't see her as often.

The other Young Kings all seem to be having their own thing going on. Iakov, as usual, is having problems with his dodgy family and their fucked up relationship. Sev, who came back to school suddenly engaged, seems to be trapped in some one-sided powerplay with his brand new fiancée. Zachary is busy with some special academic programme for the smartest kids in Spearcrest, and, as always, obsessed with his unhealthy rivalry with Theodora Dorokhova, the Ice Queen of Spearcrest.

Only Luca remains cold, untouched and unconcerned, but being around him doesn't make me feel better—the opposite.

Because Luca is part of the reason why I can never get any closer to Sophie than I am.

Normally, I can cope with this. I can slap on my careless grin and rip into Sophie for the entertainment of everybody else just so I get to be close to her. In my head and in my heart, I can think about her however I want. And that's fine.

But nowadays, that's getting more and more difficult to do.

Up till now, I never had to worry about anything. Up till now, it felt as though Sophie would always be in my life. But now, she's slipping away. Our time at Spearcrest is slowly but inevitably coming to an end, and Sophie apparently already has one foot out of the door.

How the fuck did she manage to get a boyfriend?

I was so fucking careful to keep her alienated from everybody at school it never occured to me I would push her straight out into the arms of boys *outside*. The thought of it sickens me—and it's all I can think about.

Everytime I close my eyes or stop to think, Sophie is in my head, sitting next to some anonymous boy—some nameless, faceless nobody. Everytime I close my eyes, she's with him, smiling at him, talking to him the way she used to talk to me back in Year 9. Earnest, self-assured, and a little too serious.

What if he holds her hand and touches her and kisses her cheeks, her mouth, her neck? What if he gets to see what's under those black tights and grandpa sweaters? What if he gets to take her back to his, to spread her on his bed all bare and soft and needy?

My stomach twists and my fists clench at the thought. *I* don't get to touch Sophie—why should anybody else?

Since I can't say any of this to anybody, I end up stuck in an endless loop of imagining scenarios and repressing my anger and frustration.

I must have underestimated the effect this is having on me, because it all comes out explosively the next Monday at school. I'm sitting on the steps of the Old Manor—the central and oldest building on campus—with the other Young Kings, the giant column-born roof shielding us from the rain. Iakov is chain-smoking as usual, filling the air with tendrils of smoke, and Sev is, as he so often is these days, ranting about his fiancée.

Out of nowhere, a voice reaches us. "You all need to get up and leave. Now."

My head turns so quickly I almost give myself whiplash. At the top of the steps, standing in the doorway into the Old Manor, is Sophie Sutton. Her hair is tied back in a low ponytail, and she's holding her clipboard to her chest like some sort of protective armour. Her eyes are hooded and her expression is about as unhappy as someone walking to their certain death. My heart leaps in my throat.

I force myself not to sit up from where I'm lying back, propped against my backpack. But my eyes find Luca; he's not made an attempt to hide his sudden interest. He sits up slowly, his pale eyes raking the length of Sophie.

Spikes of ice pierce my skin. I speak before he can.

"Here we go again, everyone. Sophie Sutton, looking for whatever scrap of attention she can get."

"Mr Ambrose sent me," she says icily.

"Oh don't worry," I smirk. "We all know you're his special little kiss-ass. Does it get you off, Sutton, doing his dirty work like this? Does it get you a nice little pat on the head for being his good little *bitch*?"

Her cheeks darken, but she doesn't even deign to send a look my way. She looks at everyone but me, which only infuriates me more.

"Couldn't you all find somewhere smarter to smoke and save us all the trouble?" she says, voice low with anger.

"*Ta gueule*," Sev mutters under his breath. Then he waves a dismissive hand at her. "Get fucked, Sophie. I don't have the patience for your shit today. Christ, you Brits are so fucking horny for rules."

"I don't think it's rules Sophie's horny for, Sev," Luca drawls. "She's clearly come here looking for something—why don't we give it to her?" He raises an eyebrow at Sophie. "Craving some attention? Do you need one of us to shove a cock down your throat, Sophie? Is that the only way to shut you up?"

I taste bile in my throat. Luca doesn't even hate Sophie—not really. He just loves playing with what's mine. Her name probably tastes delicious to him because he says it and I don't—not anymore.

The thought of his cock down her throat makes me see red. If his cock goes anywhere near her lips, I'll rip it off his body myself.

But I can't say any of this. I can't let him know I care.

"If Sutton wanted a cock down her throat," I say, moving my eyes over Sophie's black tights, her knee-length skirt, her blazer, "she would make a bit more of an effort. Those bushy eyebrows and big teeth aren't going to make anybody hard, especially when there are so many hot girls here. Nobody wants to fuck a dog when they could fuck a supermodel."

"Oh, ouch, that one really hurt." Sophie's tone is bone dry but the flush in her cheeks darkens. "A dog, huh? Be careful, Evan, you might just cut yourself on the sharp edge of your wit."

Before I can reply, she turns to Iakov. "Put out your cigarette or go smoke somewhere else."

Iakov stares at her, and she stares back.

They both have a similar gaze, actually: dark and bleak. Watching them interact is like looking at two immovable statues facing one another. Iakov lifts his cigarette to his lips, takes a long drag, then stands. He's the tallest of all of us, built like a tank, but Sophie never flinches, even as he approaches her.

I know for a fact Iakov would cut off his own hand before hurting a girl—outside of the bedroom—but my stomach still churns when he approaches her. My instinct is to stand, to get between them and tell him to stay away from her, but I push that instinct deep down inside.

Then, Iakov flicks what's left of his cigarette with two fingers, shooting the glowing butt straight at Sophie's chest. It hits her clipboard and falls at her feet. Iakov walks away without a word.

Sophie, her expression unchanged, crushes the butt under her heel and turns around.

"Leaving so soon, Sutton?" I call out lightly. "Got your fix of attention and now you're done? I feel so used."

Her head turns and she tosses me a look over her shoulder. It's a look full of scorn and dislike, but all I can see when I look at her is another guy's arms around her, another guy's mouth moving against her skin. My body is raw and electric, as if I've just been hit by lightning.

"I could be staring at white paint drying on a white wall," she sneers, "and it would still be more interesting than whatever trite shit is coming out of your mouth today."

I tilt my head back. "What are you talking about my mouth for, Sutton? Is it on your mind?"

She narrows her eyes. "Why would it be when I'd get more pleasure kissing a slug?"

I bet she's real proud of that one as well. Would hate her to think she landed a low though. So I give her my cockiest grin. "Good, because kissing slugs is the only action you're likely to get this year, Sutton."

She shrugs. "If you say so."

And then she just walks away.

Sev throws her a dirty look and mutters, "Casse-couille." He resumes his conversation with Zachary, but Luca's eyes find me, no doubt amused and waiting to see what I'm going to do next. I don't want to give him the satisfaction, but I'm too worked up to let the moment slip by.

Scrambling to my feet, I grab my backpack and climb up the steps two at a time.

"Where are you going?" Luca calls.

"I've got something I need to do!" I call back.

I don't bother looking back.

By the time I catch up with her, Sophie is standing near the pastoral office in the Old Manor, ticking off things on her clipboard. That fucking clipboard. I grab her elbow and she looks up sharply.

The surprise in her face melts away, promptly replaced by irritation.

"What is it, Evan? Have you come here to subject me to more of your clumsy insults and awkward banter?"

"Clumsy? Awkward? Projecting much, Sutton?"

"I don't have time for whatever *this*," she gestures between us, "is. So if you want something, spit it out. Otherwise go and find something else to amuse yourself with, since we both know you're not exactly spending your time studying or cultivating your mind."

"You're on fire today, Sutton. Every word coming out of your mouth is a bullet."

"If only." She gives a sigh full of fake wistfulness. "If my words could kill, you'd die every day."

"Yeah, yeah, okay Sutton, we get it, you hate my guts." I smirk. "You hate me so much I'm all you think about. You hate me so much you dream of me every night."

"Don't flatter yourself," she snaps. "Even the monsters in my nightmares have brain cells."

"Maybe you should try fucking the monsters from your nightmare, Sutton. You might be less of an uptight bitch if you got laid—even if it's only in your dreams."

She doesn't even dignify this with a response—not even a roll of her eyes. She simply turns around and walks off towards the pastoral office.

I grab her elbow once more and turn her around to face me.

"*What do you want?*" she grinds out between clenched teeth.

"I want to talk about the tutoring programme."

She shakes her elbow loose from my grip and glares at me. "Talk to Miss Bailey."

"I want to know where you're going instead of tutoring me." I cock an eyebrow and tilt my head. "Can't exactly ask Miss Bailey, can I?"

For a moment, we just stare at one another. Her dark eyes slice into mine like black blades. Her face is hard with dislike and mistrust. But at least she's looking at me, her attention entirely focused on me.

Not on Luca, or the other Young Kings. Not on some random guy outside of school. She's here, with me, just within my grasp—exactly where I want her.

"Look, Evan," she says finally, her raspy voice low and firm. "If you have a problem with the tutoring programme, talk to Miss Bailey. If you want to grass me up for not doing the tutoring programme—talk to Miss Bailey. I don't owe you the truth—I don't owe you anything at all. And even if I did, let me make something perfectly clear to you: I do not trust you. I will *never* trust you. I would love to be able to say I have never trusted you, but we both know that's not true—and that's exactly how we got where we are today. You might not learn from your mistakes, since nothing ever happens in your life to force you to learn, but luckily for you, we can both learn from *my* mistakes. And trusting you was the biggest of those mistakes."

Her lips curl in a cold, hard imitation of a smile. "And with that said, I'm going to walk away and get on with my day. As for you, you can just go right ahead and—oh, I don't know—*fuck off*."

And then she whips around, her long ponytail following in a graceful arc, the tip whipping against my chest, and she strides away.

## *The Last Time Sophie Trusted Evan*

*My first Christmas away from Spearcrest was like waking up from a nightmare but then realising you are still asleep, just in a slightly different nightmare. My parents spent the entire holiday asking me about school, the teachers, the lesson. Asking me about the other kids, the friends I'd made.*

*I could talk well enough about the quality of the learning, about how hard I'd been working, about enrolling into after-school clubs. My teachers across almost every subject told me I'd be moving up sets after the holidays—a clear proof of my academic capabilities.*

*But this wasn't really what my parents wanted to know. Doing well at school wasn't the kind of thing they could be impressed by because it was what they expected—the bare minimum.*

*What they really wanted to know was whether I was making the most of the opportunities Spearcrest presented me. They wanted to know who I'd made friends with, if I was making connections with the kids of politicians, or actors, or lawyers, or CEOs.*

*I kept all my answers vague. I didn't want them to lecture me about the importance of making connections in Spearcrest. Equally, I didn't want them to go snooping around my friends, though of course, I only had one friend. Evan.*

*But if I told them about Evan I would inevitably have to deal with the questions, with them giving me a whole break-*

*down of his family's wealth and importance. And I didn't want that.*

*Spending time with Evan made me forget I was in Spearcrest. It made me feel, even for a little while, like I was a normal teen with a normal school. Evan didn't talk about his family, or his money. He talked about films he liked, comics he read, his favourite sweets and snacks, about his sister and his dog. Normal things, like a normal person.*

*So I spend most of the holiday hating my time away and simultaneously dreading the new term, but when the new term starts, it's not as bad as I thought. Lining up outside the main hall for the start of term assembly, I'm just staring out at the pale grey sky and the snow crowning the naked branches of the trees when a hand grabs my elbow.*

*I turn and see summer sky-blue eyes and a headful of curls gleaming like pale gold. A smile rises to my face. "Hey."*

*"Hey, you." Evan's grin is all dimples and bright white teeth. He pulls a box from his pocket and hands it to me. "Merry late Christmas."*

*I take the box. "Is this for me?"*

*"Yeah. It's your Christmas present. Open it."*

*My heart beats so hard in my chest it's practically bruising my ribs. The box is small, but beautifully packaged in powder-blue paper, with a silver bow and curly ribbons.*

*Tearing open the wrapping feels almost rude, but Evan's eager expression urges me on. I open the small box to find a small silver necklace, a tiny silver bear hanging from it.*

*Not a teddy bear, but a real bear, a tiny real bear with a long snout. I look up.*

*"Bears are my favourite animals."*

*He smiles. "I know. They are super smart and are some of the only animals who grieve for each other—I remember."*

*I swallow back a lump in my throat and close the box. "I didn't get you anything."*

*He shrugs. "That's fine. We didn't say we were going to get presents, but I saw it when my sister dragged me with her when she was shopping, and I thought you might like it."*

*I did like it. I liked it so much I wore it every day after that.*

*Every day—until the last day I trusted Evan.*

*It was after assembly one time, and I'd received an award for an essay I wrote. It was a humiliating ordeal as ever, to stand in front of the entire year group to receive a certificate, with everyone looking at me and whispering about my parents being cleaners.*

*But by that time I was getting pretty good at disassociating. I went to the front, watching myself from afar, and left myself vacant for the rest of the assembly.*

*After the assembly, I hastened away from the crowd of students pouring out of the assembly hall.*

*But before I could get away, a hand caught my elbow. I turned to see Evan's face once more. Blue eyes, sunshiney hair, wide smile.*

*"Congrats on your award, Sophie. Can't believe your essay is gonna get published."*

*I waved a hand. "It's nothing. It's stupid."*

*"It's not stupid." His grin was like a little campfire, bathing me with light and warmth. "It's cool. Well done, Sophie."*

*I sighed and finally relaxed, a chuckle melting from me. "Thanks."*

*We looked at each other, and the moment became strange, different. Soft. He opened his arms and raised an eyebrow at me. I laughed, and stepped into the bracket of his arms. We hugged: he was warm, and he smelled good: deodorant and shampoo. Heat flushed through me, radiating from my heart and from his body.*

*We pulled apart. His cheeks were flushed, as flushed as mine felt. We laughed and set off to our English classroom—even though we no longer shared a class.*

*The day after, everything changed, and my friendship with Evan ended as suddenly and unexpectedly as it began.*

## 10

# CAPITULATION

## Sophie

By the end of November, life has become a blur of work, the stress of Evan replaced by the stress of academia. Despite my organisational skill, schoolwork piles up. Maths is easy enough if I put in the practice work, but History and Lit are back-to-back essays. Every teacher behaves as if theirs is the only subject you're studying. And since I'm not willing to accept anything less than top marks, it means more reading, researching and writing.

It quickly becomes obvious that there are only so many plates I can juggle. So I've handed the reins of the book club to one of the Year 12 girls who's been running it with me. I still run every morning, but my night-time swims have been cut in half. I've not even had time for chess club, which now clashes with the days I'm working.

When I'm not at the café or in classes, I'm in the study hall or the library.

The last thing I need is a full-blown fight, but this is basically what I get when the taxi drops me off outside Evan's house on the last Tuesday of November.

The incessant rain has finally relented, giving way to a frosty cold that encases every blade of grass on the manicured lawn. Even though it's cold and the ground is slippery, it's still better than having to rely on Evan for a lift.

Alas, think of the devil and he shall appear.

Or, to be exact, he shall jog up the drive, in shorts and a hoodie, his sandy hair dark with sweat. The devil's been running, and his cheeks and nose are red from the cold.

When he sees me, he pops out his earphones and greets me with a bright grin, his friendliness a glass mask for the tension thrumming through him.

"Well, *hey* Sutton. Just the person I was hoping to run into."

He is up for a fight today. I can tell. His thinly-disguised aggression radiates from his strut, the crooked tilt of his grin, the directness of his gaze. His eyes are violently blue, challenging the colour of the sky.

I should have been ready for this. It was obvious last time we spoke that he's been having second thoughts about our so-called alliance. I should have seen it coming, really. And since I got away from him last time, I doubt he's going to drop the matter this time.

Still, evasive manoeuvres are worth a try.

"As always, it's been a pleasure," I say drily, "but I have somewhere to be. So unless you have some work you need me to do, I'll be off."

"Mm," he walks up to me and stands the way he always does: right in front of me, too close for comfort. My heart starts beating faster. "Not today, Sutton. We need to talk."

"Then make it quick," I say, stifling back my annoyance. "I need to go."

"Whatever plans you have, you're going to have to cancel," he says, tilting his head and speaking with disturbing gentleness. "I'm not joking around, Sutton. I wanna talk."

This does not bode well. A sinking feeling pits through my guts. I glance up into Evan's eyes, gauging him. He's not going to budge on this. I'm going to have to weigh my options quickly.

If I go to work at the risk of pissing him off, he might renege on our deal altogether and break our tenuous alliance. If I cancel on work and keep him sweet, I risk letting down Freddy but might salvage my deal with Evan. Christmas is coming up, and there'll be a lot of shifts I can pick up over the holidays, lots of money to tuck away into my university jar.

I'm going to have to take a loss now in exchange for a victory down the line.

"Fine," I say, trying to keep the resentment out of my voice. "Go on inside, I need to make a call."

He doesn't budge, and I add with a sigh. "I'm not going to run away, Evan. I'll be inside in a second."

He watches me, his gaze as physical as a caress as it moves slowly over my face. Heat rises in my cheeks; I'm almost disturbed by the intensity of his gaze. He reaches for me and I flinch. His fingers brush my jaw and chin in a feather-light touch, his skin surprisingly warm.

"Don't be too long," he says, gentle and threatening all at once.

I swallow and glare at him. "You're the one slowing me down."

His fingers brush up my jaw and over my hair. He takes a strand and yanks. Then he grins, steps aside and saunters off into his house. I watch him go inside, and then still make sure to stand far enough from the house that Evan couldn't hear me even if he stood right behind the door, which he probably is.

Freddy answers the phone after a few rings. Anxiety strangles me when I tell him I can't come today, but to my surprise, he doesn't even question me.

"Alright Sophie, don't worry about it," he says. "Can you still make Thursday?"

"I hope so," I say quickly. "I'll let you know as soon as I can. I'm so sorry, Freddy."

He tells me not to apologise and that he'll see me soon. Before he hangs up, he says, "Take care, Sophie. We'll miss you here today!"

When I hang up, my heart is still beating fast, but not so much from fear this time. I press my cold hands against my cheeks, which are red-hot. No chance am I going inside the house with a blush.

God knows what Evan would make of that.

I push the door open and step slowly inside. Evan's house never fails to fill me with awe: opulent décor, pale marble, light pouring in from the windows in abundance.

The house feels modern and new, yet it's full of antique statues, paintings and chandeliers. It has a sort of timeless aristocratic elegance that is in stark contrast to Evan's all-American youthfulness.

Noises lead me into the kitchen. There, Evan is breaking frozen bananas into pieces and dropping them into a blender. He's still in his shorts and baggy sweatshirt, and I can't help but notice his legs, the tan skin taught with muscles.

I'm almost irrationally annoyed by the way he wears shorts even in the dead of winter. Everything else about him becomes annoying too, by association. The way his sandy hair, pale and buttery-soft, has grown a little too long, curling around his ears and against the nape of his neck. The pale eyelashes that frame his too-blue eyes, the curl of his grin, his unnaturally white teeth.

Evan's always been beautiful, but now his handsomeness is just another aspect of what makes him so hateful.

He drops two scoops of protein powder into the blender and pours in almond milk. His eyes flick to me while he blends, and he dances a little as if the noise is music to his ears. I perch myself on one of the kitchen stools, watching him with annoyance.

"Banana milkshake?" he asks once he's finished.

"I'm alright. Just say what you need to say."

He pours his milkshake into a tall glass and sighs. "All business as always, huh?"

"Unlike you, I value my time too much to waste it."

He pauses and glances at the glass in his hand. "This isn't a waste of time. Protein is important, you know. It's the building block of muscles."

"Wow, so at least you listened in science class."

"Mm," he takes a sip and licks some milkshake from the corner of his lips. "I'm more than just my good looks."

*Hardly*, I want to say, but I keep my mouth shut. His blue eyes are still fixed on me as he walks over to the kitchen island in slow, relaxed steps. To my relief, he stays on the other side, propping both elbows on the marble countertop. He takes a deep drink of his milkshake, wipes his mouth on the back of his hand, taking his sweet time.

Making me wait. Testing my patience.

"I need us to put our deal on hold for now," he says finally.

"Absolutely not."

"Hear me out, Sutton."

I clench my fists but stay quiet, waiting for him to carry on.

"We have a literature exam coming up the week before winter break. You know I'm not lying; I'm guessing you have an exam too."

I do. I've been revising for it for several weeks now. It's an exam I have every intention of getting full marks on.

I doubt Evan has even read the books for it.

"So?"

"*So*, Sutton, I'm going to be sitting that exam, same as you. Except I'm not ready for that exam."

"It's not my fault you refuse to study for your own A-Levels."

"No, but you are the one who's meant to tutor me for this particular A-Level. So how do you think it's going to go down if I fuck up the exam?"

Anger flares in my chest. "You wanted out of those tutoring sessions as much as I did!"

"I'm not saying I didn't. Jesus, Sutton, quit being so defensive. I'm just saying, if we want to carry on our little arrangement, it would work out in both our favours if you help me get at least a passing grade on this paper."

"If that's what you wanted, then why not ask earlier?" I exclaim, this time unable to suppress the anger from rising in my voice. "The exam is in less than two weeks!"

"Honestly? I had no idea we had an exam because sometimes I just don't listen to Mr Houghton at all."

"*Sometimes?*" I ask in derision. "When do you listen to him, then?"

"Hey! I actually know that Hamlet is set in Denmark, so get off my case."

I sigh, pressing my fingers to my temple. The headache throbbing there has been brewing for a few days now, but it's really hammering into life through this conversation. I'm so furious my hands are shaking. Evan has been fucking about all term, he's even blackmailed me into doing his homework for him. Now he wants me to *actually* tutor him?

"I'm not going to do it," I say, sliding off the stool to stand. "Forget it, Evan. If you want to do well in the exam, then do what the rest of us are doing and study for it."

Evan narrows his eyes then slowly sets his glass aside. Wiping his hand on the back of his mouth, he skirts the kitchen island to stand in front of me.

If he's hoping to intimidate me with his height, his broad shoulders and big arms, then he's wrong. I cross my arms, waiting for him to make his move.

"Have I not been covering for you this whole time?" he asks. He speaks with that low voice, that half-smirk. Amiable and threatening all at once. "The least you can do is help me pass a fucking exam."

"How much of a difference do you think a couple of tutoring sessions are going to make?" I meet his gaze and hold it, even though I have to step back and tilt my head up to do it.

"Then give me more sessions," he says, and his smile unfurls, widens, becomes full of self-assurance.

"You really think I'm going to waste *my* free time so I can help *you* pass an exam?" I say, incensed. "You're not just stupid, you're delusional."

Now his smile grows dangerous. He steps closer. Heat emanates from his skin, brushing against me. My heart is hammering, but not the way it did when I talked to Freddy. It knocks against my ribs, my pulse pounding in my throat. My gut squirms and heat burns in my cheeks.

It's crazy how similar adrenaline can feel to lust sometimes.

"Anything else you want to say, Sutton?" Evan's voice drips with arrogance. "Get it off your chest. Go on. I can take it."

He's goading me. But he's so close, and even though I'm forever cold, I'm running too hot under my coat and scarf. I want to grab him by his stupid baggy sweatshirt, shove him, punch his chest and slap the smirk off his face.

"Step back," I snap. "You're standing too close."

"Too close?" he asks, his voice rough. "Too close for what? What is it you're afraid of, Sutton?"

"Certainly not you."

"Are you sure?"

He reaches for me and I resist the urge to stumble back. I stand my ground as his hand closes around my thick scarf. With slow movements, he unwinds it from around my neck and pulls it off.

"Let me help you with that," he murmurs. "You look like you're too warm. Your cheeks are very red right now, Sutton."

I try to grab the scarf from him but he tosses it behind his back.

"I would love to know what you're so afraid of, Sutton." His hands slide down the lapels of my coat. "What could possibly frighten someone as brave and strong and tough as you?"

He unbuttons my coat, pulls it off my shoulders. Underneath it, I'm wearing a white shirt, an oversized jumper, a skirt, black tights—enough layers that he gets nowhere near my skin—and yet the way he slides my coat off me is so intimate it sends a strange, gliding heat deep into my belly. My breath is short, and I have to swallow hard before I speak.

"Why don't you just stop playing games and tell me what you want?" I ask, imbuing my voice with all the disdain I have for him.

"Want?" he repeats in a soft murmur. He leans down until his face is inches from mine, and I can smell him: banana milkshake and fresh sweat, cedarwood and frost. He's close enough for his breath to ghost across my lips. For a terrifying, tantalising moment, I'm sure he's going to kiss me. "I want you," he continues, his voice low and rough, "to prepare me for that *stupid fucking exam*."

Then he steps away from me and strides out of the kitchen.

I stumble back and almost collapse onto a stool, my legs buckling underneath me. Whatever mind games Evan is playing, he must be getting better at them, because I'm definitely more shaken than usual.

I'm trembling, blushing and panting, absolutely furious, and utterly humiliated.

He comes back with a shit-eating grin, carrying a pile of books, notebooks and papers, asking in a bright tone, "Where do we start, then?"

I glare at him, but he settles himself on a stool across the kitchen island. The space he's ceding is about as much as I'm going to get from him in terms of victory. So I swallow back my anger, my confusion, my resentment—and whatever strange other feeling is lurking deep inside me.

"Since the exam is about Hamlet," I say, trying to keep my voice from betraying how shaken I am. "I guess we should start with that."

It's a capitulation.

But the war's barely starting.

## 11

# AGGRESSION

## Sophie

When I return to the battlefield on Thursday, I'm better prepared and better armed. Last time, Evan caught me unawares, on the backfoot. It took me all of Tuesday night and Wednesday to recover, but I'm not known to let myself be flattened by a defeat.

Thursday afternoon, I arrive at his house with an accordion folder full of textbooks and printouts. If Evan thinks he's going to be wasting my time for two hours every Tuesday and Thursday until Christmas, he's going to find out very quickly how wrong he is.

I slam the door knocker, and Evan opens the door in less than ten seconds. His hair is damp, loose curls obscuring one eye. He smells like he's just showered, the crisp, masculine perfume of cedarwood and frost. He's wearing a long-sleeved white t-shirt and black sweatpants, a go-to look for him. Even in baggy clothes, his tall, muscular frame stands out.

He greets me with a grin, but before he can say anything I shove the box at his chest.

"What's this?" he asks with a frown.

"Your work. This is how I'm going to get you to pass the exam."

"Fucking hell, Sutton," he says, peering inside the box. "You're worse than Mr Houghton."

"Mm," I say drily. "Should've listened to him, then, shouldn't you?"

"I'm starting to wish I had," he mutters. "Come on, then, you fucking killjoy."

We take our usual places on opposing sides of the kitchen island. I pull the books and sheets out of the folder, forming neat piles between us. He watches me, his eyes flicking from my hands to my face as I organise the work.

"Wanna drink?" he asks finally.

"No, I don't think that's appropriate," I snap.

He glares at me, "I mean like a hot drink or something. I know how much you Brits love your tea."

I actually prefer black coffee, and caffeine would certainly not go amiss right now. But accepting Evan's hospitality would indebt me to him somehow. And that's the last thing I want.

I glance at his big hands, suddenly remembering the way he pushed my coat off my shoulders last time.

Okay, *one* of the last things I want.

"I'm alright," I say quickly. "But thank you."

"So much for trying to be nice," he mutters, as if offering one cup of tea was going to redeem him for years' worth of shit.

I'm tempted to say this out loud, but we've already wasted enough time, so I get straight to it.

"Right, so last week we covered the basic plot of Hamlet. Do you remember it?"

"Yeah, yeah," he says, waving a hand. "Angsty prince, incest, suicide. I remember."

"Anything else?"

"Dead girlfriend."

"So succinct."

"Oh, Sutton," Evan says, tilting his head and biting his lip. "I love it when you talk dirty to me."

"You do?" I lower my voice and lean towards him. "Then let's get really filthy, Evan."

He blinks at me in shock for a second. "Really?"

"Yes. Let's talk about the motif of disease and decay in the play and how Shakespeare uses it to symbolise corruption."

The only reason I say it is to make him feel stupid; I doubt he has any idea what I'm talking about. But he doesn't fall for my trap. Instead he sighs and, to my surprise, flips open his tragically underused notebook.

"Go on, then, my dirty little slut," he says with a wicked grin, clicking his pen open with his thumb. "I'm all ears."

For a moment, I can do nothing but stare at him, speechless and hot in the face. But he waits patiently, and to my surprise, he even takes notes of what I tell him. He asks relevant questions and follows my annotating instructions to the letter. He picks up on things pretty fast, which is irritating. If he had paid this kind of attention in class, I wouldn't have to be wasting my time here.

If I think about it, I must be just repeating stuff that Mr Houghton's already told him, except he chose not to listen then. I banish the thought from my mind, because it does nothing but fill me with a quiet, bubbling rage.

An hour in, Evan tells me we should stand and do stretches. I roll my eyes and stay on my stool. He hops towards the middle of the kitchen, twists his torso, swings his arms, touches his toes. His effortless athleticism, the rolling of his muscles underneath his clothes, is strangely captivating.

"I gotta stay limber," he explains, probably in response to my stare. "Otherwise my muscles will seize up like crazy."

"Yes," I say drily. "I forgot you're the star athlete of Spearcrest. A champion in the making."

"Not anymore," he says, impervious to my sarcasm. "Dad's made me drop rugby, and it was the only thing I was really good at."

Although I wouldn't have been caught dead attending one of his matches, I'm more than aware of his reputation as a rugby player. After every match, the girls would fall over themselves praising his strength, his stamina, his resilience. I'm pretty sure Evan could have slept with any girl in Spearcrest on the strength of his rugby prowess alone.

Well. Almost every girl.

The logical part of me understands why girls might find athleticism attractive. You'd have to be blind not to notice how good Evan's muscles look under his smooth skin.

I just happen to think rock-hard abs aren't a substitute for a personality.

Still, it's sort of weird imagining Evan not doing something he wants to do. He always seems to act on every impulse and caprice, and it's always been clear how much he loved rugby. Even if his dad wanted him to stop, it's still a surprise to me that he obeyed.

"Well, now you might get to grow old without any brain damage."

He laces his fingers together and stretches his arms behind his back. "It's not healthy for a teenage boy to not have an outlet for his aggression."

"You seem pretty adept at finding yourself a punching bag when you need one."

It's a barbed comment and more than a little unwise. He doesn't seem fazed though.

"Mm, cute, Sutton. But that's not the kind of aggression I mean."

He stops his stretches and prowls over to me. My heart quickens at his sudden approach, the heaviness of his gaze as he speaks.

"I'm talking about the kind of aggression where you want to just grab someone." His arms shoot out, and he grabs me by the neck, making me jump so hard my pen flies out of my hand. "Slam them into the wall. Pound them into the ground. Overpower them. *That* kind of aggression, Sutton."

He's not holding my neck hard enough to hurt, but his grip is firm, hinting at the strength he could be using, should he wish. He's trying to intimidate me like he did when he took off my scarf and coat. So I force myself to stay still and serene.

"I wouldn't know," I say coldly.

"No, I bet you wouldn't," he grins, his fingers digging a little deeper. A pulsing deep between my legs echoes the mad flutter of my heartbeat. "But you're wound so tight—I bet there's all sorts of pent up tension inside you. I'm sure I could find a way of bringing that aggression right out of you."

I look him straight in the eyes, refusing to be cowed.

"If you're offering yourself up as a punching bag, I'm sure you could."

"Anywhere, anytime," he says, low and husky. "Oh, I wouldn't even fucking hold back with you, Sutton. I'd give you everything I have."

Even though we're talking about sports, suddenly it doesn't feel like we are. My breath is halting, my skin burns under my clothes. Heat pools low in my stomach, trickles between my legs. I remember the first time we touched, the innocence of that moment. But the memory of that hug is consumed like kindling in the fire of whatever is happening right now, it flies away in a flurry of embers.

Because this isn't sweet and innocent.

This is aggression in a different form. The scarlet of lust disguised as the crimson of violence.

I lick my lips nervously. His gaze drops to my mouth immediately.

"There's nothing you've got to give I couldn't take, Evan. I know you too well. You're all talk."

"I wouldn't be so fucking sure, Sutton."

He drags me to him by my neck, forcing me down from the stool, almost closing the distance between us. Sirens scream in my mind, warning me I'm treading too far into dangerous territory.

"If you get an A on the exam," I say quickly, my voice coming out a little rough, a little panicked. "Then I'll let you get a free punch in."

He swallows, his throat shuddering. His voice comes out as rough as mine did. "I'd fucking kill you."

"I said *if* you get an A on the exam," I repeat. "So I'm not going to lose sleep over it."

I pull away and to my surprise he immediately releases my neck. I back away, resisting the temptation to touch my neck, to erase his touch from my skin.

"In this case," he says with a wicked glint in his blue eyes, "I'll have to think of another way of making you lose sleep."

"You can try," I say, perching back on the stool and waving a hand at him in a dismissive gesture.

"Be careful what you fucking wish for, Sutton," he smirks, and saunters off to make coffee.

My pulse is still pounding in my throat as I watch him with narrowed eyes. Evan is as simple as they come, but I'm finding him harder and harder to understand lately.

I almost find myself missing our relationship of the past few years. It was intense only in the way it was unpleasant. Encounters with him and his rich kid buddies always ended in the same way: with cruel comments, childish acts of bullying and smug sneers.

But there was a sort of comforting reliability to that viciousness. After a while, I adapted to it. I became adept at avoiding it and, failing that, at withstanding it.

This, however… This is far from anything I'm used to. I no longer know how to handle it. It's as though by being in his house, Evan has realised he is on a whole different kind of battlefield.

Instead of trying to defeat me with insults and mockery, he is using a completely different arsenal. An arsenal made of his body, his eyes, his voice. His ambiguous comments and the sensual suggestions within them.

If I didn't know better, I'd think Evan was flirting with me.

But I *do* know better. I know better than to trust him, to give in to his games.

Because for all his appearance of sincerity, Evan is more duplicitous than anybody else I know. I'm still ashamed that he burned me once.

He won't burn me twice.

12

# HONEY

## The First Time Evan Burned Sophie

*THE FIRST TIME EVAN burns me is in the dining hall at lunch. I'm sitting at my usual table by one of the windows, eating with a book propped against my tray. Evan doesn't always join me for lunch—I never expect him to. But today, he stops at my table with an apple in hand. I look up, and my smile freezes on my face.*

*At his sides, Luca, Iakov, Séverin and Zachary, the most popular boys in the year, stand staring down at me. Their faces are closed and mocking—so is Evan's.*

*I frown at them. "What do you want?"*

*"Nothing from you," Evan says, the aggression in his voice startling me.*

*"Just having a look at Evan's new admirer," Luca says with a leer.*

*"What are you talking about?"*

*It's like being awake in a nightmare, but a really realistic nightmare, where everything feels real but something is off.*

*I'm on the backfoot, underprepared and disoriented. My heart is beating fast, like I'm in danger. If I could follow my instincts, I would grab my tray, throw it at the whole group of them and run away. But they have formed an arch around me; if I wanted to walk away, I'd have to push past them, something I don't want to do unless my hand is forced.*

*"Do you really think a girl like you stands a chance with one of us?" Luca continues. "Have you seen yourself?"*

*"I know what a mirror is, yes," I answer. "Don't you have anything better to do than tell me stuff I already know?"*

*"If you already know how disgusting you are, then what made you think it would be a good idea to try to get with Evan?"*

*I look at Evan, but his grin hides any true expression on his face. It's impossible to tell what he's feeling or what he's thinking in this moment. But it's clear that something happened. The Evan standing in front of me isn't the Evan from English class. The Evan who sat next to me with his chin propped on his fist as he watched me playing chess. The Evan who gave me a tiny bear necklace for Christmas and hugged me outside the assembly hall.*

*That Evan is nowhere to be seen—I'll never see him again after that.*

*"I'm not trying to get with Evan," I snap. "So you can all go away and leave me alone."*

*But by then, the damage isn't done—it's growing. A crowd assembles, not just Year 9s but Year 10s and Year 11s, too. Girls who have always found reason to look down on me are now gleefully observing the scene unfolding in front of their eyes.*

*And no matter what I say or reply, I've already lost.*

*I lost the moment I stepped foot in Spearcrest.*

*Voices rise, become faceless.*

*"She's just been clinging on to Evan—so desperate."*

*"Her parents are cleaners. She only got a place here because they begged the school to let her."*

*"I'm so embarrassed for her."*

*"I hear she has a crush on Evan—I'd be so offended if I was him."*

*"Have you seen those gross spots on her face? Does she even wash?"*

*The voices all melt into one, anonymous, amorphous mass. But one voice stands out; the voice I know best.*

*"Yeah, at first I just felt sorry, because her parents are so poor and literally nobody likes her, but it's like she's obsessed or something, she's always hanging about and trying it on. It's just awkward—it's not like I'm going to date her just out of pity, maybe that's what she hopes. I guess she'll just go for anybody who gives her attention."*

*"Maybe you've been too nice to her, Ev," Luca says with a cocky little smirk. "Poor people can't tell the difference between a gift and a handout."*

*But my eyes are fixed on Evan's. Fury swells in my throat, my eyes are burning.*

*"I don't want to be your girlfriend," I say loudly, loud enough for everybody to hear. "I don't want to be your girlfriend, or even your friend, and I definitely don't want your handouts." I pull on the necklace he gave me, snapping the clasp, and drop it into my plate of spaghetti. "So you can take it back."*

*An expression flashes across Evan's face, fast as lightning. A strange, unreadable expression, almost feral. Then it's gone, and there's nothing left but the amused grin, the cocky confidence.*

*"Nah, I don't want it back. Keep it, Sutton."*

*And then, with the quick strength of a school athlete, he flips my tray at me. I don't even have time to react before spaghetti and apple juice fly at my face. Laughter explodes through the dining hall. I sit, frozen, sauce smearing my face, my white shirt. Pasta dangles in my hair, on my shoulders. Apple juice drips down my cheeks like tears.*

*But I'm not crying.*

*They can take everything from me. But not my tears. For as long as I'm here, I'll never give them this. I'll never let them see me cry.*

*It doesn't take long for everybody to grow bored with the spectacle. Evan and his friends walk away without another backward glance. The crowd disperses. I sit, and don't move until after the bell rings.*

*That was the first time Evan burned me, but not the last.*

*He burned me many more times after that, for years. Countless trays flipped, countless plates of food thrown at my face. Countless uniforms ruined. Notebooks wrecked, pens snapped, handfuls of dirt shoved into my backpack, my pockets, down my back. Hurtful words, unbearable humiliations, litanies of insults and mockeries.*

*But nothing hurt quite as much as that first burn. That scar still serves me as a reminder of who Evan truly is, and exactly what he's capable of.*

## Evan

I FOCUS ALL MY attention on making coffee: pulling out the filter, scooping in the grounds, evening them out—exactly how Dad taught me. Winding Sophie up is intoxicating, but I'm starting to realise the danger of it.

Flirting with girls is fun. It's light-hearted and playful, like playing a game you can't lose.

But what I'm doing with Sophie is different. It could never be just flirting, because handling Sophie will never be like handling just any girl. Sophie is something else, and so flirting has to be something else, too.

So this isn't flirting. Whatever this is, it's reckless, heavy and intense. Not like playing a game, but like sparring. It's dangerous and wild, and it makes my blood run hot in the same way rugby used to. It makes my skin hot and my cock hard.

Sophie might think I'm stupid, but I know what I'm doing. Flirting with girls is one thing: I never have to worry about the consequences of that. But flirting with Sophie is like playing with fire, except she's not the one who would end up in flames.

Because nothing ever gets to Sophie.

I should know. I've done plenty over the years to test her armour. I've never seen so much as a crack or a chip. Her armour is made of the most impenetrable ice. Sophie could walk through an inferno and it would never melt.

When the coffee is ready, I pour two cups and return to the kitchen island. She's sitting with her chin in her hand, absent-mindedly doodling on a pale yellow sticky note. I slide one of the cups of coffee over to her and she gives me a wary look.

"It's just coffee," I say. "I know you need it."

"Because you're such hard work?" she asks with a pointed look.

I shake my head. "No. Because you look fucking exhausted all the time."

She looks at me, blinking slowly. I can't tell what she's thinking, but she reaches for the cup and curls her fingers against the grey ceramic.

"Thanks," she says eventually.

I nod and without ceremony, she resumes talking me through the key themes of Hamlet. Even though Shakespeare bores me to tears, there's something mesmerising about listening to her talk about it.

Part of it is Sophie's voice.

She has this very dry, kind of deep voice, like she has a sore throat all the time. It scratches against me as if there's an itch so deep inside me I don't even notice until her voice reaches it.

And another part of it is the way Sophie speaks about this shit. Normally, Sophie is curt and non-committal when she speaks, as if she wants to contribute to conversations as little as possible. But when she's talking about stuff like the morality of revenge, the deaths of women and metafiction, she speaks long and eloquently.

She's so interested in what she's saying I can't help but be interested too. When she reads aloud chunks of monologues like they are as beautiful as music to her, I want to hear what she's hearing, feel what she's feeling.

Shakespeare's words, in her mouth, take on a whole new meaning. They sound heavy with implications, hot with desire, full of hidden emotions.

"*And I, of ladies most deject and wretched,*" she reads, her long eyelashes fanning on her cheeks as she looks down at her book, "*that sucked the honey of his music vows—*"

A sudden rush of blood straight to my cock startles me. This isn't the first time her voice has made me hard—but it's the first time Shakespeare's words have. I sit up, the trance of her words now broken.

"Wait, what?" I interrupt, leaning forward. "That sounds dirty."

She stops and raises a stony look to my face. "It's not dirty. She's saying that she's miserable for having listened to all his sweet words and promises. She's literally calling herself a sucker for falling for his bullshit."

"Bit harsh," I say. "Maybe it wasn't bullshit. Maybe he meant what he said at the time."

"How could he?" Sophie says. "You can't take something back if you truly mean it."

I tilt my head and watch her closely. She doesn't give anything away, just watches me back with the same mild irritation as always. But this is interesting insight into the way Sophie thinks, the way she feels.

"You can say or feel something true, and then it *stops* being true," I try to explain. "Doesn't make it a lie, because it was true at the time."

She scoffs. "Things are either true, or they're not. If something was true and stops being true, then it's no longer true."

"I'm starting to understand why you have so few friends."

For once, I don't speak out of the urge to hurt or irritate her. It's a genuine observation, a sudden realisation. If she's offended by it, she doesn't show it.

"Nothing wrong with putting value in sincerity," she says icily.

"No, but the bar you set for sincerity sounds like it's pretty damn high."

"It didn't use to be so high," she says, "but all sorts of shit managed to get through."

She's smiling, something she rarely does, but this isn't a true smile. It's a curling at the corner of her lips that makes her look both sad and cruel all at once.

She's talking about me.

This is interesting. I thought she had all but forgotten our fleeting friendship in Year 9, that she had left it in the past with her spotty cheeks and awkward feet. But it seems like that's not quite the case.

I see this for what it is: the little loose thread I've been looking for.

Something I can pull on to make the tight knot that is Sophie come undone. Sophie is the kind of knot you couldn't even cut through with the knife, she is wound that tightly, completely closed in on herself. But this is something to hold on to, something to pull on.

Except that today is not the day, now is not the time. This is something I'm going to have to approach carefully, tactically. Now there is a new battlefield on which to meet Sophie, I'm not going to show up unprepared.

"Looks like you've learned from your mistakes, then," I say lightly, watching her. "Unlike our poor boy Hamlet."

"You can't learn from your mistakes when there are no consequences for them," she retorts.

This time, the insult is even more thinly veiled. But right now I feel no anger, no resentment. I kind of enjoy this sudden act of aggression. From Sophie, it's almost intimate. Like she's stabbing me but has to be in my arms to do it.

"Let me make sure I write that down," I say sweetly. "It would make a killer line for an essay. Mr Houghton would be very impressed."

"He'd probably be even more impressed if you wrote down something he actually taught you instead."

"I'll pass, thanks." I finish writing my note and look back up at her. "I'd much rather listen to you go on about Shakespeare."

"Yes, because I'm much better than an Oxford-educated, professionally-trained teacher."

I give her a slow smile. "Mr Houghton's boring. You make Hamlet sexy."

Her cheeks go slightly pink, but she still speaks in her cool, dry tone. "What could you possibly find sexy about madness and suicide?"

"I dunno, Sutton. Listening to you talking about sucking honey definitely made me a bit hard."

Finally, the facade cracks.

Her mouth falls open. A dark, uneven flush spreads across her cheeks.

"And on that note," she says, standing up and grabbing her coat off the stool next to hers. "Your two hours are up and I'm off."

"So soon, Sutton?" I watch her with amusement as she wraps her scarf around her throat and buttons her coat all the way up. I glance at her clothes, letting myself imagine idly pulling them off her. "Aren't you going to take the taxi back to school with me?"

"I'd rather walk," she says, shouldering her backpack. "I need the fresh air."

"So do I!" I exclaim, springing to my feet. I'm not lying, though I need fresh air for probably very different reasons to her. But now she's going, I can't bring myself to let her go—I want *more*. "I'll walk with you."

"I don't think so." She grabs the thickest booklet off the kitchen island and throws it over to me. "You need to finish working through this before you forget all the stuff I told you today. Don't waste my time."

"Fuck!" I glare at the booklet. "Can't I do it later?"

"You know you won't. Do it, or I won't show up next week."

I sigh and slump back down onto my stool. "For fuck's sake, fine! You're worse than Mr Houghton."

"By all means, go back to him. I won't stop you." She gives me a brief wave. "Don't bother standing, I'll see myself out."

She strides out of the kitchen and I shout after her, "Is it my punishment for saying you made me hard?"

The only reply I get is the sound of the front door slamming shut.

I'm still horny after she's left and have no choice but to stroke myself to the mental image of Sophie sucking honey off my cock.

# 13

# CURSED STAR

## Sophie

THE SPEARCREST LIBRARY IS my favourite place on the whole campus. I love it more than the corridor of aspens and poplars leading towards the astroturf and tennis courts, more than the austerity of the study hall, more than the Victorian greenhouse on the lower school campus.

The library here has its own building, tucked away from view behind a shield of ancient oaks and tired willows. Inside, it's all wooden panelling polished by the years, tomb-shaped windows and bronze railings. Three glass cupolas crown the ceiling, huge bronze lights hanging from their centres. Amongst the bookshelves, long desks are set with green bankers lamps.

Here, the smell of leather and old paper permeates the air. A peaceful, contented silence reigns. It's a sort of oasis in Spearcrest. Even the most obnoxious kids sense the consecration of the library when they enter.

With the winter exams having already started for many subjects, I'm not the only person who's chosen to spend their weekend in the library. Tucked away in a corner of the

Modern History section, I sit across from Audrey, who is also taking History.

We take turns holding our notebooks and quizzing each other about Stalin.

Night is falling outside. The soft gold lights and green lamps keep the darkness at bay. An icy drizzle patters against the windows and the cupolas, the sound filling the air like static. After several hours spent going over dates and details of Stalin's atrocities, we take a much-needed mental health break.

Audrey takes out a thermos from her bag and pours two tin cups of tea.

"Do you think he actually ever had good intentions?" Audrey asks, passing me a cup.

I prop my chin into my palm and stare thoughtfully into the dark amber tea and the steam rising from it. "I mean, even if he did... does it matter?"

"I think so," Audrey says. "I think I'd respect someone more if they did something bad with the intention of doing something good. You wouldn't?"

"I don't think I would. Your intentions can't affect others, but your actions can. I think if someone did something bad, I wouldn't give a shit about their intentions." I raise a pointed eyebrow. "Especially if the bad thing in question is the murder of millions."

"I mean, I guess that's fair, and it's not like I'm saying those murders would be justified even if he did have intentions. But it would make him a slightly different person."

I try to take a sip of my tea, but it's still too hot to drink. "Not to me."

Audrey laughs. "Everything is so black and white to you, Sophe. I kind of love that about you. I always know where I stand with you."

I laugh too. Crossing my arms on the table, I lie a cheek against them and close my eyes. "Do you think I'm too judgemental?"

Audrey doesn't answer straight away, which makes me realise she has to think about it.

"No, not judgemental," she says eventually. "More like... you have high expectations of others. Do you think people think you're judgemental?"

"No. But Evan implied that's the reason I don't have a lot of friends."

Audrey scoffs. "What would he know? He wouldn't recognise true friendship if it slapped him in the face. The Young Kings aren't friends, they're more like teenage mobsters."

I laugh, genuinely amused by the image.

"He said I set the bar too high for sincerity," I add after a moment of silence.

"So what if you do? Good for you for not surrounding yourself with fake friends. Since when have you been talking to Evan anyway? I thought you'd been working at the café instead of tutoring him."

"I was, but he made me stop so I could prepare him for the Lit exam."

Audrey leans forward. "What? You didn't tell me."

I rest my chin on my arms so I can look at her properly. "I've only been doing it since last week."

"Since when does he even care about the Lit exam?"

"That's what I said. But he said if he tanks it then it won't look good since I was meant to be tutoring him. He said it'll be easier to keep our deal going if he passes the exam."

Audrey sits back. "Okay, I get the logic. But why doesn't he just revise if he wants to pass?"

I sigh. "Because he's a lazy moron who literally knows nothing. And I mean *nothing*. He didn't even know the plot of Hamlet."

"Hamlet? I thought you were studying Othello."

"I am. My class is doing Othello and his is doing Hamlet."

Audrey's eyes narrow in their nest of long, curly lashes. "So let me get this straight. Not only have you had to do this idiot's homework, but now you're basically studying and teaching a text that you're not even sitting an exam for?"

"Do you understand my frustration?"

"Understand it? I'd be *livid* if I were you. Why don't you send him packing?"

"I'd love to. But if he passes then I can go back to working at the café and putting money away for next year."

"Well, alright," Audrey says more calmly. "I see what you mean. It's still annoying, though."

I laugh quietly. "You're preaching to the choir, Audrey."

We lapse into a cosy silence, lulled by the dull rush of the rainfall. Sleep tugs at me, my eyelids growing heavy and slow, like I'm blinking through thick honey. A dull buzz vibrates through the table. Audrey picks up her phone, peers at it, puts it down. She picks it up again, pouts thoughtfully at it, puts it back down.

"Is it him?" I ask, blinking blearily at her.

She's not mentioned the boy she met over the summer holiday, but it's clear he's still on her mind and in her life.

"Mm-hm," she says, pushing the phone away.

"Are you not going to text him back?"

"He wants to meet over the Christmas holidays."

"I didn't even know you two were still in touch."

It's a familiar story. Audrey always knows everything about us. She was the first person I told about my secret job, about Evan. And yet it always takes her the longest time to open up to us, to tell us about the things going on in her life.

It takes patience, being Audrey's friend, but she is worth the time.

"He's been texting me all term. Now he's offering to come to London for the winter break. He's even offered to pay for me to come to Switzerland if I want."

"Is that where he lives?"

"It's where he goes to university."

I watch her, waiting for more information, but she seems deep in her thoughts.

"Well. Are you going to meet him?"

"Is it bad that I really want to?" she asks, finally looking up at me.

"Why would it be bad?"

"Because he's a rich arsehole, exactly like all the rich arseholes here at Spearcrest. His parents are investment bankers, he went to a private school in France. I've spent all these years avoiding the boys here, but how is he any different?"

"Well... what attracted you to him in the first place?"

Audrey pauses to think, reaching absent-mindedly for her hair and pulling on a thick curl that doubles in length when she extends it. Her voice softens as she speaks, taking on a softer hue, soft as the gold and green lights of the library.

"I liked how smart he was, how well-spoken. He speaks with a French accent and he's a little self-conscious about that. He's sort of quiet, and a little bit shy."

"Well," I say, sitting back in my chair and raising my eyebrows. "He sounds nothing like the boys at Spearcrest. And even if he was, then so what? If you like him, and he likes you, and you want to spend time with him, then why shouldn't you?"

Audrey gazes at me for a long time. I can't help but admire her hazelnut-brown eyes, her dark, smooth skin. Her beauty is unlike anybody else's: a maturity and poise that makes her look older than she is, almost regal.

A smile dawns on her beautiful face, making it more beautiful still.

"Yeah, you're right... you're totally right, Sophe."

She picks up her phone and types out a quick text. When she's done, she puts the phone away and peers at me with a grin.

"How about you, then? How's your love life coming along?"

Immediately, my mind is flooded with images of Evan. Evan with his towel around his neck and his bare chest and his hard muscles. Evan slowly sliding off my scarf and coat. Evan standing too close, the cedarwood scent of his cologne curling around me. The sharp line of his lips and the way they crook into that wicked grin of his. His eyes, bluer than winter skies.

His hand around my neck, fingers digging into my skin.

My cheeks burn and I quickly shake my head. Thinking about him like this is a mistake. I should know better.

"What love life? I don't have a love life."

"No progress with Freddy, then?" Audrey asks with a little pout of disappointment.

Oh. She was talking about Freddy. I'm immediately red-hot with embarrassment and infinitely thankful Audrey can't read my thoughts.

"He's technically speaking my boss," I explain, "so I don't think there's ever going to be any *progress*, as you put it."

"That only makes it more scandalous," Audrey says, waggling her eyebrows. "An illicit workplace romance. This is what rom-coms and erotic novels are made of."

"Oh, sort yourself out!" I reached over the tablet and grab the book in front of her. "Your brain should be filled with key dates of the Russian Revolution, not this nonsense."

"There's always room for both," Audrey laughs. Still, she reluctantly picks up her perfectly crafted flashcards. "Agricultural developments in communist Russia and Stalin's use of propaganda to create a cult of personality isn't quite as sexy as your little adventures with your coffee shop boss, but if we must."

We resume taking turns quizzing each other and spend the rest of our Saturday night drinking tea and revising. As the evening goes on, the rain doesn't relent but grows more frosty and aggressive.

By the time we make our way back to the sixth form dormitories, the ground is a mess of sludgy puddles. We run with our backpacks over our heads all the way from the library.

Later, I fall asleep thinking about Freddy, but somehow end up dreaming about Evan.

I spend Sunday in the study hall working through piles of practice exams for Monday's Maths exam. Although I had every intention of going to the dining hall to buy something for lunch, I end up skipping it altogether.

My chest is crushed by an invisible pressure, a sense that I'm running out of time and that doom is impending and inevitable. I usually get this every time I have exams coming up, but it's been getting worse.

The study hall slowly empties itself as the afternoon passes, until there's a handful of us left. We are all sitting apart, and the room is as silent as a tomb. When my phone buzzes from under a pile of books, it startles me so much I jump.

I check it with a frown. The only texts I get tend to be from one of the girls arranging to meet somewhere, or from my parents checking in. I unlock my phone, hoping it's not the latter.

It's neither. It's actually from Freddy.

**Freddy**: Hi Sophie, we've been missing you at the café but we both hope your exams are going well. Just wondering if you fancy picking up some shifts over Christmas, it gets pretty busy around that time of year so could do with the help if you're around. Let me know x F

The little innocent $x$ at the end of the message somehow feels more intimate than a kiss, and I can't believe it, but I feel a little flustered. I text back quickly.

**Sophie**: Hi Freddy. I hope I can pick up some shifts but I'm not sure yet. I'll let you know as soon as possible. Say hi to Jess.

I hesitate. Should I respond with an $x$ too? His is so casual, so... Freddy. Just soft and kind like him.

But if *I* add an *x*... I don't know if I can pull it off. I'm not soft and kind like Freddy.

**Sophie**: Say hi to Jess. S.

The *S* hopefully is casual enough, and it's not like I have any reason to send Freddy a kiss. Even if Audrey seems to imagine some cutesy workplace romance, I live in the real world. And in the real world, Freddy is just the guy I work for, and I have bigger problems to think about than the way I end my texts.

Like the impending Christmas break, and how I'm going to work out a way to pick up shifts. I usually spend the first week of the holidays at Spearcrest because my parents work that week, so I might be able to manage at first. There won't be many people at school, and technically we are allowed into town during school holidays.

But the second week, I usually spend with my parents in our small house away from the school. I'll still be close to the café, but I'll also be right under my parents' watchful eyes.

If they found out I was working, I can't even imagine how disappointed and hurt they'd be. They've spent all my life at Spearcrest telling me how hard I have to try, how amazing an opportunity this is, how perfect I need to be to ever compete with the kind of kids I go to school with. If they knew I'd been knowingly breaking the rules, they would be both furious and devastated.

And if they found out I was doing it to earn money, that would be a whole different level.

They've worked hard their whole lives to provide for me, to send me to the best school possible. I know how ungrateful they'd think I am if I told them I needed more money. I've not even told them I'm applying to universities in the states yet. They think I'm going to Oxford or Cambridge, they have practically already told everyone about it. But I don't want to escape Spearcrest only to end up somewhere exactly like it.

I just have to find a nice way of saying this to them.

The rest of the afternoon is a write-off. I can barely concentrate on my practice exams. My mind keeps being tugged back towards my parents, towards work, towards the difficult conversations ahead, and beyond that, the uncertain future.

I spend several hours forcing myself to concentrate, but my answers get increasingly worse until I realise I'm doing worse on the practice exams than I was when I arrived at the study hall.

In the end, I pack all my books and leave the study hall, defeat weighing me down. I've not had dinner yet, but I'm not hungry. I dump my things in my room and go for a swim, hoping it will release some of the tension building inside my chest.

The pool is empty, half the lights turned off. The water casts shifting dapples of blue light onto the walls and ceiling. Combined with the rush of the rain falling outside the open windows near the ceiling, it makes the pool feel quiet and eerie.

I dive into the water and swim all the way to the bottom. The cold water shocks my system, but my body adjusts quickly. I swim to the surface, breathe, and dip back in. I break into slow, strong laps, up and down, until my body is as tired as my mind.

The sky outside the windows is pitch black by the time I finally take a break, floating on my back on the surface of the water.

I watch the vaulted ceiling, blinking slowly. The glowing blue dapples there tremble and shift ceaselessly, strangely mesmerising. For the first time since receiving Freddy's text, my mind is quiet.

Then droplets of water splash over my face. I flounder for a second, righting myself in the water as I look around.

My heart sinks.

The last person I could possibly want to see right now is sitting at the edge of the pool, feet tickling the surface of the water.

In my dream last night, Evan wore his school uniform, the tie undone, the crisp white shirt unbuttoned. I was kneeling on marble, and he stared down at me. He held a bottle of expensive champagne, and he tipped it, pouring it down into my open mouth.

His eyes never left mine as I drank, champagne running down my chin and chest. I woke up as shocked and embarrassed as if I'd had the filthiest sex dream, and thanked my lucky star I wouldn't have to see him until Tuesday.

Of course, my lucky star has never been all that lucky.

If anything—it's more of a cursed star.

14

# TREACHERY

## Evan

SOPHIE ALWAYS APPEARS, AS if conjured by some spell or curse, just when I'm trying my best to get her out of my head. It's almost as if she can somehow sense what I'm trying to do and chooses that very moment to materialise into my day.

Of course, this time she doesn't so much materialise into my day as float into it like some dream mermaid.

I'm standing at one end of the pool stretching when I spot her in the water, floating with her arms out and her legs gently paddling. Her dark hair is in a plait, she's wearing a plain black swimsuit and her eyes are wide open as she stares up at the ceiling. She is almost otherworldly in the bluish light of the pool, her skin ghostly in the water.

I end up sitting at the edge of the pool and staring at her. I'm surprised she hasn't noticed she's not alone yet, but she is too deep in thought to have any awareness of her surroundings.

Not just deep in thought, but... sort of sad. Melancholy.

It makes my chest clench uncomfortably, and I act on instinct. Kicking out my foot, I send a tiny wave of water splashing towards her face.

She's startled, and flounders for a moment in the water, arms splashing as she rights herself. She turns around and faces me. The sad look on her face is gone, replaced by a frown. "Are you following me?"

I scoff. If only she knew that it's quite the opposite, that I've only come here tonight to clear my mind of her. But the last thing Sophie needs is for me to give her the ammo she needs to shoot me with.

"Are *you* following *me*?" I fire back. "You know I'm on the swim team. I doubt you're here by pure coincidence."

"I happen to come here every other day," she says coolly, "I've never bumped into you before."

"Every other day, huh?" I lock that useful morsel of information away in my mind for later use. "That's a lot of exercise for a scholar like you, Sutton."

She gives me a little fake smile and answers tritely, "Healthy body, healthy mind."

She kicks herself into a quick crawl to the edge of the pool and climbs out of the water. It's hard to not look at her, with her black swimsuit sticking to her body, water running down her long limbs. But it becomes quickly obvious how much my body appreciates the sight of hers, because blood immediately rushes to my cock.

I'm not about to irrevocably embarrass myself in front of Sophie Sutton by being caught in the pool with an erection, so I make sure my eyes rush to her face and stay stuck to it.

"Don't leave on my account," I tell her. "Plenty of space for both of us."

"Oh, I couldn't possibly swim next to an elite of the swim team," she says, dry as dust.

She walks up to her towel and picks it up. She's not going to stay if I'm here. Why would she? She can't stand me.

But the look of sadness on her face when I spotted her is like a fucking dagger to the chest. It's stuck in my ribs, too painful to ignore, and I can't repress the impulse to be nice to her.

"I'll go if you want," I say, glancing away, keeping my voice light and casual. "If you want the pool to yourself or whatever. I've not even gone in the water yet. I'll go."

She pauses, towel wrapped around her shoulders. Her brown eyes, almost black in the dim light of the pool, fix me with a long, searching gaze. It's difficult to tell what she's looking for, or whether she finds it. But she retraces her steps to the edge of the pool and sits down, facing me across the water.

"Don't be stupid," she says, but there's definitely a lot less of the usual impatience and irritation there normally is behind the words. "You came here to swim, didn't you? So swim."

I drop off the edge of the pool and sink to the bottom, letting the temporary shock of cold travel through me before I kick myself back up. Once I break through the surface, I swim slowly towards her.

"I didn't come here for swim team practice," I admit to her. Something about the fact that she's staying melts me like butter, making me softer, sweeter. Not something I can explain, just something I can feel in my chest. "Swimming just helps take my mind off things."

She gazes at me with the same searching gaze as before. Maybe she's trying to work out how sincere I'm being. I meet her gaze with a frank grin.

"Same," she says after a moment of silence. "What could possibly be troubling you anyway? I thought your life was just a series of carefree adventures, girlfriends and parties?"

I laugh. "And that doesn't sound stressful to you?"

She smiles. It's only a tiny lifting of the corners of her mouth, but it's sincere. A sincere, shy little Sophie smile. It makes my chest tight and warm. I can't help but wade slightly closer to her.

"It sounds appalling," she says. "Never realised how harrowing your life actually is."

"The worst."

I stop until I'm only an arm's reach away from her. She sits with her feet in the water, her towel around her shoulders. Droplets fall from her hair like tiny raindrops, sliding down her face and neck.

"What brings you here, then? What could possibly be troubling the perfect Sophie Sutton?"

"I'm overwhelmed by the enormity of what lies ahead," she answers quietly, her eyes intently fixed on mine.

I can't believe she's opening up like that. For a moment, I'm frozen in shock. Then I swim to the edge, placing my hands on either side of her legs to bring myself closer to her.

"What do you mean? What lies ahead?"

She leans down until her face is so close to mine droplets from her wet hair tickle my forehead and cheeks.

"My Everest, my white whale," she murmurs. "Getting you to pass that fucking English exam."

All the tension leaves my body and I let out a groan of annoyance. I can't believe she got me so easily.

"Oh, fuck you!" I say, pushing myself away from the wall and splashing water up at her.

"No thanks," she retorts. "I can do better."

"Are you sure?"

"Absolutely certain."

"We'll see." And with that threat, I grab her by the arms and pull her into the water.

She falls forward with a big splash and remerges, spluttering.

"Evan! My towel!"

I hold up my middle finger. "Fuck your towel, too."

She grabs the towel, now sopping wet, and tosses it out of the water. Then she turns around, her eyes searching the pool.

She seems to find whatever she's looking for, and I turn to follow her gaze.

My eyes land on my clean, dry, monogrammed, Turkish cotton towel, folded and sitting innocently at the other end of the pool.

"Oh no, you fucking don't!"

I dive into the water and catch up with her, yanking her leg back. She sinks and flails, then breaks the surface and pushes a big wave at me. My goggles are still around my neck, so my eyes are already burning from the chlorine, but I still turn my head to avoid the splash.

She tries to swim away, but she's not fast enough to get away from me. I grab her by the waist and swim her away to the other side of the pool.

"Let me go, you giant moron!"

She struggles against me, but I keep her pinned by her waist. It's not easy, because she's stronger than she looks. She presses her hands to my chest and pushes, but I refuse to let her go. By the time we both realise her thighs are wrapped around my hips and her breasts are at my eye level, it's too late.

Her indignant laughter dies in her throat. Wet black hair coils against her neck and shoulders. Droplets of water slide across her skin, disappearing between her breasts. Her nipples are hard underneath the smooth black fabric of her swimsuit. She stares at me, lips slightly parted. I stare back, praying to God almighty she can't tell I'm suddenly really fucking turned on.

She takes my face in her hand, holding my jaw in her fingers. For a crazy second, I think she's about to kiss me. I tilt my head, raising my mouth to hers. Every inch of me wants this—a dark, yawning hunger inside me I didn't even know was there.

Her lips ghost across mine.

But of course, she doesn't kiss me.

"Race me," she says instead, her breath tickling my lips, her voice low and husky.

The way she's looking down at me with those dark, hooded eyes is authoritative, almost dominant. My breath catches, my cock hardening. She looks so fucking hot I can barely stand to look at her. All I can think of is claiming her mouth with mine, palming her pretty tits roughly and shoving aside her swimsuit to thrust myself inside her to the hilt.

"W—what?" I ask hoarsely, realising I didn't register what she said.

Her fingers dig into my cheeks and she pushes my head back with a slow, cocky smirk. "You heard me. *Race me*, swim team champ."

I swallow hard. I can think of a thousand things I want to do to her right now, and racing her is the last thing on the list. By now I'm really fucking hard, my cock desperate for friction, contact—anything. If she was anybody else, I'd already have my tongue in her mouth and my cock buried inside her—but she's not anybody else, and I'd rather die than let Sophie know how hard I am for her.

So I push her away from me in the water and paddle away, calling over my shoulder, "You're on!"

We both go to different edges and wait. I take my goggles off my neck and shake the water off them, then pull them on. If nothing else, this race will reroute the blood through my body and hopefully away from my cock.

I glance over at her and she nods.

"On my mark. Ready.... Steady..."

I grin. She has no idea what she's signed up for.

"Go!" she calls.

I shoot forward, piercing through the water like a spear. I keep my head down, emerging only to breathe at timed intervals. I reach the end in minutes, and emerge triumphantly, looking around so I can watch her catch up with me.

"Trust you to have the fanciest towel imaginable."

I whip around. Sophie is standing by the edge of the pool, my towel wrapped around her, patting her face and neck with a corner.

"You little fucking cheat!"

She doesn't even have the courtesy of looking sheepish. Instead, she shrugs and sneers down at me in the same dominant way she looked at me before.

"I said 'let's race'." Arrogance drips from her voice. "I never said anything about swimming."

And with that cocky smirk plastered all over her face, she gives me the middle fingers, turns around and walks away.

After she's gone, what lingers with me isn't her dishonesty and treachery—part of me *liked* her dishonesty and treachery.

Instead, what lingers with me is the red-hot memory of her waist pinned by my arms and her thighs wrapped around my hips. The husky arrogance of her voice, her heavy-lidded eyes as she stares imperiously down at me.

Sophie fucking Sutton. She really is full of surprises this year. And yet I can already tell the memory of this moment is going to be making frequent invasions into my fantasies. Especially when I'm in the shower.

So much for coming here to get my mind off Sophie fucking Sutton.

15

# DEADLY SERIOUS

## Sophie

BY THE TIME I get to Evan's house on Tuesday, I'm too tired to worry about the repercussions of my actions at the pool. To my surprise, he doesn't even bring it up. Instead, he lets me in, makes coffee and we pretty much get straight to work.

I find myself wondering if he does care about the exam after all. He's done all the work I set him and has even been revising his notes. I pull out some practice papers for him to work on, and he doesn't even complain when I do.

He looks through them for a moment and then looks up. "You're not doing Hamlet for your exam, are you?"

"No," I answer, a little taken aback by the question. "Our class is doing Othello. Why?"

He gestures at the papers. "These have got all the questions in them. Do you wanna do some Othello questions while I work on Hamlet?"

I frown. Has some form of guilt finally gotten to him?

I'm not sure how to respond, and he adds, "The exam's tomorrow, and I can pretty much work through these on my own. Why don't you just work on your stuff while I write, then you can tell me how you think I did at the end?"

It's more than reasonable, but reason is a little unexpected from him. Still, I haven't been doing anywhere near as much work on Othello as I should have, and could definitely do with the practice.

"Alright. Let's do that, then."

We work in a sort of strangely amicable silence for a long time. After several rounds of extended analysis, we finally stop so that I can have a look at Evan's work.

He stares at me expectantly as I read through what he's written. Today, he's wearing a baggy grey sweatshirt that makes his eyes look lighter than usual. His sandy curls fall over his forehead, the tips hanging over his eyes.

I don't know how he can't find it distracting—it's distracting me just looking at it.

"Well?" he prompts.

"I mean, it's not exactly profound or even perceptive... but you sound like you at least know what you're talking about."

"I don't get it. What are you saying? Is it good or not?"

"Well, it's good *for you*. I'm not saying that to be mean. Given where you started, this is decent."

"Right, right," he says, narrowing his eyes. "But will I pass?"

"Mm..."

I gaze down at his work. Passing is never something I've worried about. My parents never set "passing" as a goal for me, it's always been "excel" and "exceed" with them. I can't exactly say this to Evan, but I try to give him an honest answer.

"It looks good enough to me, but remember, I'm not a teacher. Really, if you'd done mock papers with Mr Houghton, he would have been able to tell you."

"What is it with you and Mr Houghton?" he says, taking his work back with a pout. "Why don't you just marry him, if you're so horny for him."

"If only. Unfortunately for me, he's already married."

"Hah, I knew you liked your older guys!" he exclaims, staring at me with wide eyes. "I can't believe I guessed your type. You're so damn predictable, Sutton."

I roll my eyes. "I don't like *any* guy, so there's no type to guess."

"Oh?" he props his elbows onto the countertop, lacing his fingers and peering at me over them. "Then who is it you're meeting in town every Tuesday and Thursday?"

I stare at him in complete shock for a moment, then I burst out laughing.

"You think I'm sneaking off on *dates*?" The mere prospect brings irresistible laughter out of me. "You really are a complete fucking idiot."

"Well, you're always acting so suspicious and shifty, like you're up to some secret stuff."

"I *am* up to some secret stuff," I tell him. "But it's definitely not dating. As if I have the time."

"Then what are you up to?"

I lean forward. "Not for a second would I trust you with that information. You'd run your mouth and get me in trouble."

He imitates me, leaning further forward so that we are now both half-draped over the kitchen island and whispering for no reason.

"Oh my god. You're breaking school rules, aren't you?" His eyes search mine as though he thinks he can somehow see into my mind. "Fuck. Perfect prefect Sutton, breaking the rules?"

"And this is why I'd never tell you. Because you have the mental capacity of a five-year-old and all the self-control of an alcoholic drinking mouthwash at a rehab centre."

"That's dark, Sutton, real dark," he says. "But if you think about it, it would be in your interest to tell me."

"Oh? How so?"

"Well, we have our alliance, and you're meant to be here with me, so it makes sense if I knew about it. Besides, if you told me what you're up to, I might even be able to help you."

Of course, what he's saying makes sense. Except that this is Evan, and I know all too well how easily he can turn his back on his "allies" when he wants to. Just because I've not seen him around school much and I get to see this different side of him here doesn't mean he's changed.

I don't think I even believe that people can change at all.

"Look," he says with a sigh. "The truth is that Dad went ballistic when he found out I'm failing Literature, and he begged Spearcrest to get me this tutoring. So if he finds out that I've been fucking it off, I'd be the first one to get in trouble. It wouldn't even surprise me if he just yanked me out of Spearcrest, he's tried before."

I stare at him in surprise. I didn't expect this admission from him. I didn't expect *any* of this from him at all. He seems so easy-going and happy-go-lucky at all times, so careless of the world around him it's difficult to imagine him suffering the repercussions of his action.

Evan watches me watching him and slowly shakes his head. "Oh my god. I can hardly believe it. You *are* seeing some older guy, aren't you?"

I roll my eyes. "I got a job, alright?"

Clearly, this is not the scandalous revelation he was expecting. At all.

He blinks, mouth wide open, revealing those obnoxiously white teeth of his. "A *job?*"

"Yes. What else would it be?"

"I don't know. Something darker. Something more... deviant."

"No. That's just your overactive imagination. I just got a part-time job so I can put some money aside for university next year. That's it."

"Oh."

We sit staring at one another. My heart is too tight in my chest, as if it's been tightly wrapped in cellophane. I can't tell whether it's because I'm nervous that my secret is finally out or because I'm terrified of being betrayed. A bit of both, I suppose.

I know he's not to be trusted. If this comes back to bite me in the arse, it'll be completely my fault.

"Why is that even a secret?" he asks finally. "Is it a... dodgy job?"

"Of course not. It's a job at a café."

"Oh! Oh... well, what's the problem then?"

"It's against the Spearcrest rules, Evan," I say, resisting the urge to roll my eyes at him again. "Not that I would expect you to concern yourself with something so insignificant."

"Yeah, it's a rule, but not a *rule* rule," he says with a frown. "It's like the rule about the head boy being allowed to keep a mistress or Friday being the official day for floggings. The kind of old rule nobody gives a shit about."

"My parents give a shit," I say, unable to keep the resentment from creeping into my voice.

"Ah, yeah... they work for the school, right?" He taps his index finger to his chin. "Well, I'm sure they're not going to find out. And now that I know your dirty little secret, Sutton, I can actually help you."

"No, thanks. I've been doing grand without your help."

I stand off my stool and stretch before packing away my things. I've been at Evan's house for almost three hours now, which feels far too long. He stands up too.

"You don't always have to be such a strong, independent woman and all that stuff," he says in a serious tone. "If you need help, sometimes it's okay to ask."

"I know it's okay, and if I do need help, I'll ask one of my friends," I tell him with my most polite smile.

It would have been the perfect line to leave on, but unfortunately, I end up sharing the taxi back to Spearcrest with him. I sit tucked against the window, my chin in my hands, watching the dark outlines of the trees and hedges framing the countryside roads.

Outside the window, rain and fallen leaves swirl in the air. Evan doesn't say anything for a while, then his voice reaches me through the quiet music the taxi driver has got on.

"Are you going back there on Thursday?"

He's talking in a whisper, which I guess is his way of showing he's keeping my secret.

I nod. "Yes. Hopefully."

"Oh."

He's silent for a while, and I thought he was done until he spoke again.

"You're going to be working there Christmas too?"

I sigh. "I don't know if I can. If I have to stay with my parents, then they'll definitely suspect something, and I absolutely can't let them find out."

He nods but doesn't say anything. We lapse into silence, and the lights and spires of Spearcrest have appeared in the distance by the time he speaks again.

"Do you want to stay over at my place during winter break?"

For a second, I think I've misheard him. I turn to look at him. The inside of the car is dark, and there are only distant streetlights to occasionally cast a pale orange light inside. In that dim light, Evan's face looks perfectly serious.

"What do you mean?"

"I mean, *do* you want to stay over at my place during winter break? My parents are working over Christmas and my sister is going to New York to stay with her boyfriend, so it's basically just going to be me. The house is close to town, and you can tell your parents you're staying with a friend or whatever."

"Are you serious?"

He stares at me. "Deadly serious. Why the fuck not? It's a win-win. You can go to work whenever you want, and I get free coffee out of it. Right?"

I don't say anything. The idea is so wild it doesn't even feel worth dignifying with a "no". Except that the more I think about it, the more it feels like it's not so much wild as too good to be true. It *would* be perfect.

Except for the living with Evan part.

That would be... no, that would be too weird.

"That sounds like a terrible idea," I say finally, not quite sure I mean it.

"I dunno, it wouldn't be *so* bad," he says.

I envy how calm and casual he sounds because I am inexplicably and embarrassingly flustered. The taxi is parking up outside the Spearcrest gates, and we thank the driver and get out.

"Well, it was just an idea," Evan continues, waving the taxi off.

"Sure."

"Just give it some thought, yeah?" he says. "Might be nice having some company at Christmas, and you wouldn't have to worry about your parents nagging you."

We cross the ornate arch of the gateway and stop where the path splits up. The girls' dormitories are left past the library, and the boys' dormitories are behind and past the Old Manor, at completely different ends of the campus. I'm not sure what to tell him, so I end up saying, "Alright. I'll think about it. Goodnight."

"Alright, Sutton, I'll see ya."

He gives me a casual wave and strides off, stuffing his hands into his pocket. A strange impulse of kindness pushes me to call after him. "Good luck with the Lit exam!"

"I don't need luck!" he calls back. "I wouldn't dare let you down!"

I don't respond and hasten away before he can realise I'm smiling.

# 16

# DRAGON

## Sophie

WITH ONLY FIFTEEN MINUTES to go before the exam, I'm sitting on the chessboard tiles of the assembly hall foyer floor. The gloomy daylight falls through the high stain glass windows above the door, turning the grey light blue and red.

I'm sitting in a patch of red light and reading through critical theories on Othello when my phone buzzes from the depths of my backpack.

Propping my notes on my lap, I reach for it with impatience. A text from an unknown number. I open it with a frown.

**Unknown**: Good luck with the exam xo Evan

I text back immediately.

**Sophie**: How did you get my number?

His reply pops up.

**Evan**: I asked Miss Bailey.

**Sophie***:* Creepy.

**Evan**: Hardly. It's not like I'm sending you nudes.

**Sophie***:* I'd rather bathe my eyes in bleach.

**Evan**: Trust me, Sutton, if I sent you one, that's the last thing you'd want to do.

**Sophie***:* Please delete my number.

**Evan**: Relax, I'm not going to send you nudes. Unless you ask, of course. Just wishing you luck.

**Sophie***:* You should be too busy revising to wish me luck.

**Evan**: Just tryna be nice, Sutton. You should try it x

I hesitate, then text back.

**Sophie***:* Good luck with the exam x

I turn my phone off straight away. I've worked too hard to let Evan's frivolity distract me from my revision. The Lit exam is my last exam of the term, so as long as I give it everything I have, then I'll hopefully feel a little better over the holidays. Maybe I'll even wake up without my chest being crushed under some enormous rock of urgency.

When the teachers finally open the doors and we get let into the hall, I make a beeline for my desk and sit down. I arrange my water bottle, pens and student ID in front of me, then I sit back. The answer booklet, with its pink pages, sits heavily on my desk, drawing my gaze. My stomach is churning, nausea whirling through me. I'm thankful I decided to only have a banana for my breakfast today.

Finally, the invigilators hand out the question papers and the times are written down on the chalkboard at the front of the room.

"You may start."

The sound of everyone turning their papers open is like the rushing of wind through the assembly hall. After that, everything in the room might as well have disappeared as far as I'm concerned. There's only my exam questions, my answer booklet and my pen.

By the time the invigilators call for us to put our pens down, three hours have passed, my hand is aching and my eyes are burning. We get asked to pass our papers to the invigilators; I do so without looking. The relief I was hoping to feel hasn't sunk in yet. My chest is still crushed under an impossible weight.

Outside the hall, everyone is bumping into each other as they collect their bags and coats. I stand in the doorway, waiting for them to be done before I get my things.

I'm staring at the slowly dispersing crowd of students without quite seeing them when there's a tap on my shoulder.

"Did you flunk the exam?"

I turn my head in surprise. Evan is standing next to me. For once, his uniform is in order: his shirt is buttoned up and his tie is done and straight. For some reason, the crisp azure and white of the Spearcrest uniform always makes him look a little older and a lot taller.

He's standing right next to me, hands in his pockets, hair brushed back. The heat from his body somehow reaches through my clothes, brushing against my skin. His blue gaze is direct, a light smile on his lips. I take a step back, putting distance between us.

"No, of course I didn't flunk the exam. Did you?"

"No, I don't reckon I did. Why do you look so grumpy, then?"

"I'm not grumpy."

He draws a little closer, tilting his head. "You're not happy either."

I'm thrown by that. For a moment, I don't know what to say. In the end, I settle for part of the truth. "I'm just tired."

Evan gazes at me, unspoken emotions lurking in the blue of his eyes. His fingers reach out to touch my cheek with startling tenderness, sending a wave of goosebumps through me.

"Sutton..."

Before he can say anything else, a hand falls on his shoulder. Evan's fingers recoil from my cheek like it's burned him.

"How did it go, Ev?"

Zachary Blackwood appears at Evan's side and stops. "Oh, Sophie. Uh, hi. I hope your exam went well?"

Zachary is the total opposite of Evan. Where Evan is fair, Zachary is dark. Where Evan is broad and big with muscles,

Zachary is lean and angular. Evan has a sort of easy-going, arrogant carelessness, Zachary is rigidly courteous and ruthlessly self-disciplined.

Where Evan seems to barely realise Spearcrest is an educational establishment, Zachary is the emblem of academic excellence. In the lower school, he was always in the top five of every class for achievements. This year, he's even been selected as a Spearcrest Apostle—Mr Ambrose's elite group of academically-gifted students.

Out of all the Young Kings, he's the one I despise the least.

"It went fine, thank you," I answer. "I'll see you both around."

I turn to go grab my backpack from the now almost empty foyer. Evan calls out from behind me. "Don't you want to know how my exam went?"

Shouldering my backpack, I suppress the urge to sigh and roll my eyes. I pause, turn, and ask, "How did it go?"

"Pretty good, actually," he answers with a level of confidence I could never hope to achieve. "I think you'll be impressed come results day."

Zachary's eyes move from Evan to me, and I suddenly remember my goal to stay under the radar this year. I've already had more run-ins with the Young Kings than is wise.

So I bite back a sarcastic reply and instead go for a diplomatic comment and a quick escape. "Well done on your hard work, I guess. I have to go, see you later!"

I make my tactical retreat, all but running out the doors and into the icy winter sunlight. Still, even when I'm outside I can't help the feeling that Evan and Zachary's gazes are following me. I shake my head slightly.

It's probably just paranoia.

## Evan

As soon as Sophie has disappeared into the alleyway of trees leading to the rest of the campus, Zachary turns his head and lifts an eyebrow.

"Sophie Sutton," he says. "I see."

My cheeks are suddenly hot. I'm thankful for the cold breeze rushing in to cool them down.

"You see what, Zach?"

"Well, it's always been Sophie, hasn't it?"

Zach reaches down for my backpack and passes it to me. I take it absent-mindedly. "She's just tutoring me in English for Miss Bailey's mentoring programme."

"Right," Zach says as we slowly go down the steps of the assembly hall. "But I mean, it's always been Sophie. Even when it was Giselle, or Freya, it was still Sophie."

"*What* was still Sophie? Why are we talking in riddles? This is why I don't like Lit students. They always read too much into shit."

"You've liked Sophie since Year 9. No riddle there."

"Right, so I had a tiny crush on Sophie in Year 9—so what? That was fucking stupid—that was nothing. Did I not make up for it? Did you not see me make her life hell all these years?"

Zach raises an unimpressed eyebrow. "So, you figured out Luca likes having the girls you like, and you did your best to keep her as far from reach as possible. If anything, that just proves my point."

"What is this, Zach? This isn't a court of law, man. There's nothing to prove. I'm not on trial."

"Alright," Zach says, stopping in his tracks.

We stand in the middle of the path, facing each other. The day is bright and cold, and it's clear Zach is about to say something particularly annoying.

"Alright," he repeats. "Sophie is smart and pretty, so if I wanted to ask her out, that should be fine."

"No," I say immediately. "You better fucking not, Zach."

"Right," he says with a little shrug. "Because you like her."

"I don't like her. She's a stuck-up, moody, uptight little kiss-ass. We barely get on. I don't *like* her, I..." I try to figure out a way of explaining how I feel about Sophie, why the thought of Sophie going on a date with any guy feels wrong. "I *want* her."

It really is the only explanation I can give. Because I can hardly explain to Zach I want to fight Sutton, play with her, test my strength against hers, defeat her in combat. That would sound crazy.

It *is* crazy. Something that only makes sense between Sophie and me.

But Zach, as unmoved as usual, simply says, "Right. So then have her."

"I can't just *have* her. She's a human being, not a thing. And Sophie... ugh, she's such a fucking pain in the ass. You can't just *take* Sophie. You have to, I dunno... you have to *earn* her. She's like the princess in the tower: you have to fight and defeat the dragon first. Except that she's also the fucking dragon. Does that make sense?"

"Inside your crazy little American skull, I'm sure it does," Zachary says drily.

"Oh, fuck you. You sound just like her."

"Is that so? Except that I don't see you going around telling people you *want* me."

"I don't go around telling people I want Sophie—are you nuts? I told *you*. Only you, Zach, so keep that shit to yourself."

"I won't tell Luca you fancy Sophie, don't worry."

I grab Zach into a headlock. "You little shit! What are you talking about!"

"Let me go," Zach says calmly.

He's not fighting me back, so it's not even like I can beat on him. Not that I would dare to beat on Zach—his parents would have my ass in court faster than I could unclench my fist. Instead, I do something I know for a fact will annoy him: I mess up his perfectly groomed hair.

"Evan!" Zach yells. "I swear to God! You'll fucking pay for this!"

"Gentlemen!" a voice bellows, making us both jump apart. "This is a hallowed educational establishment—not a wrestling ring! I will thank you both for keeping your hands to yourselves."

"Forgive me, Mr Ambrose," Zachary says stiffly, slicking back his hair. "They are not taught manners in the colonies."

"The *colonies*?" I exclaim, incensed. "Mr Ambrose, are you hearing this?"

"Alas, I can only wish that I wasn't burdened with having to listen to any of your trite conversations," Mr Ambrose says witheringly. "And I expected more from you, Mr Blackwood. Now both of you fix your uniforms and get out of my sight."

We obey; Mr Ambrose isn't someone to piss off at Spearcrest.

We're still arguing on our way to the dining hall when we pass a small group of girls sitting on the stone benches by the tree. I don't notice them until Zach stops in his tracks to look at them. I turn around and follow his gaze.

It's Sophie and her friends, Audrey and Araminta—with whom I share a class. Araminta is sharing a muffin with Audrey on one bench and Sophie lies across the other bench, her head on Audrey's lap.

My heart skips a beat. Seeing Sophie off her guard and relaxed is not a common sight. It barely even feels real, like seeing a wolf without fangs or a shark asleep.

It's completely mesmerising.

She's stretched out over her coat, one leg dangling off the bench. Gone is the stiff posture, the fucking clipboard, the carefully neutral expression. Her phone is lying face down on her stomach, and she's eating an apple and talking up to Audrey with a smile on her face. A Year 9 smile, big and goofy. The kind of smile I've not seen on her face in years.

My heart clenches uncomfortably.

It's the kind of smile I haven't seen on her face since our short-lived friendship.

Zach veers off the path and towards the benches. I grab the sleeve of his blazer. "What the *fuck* are you doing?"

He responds with a chilling smirk. "I told you I'd make you pay for fucking up my hair."

"Zach, what—"

He completely ignores me and calls out to the girls, "Ladies! Post-exam party in the peace garden Friday night. Will you join us?"

The girls turn their heads, giving us a mix of reactions: surprise, delight, annoyance. Sophie props herself up on her elbows and calls back, "You know I'm meant to report this kind of stuff, right?"

"Right," Zach calls back. "But if you come, I'll make sure you're too tipsy to fill in any paperwork. Are you in?"

The girls exchange looks. I make a mental note to kill Zach with my bare hands as soon as we're alone.

"We'll see!" Audrey calls back.

"Yeah, we'll get back to you!" Araminta adds. "Thanks for the invite, Zach."

"It's my absolute pleasure," Zach calls back.

We leave. I turn to cast a final look at Sophie, but she's already lowered her head back onto Audrey's lap, talking up to her. She doesn't so much as glance my way, so I just turn around and follow Zach towards the dining hall. When I'm sure we're out of earshot, I grab his arm.

"What the fuck was that all about?"

"Payback and a favour rolled into one."

"How is that a favour?"

He smirks. "I don't know, Evan, let me think. What do girls and boys do at parties?"

"Yes—obviously I know what girls and boys do at parties. But what if Sophie does what girls and boys do with *another boy* at the party?"

Zach snorts. "Please. She hates everyone at Spearcrest."

"True," I admit, suddenly calmer. "You're right."

"Everyone, including *you*," Zach adds mercilessly. "So make an effort, eh?"

"Right, right..."

His words stay with me for the rest of the day. By the time I get back to the dorms that evening, my mind is full of thoughts of Sophie at the party.

Sophie being chatted up by boys who are finally realising how attractive she is. Sophie being chatted up by Zach, who would probably do it just to wind me up. Sophie liking Zach, because he's hard-working and intelligent and sarcastic, just like her.

Worst of all, Sophie being chatted up by Luca. Luca would do it just because he can, just because Sophie is mine and Luca always wants what doesn't belong to him.

All of this is unbearable to think about, and I make a silent but deadly promise to myself that I'll smash in the faces of anybody who goes near her.

But then my mind goes down an even more unbearable road.

Sitting with Sophie and chatting and having a drink with her. Dancing with Sophie under the canopy of the trees, stumbling drunkenly in the frosty grass. Pinning her against a tree trunk, kissing her mouth, her neck, her throat. Holding her up against me, her thighs wrapped around my hips. Her rough voice rasping a low moan against my ear while I push my cock slowly inside her. Making her wait, making her tremble and beg.

I roll around on my bed, burying my face into my pillow. I'm hard just thinking about it—really fucking hard—but I have to resist the urge to slip my hand into my boxers. Not just because my roommate could come back into the room at any time, but mostly because I don't think I could face Sophie tomorrow after having jacked off thinking about her... again.

I end up falling asleep still half-hard, and spend the entire night dreaming of nothing but Sophie.

Turns out facing Sophie after jacking off to thoughts of her is not something I should have worried about. Thursday afternoon comes, and Sophie is nowhere to be seen. I text her even though I know she probably doesn't like it when I do.

**Evan**: Are you not coming today?

She texts back a few minutes later.

**Sophie**: No. Lit exam is over. Gone straight to town.

I sigh in disappointment, then see that she's typing again.

**Sophie**: Is that ok?

From Sophie, this is inexplicably cute. I sit down at the kitchen counter and hesitate before texting back.

**Evan**: Yea yea. Are you coming to the party tomorrow?

I wait for her response, tapping my fingers in impatience. She responds three minutes later.

**Sophie**: No.

**Evan**: Why not? It'll be fun. Come.

**Sophie**: Not worth the trouble if I get caught.

**Evan**: Then don't get caught.

**Sophie**: That's what I'm planning to do by not going.

**Evan**: Ha ha. You deserve to have fun sometimes.

**Sophie**: I DO have fun sometimes

I sit up, lifting my phone up to my face. I text back quickly.

**Evan**: Not the kind of fun I'm thinking of.
**Sophie**: How would you know?

This is the problem with Sophie. That wicked streak in her, those vicious claws she has a way of digging into my skin.

**Evan**: Come to the party. We can find out.

She types something, stops. Types something, then stops. I'm wondering if I'm finally getting through to her, if she's going to give in. Her reply finally pops up.

**Sophie**: Maybe.

I lock my phone and shove it away from me. I'm not quite sure whether I emerged from this exchange victorious. Let's be honest, a *maybe* from Sophie is as good as a no. I should have known she'd be too uptight and rule-obsessed to party. Sophie doesn't *know* how to have fun.

But I could show her. If only she wasn't such a coward.

Now I've got nothing but disappointment and the pent-up tension leftover from texting Sophie. I glance at my phone. If she doesn't come to this party then I'm not going to get to see her until... when? Next term?

Not if I can fucking help it. I pick up my phone again and text Sophie.

**Evan**: Hey, if you need some time away from school and your parents, my offer is still open if you wanna stay over during the holidays.

She doesn't reply in so long I almost forget I sent her the text. By the time she responds, I've gone for a short run and a workout, I've taken shower and made myself an omelette. My phone buzzes and I pause before I unlock it.

When I see her message, I let out a shout of triumph and punch the air.

**Sophie**: Why not x

# 17

# DESPICABLE CINDERELLA

## Evan

THE PEACE GARDEN IS one of the best party locations in Spearcrest. It's split into eight quadrants, with pathways of broad flagstones dividing each quadrant. An enormous marble gazebo overlooks the garden, its wrought iron dome laced with ivy, and cedars and oaks shield it from all the main buildings, so we don't have to worry too much about getting caught.

Still, I'm in a despondent mood when I arrive at the party.

The thought of hanging out with the other Young Kings—listening to Sev rail on about his fiancée when it's clear he just needs to get over himself and fuck her, watching Luca make out with any girl he thinks we might want or helping Zach find reasons to start a fight with Theodora—brings me no joy. There's no girl I want to dance with, nobody I want to talk to.

I'd rather be at home, waiting for one text from Sophie than speak to pretty much anybody at the party.

I make a beeline straight for the gazebo, where the drinks are usually kept. I immediately spot Sev, who looks like some fairy tale prince in tight black pants and a loose white shirt that's unbuttoned halfway down his chest.

He's looking around distractedly and running his hand through his pitch-black hair, a sure sign that he's stressed or nervous. I can only guess he's looking for his fiancée. For somebody he claims to hate so much, he spends a lot of time thinking about her, talking about her or looking for her—but who am I to judge?

"What's up, Sev?" I ask, grabbing a bottle of beer from one of the ornate marble plant pots somebody has thoughtfully filled with ice.

"Fuck, nothing," he says.

His gaze sweeps the crowd anxiously; it's obvious he's lying. Instead of pressing him for information, I grab another beer and hand it to him.

"Nothing is right," I sigh, following his gaze to the crowd. The Sophie-less, pointless crowd. "Let's just get fucked up tonight."

Sev finally meets my gaze and gives me a grin: his signature Sev grin, full of French arrogance. He raises his beer bottle, tipping the neck towards me. "*A la tienne.*"

I clink my bottle to his and we both drink—and keep drinking.

Sev is a good person to get fucked with because he can hold his alcohol and at the same time alcohol brings out the more belligerent, ostentatious aspects of his personality. By the time I realise we're drunk, we're both holding bottles of red wine and lying half-slumped into lavender bushes. The music surrounds us, and the crowd moves to the beat like an ocean, rising and falling.

"What really pisses me off—" Sev is shouting over the music, his French accent ten times more pronounced now he's drunk, "is she's acting as if she's, I don't know, so bored with the whole thing. I told her to do what she's told—I told her how things work here. But she just acts like she doesn't give a shit about any of it! She acts like she's not even interested in *knowing* me. Can you fucking believe that shit?"

"I thought you didn't want her to follow you around like a puppy?" I shout back, trying to keep his face in focus "Isn't that what you said at the beginning of the year? I don't want her to follow me around like a puppy—*comme un*, a, a...*chienne*?"

I'm pretty sure that barely counts as French, and Sev shakes his head and waves a dismissive hand.

"*Comme un toutou!*" he shouts back, but I have no idea what that means, so I just stare blankly at him. Clearly my contribution to this conversation is unnecessary, because he continues anyway. "I don't want her to follow me around *comme un toutou*! It's the modicum of respect to try and at least come to me, to—it's not like *I'm* marrying into *her* family, for fuck's sake. *She's* marrying into *mine*. It's *my* name she's after, so why the fuck does she think she doesn't have to listen to a thing I say, or—it's the disrespect, you know?"

I nod vigorously.

Sev is a lot more worked up about this fiancée situation than I thought. After all his talk about not wanting this girl to follow him around and steal away all his freedom to do what he pleases and fuck around—Sev's favourite thing to do—I can't understand why he isn't happy she's left him alone.

Actually, I'm pretty sure I know exactly why.

"Maybe you should just go ahead and fuck the shit out of her!" I shout in Sev's face.

"Fuck her? And let her think for one second that I want her?" Sev's face goes red. "*Mieux vos la mort!*"

I have no idea what he's saying—something about death, which does not bode well—but since his fiancée is French, I'm sure she'll be able to handle his bilingual wrath better than me.

"You wouldn't be doing it because you want her, though," I explain slowly, working out what I mean as I speak. "You'd be doing it to remind her of her place here. She won't dare disobey or disrespect you if you fuck her into submission. Right?"

Sev's cheeks are flushed, but he's nodding now. I can tell he likes the idea. Grim determination draws his thick black eyebrows together. "Yes—yes, you're right, man!"

Before I can say anything to convince him, he's struggled upright from our lavender bush and is standing in front of me, sweeping his hair back with one hand. "She's my fucking toy—why shouldn't I play with her?"

Looks like Sev doesn't need to be talked into this idea, because he's clearly only too happy to talk himself into it. "Right—exactly."

I extend my hand to him, hoping he can help me up, but he's already striding away in a determined zigzag. He disappears into the darkness of the peace garden and I sigh and roll myself up.

Time to go latch on to another Young King and inspire him to action, since I'm powerless to do anything about the things *I* want.

I'm walking slowly and carefully back to the gazebo when I spot a face in the corner of my vision. I stumble to an abrupt stop and turn my head so fast I almost pull a neck muscle.

The world crystallises. Have I blacked out and woken up into some sort of dream?

Because right there, standing amongst the trees a little away from the broad flagstone paths, is Sophie fucking Sutton.

She looks good, too. I don't even think I've ever seen her in a dress, but the look still screams rule-abiding prefect with the personality of an uptight librarian: black fabric, square neckline, long sleeves. Her hair is loose on her shoulders, the lustrous brown strands too thick and heavy to fly in the wind.

She's standing with Araminta, the girl from my Science class. They are holding hands and dancing to the music, with Sophie twirling Araminta around then catching her by her waist.

I veer in their direction. My mind has gone blank—blank except for the single thought of Sophie, and Sophie's long brown hair, and Sophie's waist in my arms and her thighs around my hips. I walk with grim determination.

Tonight, I'm going to put my hands on Sophie. I don't care what excuse I find, or how weird I might come across. But tonight—as soon as possible, in fact—I'm going to touch Sophie.

A blur of pink and gold fills my vision, blocking Sophie from my sight and stopping me in my tracks. I look down and let out a sigh of barely repressed frustration.

"What do you want, Rosenthal?"

Seraphina Rosenthal, the Rose of Spearcrest, stands in front of me with wide doll eyes and an innocent smile on her face. She's wearing a bright pink corset stitched with dozens of actual roses, a puff of tulle skirts, fishnet tights and combat boots.

Her colourful exuberance is a direct contrast to the austerity of Sophie's plain black dress, and as a result it holds no power over me.

I gaze down at Rose, wondering whether I could fancy her if she wore her long gold hair in a severe centre parting, wore big boots and matronly outfits. Somehow, I doubt it.

If it was that easy, then I could get over Sophie and finally live a normal, happy life.

"Won't you dance with me, Evan?" Rose asks, drawing closer. "It's my favourite song."

"Uh... I'm busy right now." I shrug. "Maybe later?"

"Oh, you're busy?" She flutters her eyelashes. Her make-up is a work of art, pink and gold glitter artfully decorating the bright blue of her eyes. "Anything I can help with?"

"Uh, no."

I side-step her and resume my lurching journey over to the trees, where Sophie is now leaning against the rough trunk of an oak, talking to Araminta and a boy with dark hair. I don't recognise the boy, so I can only assume he's in Year 12, but he leaves almost as soon as I arrive anyway.

Araminta turns with a start when I appear at her side and her eyes immediately narrow. Sophie's reaction is almost imperceptible: a slight raise of one eyebrow.

"Can we help you?" Araminta asks icily.

"I wannna—" I look straight into Sophie's eyes. She holds my gaze and says nothing. "I wanna see if Sutton's having a good time."

"She's having a grand time," Araminta snaps.

It's clear she doesn't like me. I can understand why. But she could be stabbing me straight in my chest right now and it still wouldn't be enough to draw my attention away from Sophie's direct gaze.

"I thought you were scared of getting caught," I say to her.

"I thought I deserved to have fun," she answers drily.

Her voice is like a match set to my alcohol-fuelled veins. Heat rushes through me. "What kind of fun, Sutton?" I step a little closer. "You'd have a lot more fun with me."

"I doubt it," Araminta snaps. "Come on, Sophie, let's go get another drink."

She takes Sophie's hand and pulls her away. Sophie follows without protest, but she turns her head slightly as she goes, and pokes her tongue out at me.

That's when I realise she might be a little tipsy.

The sight of her tongue peeking out between her pursed lips is like an electric shock right to my system. I am instantly and embarrassingly aroused, but I resist the urge to follow Sophie. It's clear Araminta doesn't want me around them, and if I'm honest with myself I know exactly why.

I turn and jump when I find myself once more face to face with Rose. The doll-like expression of innocence and sweetness is gone, replaced by a disdainful sneer.

"Really, Evan? Her?"

I sigh. "I have no idea what you're talking about."

"Sophie. Fucking. Sutton."

This is dangerous ground. Rose is a powerful influence in Spearcrest—not enough to call my power into question, but enough to make Sophie's life unpleasant in the way it used to be.

"I'm not even angry," Rose says (a blatant lie, since her face is flushed with fury), "I'm just disappointed. Don't you know you could do much better?"

My jaw clenches. The mist of alcohol seems to evaporate in the sudden gale of annoyance blowing through me. "If I wanted to hear your opinion on anything, Rose, I'd ask for it. But since you have nothing intelligent or relevant to contribute to a conversation, you might as well keep your mouth closed."

"Don't be so fucking defensive, Evan. It's a bad look." She gives an airy laugh which doesn't quite manage to make her appear as careless as she wishes. "Over Sophie Sutton of all people? Just because she acts stuck up and dresses like she belongs doesn't mean she's one of us, or that dating her would be anything more than a fucking charitable act."

I stare at her as she speaks, at her expensive clothing and empty blue eyes, and my fury goes out like a blown candle.

"You're really fucking pathetic, Rose." Her eyes widen, but I don't stop. "You might be wearing the prettiest dress and the most expensive makeup, but it doesn't hide what you really are: some vapid, brainless, jealous fucking *baby*. Grow the fuck up, yeah?"

Then I turn around and walk away from her. And it might just be the alcohol, but for the first time, I realise there isn't a single person at this party I actually want to spend time with.

Well—one person—but no matter how close I get to her, she's forever out of reach.

"Fuck this," I mutter to myself, and leave.

I'M CROSSING THE NARROW belt of trees on the way back to the dorms when I collide with a figure as it emerges from behind the enormous trunk of an oak. I throw my hands out to catch the figure as it stumbles back and look down into a pair of dark, hooded eyes.

"Fuck." Sophie gives a low, lazy laugh. "Why is it always you?"

She lays a palm on my chest and pushes me away, but I keep a hold of her arms. Now my eyes have adjusted to the shadows, I can see a little more clearly. Her hair is still parted down the middle severely, but her cheeks are flushed and her lips are gleaming.

She smells of vanilla and coconut rum.

She smells fucking divine. I have to use all my willpower not to bury my face in her neck and breathe her in like some deranged sicko.

"Where are you going, Sutton?" I ask, forcing my voice to remain light.

Her hand is still on my chest, but instead of pushing me away again, she curls her fingers into my T-shirt, digging into my chest. "I'm leaving before I get myself in trouble."

Her rough voice claws across my skin. With the alcohol still in my system, my barriers have all crumbled down, and there's nothing to protect me from the effect of that unbearable fucking voice. Blood rushes straight to my cock, and I grow so hard so fast I have to clench my jaw to suppress a groan.

"Trouble, Sutton?" I slide my hands slowly from her arms to her shoulders, gently cradling her neck and slowly drawing aside strands of her hair so my fingers can rest against her skin. She doesn't make an attempt to stop me. "What kind of trouble?"

I slide my thumb gently up and down her neck, my eyes on her lips. They're wet and parted in a scornful half-smile—they look good enough to fucking eat, and for a moment I have the wild urge to slide my thumb into her mouth, to part her lips just so I can press my finger against her tongue.

I want to taste the alcohol on her breath, I want to claim her mouth with mine, to kiss her so fucking good she'll never be able to even dream of kissing anybody else.

But Sophie with some alcohol in her is bolder than I could ever have expected. She tilts her head back and arches her neck, watching me from under her heavy eyelids.

With her hand still fisted in my T-shirt, she lifts the fabric, exposing my stomach to the cold. Her eyes rake over my skin, my abs.

She smirks. "More trouble than it's worth, I reckon." And then she drops my T-shirt and pats my chest with supreme condescension.

I tilt my head, keeping my voice low and calm. "Liar. Everybody knows you want me, Sutton."

She must have either had too many drinks or she's got low tolerance, because instead of her usual glare, she laughs. "You're about as wanted as a brain tumor."

"You're one vicious little fucker, aren't you?" I tighten my fingers around her throat ever so slightly, but she doesn't seem alarmed at all. Her cheeks are darkly flushed now, and her teeth tug slowly on her bottom lip.

"Oh no," she says, low and rough and mocking, "I'm not going to make you cry, am I?"

"In your dreams."

"You don't belong in my dreams, Evan Knight," she rasps. "You belong in my fucking nightmares."

And then, to my complete and utter surprise, she fists my collar and pulls me down, dragging my lips to hers. I open my mouth in a half-moan. Her lips part and I glide my tongue against hers, tasting rum and sugar.

I'm so fucking hard I'm certain I could come without being touched. My mind is a crimson blur of urgent lust. Lifting her up against me, I hurtle forward, slamming her back against a tree trunk. Her legs hug my hips the way they did in the pool. Her fingers dig into my neck, pulling me closer.

"Fuck, Sutton," I groan against her mouth. "You taste so fucking good."

Kissing Sophie Sutton feels exactly as dangerous and forbidden and exhilarating as I always imagined it would. But it also feels completely right, profoundly satisfying, like the final piece of a puzzle slotting into place.

And it feels good, so good I could fucking die.

Her open mouth and the squeeze of her thighs around my hips tells me she's enjoying this as much as I am. Who would have thought Sophie Sutton could be like this? Austere Sophie, tightly wound, so fucking controlled—would would have thought she could kiss so good, arch her back with such abandon?

I want more—so much more. Now I know how good it feels to kiss her mouth, I want to kiss the rest of her—every part. I want to touch her, taste her. I want—I *need*—more of this, more of *her*.

My hand slips up her leg, gripping her thigh, dragging her skirt up. Her skin is hot through her tights—there's too much fabric, all I can think of is tearing her tights off, pushing up her skirt, taking off her dress and—

And then her hand clutches my throat and she shoves me away.

I freeze, staring at her in shock and confusion. Her lips are gleaming and dark. Her eyes are wide and panicked.

She pushes against my chest again. I immediately move away, setting her carefully down. She wipes the back of her hand across her mouth, tucks her hair back behind her ears and straightens her skirt.

"Sutton—" I can barely think, my mind foggy with lust, my entire body a flame. "What—"

She slaps her hand down on my chest and laughs up at me.

"Fuck-ups like *this*," she says, "are why I should never drink."

And then she just turns and runs away with a mad giggle. I stand, frozen in shock and still hard, and watch as she disappears into the night like some sexy, despicable fucking Cinderella.

## 18

# COOKIES

## Sophie

I STAND IN FRONT of Evan's front door with my suitcase at my feet. My pulse pounds erratically, as if I'm in the middle of being chased by a crazed killer or trapped in a fight to the death. My mind is full of blaring alarms, and every part of my body is urging me to turn around and run.

Really, what the fuck am I thinking?

I lied to my parents, asked Audrey to cover for me, and willingly agreed to spend two weeks living under the same roof as Evan Knight. Not only that, but I decided to do all this in spite of what happened at that stupid party.

Going was a bad idea—I'd known that all along. So why did I go? Out of curiosity? Because I *did* deserve to have some fun?

I went because I'm an idiot, that's why. And I'm here right now also because I'm an idiot.

If my Year 11 self could see me now, she would probably slap me in the face, or else take me to a hospital to have my head checked for significant brain damage.

Because what I'm doing is not only willingly entering the monster's den, but agreeing to live with the monster for two weeks... after aggressively making out with said monster against a tree.

When I inevitably get devoured alive, I'll have nobody but myself to blame.

I shake my head and pick up my suitcase. No. I know exactly what I'm doing. I'm not here out of stupidity—I'm here out of strategy, to serve my own interests. And I've picked up so many shifts at the café I'll barely be in Evan's house anyway.

Besides, I'm sure he'll be up to his own stuff. He might not give a shit about his A-Levels, but he definitely gives a shit about sports, so there'll be that, and I can't imagine he wouldn't have plenty of friends and girls to hang out with.

I ascend the steps to his door like they're gallow stairs, bracing myself.

Before I can even knock on the door, it flies open and I'm faced with a beaming Evan. He's in normal clothes, for once: jeans and a long-sleeved t-shirt. Loose curls of sandy hair fall over his eyes and his cheeks are flushed as if from exertion. He smells... like cookies.

"Have you been baking?" I ask, peering around him.

"I've tried making cookies," he responds brightly, taking my suitcase from my hands.

"Right... how come?"

I follow him inside and he closes the door behind me. The warm, sweet scent of cookies fills the foyer.

"I dunno, I thought it would be kind of a homey thing to do. It's been ages since I've had company over for Christmas."

I frown slightly. "Do you not spend Christmases with your family?"

"Eh, sometimes." He shrugs. "But it's difficult to get everybody in the same country at the same time. Where's the rest of your stuff?"

"What stuff? I've got my suitcase and my backpack."

"That's all?"

"It's not like I'm going to Paris Fashion Week. I'm going to be working most of the time."

"Oh." He stares at me for a moment, his smile wavering. I expected him to be cocky or obnoxious, but he's not. In fact, he seems almost nervous. "Come on then, let me show you around."

I nod and follow him on a tour of the house. It's beautiful throughout: the dining room is simple yet tastefully decorated, the corridors upstairs all feature vases of flowers, paintings, plush rugs. Velvet curtains frame the tall windows and plant baskets hang in little nooks over armchairs. Even the bathrooms look amazing, with their marble flooring, lion-clawed bathtubs and enormous plants.

"This is my room," Evan says, stopping in one corridor with his hand on a door handle. He gives me a sheepish look, and colour clouds the sharp plains of his cheeks. "Nothing much to see, I guess. Um, let me show you the guest room."

He takes me to a room down the corridor. There, Chinese silk wallpaper in pale shades of green and gold adorns one wall, and the large French window gives way to a small balcony overlooking an enormous garden. A large bed with a headboard of padded green velvet dominates the room, complemented by sparse, tidy furniture.

"Uh, so this is your guest room," Evan says, ruffling the back of his hair in a sheepish gesture. "There's an en-suite, but it's only got a shower, so if you fancy a bath, you have to use the big bathroom down the hall. And I think that's everything."

He stares at me while I take in my surroundings, and I realise my mouth has been wide open this whole time. I close it quickly and put my backpack down on the ottoman at the foot of the bed. Evan props my suitcase next to it and points to the wardrobe on the other side of the room.

"That's the wardrobe," he says uselessly. "So... yeah."

We stare at each other for a moment, and I'm suddenly aware of the strange intimacy of the situation. And with our disastrous and messy peace garden kiss hanging between us like a spectre, the situation is quickly becoming too tense to bear.

I clear my throat and say, "Thank you for letting me stay."

"It's my pleasure," he replies with a grin. "I'm gonna go check on the cookies if you want to get settled in or whatever?"

"I'm working later, so I'm just going to get ready and set off."

"Oh." Again, his disappointment is obvious. "Well, do you want a lift?"

Sitting alone in a car with Evan after everything that happened? Now *that* would really be a stupid thing to do.

"No, I have plenty of time to walk."

"Right," he says. "Right, right. Alright. Well, grab a cookie before you go."

"Yes," I nod. I'm blushing, and I don't even know why. "I will. Thanks."

"Right," he repeats. "I'll be downstairs, then."

"Okay."

Even though he's so tall and broad-shouldered, there's something childlike in the way he shrugs and marches out of the room. I stare after him, shocked at the realisation that I'm finding him kind of endearing. Maybe it's the cookies, or that mop of curls falling softly into his eyes, or the way he's being so weirdly courteous.

Or maybe it's just a dangerous lapse in self-preservation on my part.

After emptying my backpack of everything apart from my travel essentials—earphones, purse, a book and a case for tissues, lip balm and hand sanitiser—I head downstairs. My coat is waiting for me on the coat hanger and I put it on before going into the kitchen just in case I need to make a quick exit.

I enter the kitchen to a scene of chaos: bags of flour and broken eggshells litter the counters, trays of cookies propped precariously wherever Evan found space to put them. He's standing by the kitchen island, a look of intense concentration on his face as he carefully pipes icing onto flat white biscuits.

The artwork is dubious, but there's something incongruously adorable about the way his tongue is sticking out, looking like he's about to create the biscuit equivalent of the Sistine chapel.

"What did you make, then?" I ask, peering at the trays.

He looks up eagerly. "I've made chocolate chip cookies, sugar cookies and snickerdoodles."

Not exactly the kind of word I expected to come out of his mouth.

"Snickerdoodles?" I repeat, leaning over the tray. "I don't think I've ever had those."

"Oh, what? My mom made them every Christmas when we lived in Massachusetts. Here," he grabs one off the tray and lifts it to my face. "Try one."

I take the cookie from his hand because as homely as this is, letting him feed me a cookie would feel a bit too much like we're playing mum and dad. He watches me expectantly as I take a big bite. My eyes widen.

"Fuck!" I say through my mouthful. "That's amazing."

Who would have thought the devil would be such a fine baker? I finish the cookie in a couple of bites, Evan watching me with delight.

"You like it?"

"Yes," I say with some reluctance. I hesitate, then point at the cookie tray. "Can I take a couple for the road?"

"Yeah," he beams, "have as many as you want. These will still be here when you come back anyway. You sure you don't want a lift?"

I shake my head, wrapping two cookies in some kitchen towels. "No, I have plenty of time to walk. See you later."

"See ya..."

Evan sounds like he's going to say something else, but he doesn't and I leave before things get awkward again.

---

When I arrive at the café, it's bustling with customers, and Jess and Freddy are both behind the counter, taking orders and making coffees. Freddy looks up with a warm smile when I come in.

"My saviour!" he says when I slip behind the counter. "Do you know how glad we are to have you back?"

I laugh and point at the clock, which shows that there are still fifteen minutes to go before my shift starts. "Is that a hint to jump on now?"

Freddy grins. "I'll pay you for the hour and you can have as many muffins as you want."

"Fair."

I drop my bag and coat off in the office, and hastily pull my apron on. Jess gives me a quick hug when I join her, and hands me two lattes in massive cups. "Will you be a sweetheart and take those to these two ladies over there?"

I nod and do what she asks. After that, the hours become one long blur of taking orders, popping muffins, cupcakes and brownies on little plates and making drinks, bringing them to tables, being kept chatting with chatty old ladies and clearing tables once they leave. Freddy makes sure to keep everything stocked up and helps with the drinks, since he's brilliant at latte art and the customers love it. Jess, who is normally reserved and deadpan, always somehow becomes more animated and friendly the busier the café gets.

Eventually, night falls outside and there is finally a lull. Jess hops back onto the counter to rest her feet and Freddy immediately hands her a key lime cupcake, which she takes gratefully.

"How about I make you two a drink?" Freddy says. "What do you feel like? I'll even make you a fancy latte if you want."

"It's too late for caffeine," Jess says with a grimace. "Can I have a hot chocolate? With lots of marshmallows and cream?"

"Anything for you," Freddy grins. "Sophie?"

"Same, please."

My feet hurt, so I hop up next to Jess with a sigh of relief.

"How did your exams go?" Jess asks through a mouthful of cupcake.

I shake my head. "Stressful. Exhausting. Relentless."

She laughs. "Yeah, sounds about right. I can relate. I'm surprised you're not taking time off work to rest and chill."

"I probably will take a few days off at Christmas, but I'm trying to make money while I can."

"Fair, fair."

Jess takes the mug of hot chocolate Freddy hands her and immediately takes a big bite of her whipped cream. Freddy hands me my cup and I take it with a smile.

"Thanks."

"What are you saving up for, then?" Freddy asks, leaning against the counter with his own drink.

"I'm applying to universities abroad, so I'm saving for that."

"Oh really?" Jess says. "I thought you'd be going Oxbridge."

I laugh. "I'm applying, of course, but that's mostly because my parents expect me to."

"You don't want to go?" Freddy asks with a look of surprise. "I thought it'd be right up your street."

"Not really. After five years of Spearcrest, I'm ready to move on, and Oxbridge wouldn't feel like moving on."

"Where are you applying?" Jess asks. "If you don't mind telling us, of course."

"Well, I'm applying to most of the Ivy Leagues, but the one I want is Harvard."

"Fuck me, Sophie!" Jess exclaims. "You're not fucking around!"

"I admire your ambition," Freddy says warmly, staring into my eyes. "You're driven and unafraid of working hard for what you want. I think Harvard would be lucky to have you."

Heat floods my cheeks, but luckily I'm saved from saying something embarrassing and awkward by the arrival of some customers. After that, it's the final rush of the day, mostly orders to go, and then it's finally time to close up.

"You go home, Sophie, we'll close up," Freddy says. "Thanks for today."

"Yeah, go home and get lots of rest. You need to be full of energy for tomorrow!" Jess says giddily, bouncing around the shop watering the plants.

"What's tomorrow?" I ask, glancing between Freddy and Jess as I remove my apron.

"Only the best day of the year," Jess says with a little spin. "A magical day!"

Freddy laughs and hands me my coat and bag, which he fetches from the office.

"Tomorrow is when we put up the Christmas decorations," he tells me with a broad smile. "Our parents used to do it every year, so it's a bit of a tradition here at the Little Garden."

"I can't wait, then," I say, putting on my coat and shrugging on my backpack. "I'll make sure I've had plenty of sleep and a big breakfast, Jess."

"You better!"

On the walk home, I can't help but think of Freddy and Jess and their Christmas decorations.

The Little Garden sometimes feels like a dream world, a bubble away from the reality of my life. My parents don't celebrate Christmas in a big way, but we always have a tree and some presents at Christmas.

Are they sad I'm not going to spend Christmas with them? When I told them about staying at Audrey's for Christmas, they seemed happy, not sad at all. Mum gushed at the "opportunities" a friendship with Audrey's family could present me in the future, and Dad told me to make sure I was on my best behaviour around them.

It's not like I have anything to complain about. My parents have worked hard their whole lives and worked alongside people with more wealth and success than they'll ever be able to aspire to. Now, they want nothing but the best for me, and they are aware of how difficult the best can be to get when you don't start off with an advantage.

To them, Spearcrest is that advantage for me, and everything I do should be in service of my future, my success. There's nothing wrong with that. I am the way I am thanks to them, and I have to remind myself to be grateful for that.

When I finally reach Evan's house, I pause outside the gates. The house is enormous, towering over the pine trees around it, outlined by the faint starlight. Even amongst the massive houses on the street, this house is isolated, separated from the road by a long path and all those evergreens. I can see rectangles of light here and there, but the rest of the windows are dark. Such a big, empty house.

For the first time, I wonder how Evan feels about spending Christmas alone in this big house.

Asking him is out of the question, but when I enter the house, the first thing that strikes me is the silence. I check the kitchen, which he's tried to tidy up with surprising success. The living room is ablaze with lights but as empty and pristine as usual.

I head upstairs to the guestroom to put my things down when I finally spot Evan.

His bedroom door is wide open, revealing a sprawling room, surprisingly tidy. An enormous TV is set on a low unit of dark wood, and Evan is sprawled in front of it on a pile of cushions. A game controller rests on his stomach, and the TV is flashing brightly coloured cartoons at the room, but he's asleep. His mouth is slightly open, his chest is rising and falling slowly. At his side, there's an empty plate with the corners of a sandwich left untouched, a glass half full of milk.

It's hard to believe this is the same guy who's been making my life a nightmare since Year 9, the guy who hoisted me against a tree and kissed me like he was starving and I was the last fruit on earth.

I stare at him for a moment, a weird sensation squeezing my heart. It's not really affection, but something else, a sort of sadness—almost pity. There's no reason to feel sorry for Evan: he's as rich as it's possible to be, privileged beyond belief. He will never worry about work or money.

And yet...

Padding across the soft blue rug, I kneel by Evan and poke his arm. There's no response. From up close, it's shocking how handsome he is, and I allow myself the indulgence of looking at him properly.

He was very pretty in Year 9 when I met him, but since then he's grown more handsome—a sort of rugged, American handsomeness. Strong jaw, defined cheekbones, straight nose. His eyelashes are long and thick, just like his ridiculous hair. In sleep, he looks like a fairytale prince.

Of course, he's closer to the wolf than the prince—but you couldn't tell by looking at him.

I flick his cheek. His eyes snap open and he starts when he sees me.

"Sophie!"

My name slips from his lips like he didn't even mean to say it. He probably didn't. After all, he's not called me by name for years. He sits up and wipes his face, scrunching up his handsome features with one hand.

"I fell asleep," he explains uselessly.

"Really? Are you sure?"

He laughs. "You're such an asshole."

"Now you're telling me something I didn't know," I retort. "It's only eight o'clock. Do you always go to sleep this early?"

"I didn't do it on purpose," he says. "I was waiting for the guys to come online so we could game, but I fell asleep waiting." He checks his phone and grimaces. "Zach is probably too busy obsessing over Theodora and I bet Sev is somewhere plotting some sort of plan to defeat his new arch-enemy, the fiancée." He tosses his phone aside with a sigh. "Fucking sell-outs."

I don't see why he's disclosing this stuff to me, but I have no interest in the complicated love lives of the Young Kings.

"Well..." I say, standing, "have you eaten?"

He points at the plate. "I made a sandwich."

"That's not a meal, though, is it? I thought you were meant to be all about health and fitness."

"I am," he says with a pout. "But I'm not great at cooking, and there's nothing much in the fridge."

I frown. "How do you normally feed yourself over the holidays?"

He shrugs. "My parents send me money, I usually order take-outs or make sandwiches."

"Well," I take a deep sigh and hope I'm not making a terrible mistake. "I'm going to need to eat, so... do you want to eat with me?"

He immediately sits up, and his eyes go three shades bluer like they've been lit up from the inside. "Yes! I'll order anything you like."

I shake my head. "No, I'm going to cook."

"With what?"

"With ingredients."

"But I don't have any of those."

"Right, that's why I'm going to the shop."

"Like... a grocery store?"

I roll my eyes. "I *know* you're not too rich to know what a supermarket is, Evan."

He raises both hands. "No, no, I just don't go often. This is brilliant." He leaps to his feet, almost headbutting me in his haste. "I'll drive us. Let's go shopping."

He bounds off and I follow him. For some reason, his enthusiasm is both endearing and a little depressing. I make a mental note to buy some Christmas decorations while we're at the supermarket.

Evan might be a complete and utter arsehole, but even arseholes deserve a bit of Christmas cheer.

19

# AMERICAN DREAM

## Sophie

Over the next few days, it becomes painfully obvious how empty Evan's life is. All he does is go for runs, work out in his massive home gym, walk around the kitchen looking for snacks and play video games.

Nobody visits him, since his friends, like mine, are all home with their families or holidaying abroad. He doesn't seem bothered about university applications or homework or revision—or about much at all, actually. He just ambles aimlessly through his days, looking for stuff to do.

Whenever I return home from the café, he comes bounding down the stairs like an eager puppy. We get into the habit of cooking together, which mostly involves me doing the cooking and Evan looking over my shoulder and asking a million questions. I give him tasks, and he does them without complaint: washing up, peeling veggies, emptying the bins.

We eat together at his kitchen island and then watch TV for a bit in his fancy living room. Sometimes, we'll play some video games, but I'm not very good at them, and Evan isn't the best teacher, so I always end up giving up.

Other times, we'll play some music and I'll sit and chip away at my homework while Evan lies on his back on the floor with his legs on the sofa, playing games on his phone.

On Friday evening, I come home exhausted after five consecutive days at the café. I have Saturday and Sunday off, so I put away my coat and backpack and go find Evan. Although we never talked about the kiss at the party, it no longer feels like a phantom haunting us every time we're together, so most of the awkwardness has dissipated by now.

He's perched on a stool in the kitchen, watching something on his phone and sipping a massive protein shake. His blue eyes light up when I enter the room and he holds up his glass.

"Want some?"

"After I'm done working out in your basement, maybe."

"You're going to work out?" he asks with honest surprise.

I give him a look. "No, Evan. No, I'm not going to work out. But there *is* something I want us to do."

He stares at me wide-eyed, and his phone slips from his hand, landing on the marble tabletop with a thud. A dull flush colours his cheeks. Immediately, the ghost of the kiss rises between us. I have to intervene quickly if I don't want this to become unbearably awkward.

"Not whatever it is you're imagining," I snap.

"Oh." He blinks at me with a slight frown. "What, then?"

I raise my eyebrows. "Do you remember the decorations we bought at the beginning of the week?"

He sits up. "Fuck off. Yes. Yes, I remember! What about them? Is it time?"

I nod solemnly. "It's time."

He runs from the kitchen, abandoning both his phone and his protein shake. The decorations are in bags and boxes in the hallway. I walk over to find Evan flitting around them like a giddy kid.

"Where do we start?"

Decorating takes us the rest of the afternoon and most of the evening. But when we finally finish and walk around to admire our handiwork, it doesn't feel like we wasted our time. The austere elegance of the rooms is transformed by the soft glow of coloured fairy lights, the strings of tinsel, the garlands and wreaths.

Even our small Christmas tree, tucked by the ornate fireplace in the living room, looks pretty good now it's decorated.

"Does that mean we're doing presents, then?" Evan asks as we both stand admiring the tree.

"I mean, it's a little late now. Do you want to?"

"Yeah! It would be weird to have a tree with no presents under it."

I shrug. "Alright. We'll do presents."

I still remember the present Evan gave me in Year 9: a silver necklace with a tiny bear on it. The present was too nicely packaged for him to have wrapped it, but he had remembered what my favourite animal was, which had touched me profoundly.

It's one of my last good memories of him.

I glance away from Evan. As hurtful as the memory is now, it's a much-needed reminder of the reality of a friendship with Evan. Just because we've reached a sort of friendly civility during my stay at his house doesn't mean we're friends, and there's no chance I'm letting him hurt me again.

Still, when I go to town the next day to look for a present while Evan is out for a run, I can't help but feel a strange pressure. Rationally, I know that it doesn't matter what I get him. This whole thing isn't real, it's more of a play-acting between us. Despite that, I can't help but want to get him something he'll like.

I spend hours looking, ambling from one shop to the next. What do you get someone who can have anything he wants?

The answer is... anything.

In the end, I settle on a soft, oversized hoodie the same summer sky-blue as his eyes. I buy blue wrapping paper with silver stars, and a Christmas card with a mischievous looking snowman on it.

When I get home, Evan is nowhere to be found, and I'm guessing he's either sweating away in his gym or out doing the same thing I'm doing. So I carefully wrap his present, place it under our little tree and amble into the kitchen to cook some dinner.

He returns a little before I finish cooking. To my surprise, he apologises for not being back in time to help. Then he sets the kitchen island with cutlery and pours two glasses of wine. He offers me wine with every meal, which I always decline. But since I don't have work the following day, and either I'm tired, or his candour has managed to lower my defences somewhat: I end up accepting the glass he gives me.

We sit and eat, Evan regaling me with tales of American Christmas extravagance and overzealous house decorations. I take a slow sip of wine and watch him over the rim of my glass.

He's animated, cheeks flushed, blue eyes bright. I never realised how much of a fan of Christmas he was, but maybe all Americans love Christmas this much. He pauses in his stories to shovel stew and bread into his mouth, and I take the opportunity to ask the question that's been on my mind.

"Do you miss America?"

He shrugs. "Kind of. I have good memories there, especially my aunt's house in New Haven when the whole family gets together. And New York is pretty cool too. Everything in America feels bigger and newer compared to here."

"Would you ever move back?"

"I mean, yeah, I think I'm gonna have to. I'll probably intern for my dad in one of his offices or something. Who knows."

"Well, I might end up moving there before you," I say.

Evan freezes with a spoonful of stew halfway between his bowl and his mouth.

"You want to move to America? I thought you were going to Oxford or Cambridge. That's where most of the kids in our year seem to be planning on going."

"Exactly."

He smirks. "Oh, of course. I forget how much you hate being associated with the rest of us Spearcrest kids. Wouldn't want anyone thinking you've been handed anything, right?"

It's an odd comment from him, subtly pointed. Evan might be many things, but subtle's not one of them.

"Nothing wrong with that," I say drily, taking another sip of my drink. I don't particularly like wine, but this is good wine, and it warms me up from the inside on its way down.

"No, nothing wrong with that," Evan says with a sudden smile. "They're going to love you in America, you know."

That, I did not expect. "Really?"

"Yeah, really. You've got this sort of stuck-up British sophistication, but you're also an underdog. It's a winning combination. All the American boys are going to fall head over heels in love with you."

I try to imagine it. Being noticed by tall, smart American boys at Harvard. After years of being poked at from a distance like a roadside show bear by the Spearcrest boys, I can't honestly say it's not a pleasant image. It would be quite nice to be wanted for once.

"I wouldn't hate that," I say with a little shrug.

Evan looks scandalised. "What are you talking about? You'd never date an American!"

"What are *you* talking about? Since when are you such an authority on who I would or wouldn't date?"

"I'm not saying I'm an authority. You've made your opinions on us thick, bull-headed Americans pretty clear."

"I don't think *all* Americans are thick and bull-headed. Americans have plenty of qualities too."

He stares at me with his mouth open in an expression of incredulity. "*What?* Like what?"

"They can be friendly, optimistic, full of hope. There's something kind of romantic about the American Dream, the belief that anyone can make it if they work hard enough. It might not be realistic, but it's idealistic. I like that."

Evan narrows his eyes and leans forward. "So what about me?"

"What *about* you?" I laugh. "You don't count."

"I don't count? What do you mean, I don't count? I'm American, aren't I?"

"Yes, but," I shake my hands, trying to think of the best way to explain what I mean, "you're not an *American* boy, you're a... a *Spearcrest* boy."

I laugh and realise at exactly that moment that even though I'm not quite tipsy yet, the wine has definitely loosened my tongue a little. I make a mental note to reel myself in, because I'm not about to have another repeat of the party disaster. But there's something about talking with Evan without a filter that's somehow more intoxicating than the wine itself.

"So what you're saying is that you wouldn't refuse to date me on the grounds that I'm American, but rather on the grounds that I go to Spearcrest?"

I shake my head, then realise he's not completely wrong. "Right, yeah."

"You realise you go to Spearcrest too, right?"

I nod. "I wouldn't date me either, if that's what you're asking."

He sits back. "Oh my god, Sutton. You're drunk."

"I'm not drunk. I'm not even tipsy. I'm just being honest."

"Okay. Alright. Then how about this: what if a guy asked you out, and you liked him, but he was from Spearcrest?"

"Don't be stupid," I say, pushing aside my empty bowl and grabbing some more bread. "That would never happen."

"Because you'd never like a guy from Spearcrest?"

"Because nobody in Spearcrest would ever ask me out. You made sure of that."

"Oh." Evan looks away for a moment. His cheeks go several shades redder, as if he's blushing. I narrow my eyes at this unexpected reaction, but then he turns back to look at me. "Isn't that what you want, though?"

I let out a bark of laughter. "What, to be a social pariah because you and your shitty friends picked me out to be your personal pinata for the last few years? No, that's not really what I want, Evan."

He frowns. "We didn't—come on, we never went too far. Mostly it was just teasing."

"*Teasing*? You insulted me every chance you got, made my life a fucking nightmare for years and somehow made me out to be both a freak weirdo loner *and* an attention-starved social climber."

"Well, you didn't help yourself, did you?"

It's my turn to blush and stumble. "What are you talking about?"

"Sucking up to the teachers, being a prefect and ratting everybody out, acting stuck-up all the time just because your parents work at the school."

"It's almost as if I was putting in the effort to make sure I would leave Spearcrest with excellent grades and references, something you and your millionaire mates clearly don't worry about. And—and stop saying I'm stuck-up, I'm not stuck-up!"

Evan raises his eyebrows. "You think you're better than the rest of us because our parents make our lives easy and we don't ever have to do anything for ourselves or face consequences."

"But that's the truth!" I protest angrily.

My face is hot and I'm no longer laughing. Even though I don't want to be, I can't help but be offended that Evan thinks I'm stuck-up.

There's a difference between having dignity and self-worth and being stuck-up, and Evan doesn't seem to be understanding that.

"Sometimes, yes," Evan admits. "But it doesn't mean you're better than us just because your life is more difficult."

"I don't think I'm better than you."

That's definitely a lie, and I hope Evan doesn't realise. He leans forward again and speaks in a low, serious tone. "Fine. Then let me rephrase my question from before. If *I* asked you out, on a date, would you say yes?"

"Absolutely not."

"Why not? It's not because I'm American, and it's not because I go to Spearcrest, right? So why not?"

"Because—" I stare at him, astounded that I even have to explain my answer after everything that's happened between us all these years. "Because it's not—this whole scenario isn't real, you're obviously not going to ask me out. We're barely even friends. Why are you even asking? To prove your stupid point?"

"I'm asking. Go on, Sutton. Let me take you on a date. It can be your practice run at dating an American boy."

His blue eyes are fixed on mine, intense and unyielding, daring me to look away. A smile plays on his lips, impossible to read.

It's hard to tell how sincere he's being, or even what point he's trying to make anymore. But I'm completely out of my depth, like I've waded too far into the surf and am now being pulled under by a powerful, treacherous current.

A current alive with memories of cold night air and alcohol and Evan's tongue sliding against mine.

Time for some evasive manoeuvering.

"Fine, I'll make you a deal." I lean toward him and meet his gaze. "If I get accepted into the US universities I'm applying to, then I'll go on a date with you and *you* can tutor *me* on how to date an American."

He tilts his head and narrows his eyes. "What universities are you applying to?"

"Harvard, Yale and Stanford."

"Fuck me, Sutton." He glares at me and then extends his hand out to me. "But fine. If anybody can do it, it's you. Shake on it."

I shake his hand, relieved that he's fallen for my distraction tactic and more than a little triumphant at my trick. Except that when I try to pull my hand away, his fingers tighten around it, pulling me closer across the countertop.

"But we're making out on the first date."

I glare at him.

"Absolutely not."

"Too late," he says with a wicked grin. "We shook on it."

And he releases my hand. My triumph vanishes as quickly as it appeared. Instead of tricking him, I think I might have just tricked myself.

## 20

# INTOXICATION

## Evan

I STRUGGLE TO FALL asleep that night, too excited to keep my eyes closed. I roll restlessly around my bed, kicking my blankets off, pulling them back on, sitting up, lying back down. A heady, dizzy excitement fills me like an electric current.

Of all the times I've gone toe-to-toe with Sutton, I've never once emerged with such a staggering victory. More than a victory—a prize. Even our kiss at the party barely counts as a victory, not when she left me standing alone in the trees with a hard cock and a mind full of questions.

This time, I've not just managed to beat her, to *win* against her, but I've managed to win something off her.

A date.

A date with Sutton.

A date with Suttton wouldn't be like a normal date with a normal girl. I wouldn't take her out because I like her, because I want to buy her flowers and hold her hand. A date with Sutton would be like fighting her on a completely different battlefield, with a whole new set of weapons.

Because I don't have to like Sutton to want her. In fact, the more I dislike about her, the more she mocks me and scratches at me with the talons of her words, the more I want her.

I want to hold Sophie, touch her and kiss her again, just to prove to her I can. I want to kiss every part of her she hides beneath her tidy uniform, her baggy sweaters. I want to make out with her in my car until she's so turned on she has to beg me even though she hates me.

Just thinking about it makes me painfully, achingly hard.

I slide my hand into my boxers. My cock twitches at my touch. My head is full of all the things I want to do with Sophie, all the things I want to do *to* her.

Her room is only a couple of doors away. She'd probably be disgusted if she knew I was touching myself thinking about her. But her proximity only makes this more forbidden, more tantalising.

Wrapping my fingers around my cock, I close my eyes.

What would I do if Sophie were to walk in right now? I'd look her right in the eyes, touching myself. Willing her to know my cock is hard for her. Pulling on my cock, pushing myself closer to the edge.

What if she came closer? I can think of a thousand things I'd do. Kissing a wet line from Sophie's mouth to her throat, tasting her pulse. Exposing Sophie's breasts to admire the colour of her nipples, to suck on them until they hardened under my tongue. Pushing up her skirt to reveal the pale skin of her upper thighs, licking her through her underwear, teasing her clit, making her squirm.

My eyes are clenched tight and I'm pumping my cock hard, now.

Sophie is so fucking harsh, so hard to crack, I couldn't possibly go easy on her. I couldn't just suck on her nipples—I'd have to bite them. I couldn't just slide my fingers between her legs—I'd have to bury my face there. It could never be just sex with Sophie—it would have to be fucking.

Hard, rough fucking.

I'd have to fuck her hard enough to knock every thought from her head, to make her forget how much she dislikes me, to ensure she could never want another guy. I'd have to fuck her hard enough to make her scream, to break her voice, to make her shake in my arms.

I'd have to fuck her until she threw her head back and came on my cock and—

I come with a cry of surprise—I come so hard my back arches off the bed. My eyes blink slowly open as I try to catch my breath, and then clarity sets. I'm in big fucking trouble.

"Fuck."

The next morning, I wake up both happy and sheepish. Luckily, Sophie's already gone by the time I pull on my clothes and amble downstairs to rifle around the kitchen for some breakfast. The relief I feel is short-lived, though. On one hand, I don't have to face her knowing I jacked off to thoughts of making out with her in my car, but on the other hand... I'm not going to see her all day.

She ends up working every day until Christmas Eve. I try to stay busy while she's out, but it's getting harder and harder to not spend every waking hour thinking about her.

Spending time with Sophie is like eating when you're starving, except that no matter how satisfied you are while eating, you're left feeling even hungrier than before. No matter how many evenings I spend with her, cooking with her or playing video games or just lounging around while she reads a book, I just end up wanting to spend more time with her.

Christmas Eve finally comes, and it must be a pretty special day because it's the first time Sophie accepts my offer to pick her up from work. To be fair, it's also been hailing through most of the day, and the cold is brutal by UK standards.

So I throw on a big sweatshirt and get in the car, trying my best to forget about all the fantasies I've had featuring the tinted glass and reclining seats.

I park up outside her café and try to peer through the strings of Christmas lights dangling inside the window. I'm desperately curious to see who she works with, but all I can make out are plants and the outline of big armchairs.

A minute later, Sophie comes running out of the door, holding two cups in her mittened hands. I reach over her seat to open the door, and she slumps inside with a sigh and hands me a paper cup.

"What's this?" I ask, taking the cup.

"It's hot chocolate and arsenic," she answers drily.

"What do you mean?"

She rolls her eyes. "I'm joking. It's hot chocolate, marshmallows and cream."

"For me?"

"Evan," she says, giving me the kind of impatient look she would give me when teaching me Shakespeare, with a tilt of the head and a raised eyebrow. "Yes, it's for you. I made it myself. Happy Christmas Eve."

She holds up her cup and taps it against mine, then takes a deep sip.

My heart clenches uncomfortably, and my throat suddenly feels a little swollen. I'm not one to get emotional, but for some reason, this hits me right in my feelings. I swallow hard and take a sip.

The drink is hot and creamy and sweet, warming me up straight away.

"How is it?" she asks without looking at me.

I cast her a quick grin and start the car. "It's hot and sweet—like you."

She laughs almost reluctantly. "Oh wow, how very smooth."

"I thought so too. Practising for that date of ours."

"I can already tell it's going to be life-changing."

"Really?"

She gives a low, rough laugh. "No."

We spend the rest of the drive in a sort of amicable silence. When we get to the house, we go around the rooms turning on the Christmas lights. Then Sophie lights candles while I light the fire in the big fireplace. We carry armfuls of food and alcohol into the living room and settle ourselves on the soft rug in front of the fire. I offer to put on some Christmas music on the big speakers, but Sophie grimaces.

"I know you love Christmas, but please. No Christmas music. I'd rather you shoot me between the eyes."

"It's because you've not had enough alcohol yet," I tell her, making myself a pile of cushions to lean against as I recline on the rug. "At Knight family Christmases, everyone would be tipsy before nightfall on Christmas Eve."

She laughs and extends her glass towards me to let me pour her a drink. "My family just play board games and make passive-aggressive comments."

I fill her cup, put the bottle away and stand. "Hey, we can do that too!"

I rush over to one of my mom's expensive cabinets and grab a stash of board game boxes. I dump them in front of Sophie and slump back into my mountain of cushions. Sophie tucks a strand of hair behind her ear and rifles through the boxes: Scrabble, Monopoly, Trivial Pursuit, Cluedo.

She runs her hand over the glossy, colourful cardboard with a little frown.

"These look brand new," she says, looking up.

I shrug. "Yeah, my mom wanted to do this family night every weekend where we would all have dinner as a family and play games, but that didn't last very long."

"You and your sister weren't up for it?"

"No, nothing like that. We were all up for it. But Mom and Dad had calls to take, and sometimes they had to work, and

Adele sometimes had cello lessons, so in the end, Mom just accepted that family night just would have to wait."

She's looking at me with a slight frown that's not her usual expression of stern disapproval, but more of a look of polite concern. I grin at her and say, a little mischievously, "Don't give me that look, Sutton. This isn't exactly a sob story when I live in a million-dollar house, right?"

She rolls her eyes and holds up the pile of games. "You want to play or not?"

We spend the next half hour working out which game to play. Most of them need too many players anyway, so Sophie sets those aside. We agree Monopoly is too much of a time investment and vow to play it tomorrow instead and just start earlier.

I veto Scrabble straightaway.

"Come on, you're a walking fucking dictionary. I can't compete."

"My vocabulary's the least of your worries," she says, holding up the box. "Your mum seems to have bought the British version of Scrabble."

"And?"

"And your spelling is still pretty bloody American, especially given how long you've been studying here."

I give her a dirty look, but can't really contradict her. In the end, we settle on Trivial Pursuit. I relax back into my cushions, one arm behind my head.

"Feeling confident?" she asks, pausing as she sets up the game.

I grin. "You'll get stuck on the Sports section for so long it'll give me plenty of time to catch up, smart-ass."

She gives me the middle finger, which is unexpected coming from her and a little sexy.

There's something particularly pretty about her today: she's wearing black tights, a short denim skirt and a big grey sweater that looks irresistibly soft. She's tied her hair back in a low, messy knot, and her cheeks are flushed from either the heat or the alcohol, reminding me of how she looked on the night of the party.

I need to stop getting distracted by her if I hope to get anywhere in this game. Or if I'm hoping to get through the night without embarrassing myself…

Sophie starts off exactly as one might expect: savagely competitive and mercilessly efficient. She pile-drives through the first half of the game with intimidating fervour. I'm not all that bothered about winning, mostly I'm just trying not to seem too stupid and not to let Sophie notice just how tipsy I'm gradually getting.

As the game goes on, however, it becomes pretty obvious that Sophie is getting quite tipsy herself.

She gives me long, glassy looks when I read the questions to her and then starts going off on wild lecture-like tangents instead of answering. When I get the answers to my own questions wrong, Sophie leans over to whisper clues and anagrams of the answers to help me.

Soon, I realise that Sophie Sutton isn't quite so competitive at all when she's had a few drinks.

"Come on, Evan, come on," she says, patting my arm bracingly when I get stuck. "You've got this. You've got this, okay? Look, you're already catching up with me."

Just as I predicted, she's been stuck on Sports for ages now, giving me time to slowly catch up to her. Of course, it's not too hard catching up with her when she's practically telling me the answers, but there's something too endearing about her attempts to motivate me.

While I'm still lying in my initial position propped against a pile of cushions, Sophie has been slowly collapsing as the game has gone on: at first she was sitting with her legs tucked under her, then she went lower, propping herself on one elbow, then she was lying on her side, now she's lying on her stomach, her chin cupped in one hand.

"Do you *really* think I can win this?" I ask her in my most heartfelt tone. "I'm not as smart as you."

"Bullshit!" she exclaims, tapping my shoulder. "You're smarter than you look. You just have to work harder. But I'm here to help, ok?"

"Ok, ok. But what do I get if I win?" I ask her, wondering how much I can push my luck.

"You can have more wine," she says with a smirk.

"No, no, I'm pretty drunk."

She laughs out loud, a big goofy laugh that makes my insides all warm and gooey.

"What are you talking about?" she exclaims. "*You*'re not pretty drunk, *I*'m pretty drunk!"

"I can see that," I say, unable to stop myself from laughing. I sit up from my pile of cushions to lean over her and speak before my courage evaporates. "If I win, will you let me kiss you again?"

She shakes her head and sits up to face me. At first, I think she's going to make one of her usual caustic replies, but she doesn't. She leans forward, narrowing her dark eyes at me, and her lips curl into a slow grin.

The soft rainbow glow of the Christmas lights halos her pretty face like some strange angel as she speaks in a low, scratchy voice.

"You don't have to win for that."

# 21

# OBLITERATION

For a second, I'm too stunned, both by her beauty and by her reply, to process her words. I blink at her, my heartbeat pounding in my throat.

"I don't have to win?" I repeat faintly. "What do you mean, I don't have to win?"

She gives a low laugh with that rough, hoarse voice, sending shivers down my spine. She's close enough that I can smell her, the sweet vanilla smell mingled with the fragrance of wine.

Her hand reaches for my chest, and I stay utterly still, half-afraid that if I move I'll scare her off. Her fingers curl in a fist in my sweatshirt, and she slowly pulls me towards her like she did that night in the peace garden.

An embarrassing sound escapes my throat, a sort of low groan that I can't quite help. My heartbeat is now deafening, the rest of my senses all focused on Sophie. Sophie's dark eyes, fixing mine with a half-bold, half-amused look. Sophie's flushed cheeks and pretty lips. Sophie's smell, sweet as caramel.

And then she pulls me to her, closing the distance between us and pressing her lips against mine. They are warm and soft and slightly wet.

It's different from the party kiss. This is a chaste kiss, just her lips against mine, almost innocent, but a shock of pleasure surges through my body like an electric current.

I close my eyes and open my mouth, leaning into the kiss, but find only air. My eyes blink open, in time to see Sophie pull away, a thoughtful pout on her mouth.

While I feel like I've been set on fire with desire, Sophie looks like a mathematician pondering some tedious equation.

"Haha, no," she finally says, loosening her hold on my shirt. "Definitely doesn't feel right."

A spike of annoyance and pain pierces through me. I remember the stunt she pulled on me at the party, running away into the darkness. But it doesn't shatter the spell of desire I'm under—if anything, it fuels the flames of it. I let her run away last time—I'm not going to let her get away so easily this time.

Wrapping my hand firmly around the nape of Sophie's neck, I pull her back to me. A tiny gasp of surprise springs from her lips, but I stifle it with mine.

I don't kiss her like I did in the peace garden—instead I kiss her slowly, achingly, to give myself time to calm down, to allow myself to revel in the taste of her. Then I open my mouth against hers, tilting her head gently with one thumb on her jaw.

"Feels right to me," I whisper hoarsely against her lips.

I'm shit-scared she's going to push me off, scramble back, run away—but she doesn't.

She opens her mouth without resistance. I gently caress her lips with my tongue, tasting wine, and she responds with a soft, low moan.

The rough, sweet sound pulls at the last of my restraint, and then I'm taking her by the waist and pulling her against me. She straddles my lap, burying her fingers in my hair. Now my kisses aren't slow and tender, but hard and hungry and wet.

She pulls back for air, and my name slips from her mouth in a ragged sigh.

"Evan..."

But I'm like someone who's been starving and finally allowed to eat. I can't stop.

I kiss her jaw, her neck. I'd kiss every inch of her if she wasn't wearing so many fucking clothes. She arches against me when I suck gently on the sensitive corner where her jaw meets her neck, and I slip my hands under her impossibly soft sweater.

My fingers glide over hot skin until I reach the soft curve of her breasts. Her nipples are hard underneath the thin fabric of her bra, and I catch them between my fingers, tugging ever so slightly.

A low moan slips from her lips and she pulls away, looking at me in surprise. Her dark eyes are hooded and glittering with desire. I can't help the slow, arrogant smile that spreads on my face. I lean forward to speak against her ear.

"If you like that," I breathe, "you have no idea how fucking good I'm about to make you feel."

Then I take her by her waist and tip her back, laying her down on the carpet. She looks up at me but says nothing. Her teeth dig into her bottom lip—gone is the cocky smirk from the night of the party, or the tipsy sweetness from before.

Now, she looks nervous, but hungry.

I slide down between her raised thighs, kissing her neck, her throat, just like I did in my fantasies when I touched myself the other night. Except reality is far better than fantasy. Her skin is hot and smooth as silk under my lips. My senses are filled with the sweet vanilla scent of her, because the low sound of her breathing is like the husky rush of the ocean.

Tugging on the hem of her sweater, I pull it up. Underneath, I'm barely surprised to find she's wearing a plain black triangle bra, free of any adornment. It makes my cock twitch in my pants. I swallow hard before pressing my mouth right between her breasts. She arches slightly underneath me and I suppress a groan. Hooking a finger under the underband of her bra, I pull it up and catch my breath.

"Fuck, Sutton..."

Her nipples are the dark pink of crushed berries, the most delicious sight I've ever seen. I take her breasts in my hands, first brushing my fingertips gently against her, then dipping down to capture a nipple in my mouth. I'd fantasised about being cruel to Sophie, about punishing bites—but that's not what I want right now.

Right now, I want to make her molten and aflame with pleasure, so I lick her slowly, teasing her with my tongue, first one nipple than the other, until her back is arching off the floor and her hands are curled into fists and her voice is an incoherent rasp of desire.

Even though I'm achingly, torturously hard, the thought of my own pleasure isn't important. Right now, there's only one thing I need—one thing I *crave*.

I want to make Sophie come. I want to make her come so hard she can't ever have another orgasm without thinking about me.

So I leave her nipples wet and exposed and I kiss a line down her abdomen, I kiss the ridges of her hip bones and the soft skin of her lower belly. I unbutton her skirt, and look up at her.

"Lift your—" My voice is so rough it breaks. "Lift your hips for me, Sutton."

She obeys without protest, letting me slide her skirt, tights and underwear off her. She pulls down her sweater, covering herself up, but I grab her wrists with a low groan and push them above her head.

Then I catch her lower lip between my teeth and pull, and I kiss her mouth, her cheek.

"Don't fucking move," I command against her ear. "I've waited too fucking long for this."

She doesn't say anything, but her hips squirm, and the way she's squeezing her thighs together tells me how much she wants this.

I part her thighs and lower myself between them, kissing her hips, her thighs. I suck on the tender skin there, and pull away to see tiny crimson marks on the silken fresh. It makes my cock twitch with satisfaction.

Then I move my mouth to her pretty pussy, the triangle of dark, shiny hair. I slide my tongue along the slit; she's dripping wet. Wet for *me*.

"Fuck, Sutton." I groan against her. "You're so fucking wet."

"Stop talking," she hisses.

"Or what?" I stare at her defiantly, my mouth inches from her pussy. "You *are* wet, Sutton, so fucking wet I can see it trickling down your thighs. And I'm going to enjoy every drop, and I'm going to fuck you so good with my tongue you'll be begging me to make you come."

I bury my face against her pussy. She tastes exactly as I expected, sweet and addictive. I can't get enough. I feast on her, triumph burning through me. Because I'm between Sutton's legs, tasting Sutton's pussy. Uptight, perfectly behaved Sutton, who hates me so much. I lick her in long, slow strokes, finding the tiny, wet point of her clit. I flick it with the tip of my tongue until her hips are bucking so hard I have no choice but to pin them to the floor with my hands.

"Where are your manners, Sutton?" I ask, looking up with a smirk. "Say please."

She glared down at me. Her cheeks are flushed, her lower lip wet and bruised where she's been biting down on it. "Fuck you," she rasps.

"Yeah?"

My eyes still on hers, I lick up and down her pussy, building a slow, torturous rhythm with my tongue. I don't stop until Sophie's hips are struggling against my hands, until her thighs begin to quiver.

Then I stop and look up.

"Come on, Sutton, be a good girl. Say it."

Sophie's head is thrown back, her back is arched. Her hands are still above her head, her fingers clawing the floor. When she looks at me this time, her expression is both pitiful and imperious.

"Please," she rasps. "Please, Evan."

"Please, what?"

"Fuck you—please, I wanna come—God, you fucking bastard, please let me come."

With a groan of pleasure, I bury my face between her thighs, Sutton's mixture of pleas and insults urging me on. My fingers digging into her hips, I lick her delicious pussy, slow and firm until she's shaking, then faster, until her voice explodes into a harsh cry and her hips are bucking uncontrollably.

She comes on my tongue, grinding herself against my face, riding the waves of her orgasm. My cock twitches and I have to resist the urge to slip my hand into my boxers and stroke myself to her sounds of pleasure.

When she finally grows still, I lower her hips back to the floor and sit up. Her trembling thighs meet and fall to the side. I stare down at her, wiping her juices from my mouth with the back of my hand.

Sophie post-orgasm in a grey sweater is the most erotic sight I've ever seen, and my cock strains at the sight of her. All I can think of right now is parting her trembling thighs, pulling out my cock and burying it deep into her hot, dripping wet pussy.

But Sophie sits up, startling me. Her hooded eyes have become wide, and her mouth is open and trembling. Loose strands of hair frame her face, and her lips dark and wet and bruised with kisses. But then she brushes her fingers over her mouth and begins tucking her hair behind her ears and shaking her head.

"Fuck," she says. "Fuck, Evan."

I frown, and my heart sinks. Already, pleasure is giving way to horror on her beautiful face. She sits up and grabs the pile of her discarded clothing, hugging it to her chest as she says, "I'm sorry. I'm so sorry."

My stomach is clenched. I curl my hands into fists so she doesn't realise they're trembling. "What are you talking about?"

"I'm sorry," she repeats "Look, um, obviously, we drank too much, so..."

She scrambles to her feet and stands, her legs still trembling. Hot arousal and cold anger rage inside me, battling each other.

If she wants to explain and justify her way out of this, she can try. But I'm not going to make it easy for her. Not when pleasure and want are still rushing through me, coursing through my veins like poison.

"You're not stupid, Sophie," I say, my voice low and hoarse. "You know how much I like you."

A look of panic crosses her face. She bites her bottom lip nervously and shakes her head, slowly backing away from me.

"No, you don't. You're just bored and lonely because everyone's away and I'm the only person here."

"I didn't kiss you just because you're here," I snap, sitting up sharply. "I didn't make you come just because I was *bored*."

"Look," she says, raising both hands like she's trying to calm me down. "I'm not saying there's anything wrong with it. I guess I also kissed you just because you're here, and we were both, well... clearly, we both needed to relieve some tension and—"

"I kissed *you* because I fucking wanted to kiss *you*." To my complete and utter mortification, my voice breaks as if I'm about to cry. But I'm not upset, I'm angry. "I made you come because I want to make *you* feel good. You can make whatever excuses you want for yourself, Sophie, but you can't make excuses for me."

"You wouldn't be saying any of this if you weren't drunk," she says, shaking her head. "And you're going to regret everything that's happened tonight when you sober up tomorrow."

"This isn't fucking Literature class, Sophie! You can't make up your interpretation of someone else's actions and explain it into truth. I know exactly how I feel because *I'm* feeling it, so stop trying to explain my own feelings to me."

"I'm not explaining anything," she says, slowly inching away. "I'm, I'm—" she holds her face in her hands like she's trying to work out what to say, and there's definitely more than a little panic in her eyes. "I've made a fucking mistake, alright? I shouldn't have let things get this far. I'm sorry I did."

She could have smashed the empty bottle of wine into my face and hurt me less than her words do.

I watch her, speechless with shock, as she straightens herself, pulls down her sweater to cover herself and smoothes back her hair.

"I apologise for my actions tonight," she says stiffly.

"Why are you apologising?" I say, scrambling up to my feet so I can face her. "You actually did something you wanted to do for once. I'm not fucking sorry, so you don't have to be either."

"I didn't want this," she says, blushing so intensely the red spreads from her cheeks to her forehead.

"Don't lie to me," I say, stepping towards her. "You wanted every second of this, my hands on your tits, my mouth on your pussy. You wanted to come on my tongue—you wanted it so much you fucking begged for it."

She takes several hasty steps back, putting distance between us. Her face is so red I can almost feel the heat exuding from her cheeks.

"I didn't want this," she repeats. "I—I like somebody else, okay?"

Her words fall like a bomb down the well of my mind. The bomb falls and falls for ages, leaving me completely still and speechless. Then it drops and explodes, and my mind is obliterated by flames, and then it's completely blank.

And then, like the fucking coward she is, Sophie runs out of the room like a murderer fleeing the scene of the crime.

# WINTER

◆

*"You pierce my soul. I am
half agony, half hope."*

**Persuasion**, Jane Austen

## 22

# NETWORKING

**Sophie**

Running away to my parents' house to get away from Evan is like trying to escape a dragon by hiding in an ogre's cave.

Even though I'd made up a vague excuse about being homesick and wanting to see them over Christmas, my parents still lectured me about leaving Audrey's house and "giving up on important opportunities". Christmas day is tense and mostly unpleasant.

The rest of the holiday becomes one long lecture about how being homesick is one thing, but ultimately everything I do now will have a domino effect on my life as an adult, and why am I not making more friends at Spearcrest, these connections will one day come in handy, and so on and on, *ad nauseam*.

In the end, I give them my word to make more of an effort to socialise and network when I return to school, and then things calm down a little. We even manage to last the rest of that evening without Spearcrest being mentioned once.

But for the rest of the holiday, in between what happened with Evan—which I'm refusing point blank to relive or think about or mentally address in any way, shape or form—the crushing anxiety I generally feel around my parents and the week I wasted not being able to work, it's basically impossible to relax. The only escape is inside the pages of books, but even reading becomes stressful when your brain is trained to analyse every sentence for meaning.

On the last Sunday of the holiday, when I finally return to Spearcrest, I'm actually glad to be back. Even though I've brought my stormcloud of worries with me, being here is still better than being back at home. After I've unpacked my things and put everything away in its proper place, I pick up my books and head straight for the sanctuary of the study hall, which is blissfully empty.

And end up spending almost an entire hour staring blankly at the pages of my workbooks, crushed by the terrible feeling that I have massively, disastrously fucked up, and that nothing is going to be okay.

After an hour of this, I let my face drop to the desk with a sigh.

Anxiety is pretty familiar to me, but it's unlike me to be so easily crushed by a defeat or mistake. If there's one thing I can do, it's take a punch. But it's getting harder and harder to get back up these days.

"There she is, I told you!"

I raise my head from the desk and peer around my table lamp. Audrey is striding across the study hall, Araminta in tow. They must have arrived not long ago—Audrey is still wearing her coat and scarf.

"What's up with the radio silence, Sutton?" she asks as she draws close. "You know a phone is a tool of communication and not just a paperweight, right?"

"I know," I say, dropping my head back down.

I hear the shuffle of the girls pulling up chairs to sit close to me. An arm wraps around my shoulders, and Araminta's familiar perfume fills my senses. A warm, floral smell, like cinnamon and jasmines.

"There, there," she coos.

I laugh weakly. "I'm not a baby."

"You *are* a baby," she says, pulling my head up to rest it on her shoulder and gently stroking my hair. "You are a big sad baby that needs a big hug and a kiss."

Audrey huddles close and they both kiss my cheeks until I can't help but laugh and push them away. "You're such idiots."

"Idiots? Why?" Araminta says indignantly. "Because we *wuv* you?"

"Oh God, please stop!" I laugh and sit up, and realise there are tears in my eyes that I hadn't even noticed. "Look what you've done," I say, rubbing the sleeve of my woolly jumper against the corner of my eyes.

"We can keep this up as long as we need," Audrey says with solemn determination. "We'll shower you with love until you're ready to talk."

"There's nothing to talk about," I mumble into my sleeve.

There's a moment of silence and I look up to see three identical expressions of unimpressed scepticism.

"It doesn't take a genius to tell something happened," Audrey says. "Anyone with two brain cells could tell. You look like some tragic Victorian ghost."

"Hey now!" Araminta hisses. "Do you not remember the briefing outside? We agreed on a delicate, tender approach, remember?"

Audrey looks down. "Sorry."

"You don't have to tell us anything if you don't want to," Araminta says, brushing aside the strands of hair now stuck to my wet cheeks. "We just want you to know that we love you and that we want to help, even if it means you want us to leave you alone."

"I don't want you to leave me alone."

Audrey smiles. "We know."

I sigh, tuck my legs against me, propping my heels on the edge of my seat. I take a deep breath and speak half into my sleeves.

"I kissed Evan Knight at his house on Christmas Eve."

"That's hot," Araminta says at the exact same time Audrey says, "Oh God, why?"

"I don't even know why! I was tipsy—we both were—and he asked for a kiss. He seemed lonely. I guess I was lonely too. I guess also I sort of wanted to. I mean he might be a complete arsehole but it's not like I don't have eyes."

Araminta nods. She's cut her thick hair into a bob, and the strands curl around her chin and bob when she moves her head in a way that's both adorable and distracting.

"I know what you mean," she says. "He's a walking wet dream. I don't blame you for wanting to make out with him."

"How did you know we made out?" I ask, my face flooding with heat.

"You made out with him?" Audrey frowns. "You said you kissed."

"I did!" I say, covering my red hot cheeks with my palms. "I did, and then I moved away, and then he kissed me. And then we made out."

"How far are we talking?" Araminta asks, leaning forward, her eyes boring into mine. "Are we talking heavy petting? Under-shirt action? Did you—" she moves back with a scandalised gasp "— did you touch *his cock*?"

"Oh my god, are you a child?" Audrey snaps at Araminta. She turns back to me, cocks an eyebrow. "Did you, though?"

"I didn't touch it, no." I hesitate, then talk very quickly, just to get it out of the way. "But he, um, he went down on me and—god. I don't want to talk about it anymore. I wish the ground would swallow me up."

There is a moment of suffocating silence as the girls all strive to conceal their shock.

"Well." Araminta is the one who finally breaks the silence. "Was it good, though?"

If only she knew how good. *I* barely even know how good—I have strictly forbidden myself to even think about it.

I nod.

"Wow. Fucking hell, Sophe, not what I expected, I have to say." Audrey pauses and frowns. "So then what happened?"

"So then I tried to fix my mistake. I told him we were both drunk and lonely, and I apologised to him."

"You *apologised*? It's not like you took advantage of him," Araminta points out.

"But it's not like I *wanted* wanted to kiss him, or for him to... well, to do anything—so in a way I *did* take advantage of him."

"Oh, please." Araminta rolls her eyes. "Evan's fancied you for so long this was probably a dream come true for him."

I stare at Audrey, agog. "What planet have you been living on? He hates my guts."

"No, he doesn't. He's an arsehole to you, and a complete twat in general most of the time, but he doesn't *hate* you. It's so obvious he's obsessed with you. He's like a really childish boy in primary school who throws frogs at the girl he likes."

"Except we're not in primary school, we're almost adults," I say drily. "If an adult throws a frog at another adult, it's not a cute crush. It's weird and creepy."

"Audrey isn't defending his actions," Araminta points out. "She's just saying his fucked up behaviour isn't based on hate."

"Right, but regardless of why he's an arsehole or his obsession with you," Audrey presses on. "What happened next? After your... your apology?"

She winces as she speaks the word like it pains her to even say it. I don't care, I stand by my apology. I actually have the maturity to admit my mistakes, unlike *some* people I can think of.

Well, one person anyway.

I continue with some hesitation. "Then... then he said he wanted to kiss me and that I wanted to kiss him."

"Well, I mean it's not a lie," Araminta points out.

"What did you say?" Audrey asks.

"I said that it was a mistake and that I like someone else."

Silence reigns once more. Around us, the shadows of the study hall press in, surrounding the three stunned faces blinking at me.

"You told him about Freddy?" Audrey says finally.

"What, so you like Freddy?" Araminta asks with a frown.

"No, no—I mean, of course, I *like* Freddy, he's actually nice to me. But I don't *like* him, I just didn't want Evan to think I kissed him because I like him, because I don't."

"But don't you, though?" Audrey asks more quietly.

"No, Audrey, I don't. I just... it was weird, staying with him. He baked cookies. We made dinner together. We hung out. It was like in Year 9, when things were okay, and also like having a... it was really nice. I guess I just got confused."

"Right." Audrey doesn't look convinced but doesn't push it.

Araminta prompts me on. "So then what did Evan say?"

"Nothing. I left. Then the next day I ran away and went back to my parents' house."

"Oh."

The girls all exchange glances.

"So how did *that* go?" Audrey asks.

I sigh. "As well as you might expect."

"Do you want to talk about it?"

I shake my head. "There's nothing to talk about. Honestly, it wasn't that bad. Just more stuff about making the most of my amazing connections, that sort of stuff. Apart from that, it was fine, really."

"Talk about making connections," Araminta says with a suggestive waggle of her eyebrows. "You've been making connections alright."

Audrey lets out a bark of scandalised laughter. "Minty! Stop."

"Networking with a Young King," Araminta carries on shamelessly. "Networking... with tongues."

"You're disgusting," Audrey says.

But she's laughing, and so am I. The crushing weight lifts from my chest. Things are still pretty bad, but they don't seem as hopeless now.

I take a deep breath, letting my lungs fill up properly, and slump back into my chair in relief.

"I feel like the biggest fucking idiot."

"You're not the biggest fucking idiot," Audrey says. "And you know what? I want to celebrate the fact that you finally got some action. It's been, what? Your first time since you got to Spearcrest?"

I laugh weakly. "No, no, there was that boy at my cousin's birthday party in Year 11, remember?"

"Oh, God, yes, that boy with the braces who kept texting you after?" Audrey shakes her head. "I can't believe that was your first time."

Araminta shakes her head. "And he was shorter than you."

"To be fair, every boy was shorter than me in Year 11," I point out.

"That time does *not* count," Araminta says with a wince. "It stresses me out just thinking about it."

"Then don't think about it," Audrey says. "Think about Sophie getting some hot action with the walking wet dream of Spearcrest."

I glare at her, hoping none of them notice how red I'm sure my face has become.

"Seriously, though, Sophe," Audrey asks more seriously. "What are you going to do now?"

"About what?"

"About Evan."

"God. Haven't I done enough? I'm going to do what I should have done to begin with: nothing at all. Stay as far away from him as possible."

"What about Miss Bailey's tutoring programme?"

"I'm just going to leave it. I'm sure Evan wants to see me just about as much as I want to see him after the absolute embarrassment of the entire situation, so I'm just going to not go back to his house and hope that he lets sleeping dogs lie."

"Hmm," Audrey says dubiously.

"What, you don't think he will?" I ask, fear rising in my chest.

"Evan Knight doesn't strike me as the kind of guy who would take nicely to rejection, that's all," Audrey points out thoughtfully.

"Rejection?" I stare at her incredulously. "It's not exactly a rejection, is it, though?"

"You two kissed and then he went down on you and then you apologised to him and said you liked somebody else. What would you call that if not a rejection?"

"Um, good manners? I thought I handled it in the most polite way possible."

The girls all shake their heads. Audrey stands and stretches. "I don't know how you can be both so smart and so clueless sometimes, Sophe."

"Yeah, you genuinely concern me," Araminta says, patting my head. "You're like a little pretty alien who studied everything about being human but never really got the hang of it."

"I really love how good you guys are making me feel," I mutter, packing my books away into my backpack.

"But do you actually feel better though?" Araminta asks, wrapping her arm around my waist and kissing my cheek.

I squeeze her in a hug. "You know I do."

"Right, well, let's go back to the dorm," Audrey says bracingly. "We'll do our best to help you avoid Evan, and hopefully you'll never have to see him or speak to him again for the rest of your time here and at the end of the school year you can sail off into the sunset to Harvard and never have to think about him going down on you."

The girls' laughter drowns out my thoughts, and even though it's pretty clear they don't believe my plan of avoiding Evan will work, I leave the study hall in a much better mood than when I entered it.

After that, we head out to grab some food together, and the girls regale me with stories of their outrageous family Christmases and exotic winter holidays. Later, we all end up cuddling up on the couch in the common room to watch a film.

I don't think about Evan again until I get in bed that night, and that's when I remember that tomorrow is Monday, and the first day of the half-term, and I'm on register duty for the assembly. I squeeze my eyes shut, and do my best to not think about it.

And even though I fall asleep pretty quickly, my night ends up full of strange and disturbing nightmares featuring Evan bending me over to spank me with my own clipboard.

## 23

# COWARD

## Sophie

THE FIRST DAY OF the winter term begins under a bleak, dry sort of snowfall. Brittle flakes flutter from a slate-grey sky. As usual, I've been hoisted with the duty of taking down the names of latecomers to the headmaster's assembly. I stand in the archway of the assembly hall entrance, pressing myself deeper into the shadows, hoping the red bricks of the building swallow me into them.

Becoming forever trapped in the brickwork of Spearcrest would still be a better fate than whatever awaits me when I next meet Evan.

Hoping and praying he is already in the assembly hall is a complete waste of my energy, but I do so anyway. The truth is that ever since I woke up this morning I've not stopped thinking about him, no matter how hard I've tried. All my self-control and discipline snapped, allowing my mind to replay the scene of us tipsy and making out in his living room in a maddening loop.

In the trophy hall of my greatest mistakes, this is by far my biggest, shiniest trophy.

What a catastrophic error—what a devastating lapse in judgement. And it's not even like I can place the majority of the blame on Evan, because for once, he chose to stand by what he did.

Of all the times Evan would decide to grow a spine and a moral compass and take ownership of his actions, why did he have to choose this particular time? I offered him an easy way out on a silver platter—all he had to do was to take it.

"I kissed *you* because I fucking wanted to kiss *you*."

His words burn in my mind like he's branded them there with a red-hot iron. What a thing to say.

What a thing to say to somebody whose friendship you threw away like a dirty towel, somebody you've treated like absolutely human garbage for several years. How can you be okay with treating someone like shit and then bold-facedly telling them you want to go on a date with them, or that you want to kiss them? Why torture me all these years if his plan was to get me drunk on his living room floor and make me come with his mouth? What exactly did he expect me to think and feel?

*I* don't even know what I think or how I feel. I told him I liked somebody else because it was the quickest way out I could think of and because it sort of felt like the truth at the time.

It still does. It's not a lie that I like Freddy. I *do* like Freddy. He's the opposite of everything I hate about Spearcrest kids—about Evan. And he's smart and kind.

He makes me feel *safe*.

Evan doesn't make me feel safe, at all. The opposite. He makes me feel like I'm seconds away from entering into combat to the death. Around him, I'm so on edge my heart beats faster, my breath comes quicker, my skin becomes alive with pinpricks of awareness. Evan definitely didn't feel safe when he pulled me against him like he was afraid he would die if he let go.

Safe was the last thing I felt when he kissed my neck and licked my nipples and sucked on my thighs. The sudden memory of my brutal orgasm at the tip of his tongue flares in my mind like a war flashback.

I groan and slam the clipboard down over my face. So much for staying under the radar and getting through this year with as few complications as possible. So much for careful planning and stringently faultless behaviour.

Voices reach me and I peer around the archway. My heart drops like a sack of rocks through me, an almost sickening sensation.

Strolling down the path under the anaemic snowfall, the Young Kings are approaching. Some girls accompany them—girls who have relentlessly mocked me throughout my time at Spearcrest: Giselle, Seraphina Rosenthal and her roommate, Camille Ferrera. They all chat and laugh, projecting good cheer and arrogant amusement.

My eyes find Evan like there's a spotlight shining right on him. He's the only one not wearing a coat (of course) and he's walking with his arm slung over Zachary Blackwood's shoulders. Easy laughter flows from him, and whatever he's saying seems to amuse Blackwood too, because the granite of his austere face is cracked by a rare smile.

I retreat behind the archway. My heart is slamming against my rib cage, probably desperate to escape and start a new life somewhere far away. I know what I *should* do to deal with this situation. What I *should* do is stand there with my clipboard and my down-turned eyes, let whatever unkind comments the Young Kings and their companions want to level my way slip right off me like water off a duck's back, avoid all eye contact and let the moment become just another tragic memory.

This is what I *should* do. This is what I *would* do if I hadn't made out with one of those stupid so-called Young Kings.

But what I do instead is dive through the nearest doorway and skitter like a startled mouse down the corridor leading to the backstage cupboard where spare tables and podiums and music stands are stored.

I crouch in a darkened corner, hugging my clipboard to my chest. There's only one thing left for me to do now: wallow in the murky swamp of shame and humiliation my life has become.

How have I ended up like this?

Because I'm a fucking idiot who obviously doesn't learn from her mistakes. Because—

"Sutton." I freeze at the sound of his voice, clutching my clipboard so tight the edges dig painfully into my fingers. "I fucking know you're in here."

The door opens and I jump to my feet, refusing to be caught crouching in the dark like some cowering animal. I back away quietly, praying the shadows and towers of chairs and furniture will offer me asylum and conceal me from the predator slowly prowling through the door.

I hear his slow footsteps, then the door closing with a dry click.

"Don't make me look for you, Sutton. It won't end well."

This isn't going to end well regardless of what I do—but I may as well get it over with. I close my eyes, take a deep breath, and emerge from my hiding place.

So much for avoiding Evan and leaving Spearcrest without ever seeing him again.

He stands in the dim square of light cast by the small dusty window high in the wall. Gone is the easy laughter, the careless grin. His blue eyes look sharp, not summery, almost cutting in the grey light. His face is pale, the muscles of his jaw twitch, betraying the tension within.

In the space between us stretches everything binding us—everything keeping us apart: our old friendship, so quickly destroyed, every cruel word he's ever spoken, years of mockery and insults and pain, resentment, humiliation, hatred.

But now we're facing each other in the darkness, there's something else between us—something new. Something wild and smouldering, something volatile and terrifying.

Something that makes my breath catch and heat trickle through my body like liquid fire.

"What do you want, Evan?" I ask finally.

I don't want him to realise how nervous I am, but my voice comes out pathetically low. He steps forward, narrowing the distance between us.

"I want to talk."

My heart is beating fast and loud, drowning out my own thoughts. Panic sets in, making my breath come out in halting puffs. "There's nothing to talk about."

He lets out a cold, hollow laugh. My neck prickles at the sound. This isn't the Evan I'm used to, carefree and cruel. This is something different. I've hated Evan before, but I've never been afraid of him. Now, I have the sudden, electrifying sense of being in danger. I need to leave, and fast.

"I need to go now," I say stiffly, brandishing my clipboard like a weapon. "I have to take the reg—"

He yanks the clipboard out of my hand and tosses it aside. In that split moment of distraction, I take my chances. I dash past him in a desperate bid for the door. His arm flashes out, catching me by my waist and spinning me around. He slams my back to the door and pins me to it with his arms framing my head.

His body isn't close enough to touch, but it's close enough for the heat of him to radiate against me. I look up at him breathlessly, wishing we were still the same height, wishing he weren't this strong.

"You fucking coward," he says, low and husky and hateful.

"I'm not the fucking coward—you are." I look at him defiantly, so he knows I'm not afraid of him. "We both know you didn't come here to talk, Evan."

His jaw twitches as he pierces me with his eyes. "You think you know everything, don't you, Sutton?"

I might not know everything—but I know more than he guesses. I know what's thickening the air between us, and I know the warmth currently trickling between my legs. And most importantly, I *do* know exactly what Evan wants.

He wants what he's always wanted: what he can never have.

He's spent so long alienating me and making me the most undesirable girl in Spearcrest that he's somehow tricked his own stupid brain into wanting me. But he only wants me because I feel unattainable.

If I become attainable in his eyes—if this no longer feels like a game to him because he's already won—he'll move on before the sun sets tonight. I'm certain of this.

And if fucking Evan is the only way of getting rid of him, then that's a bullet I'm ready to take.

So I peel my back away from the door, standing closer to him. With slow, deliberate movements, I loosen my tie and begin to unbutton my school shirt. His gaze follows the movement, his eyes narrow.

"What are you doing?"

"Isn't this what you want, Evan?" He steps sharply away at my words, staring at me with mingled disbelief and anger. But I grab him by the lapel of his blazer, pulling him back to me. I tilt my face to smirk at him. "Who's the fucking coward now?"

My words work like magic. In the next moment, he's lifted me up by my hips and is hurtling through the dim room. He pushes me roughly back against an old oak table, and pulls away only long enough to unbuckle his belt. I knew he would be hard, but I wasn't quite prepared to see how hard he would be.

I'm definitely not prepared for the dark arousal slithering through me at the sight of his hard cock—surprisingly large for someone with such a fragile ego. I suppress a shiver, but when Evan lowers his face to mine, I block it with my hand.

"I don't want to look at your face."

For a moment, he does nothing but stare at me, his expression unreadable.

I push him away and turn around, facing the table, my back to him. The muscles in my stomach twitch. Somehow, this feels ten times more depraved. But I'd rather completely surrender my modesty doing it this way than look Evan in the face while he fucks me.

When it comes to him, I'll take depravity over intimacy. Anytime.

Reaching under my skirt, I pull down my tights and underwear. The hissing sound of his breath hitching in his throat rushes through the air.

Before I can brace myself, his hand lands on my back and he pushes me roughly down, flattening my chest against the table. The weight of his body leans against my back, and his voice is low and rough in my ear.

"Is this how you fucking want it, Sutton?"

"I wouldn't expect anything better from you."

He laughs, low and dark. "Don't lie to yourself. You've been a good girl so long all you want now is to be treated like a dirty little slut."

Then his weight leaves my body. He yanks my skirt roughly up. He palms my arse, gripping the soft flesh. His fingertips brush the over sensitive skin at top of my thighs and my hips buck uncontrollably. I bite down on a moan—I'd rather die than give him any indication of pleasure. I'd rather die than allow him to think I want this as much as he does.

But then he slides two fingers between my legs. I'm embarrassed at how easily his fingers slip between the sensitive folds. I'm so wet I feel warmth trickling down my thighs.

A dark laugh rumbles from Evan.

"Oh, you want this as much as I do," he sneers.

"I do," I say, just because I want to hurt him, "but not from you."

My blow lands. With a growl of anger, he captures my hair, wrapping it around his fist. He pulls hard, forcing me to arch up from the table. There's no tenderness, this time. No warm, velvety pleasure.

There's only anger and resentment and hot, wet lust.

The blunt tip of his cock slides between my legs. It rubs against my pussy, smearing wetness. Then it pushes against my entrance, sending a shudder of mingled dread and desire through me. Dread because it's Evan doing this to me. Desire because it's *Evan* doing this to me.

"You dirty fucking liar," Evan hisses against my ear. "Look at how fucking wet you are—for *me*. It was *my* tongue you came on last time, and it's *my* cock you'll come on this time, Sutton."

My insides clench at the thought—my own body betraying the truth in his words.

"Stop talking," I gasp.

He pushes against me and I tense, suddenly nervous.

But he pauses. The flame of his mouth presses against my cheek. He speaks right against my ear.

"Oh, don't worry, Sutton, I'm not going to hurt you. I'm going to make you feel good—so fucking good you'll never get the thought of me out of your head ever again."

And then he pushes himself slowly inside me. I bite down hard on my lip, forcing myself to remain silent. I'm nervous. This is my first time in a while—my first time with someone as big as him, but I'd rather die than tell Evan this.

Except that Evan, for someone so stupid and so cruel, is surprisingly gentle. He pushes in slowly, giving me time to adjust, until his hips meet the curve of my arse. Then he pauses, buried deep inside me while I relax around him, adjusting to the size of him, to this new sensation. Being impossibly full, being connected to him this intimately, is both terrifying and electrifying. I tremble underneath him, fingers gripping the table, throat tight. He's still holding my hair in his fist and he pulls lightly, pulling my head back to his.

"All right, Sutton?" His voice is a low shudder in my ear—too soft, too full of emotion.

I force my voice through the thorny tunnel of my throat. "I barely feel a thing."

It's a lie, of course, but I don't want Evan to forget what this is. If he does, I might forget too. I won't be another one of Evan's conquests, another one of his string of jilted girlfriends and hapless admirers.

He can fuck me and forget me—I'll forget him faster.

"Fucking liar." His voice is angry, but his cock stiffens inside me.

He pins my hips to the table with both hands, and moves, thrusting in and out. His movements grow more desperate, more angry. But each brutal thrust comes with an explosion of sensations, the pain trailing behind shimmering pleasure, until I'm forced to bite down on my own cries, until my nails are digging into the polished wood of the table.

"Feel that, Sutton? My hard cock inside you? How good it feels in your wet pussy?"

He buries inside me with a hard, punishing thrust and a pathetic sound of pleasure slips past my lips. This isn't the wet, soft pleasure of Evan's mouth on me, his tongue lapping luxuriously at my clit. This is something altogether different: like being invaded and made hollow, like being hurt and satisfied all at once. I squirm my hips to escape his harsh thrusts, and yet arch my back every time he slows down, craving more.

"Ah, fuck Sutton." Evan's voice is so hoarse it's almost a snarl. "You fucking *want* this—you *want* me, I know you do."

He suddenly pulls me up against him, one arm wrapped around my waist, one hand around my neck. There's no pressure in his fingers; he's simply holding me against him, my head falling back against his shoulders. He thrusts inside me with a low groan. His mouth moves against my temple, my hair. He bites my earlobe and pulls, then kisses my neck, sucking on the skin there, sending hot, sharp pleasure spearing through me.

Like water through a dam, a moan finally breaks through my barrier of silence.

I stifle it, but not in time. Evan hears it—I know because he suddenly pulls out of me, startling a gasp from me. He flips me around, propping me up on the edge of the table by my hips.

Our eyes meet.

His expression is wild with hunger—with something else. I turn away. I don't want this—he pulls me to him, and thrusts into me, fucking me with fervour, with aggression—with insistence, as if daring me to ignore him.

He reaches for my face, grasping it in his hand, forcing me to face him.

"Look at me," he commands. "Fuck, Sophie—"

He falls forward—his mouth almost catches mine but I turn at the last minute. He buries his face in the crook of my neck as his thrusts become frantic, desperate. I arch against him, bracing against each thrust. His mouth moves in hot, hungry kisses against my neck, making me tremble with pleasure. I reach up, grabbing a handful of his hair. I pull sharply, yanking his head away from me.

He looks down, our gazes meet.

His blue eyes widen. "Ah—God, Sophie, I—fuck!"

Even though I'm on the pill, the thought of Evan coming inside me is so shockingly intimate it sends a bolt of terror through me. I push his hips away in sudden panic, but he's already pulling out. He takes his cock in his fist and pulls, and falls forward against me. Hot liquid spurts against my abdomen, but I'm too shocked to move, surprised by his orgasm, by my own pleasure, by the unexpected intimacy of watching Evan Knight come.

His face is a mask of pained pleasure, his eyes wide underneath the fallen golden curls and shiny, his mouth open in an expression akin to surprise.

Who would have thought he would look so pure and beautiful while he came?

I should push him away from me, but I wait for a moment. His forehead rests against my shoulder. His face is hidden from view but I can hear the chaos of his pants. Finally, he pulls himself up; I don't dare look him in the face.

I slide off the table and turn, facing away from him, pulling a tissue from my blazer pocket. I clean myself up as best as I can, even though I'm painfully aware of what I smell like right now: like Evan's sweat, cologne and come.

Like I'm his.

Once I'm as clean as I'm going to be, I button up my school shirt and straighten my uniform. My hands shake as I do, and my thighs are still trembling uncontrollably. I'm sore and hot between my legs—still, somehow, agonisingly turned on.

I ignore the sensation, reminding myself of what this is. Just sex—nothing more.

Sex with someone I don't even really like, someone I never want to see again.

By the time I've turned around, Evan's already fixed his trousers and is standing staring at me, his hand pushing his hair from his face in a nervous gesture. He hesitates, the ghost of words moving on his lips, but I'm the first to speak.

"We're done, okay?" I meet his gaze directly, firmly. "You got what you wanted—you win. You get to tell all your cool friends you fucked the stuck-up prefect, tick another name off for your stupid bet. You can tell them all how desperate I was, that you only did this out of pity, you can use every insult in your repertory—I don't care. Just stay away from me."

And with that, I walk away, pausing only to pick up my clipboard, and leave without looking back.

## 24

# NOBODY

### Evan

Tuesday comes, and Sophie doesn't turn up. It's not exactly a surprise—far from it. I would have been pretty shocked if she'd turned up.

She made pretty clear her intention to avoid me. But if she really wanted me out of her life, she probably shouldn't have let me fuck her from behind and come all over her. Because now, I don't want anything else but to do it again.

Over and over again.

Whatever strategy was behind that move, I suppose I can sort of work out. I made her come with my mouth that night so she probably assumed I chased her down to claim the orgasm I was owed in return. It would be exactly like Sophie to assume sex works exactly like a chess match, with two opponents facing each other across the board and taking turns making moves against one another.

What did she say again?

"You won."

Like having sex with her was a victory, a way of scoring a point against her.

If there's one thing I've learned this year, it's that for someone so smart, Sophie can be really fucking stupid sometimes.

Sex isn't a game of chess where one person wins and one person loses. Sophie hasn't ceded a victory to me the way she so clearly believes. She didn't let me win the battle just so she could end the war.

Quite the opposite.

If I wanted Sophie before, fucking her only made me want her more. Because now, all I can think about is making Sophie pant and moan and arch against me. Sliding my fingers against her pussy, feeling how wet and ready she is for me. Rubbing my cock against her pussy, her breasts, sliding it between her arrogant lips. All I can think about is fucking her hard and punishingly, making her feel as broken as I did when she fucked me and refused to look at my face.

But I also want so much more than that.

In spite of how cruel she is, I still want to please her. I want Sophie squirming and moaning under my hands, my lips, my tongue. I want Sophie writhing on top of me, I want to fuck her long and slow, to dangle her off the edge of an orgasm for as long as I can, to make her come so hard she sees stars.

And I want to get under Sophie's skin.

I'm sick of being the one to lose my composure around her, of being a fucking mess while she stands there with her impeccable uniform and her straight posture and her disdainful eyes. I want to be the one to make a mess of her for once. I want to crumble her like a sheet of paper, scribble myself all over her.

So on Tuesday, even though I completely expected her to be a no-show, I still can't help peering out of the windows and pacing around, waiting for something that's not going to happen. I clench and unclench my fists and grit my teeth so hard I give myself a headache.

I made a deal with myself to not text her, and I haven't. Part of me doesn't want to give her the satisfaction of ghosting my texts, which is exactly what she would do. Part of me wants Sophie to be on the other side of the phone, staring at her notifications, wondering why I've not texted her.

I want Sophie to be as restless as I am, I want her to sit and suffer like me.

But deep down, I know how unlikely that is. Sophie hasn't been shy about telling me she likes somebody else. If it's true, then what can I do with that? This isn't a romantic film, it's not like I'm going to chase Sophie to some airport and make her pick me over someone she actually likes.

If she's telling the truth, then whoever Sophie likes is probably everything she wants in a guy. Whereas I symbolise everything she hates. So of course Sophie is never going to choose me.

If I was smart, I'd do exactly what she said and stay away from her.

Except.

Except except except.

The logical side of my brain and the hungry side crash into each other in deafening clangs of chaotic thoughts. Every thought rings with the word "except".

Sophie didn't want to kiss me, *except* she's the one who drunkenly pulled me to her at that party and kissed me first.

Sophie fancies somebody else, *except* she kissed me on Christmas eve and let me go down on her and came so hard her thighs were still shaking even while she was rejecting me.

Sophie hates me, *except* she's the one who initiated sex yesterday and let me fuck her against a discarded table in the assembly hall cupboard.

I should give up on Sophie, *except* I just fucking can't bring myself to.

Because wanting Sophie is worse than thirst or hunger or desire. It's a deep, devouring need, undeniable and all-consuming. Every night when I crawl into my bed and close my eyes, the darkness behind my eyelids fills up with images of her, of her hair in that strict centre parting, of her dark brown eyes, of her mouth opening against mine, of her raspy voice coming out in short gasps.

Thinking about Sophie used to feel good, but now it's galvanising. I don't even try to rein in my fantasies anymore. I put her in scenarios in my head that make me so hard I have no choice but to touch myself. But letting my head constantly fill with these images doesn't help, it only makes me crave her more.

And that's how I end up like this: my phone turned off so I'm not tempted to text her, pacing up and down my house still hoping she turns up. Of course, she doesn't turn up, and of course, it hurts like hell.

I wait a whole hour before I finally accept that she's not coming, but I still feel restless. The house both feels too big and too small, so I pull on a sweatshirt, swap my jeans for running leggings and shorts, and get out of the house.

Outside, it's not snowing anymore, and the cold winter sun has already melted the remains of yesterday's snowfall. The air is cool and crisp in my lungs. The pavement is wet, but no longer slippery, so I set off on a run.

Normally, I run around the residential streets and towards Atwood Heather Botanical Garden. It's quiet there this time of year, the perfect place to get away from everything.

But today, my feet take me in another direction, and I don't question it until I realise I'm jogging up Fernwell high street. It's a Tuesday afternoon so it's fairly quiet, and most of the shops still have their decorations up, the dark street bright with twinkling lights.

I know I'm making a huge mistake by being here, so I enter into a bargain with myself. I'm just going to jog past Sophie's café, that's it. I might glance inside. Just to see her, to see if she's okay. Not even just to see if she's okay. I'm allowing myself to just *look* at her—nothing else, nothing more.

A starving man should be allowed to *look* at a slice of cake even if he's not allowed to touch it.

Nothing wrong with that.

Once I've rationalised my actions, I jog up the street. Even though my pace is fairly slow and my cardiovascular health is pretty good, my heart is beating like crazy. I draw closer to the green and gold facade of The Little Garden, a sense of impending doom crashing down on me.

What if she sees me? What if she thinks I'm stalking her? What if she hates me even more than she already does?

Well. It's too late. I'm running past the shop front.

I'm slowing down.

I'm stopping.

And the impending doom actualises into brutal, painful reality.

Yes, Sophie is there. She has her hair tied back into a low bun, and she's wearing an apron over her black turtleneck top. She looks good enough to eat, good enough to love, good enough to fucking worship.

The café is empty, and she's sitting up on the countertop next to a girl with purple hair. She's talking and laughing, transformed by her smile.

In front of her is a guy in a big sweater. He has a mop of dark hair and I can't see his face because his back is to the window. But he's holding up a cupcake in front of Sophie, and she leans down to smell it, and he bops the top of the cupcake to the tip of her nose and she pulls back in surprise and bursts out laughing.

Her cheeks are flushed as the guy hands her the cupcake and she takes it, and when he walks away from her, her eyes follow him to the doorway through which he disappears. Her smile dims slightly after he walks away—because he was the one making her laugh.

Something black and monstrous rises inside me, something which scrapes and claws its way up my gut, through my throat, inside my mind.

I spring away like I've been electrocuted. I sprint all the way back to my house, my steady, calming jog forgotten.

My lungs burn and my heart pounds. I'm sick to my stomach, acid burning inside me. I concentrate on the way my body feels, trying desperately to keep my mind empty, my thoughts safe.

When I get to the house, my hands are so cold I can barely grip my key, and my fingers shake as I try to get the key into the lock.

In a burst of frustration, I throw the key at the floor and slam both my fists against the door with a yell. The hoarse sound echoes through the courtyard and fades amongst the pine trees. Then it's quiet again, and all I can hear are my panting breaths and the deafening pounding of my heartbeat drumming in my ears.

I sink down, sitting with my elbows resting on my knees, my head dangling down. My vision is obscured by my sweat-drenched hair, but that's fine. The porchlight turns itself off, plunging everything into darkness anyway.

"Fuck."

My voice is hoarse and pathetic in the darkness. The anger has seeped out of me, leaving me breathless, exhausted, completely empty.

Sophie didn't lie. She *does* like someone else. And in a way, I'd already guessed this was the reason Sophie of all people would flaunt a school rule. This isn't just any job. This is a job *with the guy she likes*. I couldn't really make him out through the window, but I know I also correctly guessed she liked an older guy.

This one seemed in his twenties, with a similar carelessly elegant style to Sophie. Exactly the type I knew she would go for.

The exact opposite of me.

It hurts like I've been physically stabbed in the heart. I grip my chest with a groan. What a fucking idiot I've been. I've been so busy treating her like shit to make sure nobody at Spearcrest would covet her that I pushed her right into the arms of some random nobody out in the real world.

I've truly cut my nose to spite my face, and now I've got nothing left to do but cry into my own blood.

No.

Since when have I become the kind of guy to think like that? I've never backed down from a fight before. I've never accepted defeat just because it hurts. I'm Evan fucking Knight, and if there's one thing the Knights aren't, it's a bunch of quitters.

So Sophie likes this other guy. So fucking what? Sophie hasn't liked me ever since I turned my back on our friendship, but I've never let that get in my way before. She might like this random nobody, but *I'm* the one who gets under her skin.

She can hate me all she likes, but she can't deny how good my kisses made her feel, or how hard I made her come.

So fuck it. If she wants this other guy, she can work for it. I'm not going to lie down and let her walk right over me on her way to this guy's arms. She's going to have to go through *me* to get to *him*, and if she wants to do that then she's going to have to get her hands dirty and actually fight me.

And I'm ready to fight as dirty as I need to.

## 25

# ROYAL SUBJECT

## Evan

THERE'S NO PARTY THIS weekend—which is good because I'm really not in the mood for fake insouciance and forced socialising. Instead, my friends and I head off campus and into London for a night of hard drinking in one of Soho's most exclusive bars.

Luca's personal chauffeur drives us from Spearcrest in a black limousine, and we start drinking the moment the limousine door closes on us. From the looks of things, I'm not the only one whose sorely in need of drowning my problems: Sev looks restless and irritated, shadows gathering under his eyes, Iakov's knuckles are red raw with bruising—really living up to his nickname "Knuckles"—and there's a brand new cut in his eyebrow, and Zachary, normally the most measured and mature one of us all, is moody and monosyllabic.

Only Luca appears amused and relaxed—but that's probably because Luca is a psychopath incapable of real human emotion.

"What a glum assortment you all make tonight," he sneers, leaning back against the white leather seats. "Not girl problems, surely?"

None of us reply. We all sip our drinks and wince—we made a deal tonight was going to be a liquor night, and the burn is real.

Luca laughs.

"Really? *All* of you?" He raises his cup towards Zachary. "Even the Bishop?"

"I don't want to talk about Theodora," Zach snaps.

There's a moment of silence in the limousine. Finally, my bad mood cracks. I grin at Zach. "I hate to tell you this, Zach, but nobody mentioned Theodora."

Iakov bursts out laughing, startling everyone.

"Fucking hell," he says in his deep voice, rubbing his hand across his buzzcut. "Zach is turning into you, Sev. Bringing up his girl at every opportunity he can."

"She's not my girl," Sev immediately retorts, glaring at Iakov. "And I didn't start it—Evan's been going on about Sophie non-stop for the past five years."

"Except that at least you're engaged to your girl," Luca cackles like the fucking cartoon villain he is. "Evan couldn't get Sophie if he was the last man on earth and her only chance at survival was to get fucked."

I glare at him, but bite down on a retort.

In spite of Sophie's assumption that I would immediately run back to my friends to tell them about my so-called conquest, I've not told a single one of them. Not even Zach—not even about the kiss at the party.

Because no matter what Sophie thinks, this isn't a conquest—a *win*, as she put it.

And whatever is between us is just between us, and that's exactly how I want to keep it.

So I keep my mouth shut, and spend the rest of the trip into London listening to others rant about their problems. By the time we get to the club, we're all a little bit fucked—apart from Luca, but that's because it's actually pretty hard to tell the difference between drunk Luca and sober Luca, since he's a cold-blooded serpent regardless.

We settle in a private booth with a bottle of the most expensive liquor in the house—on the house, of course, courtesy of Luca's dad.

Sev's already a mess, his pale cheeks flushed, his black hair falling over his eyes like some anguished prince. He's gesturing wildly with his glass in his hand, amber liquor splashing over his fingers, forcing us to come up with a plan to make his own fiancée (the fiancée he allegedly hates) jealous.

I'm not sure exactly what his end goal is, or what he's hoping to achieve, but French logic seems to be quite different to normal person logic, so I don't question it.

Then, Sev says something that makes me perk up in my seat.

"She doesn't get to just fucking sweep away my existence. I'm a Young fucking King of Spearcrest—it's time to remind her she's nothing more than a subject. She'll fucking bow down to me even if I have to force her to."

He might be talking about his little French fiancée, but there's truth in his words.

Somehow, in the coldness of Sophie's disdain and in the heat of fucking her, I've forgotten who I am. Not some lovesick puppy, not some nobody to be swept aside in favour of some other guy.

I'm Evan Knight—a Young fucking King.

And Sophie Sutton is nothing more than a subject.

IT TAKES ME A whole week to finally get her alone again. I'm leaving Mr Houghton's office after begging him for a deadline extension when I spot her.

My entire body goes into alert, vividly aware, as if a bolt of electricity has just zapped through me. I freeze, watching as she peers through the window into an empty classroom before going in.

I follow her, closing the door quietly behind me, pressing my back to the wooden pane. She's in her immaculate uniform, her hair loose on her shoulders, brown and glossy as chocolate pudding. She rifles through the bookshelves at the back of the room, gathering an armful of books. Then she turns around and jumps, dropping two books. Her eyes go wide and her cheeks go red so quickly it's almost endearing enough to pacify me.

Almost.

"You haven't been coming to our tutoring sessions."

She frowns. "I thought we had a deal."

I raise an eyebrow. "We *had* a deal. I've changed my mind."

Now the blush darkens. It's easy to tell the difference between Sophie's blush of embarrassment and her blush of anger, because her blush of anger is redder, and her eyes have a fierce spark in them that make her look a bit feral, and her hands clench into fists.

"You don't get to just change your mind."

"I get *everything* I want."

It's the truth.

Almost.

"You'll have to learn sooner or later that this isn't the way the world works," she says coldly. "You get whatever money buys you, but it doesn't mean you get whatever you want."

"In this case it does."

Her nostrils flare as she inhales sharply. "Haven't you already gotten what you want?"

Her anger is almost a presence in the room, a monster rearing itself—but the monster of my jealousy and desire is far more powerful.

"I want you to resume tutoring me. Starting this week."

"I'm not coming to your house," she bites out.

"Why? Because you're afraid you're going to have to run away from it if you kiss me by accident again? Because you're going to beg me to fuck you and then pretend you did it because you hate me?"

She can't quite stop her shock and embarrassment at my words from registering, but she recovers quickly, straightening herself up. "I've already apologised for what happened on Christmas Eve."

So she wants to pretend yesterday didn't happen? I shouldn't even be surprised. She really *is* a fucking coward.

"I don't give a shit. I neither want nor need your apologies."

She glares at me. "Then what do you need?"

"I need you to get over what happened and just do what you're supposed to do, which is *tutor me*."

"You don't need tutoring sessions!" she exclaims, her hoarse voice even hoarser in her anger. "You don't even *want* tutoring sessions!"

"Mr Houghton says that he was impressed with my effort in the exam and that the sessions are clearly helping. I have an essay already overdue and more mock exams coming up next month. So yes, I do need those sessions, and even if I didn't, I still *want* them."

Even *I* can hear the arrogance in my voice. But the way she thinks so low of me makes me want to double down on everything she hates about me. No matter how little she thinks of me, I can always be worse. If she treats me like a dog then I'll become a wolf. If she treats me like I'm evil then I'll become the devil himself.

Her eyes glitter as she glares at me. She's breathing hard, her cheeks are flushed with fury—she looks in her anger almost exactly the same way she looks when she's turned on.

Blood rushes to my cock.

"Why are you doing this?" She speaks lower now, not just angry, but strangled with frustration. "You know I need this job."

I know only too well. The memory of that cupcake, her laughter, her gaze lingering after that stupid goddamn guy has been playing in an infuriating loop in my head since last Tuesday.

"Fuck your job. I'll pay you for the sessions if that's what you want."

She recoils. "I don't want your money."

Her voice is icy, and pure hatred is on her face. I know I've offended her, possibly hurt her. But at this point, it doesn't feel like I'm attacking her. It just feels like I'm retaliating.

"Isn't that the reason you need that stupid job?" I sneer. "For the *money*? Because that's the one thing your nice uniform and clever brains can never get you? Well, I have money, I can pay you. I can pay you far more than you make at that place, too. It can be our new deal. You need the money, so I help you with that, and I need to pass the class, so you teach me."

We stare at each other across the room. She's completely silent for a moment, and I can't help but wonder what's going through her mind. Is she tempted? I'm sure she would be tempted if her job was only for the money. But I'm not making her choose between her job and me.

I'm making her choose between that guy and me.

"Let me tell you something," she says finally, her voice deathly quiet.

She picks up the books she dropped earlier, holding the pile closer to her chest, and crosses the room to stand in front of me. She gathers herself up with unshakable dignity and looks me straight in the eyes.

"I would rather jump from the top of the clock tower than ever take a penny from you."

I shrug. "This is exactly why poor people stay poor: they don't know a good deal when they see one. So since you won't tutor me for money, Sutton, then I guess you're just going to tutor me for free."

Her nostrils flare and her jaw twitches. Her anger and hatred are palpable, like waves of liquid heat pulsing out of her and brushing against me. Now she's closer, I can smell that addictive fragrance, the sweetness of warm caramel. I clench my fists, glad my hands are in my pockets so she can't see how much she's affecting me.

She's close enough to touch, but I don't want to just touch her. I want to grab her, pin her to the door and fuck her until she's filling the room with the raspy, breathless sound of her moans.

The adrenaline pumping through me, mixed with her magnetic proximity and the intensity of my desire, makes my blood burn and my cock achingly hard. But Sophie's eyes are fixed on mine, and the heat of my desire melts away against the ice of her gaze.

"Read my lips, Evan. *No*. No, I'm not going to tutor you for free, or for money. No, I'm not going to tutor you at all. It's a strange little word, isn't it? I'm sure you've never heard it before. Well, let it be the last thing I teach you. *No*. It means this time, you don't get what you want. Now *move*. I'm late for my next lesson."

She tries to storm past me, but I catch her by her arm, stopping her. I take her face in my hand, forcing her to look up at me—the same way I did when I fucked her. She meets my gaze with defiance, like she's not afraid.

"Let me clarify something for you, Sutton." I speak slowly, enunciating every word. "While you and I are in Spearcrest, you belong to *me*. You have from the moment you stepped foot here—and you will until the day you leave. You can fight me, you can fuck me—you can do whatever you please. But no matter what you choose to do, you remain *mine*."

She pulls away from me with a sneer. "You don't *own* me, Evan. You might be a so-called fucking *king* of Spearcrest, but if you grow up and look around you, you'll realise that means nothing at all. You have no power over me."

I hold her gaze, but she doesn't look away, doesn't relent. I can tell she means it; she's not going to break this time. She's putting up a fight, just as I thought she would.

But that's fine. Two can play this game.

"We'll fucking see, Sutton."

I move aside and let her leave. And then I go straight to the office of Mr Shawcross, our Head of Year, and officially report Sophie for having a job.

## 26

# BLOW FOR BLOW

### Sophie

When Mr Shawcross calls me into his office on Wednesday morning, I know what he's going to say before I even walk into the room. Even though I was prepared for Evan's retaliation, it never occurred to me he would actually grass me up to the school.

But of course, it should have occurred to me.

This isn't my first time being betrayed by him.

Now, sitting across Mr Shawcross in the frosty morning light, I know exactly what he's done. There is no surprise, just a sort of numb, grim resignation. To my surprise, Mr Shawcross doesn't express any anger or annoyance.

Instead, with a sort of awkward kindness, he tells me he understands my financial concerns, that trying to find a job is perfectly understandable. I listen to him without a word, nobbing mutely as he explains to me that Spearcrest is an establishment that champions academic excellence, that this is a school rule which doesn't allow exceptions and that the school is reluctant to set a precedent for students seeking employment.

He tells me the school, and him personally, will do their very best to help me apply for any financial aid available. He adds that with my pristine record and impressive grades, I should be eligible for all sorts of scholarships and that Spearcrest will support me all the way.

Finally, he takes a deep sigh and flounders for a second.

"Out of respect for both yourself and your parents, I thought it best if we leave the matter here and keep it between us. I've made no official record, Sophie. I implicitly trust you will do the right thing. Now, whether you wish to discuss the matter with your parents is at your discretion, but know that I will not be raising the issue with them."

I nod. There's a lump in my throat so big I can hardly breathe, but I have to speak at some point. I do so with some difficulty, my voice strangled.

"Thank you, Mr Shawcross."

"Don't mention it, Sophie. We all want what's best for you. I've also decided that for the sake of fairness, no students will be allowed away from campus, so your mentoring programme will continue here in Spearcrest. I'll inform Mr Knight's parents myself."

I nod. Mr Shawcross gives me a pained smile. Somehow, his pity is worse than anything I could have expected. "I know how much you worry about things, Sophie, and trust me, I understand. But you're a bright young woman, hard-working and principled, and things will work out. I genuinely believe they will."

I swallow hard. To my complete mortification, enormous tears pool in my eyes, blurring my vision. Mr Shawcross clears his throat. "You're dismissed, Sophie."

My voice comes out in one breath as I jump to my feet and rush to the door. "Thank you, Mr Shawcross."

Repressed sobs fill my chest like a balloon, threatening to burst. I run to the nearest girls' bathroom and slam the door shut behind me. Then, finally alone, I explode into tears, sinking back against the door and burying my face in my arms to stifle the sobs that come wailing out.

I cry harder than I have in a long time. Big sobs shake me as I pull out long ribbons of paper towels to wipe away the stream of tears and snot. I cry out of sadness, fear, embarrassment, anger, frustration, relief, and from the nightmarish, haunting humiliation of my entire conversation with Mr Shawcross.

I must have seemed so poor to him, scrambling around working some stupid job to make myself a little bit of money so I'm not just living on student loans at university. His pity for me was clear, and, more painful still, his obvious sympathy for my parents.

No matter how much I appreciate that he chose not to tell them what I've done, they would have died from the shame of it, and he was just sparing them from that shame.

The shame of my actions.

The shame of *me*.

In a way, this was bound to happen. Someone at some point would have seen me at the café. If anything, it's a miracle I got away with it for so long. In a way, I'm almost relieved: no more secrets, no more sneaking around. I'll have more time for my schoolwork, which is getting overwhelming, and all the things I've been neglecting, like my running and my neglected extracurriculars.

By the time my sobs finally ebb away and my tears stop flowing, I'm a lot calmer. The sadness and humiliation and shock fade away, leaving only anger in their wake.

No, not anger.

Fury.

A cold, hard fury, that turns my insides to ice and hardens my heart until it's a rock in my chest.

I stand up and face the mirror. My eyes, nose and cheeks are scarlet, the skin puffy and shiny. I daub cold water onto my face, cooling away the redness. I smooth back my hair, fix my uniform and check my watch. It's morning break, and I know exactly where to find Evan at this time of day.

The sixth form rec room is next to the dining hall; a long room full of low, cosy sofas, a TV set and some games. It's meant to be a place for sixth formers to relax and socialise in their free time, but it's long been claimed by the Young Kings, who hold court there and receive the tributes of their sycophants.

The sound of music and laughter fills the room when I stride into it, but my attention is focused, my icy anger urging me on.

I spot Evan straight away.

It's not hard, because as usual he's the centre of attention, and as usual, it's by doing something stupid.

He's in the middle of the circle of armchairs and couches, with two chairs on either side of him. He's using the chairs to prop his hands on and hopping into some sort of elevated handstand, and then trying to do push-ups.

His top drops down to reveal his unnecessarily hard abs. Of course, he's not even wearing the proper school uniform. Instead, he's wearing a soft, sky-blue sweatshirt on top of his school shirt.

The Christmas present I got him.

As I approach the centre of the room, I hope that he somehow slips and falls on his face, but he doesn't. Instead, he lands gracefully on his feet and receives his applause and cheers with a bow and a flourish. When he stands back up, his eyes catch mine.

He grins.

"Oh, if it isn't Prefect Sutton. What brings you here today?"

My anger flares to life, I'm so irate my hands are shaking. "You know exactly what brings me here today."

"I'm assuming you've had a change of heart about the tutoring," he says, tilting his head with a smirk.

"I could tutor you every day of your life and you would still be the most stupid person in the room wherever you go," I spit out.

I'm just being hurtful out of anger, but I'm desperate to wipe the smirk off his smug face. The room seems to have disappeared around us, everything replaced by a cold white fog of anger, and in the middle of the fog is Evan, crystal-clear, with his unbearable smile.

A smile which widens slowly as he speaks with soft, quiet confidence. "You're still going to do it, though, since you don't have a choice anymore."

Even though I already knew it was him who reported me, his subtle confirmation makes obvious his complete lack of regret. He betrayed my trust easily, shamelessly—the same way he did the first time.

I'm the complete idiot for falling for the same trick twice.

"You're such a fucking coward." My voice is so low it's almost a whisper.

Finally, his smile falters, a crack in his facade of nonchalant arrogance. He steps forward, right up to me, almost intimidating, and hisses, "*I'm* the coward?"

Heat floods my cheeks and I'm stopped in my tracks. He's too close, the heat of him and the cold of my anger meeting, misting, fogging up my mind. "I—I didn't do anything wrong."

"For someone who values honesty so highly, you sure do love lying to yourself."

"I'd rather lie to myself than to everybody I meet," I snap.

He snickers, a cold, derisive sound. "The reason you see liars everywhere, Sutton, is because you wouldn't know the fucking truth if it hit you in the face."

The conversation is not at all going the way I wanted. Evan is making me defend myself when he's the one who's wronged me—and I'm letting him.

"The *truth*," I say between clenched teeth, "is that I trusted you with one single thing, and you still managed to fuck me over."

He shrugs. "You left me no choice. You're the one who broke school rules, not me."

"You knew I needed that job!" I cry out in an explosion of anger and frustration.

"So what?" he sneers. "It's not my fault you're poor, is it?"

He throws his insult at my face like a slap—it hits me like a slap. The moment is suspended in time.

Nothing seems to exist but Evan and me and the blows we're trading.

I shake my head and my voice comes out strangled with a mixture of shock and disgust. "You really are one worthless, despicable piece of shit. You make me sick to my stomach."

If my words hurt Evan, he doesn't show it. But his retaliation is swift and sharp. "Clearly not sick enough to stop you from fucking me, though."

Surprised gasps and sputtered laughter yank me back to reality. We're in the middle of the rec room, and everyone is staring. All the Young Kings are there: Luca, with some girl draped to his side, Zachary Blackwood with a book on his lap and his eyebrow tilted in surprise, Iakov and Séverin standing in the doorway with their mouths fallen open.

Not just the Young Kings, but their retinues: the richest and most beautiful Spearcrest have to offer. Giselle, Camille, Seraphina Rosenthal. Girls who have been mocking me my entire time here—girls I always maintained some sort of moral victory over. Now, they are all staring at me with mingled shock and amusement and satisfaction.

Because now, they all know I'm no better than anybody else in Spearcrest: another notch on a Young King's bedpost.

Their eyes pierce me from every angle. I feel so exposed and vulnerable and humiliated I might as well be naked. No words come to my mouth, no smart, sarcastic reply to help me hold on to a final shred of dignity. To my complete and utter despair, tears well up in my eyes before I can stop them. They drop from my eyelashes, rolling down my cheeks.

When I arrived in Spearcrest, I promised myself one thing. To never let them see me cry. It was a promise I never broke. The one thing I could always pride myself on no matter what.

And now, it's just another thing that's been taken from me.

Without another word, without even one last glance at Evan, I spin around and walk away to the sound of laughter.

# 27

# SCATHED

## Evan

THE EXPRESSION ON SOPHIE'S face is burned into my retinas. An expression like I've never seen before: shock, hurt, disbelief, betrayal, humiliation, all mingled together in those dark, shining eyes.

Her eyes fill with tears and my heart sinks.

I've never seen Sophie cry before.

She offers no repartee, no comeback—nothing. She simply turns around and leaves without another word. I'm left feeling like I just knocked her down with a punch to the face, and instead of getting up and punching me right back, she just stayed down, bleeding at my feet.

It's not how I wanted to feel. There's no sense of victory or revenge.

I just stand there, fists clenched, bile burning in my throat.

"What was *that* all about?" Luca asks, raising an eyebrow.

I shrug and run my hand through my hair distractedly, still staring after Sophie. "Nothing."

"It didn't look like *nothing*." Luca's voice quivers with barely repressed amusement. "You fucked Sophie Sutton? You must really be taking the bet seriously."

My gaze snaps to Luca. I have the sudden, violent urgent to tell him to go fuck himself and his stupid bet, that none of this is any of his fucking business and to get off my fucking back.

But my anger would only bring the sadistic fucker more satisfaction—so I swallow back the urge and wave my hand in a dismissive gesture.

"It's not a big deal. Guess someone had to do it."

I grab my backpack and blazer from the couch where I tossed them earlier.

"I'm off to Bio."

Luca checks his ridiculous Rolex. "So soon?"

I shrug. "Mr Ahmed will have my balls if I'm late."

"Wait up," Zachary calls, putting his books away into his bag and slinging it over his shoulder. "I'm headed that way too. I'll go with you."

I give a curt nod and wait for him by the door. We walk in silence until we make it out of the building. It's snowing again, thick, fluffy snowflakes spiralling down from low, dark clouds. Students are hurrying inside, their navy uniforms blurring in the corners of my vision.

My eyes are lost in the snowfall, unfocused and unseeing. All I see, burned into my retinas like a permanent scar, is that goddamn expression on Sophie's pretty face, the tears gliding down her cheeks. A horrible, almost embarrassing pain, a pain I inflicted myself.

I *did* want to hurt her. After everything that passed between us, after every blow she got to land on me, I couldn't stand that she got to walk away unscathed.

Well, she is well and truly scathed now, and the balance of pain has been redressed.

So why do I still feel like pure, utter shit?

"What did you do, then?"

"What?" I turn. Zachary's not looking at me but straight ahead as we slowly make our way towards the Science building.

"I can't imagine Sophie would have come for you for nothing," he says, his tone neutral, almost casual. "So what did you do?"

I glance away and swallow hard.

"I reported her to Mr Shawcross."

Zachary is silent.

"You know... about her job, or whatever."

"You told Mr Shawcross she had a job?" he asks.

"Yeah."

"Why?"

I try to think of the reasoning behind my actions, the chain of events that led to this horrible, irreversible point.

"We kissed. At my house, during the Christmas holiday. We... kissed."

From the corner of my eye, I see Zachary slowly nod. He's quiet for a moment, then says, "Right. You two kissed during Christmas—so you reported her for having a job?"

"No. We kissed, and then she apologised, and told me she liked somebody else."

Zachary is silent for longer this time.

"That's truly shit, Ev. I can't imagine it made you feel great."

"It made me feel like absolute shit. Then she ran away from my house. Then—then I tried to confront her, and we had sex."

"You and Sophie had sex?"

"Yeah—but not... it was... she just did it because she thought it's what I wanted and she just wanted to get it out of the way so I leave her alone."

"Well..." Zach speaks carefully. "Isn't it what you wanted, though?"

"No—obviously it's what I wanted but—" My face burns and my throat is so tight it's a struggle to get the words out. "It wasn't... she wouldn't even fucking *look* at me, Zach."

"Hmm," Zach says noncommittally. "So you reported her about her job to get back at her because of the sex?"

I shake my head. "No. I mean, yes, but... I saw her at her job and found out that the guy she likes is some guy she works with. Some guy not from Spearcrest. Some older guy."

"So what? Now she can't go to her job, so she can't see this guy, so she's not in love with him anymore and she falls for you instead? Is that the plan?"

Zachary's tone is dry, but he's always been the first one of my friends to call me out on stupid ideas. I shake my head again. "No. So then I told her I wanted her to tutor me because I want to do well in Lit."

"Which you don't."

"What—no. You don't know that. Did you not hear Mr Houghton say he was impressed by my improvement?"

Zachary scoffs. "Since when do you care what Mr Houghton has to say?"

"I *do* care. Plus you know my dad will be royally pissed off if I fail."

"So, study."

"I don't wanna study. I want Sophie to teach me."

"More like you want to keep her to yourself," Zachary says drily. "So you told her you wanted her to tutor you, and then what did she say?"

"She said no. She said: *you don't even know what that word means, do you? If I teach you one last thing, it's the meaning of the word no. It means you don't get what you want.* And then she walked away."

Zachary cracks a rare smile. "I like her style."

I sigh. "So that's when I went to Mr Shawcross and reported her."

"Mm. And now she's found out, and presumably, she's been bollocked and told not to go back anymore. Hence that heated little moment back there."

I nod.

"So, what?" Zachary asks. "Is it everything you wanted? Do you feel as good as you thought you would?"

"Obviously not," I snap, glaring at him. "Do I look like I feel good?"

"Hardly. You look like you just got the girl you like in trouble and then called her poor in front of all your rich friends and then implied that having sex with you is something she ought to feel ashamed of."

"No I didn't." I stare at Zachary in horror. "How did I imply that?"

"Well, all I'll say is that if you *didn't* want her to feel ashamed of having sex with you, you probably shouldn't have used it as an insult in a very public argument."

My stomach clenches painfully. "Oh god."

I bury my face in my hands. Zach is—as usual—completely right. In the heat of the moment, it had been the perfect comeback. I'd felt justified, full of righteous anger, like I was just retaliating against Sophie's attacks. Maybe not in the most honourable way, but at least it had been blow for blow.

Now, I'm full of shame, remorse and horror, like I just beat up someone defenceless.

Zach sighs. "Well, if it helps, you're hardly the first person to treat someone they fancy like shit for no reason."

I peer through my fingers to give him a horrified look. "This is me we're talking about! I never treat girls like shit. My parents raised me to be a fucking gentleman."

"You never treat *girls* like shit, but you treat *Sophie* like shit. Like she's special, so instead of getting the best of you, she gets the worst of you. Hard to see how you justify that one in your head."

"What else was I supposed to do though?"

"Oh, I don't know, Evan, perhaps treat her like an actual human being and show her a modicum of decency?"

"If I was nice to her," I mumble, feeling heat rush to my cheeks, "then someone else might have become interested in her."

"Oh, charming. You're like a kid that's not allowed to play with a toy and scribbles all over it so nobody else wants it."

"Well, I don't fucking know what I'm doing, do I? I was always too busy worrying about Luca taking her away from me—I just panicked."

"You panicked for several years in a row? And then you made her lose her job and insulted her in front of everyone out of panic, too?"

I look at Zachary. "If you think I'm an arsehole, just say that."

"Oh, shall I?" He gives me a smile full of fake courtesy. "You're an arsehole. You're not stupid either—you know what you've been doing. Treating Sophie the way you treated her all these years wasn't an accident. You dug your own grave, and now there's nothing left for you to do but to try and crawl your way out."

I stare at him. "How?"

"How should I know? I'm not the architect of this whole mess, you are." Zachary is quiet for a second. "I mean, you could always start with an apology."

"Out of the question."

"Right."

By then, we've been standing in front of the Science building for a while, snow collecting on our heads and shoulders. We're probably hopelessly late, and Mr Ahmed is definitely going to have my balls, but this conversation, as unpleasant as it is, is helping somehow. Even though Zachary is being more unforgiving than the world's strictest judge.

I exhale, shoulders slumping helplessly. "If I apologise, she'll know I did something wrong."

"Oh, I can assure you she already knows that."

I glare at Zachary. He stares back, impassive.

"I'm not apologising."

"Right," he says again.

There is a moment of silence. Awkwardly, I gesture towards the doorway. "Are you not late for your class?"

He shrugs. "I don't have class. I just walked with you because you looked stressed and I wanted to cheer you up."

"Oh, wow, that was you cheering me up?"

"You're welcome, Ev."

And with that, he turns and walks away, back the way we came from. I shout after him. "I don't care, I'm not apologising!"

He waves without turning around and disappears in a white flurry of spinning snowflakes.

## 28

# APOLOGY

## Sophie

THE STUDY HALL, NORMALLY so large and cold, feels small and stifling today. Not because it's busier than usual. If anything, there are barely any students. But Evan is sitting next to me, and his presence is a vortex, sucking the air from the room.

I sit as far from him as I can, my eyes stubbornly fixed on the desk in front of us. I've not made eye contact with him since he arrived for our session.

Tutoring Evan is just like everything in my life: I don't have to enjoy it, I simply have to endure it and use it as another stepping stone to the life I want.

Deadlines for university applications are fast approaching, and my applications are strong because of everything I've done here. And that includes my participation in Miss Bailey's tutoring programme. Once it secures me some offers, once Spearcrest is in my past and I can finally live the life I want, Evan will become nothing more than a distant memory.

The pain he inflicted on me will be forgotten over time; his presence in my life will fade like a scar.

The strength and comfort of this thought are enough to allow me to turn up for our session today. This half-term, we are both studying the same text, Jane Austen's *Persuasion*, and I've brought enough work that there shouldn't be any opportunities to talk.

But of course, Evan doesn't get the memo. He keeps sneaking glances at me even though he's meant to be reading the extract in front of him. I ignore his attempts to make eye contact.

"I'm sorry," he says finally, his voice catching. He clears his throat, and repeats more clearly, "I'm so sorry, Sutton."

I clench my jaw. What I was to tell him is to shove his apology down his own throat and choke on it. What I say instead is, "Have you finished reading the extract?"

"Did you hear me? I said I'm sorry."

I finally look up. I try to look right past his handsome features and sky-blue eyes at the ugliness inside and give it a polite smile.

"I heard you. I accept your apology. Have you finished reading the extract?"

He sighs. "Yeah."

I hand him another sheet. "Right, then let's work through these questions."

He listens as I talk him through character analysis and key themes. He nods when I tell him what to do, and when I hand him a sheet of questions, he takes it and, to my relief, gets to work.

He works in perfect silence for several minutes, but the respite is short-lived. With a loud sigh, he puts his pen down and looks up.

"You can't just say you accept my apology if you don't mean it."

"I mean it," I say without looking at him, keeping my eyes on the book of critical analysis I'm taking notes from. "So get back to work."

"You're just saying that to shut me up."

I clench my jaw, forcing myself to calm down. After the humiliation he's put me through, I've decided to never let him get another rise out of me. I count down from ten in my head. Then I say, "What would you like me to tell you, Evan?"

"I don't know! Tell me the truth."

"The truth is that I forgive you and I want to move on, which is why I'm here to help you with Lit. So could you please do your work?"

He's quiet for a bit, but I can tell he's still staring at me. I refuse to look at him, pointedly turning the pages of my book. My eyes burn, but I'd rather die than cry in front of him again.

I remind myself of why he can't get to me: I don't care what he says about me. I don't care what the Spearcrest kids think about me. In a year, none of this will matter.

Evan gets back to work. He gets through the worksheet, then I give him some context notes to read and summarise. He does so without protest or comment.

This is the best way to get through all of this. In the bleak austerity of the study hall, in the sallow lamplight and the icy silence between us, the heat of his kisses, of his mouth between my legs or the quick and intense sex we had seems like some strange, fast-vanishing dream.

No, not a dream.

A nightmare.

I'm in the middle of making a bullet point list of key events when Evan speaks again, startling me slightly.

"I shouldn't have told the school about your job, okay? It was a shitty thing for me to do."

I bite the inside of my cheeks. Why won't he let it go? I'm letting it go. I'm letting *everything* go. So why won't he?

"Don't worry about it," I grind out.

"I do worry about it, though. You're right, you trusted me with one thing, and I fucked you over, and I shouldn't have, and I regret it, and I'm sorry. And I'm sorry for telling everyone about—"

"Think about it this way," I say in my sweetest voice, interrupting him before he gets any further. "I was the one breaking the school rules, so, technically speaking, you did the right thing. As you can see, there's nothing for you to worry about, alright?"

He's staring at me, but he can stare all he wants because I'm not going to look at him.

"I shouldn't have mocked you in front of everyone," he says, his voice low and rough. "I feel shit about that too. I never meant to hurt you."

I hate that he's forcing me to remember it. My cheeks grow hot, and discomfort twists my insides into knots. I swallow hard.

"I already said I accept your apology, so stop apologising. Here."

I hand him the list of bullet points. "Find some quotes for these events."

He takes the sheet in one hand and grabs my wrist in the other.

"Look at me."

I don't want to. I *really* don't want to, because the more he apologises, the more I'm getting restless and upset. I don't want to argue with him, I don't want to look at him, and I *definitely* don't want to cry in front of him again. But I'm not going to fight him, and I might as well get this over as quickly as possible.

I look at him and try to keep myself as neutral as possible.

His blue eyes are huge, almost green in the yellow lamplight. His expression, normally so open and cheerful, is transformed: full of regret and pain and sadness.

That makes me angrier than anything else. What does *he* have to feel sad about? He doesn't deserve pain, he doesn't deserve forgiveness, and he certainly doesn't deserve the time I'm sacrificing as the altar of his ego right now.

I don't say any of this—I know better.

"Sophie. I'm genuinely trying to tell you how sorry I am," he says, his voice raw and low. "So why are you being like this?"

Pulling my wrist free from his grip, I meet his eyes with a cold, direct gaze.

"Look, Evan. I came here to tutor you because that's what you said you wanted. Remember? Now I'm here, just as you wanted. Everything, exactly as you wanted. You kept everybody away from me so no boy would ever come near me—as you wanted, and we've had sex—as you wanted. Now, everybody knows you were right all along, that I've always been desperate to be with you. Everybody thinks I'm your worthless desperate groupie, just like you wanted. Now you've said you wanted to apologise, and I accepted your apology. So what more can you possibly want?"

He hesitates. His eyes search my face, almost fearfully, but there's nothing there for him to find. Everything I said is the truth.

"Nothing," he says finally.

He takes the sheet and gets on with the work. We work mostly in silence for the rest of the session, and the second our two hours are over, I pack my stuff and stand.

"I'll see you next week."

"Right," he says.

He stays sitting down while I shoulder my backpack, staring at me while I tuck my chair in. He opens his mouth to say something, but I turn and leave before he can.

## Evan

"What the fuck am I gonna do?"

My face buried into my pillow, I let out a long, angry yell. Then I bolt upright on my bed and glare at Zachary, who's reclining in the armchair by the window, his chin propped on his fist.

"Your stupid idea didn't fucking work, Zach!"

"Oh. You actually apologised?"

"I practically *begged* for her forgiveness."

"Hm. And what did she say?"

I throw myself back onto my bed with a groan of despair. "She accepted my apology."

"What else did you want her to say?"

"I didn't want her to say anything else. I just wanted her to mean it."

Zachary is staring out of the window, deep in thought. One of his ankles rests elegantly on his knee. He has a sort of cool, British energy I sometimes envy, like nothing can get to him. I bet if I was more like Zachary, more thoughtful and poised, Sophie would like me more.

"I mean, I can see why she would struggle to forgive you so easily," he says in a thoughtful tone. "But how do you know she didn't mean it when she said she accepted your apology?"

"Because she was like..." I close my eyes, covering them with my forearm.

In the darkness, I play the spectrum of Sophie's expressions. Her sardonic amusement when she used to tutor me at my house. Her icy fury when she refused to tutor me. Her hurt and betrayal when I insulted her in front of everyone. Her flush of tipsy desire when I kissed her open mouth that fateful night.

"Because she was like... empty. No expression on her face, no emotion, nothing."

"What's wrong with that?"

"Sophie always *feels* stuff. She gets annoyed or fed up or frustrated or angry or sad. She doesn't just sit there like a blank whiteboard. But that's exactly what it was like when she tutored me yesterday. She was like a wall. She barely looked at me."

"Well, she's probably still angry at you—rightfully so, I should think."

"But I apologised! I did what you said!"

"I said to *start* with an apology. She's accepted it, which is a step forward. Or if she didn't mean it, it's not a step at all, but at least it's not another step backwards, right?"

"Ugh, why are you always talking in riddles? Say what you mean, man!"

Zachary stands and leans down over me where I'm lying in my bed, glaring at me.

"Then listen up, you whiny fuckwit. An apology is like an introduction to showing someone you're sorry for what you've done. You didn't just make her lose her job, you essentially betrayed her trust and then humiliated her in front of everyone that's already been looking down at her. At this point, you should be thanking your lucky star she doesn't slap you in the face every time she sees you. Now you've apologised—great start, but it's only a start. I don't even see how you would expect her to forgive you so easily. If you want her forgiveness, then fucking earn it. But let's be honest. You don't want to be good to Sophie Sutton, because you're scared it's going to make you weak. You'd rather have the power and control of being an arsehole to her and making her hate you because that's less of a risk. But guess what—we're not fucking kids anymore. We're adults. We're about to go off into the real world, and Sophie is already basically in it. So you're going to have to step up and grow the fuck up. Sophie doesn't want you because she deserves better—you know that's the truth. So *be* fucking better. Otherwise, let her go and move the fuck on."

There is a long, heavy, tense silence. I'm staring at Zachary in absolute shock. This has got to be the first time I've heard him speak for so long—he's usually a guy of few words, but boy can he talk if he wants to.

When I don't say anything he claps his hands together. "Right. And on that note... I'm off."

He strides briskly out, and I'm left alone in my room. His words whirl like a tornado in my mind, and in the middle of that tornado, standing in the eye of the storm, Sophie.

What he said is hard to hear, but it's the truth. I do have to make it up to Sophie. I do have to grow up and treat her well. And I want to. I want nothing more than to shower Sophie with everything I could possibly give her. If I could, I would lay anything she asked at her feet: love, affection, adoration, gifts and tributes.

But Sophie doesn't want anything from me. So how on earth do I earn her forgiveness or her trust or her love, if she won't accept so much as an apology from me?

I roll over onto my back and stare at the ceiling. What the fuck am I going to do? It's not even like I can google how to win Sophie back, or how to earn Sophie's friendship. I groan. If only there was an expert on Sophie Sutton or some sort of Sophie-whisperer I could consult.

I sit up.

How could I not have thought about it before? There *is* a Sophie-whisperer, right here at Spearcrest, and not even one, but two of them. Two Sophie-whisperers who have somehow managed to get themselves right into her heart.

And I happen to share a class with one of them.

# 29
# WHISPERER

## Evan

THE NEXT DAY AFTER Biology class ends, I grab a stool and plonk myself down next to Araminta Wilson-Sing. She's sort of the opposite of Sophie: small and curvy and playful, with an impeccably made-up face and dark hair dip-dyed blond. She throws me the dirtiest look I've ever been thrown, like an actual piece of dog shit has just plopped down at her side, and angles herself away from me, packing her books into her bag.

"Go to hell, Evan."

"I've not even said anything yet."

"I don't want to hear anything you have to say."

She's not even quiet for a whole second before she turns back around to face me. "You're a real piece of shit, you know that?"

I raise my hands. "I know, that's why I—"

"When I think about—" she interrupts me, then interrupts herself, composing herself with a graceful gesture. "Sophie is a fucking *goddess* in this world. Nobody works harder than she does, nobody deserves more than she does. She has a hard time trusting other people because *you* were a dick to her and decided to ruin the first friendship she ever had in this place. And now she's actually in a better place, and actually decides to give you the tiniest morsel of trust even though you did nothing to deserve it, what's the first thing you do? Sell her out? For what?"

"But I'm sorry I did it, and I wish I could take it back, but I can't, I've tried to apologise but—"

Her eyes go wide. "Oh, you *apologised*?" she says witheringly. "Oh, why didn't you say so? A whole *apology*? My god, you poor thing." She shakes her head. "You disgust me. When I think—do you even know how much Sophie worries? She worries about things all the fucking time. She's grown up around people who are richer than she'll ever be, no matter how hard she works, and she managed to find this one tiny thing that made her feel some control over her life and future, and you just fucked that up for what? For literally no reason."

"I said I'd pay her for the tutoring though!" I protest. "It's not like I don't know she doesn't worry about money. I would help in a heartbeat, but she said no!"

"Sophie would rather die than let you help her!" Araminta exclaims.

"I know, she told me she'll jump from the clock tower before she ever takes money from me."

"And I can assure you she absolutely meant it."

"Then how the fuck am I supposed to help?"

"You didn't need to help at all! You just needed to *not* fuck things up!" Araminta pauses, then glares at me. "Why did you even sleep with her in the first place if you were going to turn around and do something like that? I knew you were capable of being a real piece of shit but that's a dick move even by your abysmal fucking standards!"

I falter. "She—she told you we... slept together?"

It's not exactly the term I would have used to describe what passed between Sophie and I but if I described it the way it happened I'm pretty sure Araminta would reach into my pants and rip my balls off with her bare hand.

She grimaces. "This is Sophie we're talking about. Unlike you, this kind of stuff is a big deal to her."

I interrupt hotly. "It's a fucking big deal to me too!"

"Clearly not, since you fucked her one second, reported her to the school the next, and then told everyone she hates she's essentially your whore."

The loathing in her eyes dissuades me from denying anything she's just said, so I don't.

"Look, I know I fucked up, okay? But I'm not a robot either!" I lean forward, lowering my voice. "She hurt me too, you know!"

Araminta narrows her eyes but doesn't speak, as if she's waiting for an explanation.

So I hurry up and explain, before she punches me, which she looks like she really wants to. "She said she was only having sex with me to get rid of me and then she couldn't—she didn't even want to see my face while we… At least I had sex with her because it was *her*, because I wanted to—she could barely bring herself to look at me. How do you think that felt?"

"Obviously it must have felt like shit," Araminta admits, "but kind of makes sense in the context of things, don't you think? And telling everyone you two fucked just to make her look bad isn't exactly going to make her feel better about the whole thing, is it?"

"I wasn't trying to make her look back, I—"

But Araminta interrupts me. "The truth, Evan, is that you've always wanted her for yourself, and because you're too much of a coward to admit it, you would just rather nobody else have her, so you make her life hell so there's nothing left in it but you. You finally made some headway, because she trusted you enough to tell you she got that job, and even somehow deigned sleeping with you, and you managed to fuck both of those things up, all for what? To maintain some last dreg of power over her while you can? Well, guess what? Your scorched earth approach isn't going to corner her into liking you—it's just destroying everything."

I'm starting to get fed up with everyone calling me a coward, but I don't say this to Araminta. Instead, I sigh and say, "What do I do, then?"

Araminta blinks. "What do you mean?"

"I mean, how do I get through to her? I was nice to her at my house, and it felt nice, and I kept her secret and offered to let her stay at mine so she could keep going to that job, and then when things were finally going well and we made out, she just turns around and says it's all a terrible mistake, she was drunk and she regretted it and she fancies someone else. What was I doing wrong, then?"

"Just because you were nice to her one fucking time doesn't mean she automatically owes you her complete and undying love, Evan! My god, are you a child? Could you not be nice to her just because you actually like her and want her life to be nice and not because you expect anything from her?"

I look down, shame flushing heat into my face. "I can, I can, but—"

"But what?" Araminta snaps. "But you get everything you ever want so why should Sophie be any different?"

"I didn't say that."

"Then what?"

In the end, I tell her the truth, and it sounds even more pathetic than it feels. "But it fucking hurts."

"Oh does it?" Araminta stands up and shoulders her bag. "Does it hurt, Evan? Is it difficult and painful, having to work for something you want without knowing if you'll ever get it? Well, that's how Sophie feels. All the time. So at least be thankful there isn't some arsehole in your life making things difficult just because they can. Oh wait, there is. *You*. You're making your own life difficult, and you're too stupid to know it."

She gives me a long, hard look. "Just so you know, you used to be Sophie's favourite person in this school. Everything you want now, you had in Year 9, and you threw it all away. You might even have had it again this year, if you'd actually tried being a decent human being for once. But you reap what you sow, Evan, so maybe you should try sowing some good for a change."

And then she turns and walks out, leaving me alone in the classroom to slump down on the high desk, my face in my arms, wondering why nobody is willing to tell me something I want to hear for a change.

Araminta's words linger in my mind. "You used to be Sophie's favourite person in this school."

I never really think about our friendship in Year 9. It happened so fast—ended so quickly. It was my third year in Spearcrest by the time she arrived, I had my own friendships. Her obvious and painful awkwardness somehow endeared her to me, and I extended the hand of friendship since nobody else seemed to have done so.

Being friends with Sophie was fun. Back then, she was an odd combination of very serious and quite goofy. A bit of a nerdy kid, hard-working and with an almost grown-up sense of right and wrong.

But we could talk for hours, play stupid games, make fun of each other. In the classes we had together, we started sitting next to each other. I'd distract her with doodles and notes, she'd explain to me all the stuff I didn't understand. At Christmas, I even asked my mom to help me buy her a nice gift.

Out of all my friendships, the one I had with Sophie was the most refreshing, the most genuine. We didn't talk about holidays, about our parents' jobs, about money. We talked about everything else.

And then, the closer we got, the more Luca and Séverin and the others noticed it. At first, it was harmless jabs: who's your new girlfriend? Are you and Sophie going to get married when you're older? Stupid childish shit.

Then, it was: are you only interested in her because you want to know what it's like to date someone poor? Do poor girls put out more easily because you can just bribe them with gifts and money?

My first and only fight with Luca was on a day I found him talking to Sophie in the dining hall. He asked her a million questions, and then touched her hair, which I particularly hated. I hated it so much I wanted to punch him.

When I confronted him later, he said, "We're going to run this school, Evan. This girl isn't one of us, she's just going to get in our way. But you want to go ahead and keep her around, then you're going to have to just accept we'll be sharing. You're not gonna be the only one who gets to stick it in a poor person."

I hit him that day. His dad called the school. The school called my dad. My dad threatened to yank me out of Spearcrest. But if I left Spearcrest I wouldn't just lose Sophie—I'd lose everything.

So I stayed in Spearcrest and made up with Luca. It came with a lot of power, everything I wanted in Spearcrest. But Luca hadn't lied about the sharing thing. From then on, every girl I ever tried to be with, any girl I ever dated, Luca always ended up getting his hands on at one point or another.

I made my peace with it. I didn't really care so long as he stayed away from Sophie.

And the more I distanced myself from Sophie, the more cruel I became towards her, the less interested Luca was. And being cruel to Sophie became so easy—she made it easy. With her combative glares, her prideful posture, her fucking prefect badge. Everything I used to like about her faded, she became someone so easy to hate.

But I never stopped wanting her for myself. And so everything I did was worth the sacrifice at the time. Because my hatred kept her in a cage, and in that cage nobody else could reach her. Not even Luca.

It had been worth it for the longest time.

But Sophie made it out of that cage. Right under my nose, she outgrew it. She became beautiful and self-assured, cool and confident. And while I was worrying about somebody in Spearcrest noticing her, somebody outside of Spearcrest—some normal, random guy with nothing to offer—swept her away. And now, we'll all be leaving Spearcrest in a few months, and after that, everything here will become meaningless. I'll have spent five years around Sophie without ever being able to get near her.

And it doesn't feel all that worth it anymore.

# 30

# VICTORY

## Sophie

THE WHOLE MONTH OF January feels like being hit by a freight truck over and over again. In between coursework piling up, preparing for the next volley of exams coming up in February and university application deadlines, there's not a second of the day I'm not spending either working or worrying about how much work I have left to do.

On Sunday, I get two unexpected texts: the first one is from Freddy.

**Freddy**: Hey, Sophie. Just a quick text to let you know we all miss you loads here at the Little Garden. Would love to meet for a coffee and a catch-up sometime, if you fancy it—and if you have time. I know how busy you must be at the moment, but maybe I can cheer you up—I know seeing you would definitely cheer me up x F

A flurry of emotions burst to life. I have to read through the text five times before I can take in its full meaning. I decide to give myself the afternoon to think about it and figure out a reply, but soon get the second text, this time from my mum.

It's summoning me off-campus for a small dinner tonight with her and dad.

My heart sinks when I read her text. We rarely see each other during term time, and my parents don't usually make exceptions to rules unless something's happened.

When the taxi drops me off outside a small restaurant in Fernwell, I half-expect my parents to be waiting inside with news that a relative has died. I enter the restaurant with my heart in my mouth, more nervous about seeing them than the bad news I'm anticipating.

I spot them straight away: Mum's dark eyes and Dad's worried face. They sit across from one another, not exchanging a word, Dad tapping his fingers against the white tablecloth, Mum sipping nervously on her white wine.

My heart drops like a crashing meteorite through my chest at the sight of them, leaving behind a crater of familiar emotions. Guilt, fear, anxiety.

"Hi Mum, hi Dad..."

They both stand up to hug me and I take a seat with them. Smooth jazz plays in the background, and the restaurant is lit softly and well-decorated, but the atmosphere is stifling. I breathe deeply, and can't seem to fill my lungs with air.

"Sophie—how are you, my love?" Mum says.

My eyes sting at the question. I'm not upset and she's not even really said anything, so why do I have the sudden urge to cry? But it's not like I'm going to be telling Mum and Dad about everything that's happened, so I swallow back the lump in my throat. "Um, fine, Mum. Just busy with schoolwork."

"I can imagine," Mum says.

My mind scrambles for reasons I've been summoned here. Did Mum and Dad end up finding out about my job or about me getting in trouble with Mr Shawcross? Did they hear I didn't do as well as last time in my Maths exam? Did they somehow find out I lied about Christmas and wasn't staying with Audrey?

"So," Dad says with painful awkwardness. "How're university applications going?"

My heartbeat falters. I squirm uncomfortably in my chair.

"They're fine. My form tutor said the applications are strong and my personal statement is perfect."

"Yes," Mum says with a smile. "I bumped into Theresa in the staff room, she was full of praise."

I gulp and wait.

"She was particularly impressed that you're applying to so many Ivy League universities."

There it is.

I wait.

"I hadn't realised you were applying to universities in America," Mum says, her voice airy. "I thought the plan was Oxbridge?"

"I've applied there, too," I mumble.

"Right, yes, well done, honey." Mum sips her wine and smiles again. "Are the Ivy Leagues in case you don't get in?"

I hesitate, licking my lips.

"You have to believe in yourself, Sophie." Dad says, patting my arm. "You're working so hard, all your teachers are telling us so. Neither of us can imagine you won't get into Oxbridge."

I know this is the time to tell them I want to go to Harvard, but for some reason, the words stay stuck in my throat, coagulating into a thick lump. No matter how much I try, I can't seem to spit it out.

"You are an ambitious girl, Sophie, you've always been." The fondness in Dad's smile somehow is worse than if he'd been angry. "There's nothing wrong with having ambitious backup plans. But university is expensive, even with student loans, *especially* in America. And a lot of your classmates will also be attending Oxford and Cambridge. You can't underestimate the power of having strong connections. I know you miss your old school sometimes, and I know Spearcrest hasn't always been easy for you, but remember, all its advantages are there for you to reach out and take."

He stops and they both look at me with expectant smiles, as if waiting for a response. So I force one out. "I know Spearcrest is a great opportunity."

The waitress arrives and takes our orders. After she walks away, Mum reaches across the table to touch my hand, which is fisted around my napkin. "We just want what's best for you, Sophie. You know this, don't you?"

My words are now a thick, glutinous lump in my throat. Words like: if you wanted what's best for me, you wouldn't have kept me trapped in this hellhole for all these years. If you wanted what's best for me, you wouldn't have forced me to endure bullying, mockery and insults all this time. If you wanted what's best for me, you'd actually ask me what *I* want for once.

But I don't say anything.

Ultimately, I know Mum and Dad mean what they say. They do want what's best for me. They have offered me an opportunity not many people like me get to have. They've always worked hard to make sure I'd be looked after and never have to worry.

It would be easier to say everything I want to say if they were worse parents. But they're not.

So I swallow everything back until I'm suffocating, until I can barely eat through the lump in my throat. When it's time to go home, I thank them, hug them, and leave with my words still stuck in my throat.

I wake up the next morning exhausted and shaky. I'm off my game for the rest of the day: I turn up too late to catch breakfast in the dining hall, I'm distracted in my Maths lesson and my free period is spent rereading the same few sentences of my book of critical theory on Austen. I arrive for my Literature class ten minutes early, so I lean back against the wooden panelling of the wall, letting my head fall back and wondering whether I could sleep standing if I just closed my eyes.

Before I can close my eyes, I catch a glimpse through the glass door of one of the other classrooms. I recognise Mr Houghton, gesturing passionately as he explains something to his students. Moving slowly and carefully so nobody notices me, I peer inside the classroom. It's definitely a Year 13 class; I recognise most of the students. It doesn't take me long to spot Evan.

He's easy to spot, with his bright hair shining like a beacon in the morning sunlight, but that's not the reason I notice him.

I notice him because every single student in the class is bent over their desks, diligently taking notes as Mr Houghton speaks. Every single student—apart from Evan.

His exercise book isn't even open, his copy of *Persuasion* sitting closed next to it. His elbows are propped against his desk and his chin rests on his fists. He's staring out of the window.

I watch, frozen in fury, as Mr Houghton says something that makes all the students bend forward to annotate their book. Evan, though, just sits completely still, staring out of the window. He doesn't even glance at Mr Houghton.

After all this, after everything... Why am I even shocked that Evan doesn't actually give a shit about Lit? It's not like I believed his blatant lies about wanting to improve. I knew he was lying then, so why am I so shocked now?

Seeing it with my actual eyes, how little he cares and how blatantly he lied to me, somehow brings everything into crystal clear focus for me.

All the work I've put in this year—all the time wasted on him just so he can do nothing at all. Evan is exactly what I always knew he was: a spoilt, selfish, deceitful arsehole with not a thought to spare for anyone or anything that isn't him.

A strange calm settles over me.

I sit calmly in my Lit class until the end, and then I calmly walk over to the other side of the building and knock on Miss Bailey's door. She calls me inside, and I sit down across from her. I tell her I can no longer tutor Evan, and that if there is no way out of tutoring him then I would like to resign from the academic mentoring programme.

Miss Bailey immediately goes into a state of panic.

"Oh, no, Sophie, there's no reason to quit!" she says, throwing up her hands. "I know you asked me to find somebody else for Evan, and I'm so sorry I didn't! I've been so busy—but that's no excuse, I know. No, there's absolutely no need to quit the programme."

She reaches for her glasses, which are resting next to a box of chocolate biscuits, and checks her computer. "Right, let's see what we can do."

I sit rigidly facing her. An icy sort of triumph fills me. I'm finally going to be free. After today, I never have to see Evan, speak to Evan or think about Evan ever again. It doesn't exactly solve all my problems, but it's exactly what I need: a symbolic victory against an untouchable foe.

"Right, well, Beatrice has just started tutoring Zachary Blackwood. He's on target to achieve his predicted grade but he wants to achieve top marks in Literature since he's applying to read Literature and Classics at Oxford. I suppose you could take Zachary and Beatrice could take Evan?"

I'm only swapping one Young King for another, but at this point, I'd take Luca Fletcher-Lowe, the devil himself, if it meant getting away from Evan.

"That's fine." I take a deep breath, trying to project assertion and determination. "I would like to start straight away, please."

Miss Bailey nods. "Well, Beatrice has been telling me she doesn't think she can help Zachary much since he's already doing pretty well, so I'm sure she won't mind. Alright, I'll let everyone know what's happening, hold on."

She makes a note in her planner then puts her pen down and looks up.

"Are you alright, Sophie?"

I nod and stand. "A lot better now, Miss Bailey, thank you."

"Did something happen between you and Evan?"

I smile. "Nothing I can't handle. And now that I'm done with him, I don't even have to worry about it."

"Right..." Miss Bailey says with a slight frown. "Well, if you ever need to talk, you know where to find me."

"Of course. See you later, Miss Bailey."

I leave, walking on air. I can't even remember the last time I felt this free and happy. To celebrate, I allow myself to actually have lunch instead of eating as I work. I fill my plate with food and go find the girls, who are sitting in the dining hall since it's too cold to hang out outside like we usually do. Araminta is in the middle of a story, and both Audrey and her jump when I appear in front of them with a bright grin.

"Oh my god, Sophie, you look insane!" Audrey exclaims. "Are you ok?"

"I'm in a good mood," I explain, taking a seat next to them and grabbing my knife and fork. "I'm in a *really* good mood."

"Your timing is good, too," Audrey says. "Guess who Araminta spoke to yesterday?"

Araminta stares at me with huge eyes and I stare back. She seems to be awaiting my guess. "I don't know... Mr Ambrose?"

"Mr Ambrose?" Araminta says, frowning. "Why on earth would you guess him?"

I shrug. "Make-up?"

Make-up is technically against the rules, although teachers are generally pretty lenient. Mr Ambrose, though, is a stickler for his school's rules, and Araminta doesn't know the definition of a natural look. Today, she's wearing purple eyeshadow, glitter under her eyes, and a sort of witchy violet lipstick. But she laughs and shakes her head.

"No, you idiot. Not Mr Ambrose."

"Think somebody in our year," Audrey says. "Somebody you feel strongly about."

"Evan," Audrey says to me, rolling her eyes.

I raise my fork in the air. "Let me stop you right there. I have literally just come back from Miss Bailey's office after officially resigning from tutoring him."

"What? Really?"

"As of today, I'm not wasting a single more minute of my life on him."

Araminta leans forward across the table, lowering her voice. "Do you not want to hear what he said to me?"

I shrug. "I imagine something either creepy or stupid. Either way, I could not give less of a fuck if you paid me to."

"You'd be surprised," Audrey says.

"You genuinely don't want to know?" Araminta asks, eyes wide.

I nod. "I genuinely don't. In fact, I would rather listen to you describe having sex with Luca Fletcher-Lowe in excruciating detail than talk about Evan for one more second."

Araminta lets out a peal of shocked laughter. "Don't be disgusting!"

"You did say you would have sex with him out of all the Young Kings," Audrey points out.

"Yeah, but not actually!" Araminta says with a grimace. "He's so creepy—I'm pretty sure he might be an actual psychopath. I heard a rumour he likes tying belts around girls' necks when he fucks them—that shit is far too advanced for me. Anyway, as if I even have the time right now."

"Yeah," Audrey agrees. "Back when they made the bet I don't think they realised how stressful and busy upper school would actually get. I saw three of the Young Kings in the study hall the other day, and they weren't even fucking about. They were genuinely working."

"It's those university applications," Araminta groans as she peels open a muffin. "I don't know about you guys, but they felt like a real wake-up call to me."

Talk turns to university applications. After this year, we might all be scattered across the world, and that unspoken fact hangs over the conversation like a dark cloud.

It reminds me I have other things to worry about than Evan—a lot of other things. And to my relief, I don't think about him for the rest of the day, I don't even think about him that night, and manage to sleep well for once. And I don't think about him in my classes the next day, and I don't think about him all the way until Friday afternoon.

Because on Friday afternoon, I'm sitting in the study hall working through a pile of Maths past papers when the door slams open. I jump, almost dropping my pen, and look up with a frown.

In the doorway is Evan. He's out of uniform, wearing his swim team sweatshirt and dark shorts. Despite that ridiculous outfit, his presence radiates light and heat, and the way he stares around the room is ferocious, almost intimidating.

His eyes find me, and he surges forward like a predator springing into a leap to chase its prey.

"Everyone out, now!" he roars.

His voice, deeper than I've ever heard it, sounds like a man's, not a boy's. It fills the cavernous space beneath the vaulted ceilings. Without question or complaint, everyone in the study hall grabs their books and bags and scrambles towards the door.

Then, there's just silence, and me, and Evan, facing each other across the bleak space of the study hall.

# 31

# DIRTY LIAR

## Evan

Sophie's hair is gathered back in a strict ponytail, and with her dark glasses and white school shirt, she looks like the poster girl for academic excellence. She looks sophisticated, elegant—beautiful. I'm devastated to realise that even though it's only been a few days, I've missed her.

But wanting Sophie and being angry at her are all mingled up, sending pure fire through my veins. Seeing her only whips my anger into a fervour. I cross the space between us in a few strides.

Before I can say anything, she glares up at me and exclaims, "You can't talk to people like that!"

"I can if I want to, and I just did," I retort. "What are you gonna do, report me for not minding my fucking manners?"

Her lips stretch into a smile that doesn't reach her eyes. "That's more your style, don't you think?"

"I've apologised for that, though! What more do you want?"

I'm standing in front of her, practically towering over her, and yet I still somehow feel completely helpless.

"I didn't want your apology then, and I don't want anything from you now," she says frostily. "So get out of my face and enjoy the rest of your life."

Her gaze slides off me as if she's dismissing me. She looks down at her exam paper as if her work is the only thing in the room. I reach down and snatch the paper from under her pen.

She looks up with a frown and a grimace. "What did you do that for?"

"I've not come here to be ignored!"

"Too fucking bad! I have work to do and you're an unwelcome, unneeded and undesired distraction."

She springs to her feet to grab the paper from my hand, but I yank my arm out of her reach. Now she's standing, her anger a mirror to mine.

"Give it back," she bites out.

"Why did you quit tutoring?"

The question spills out of me, uncontrollable. It's been eating away at me since I found out. It devoured me the whole time it took me to come here and confront her.

"You don't care about tutoring!" she explodes, her rough voice rougher the louder she gets. "You don't care about your grades at all, you don't care about anything but your stupid self and I'm sick and tired of wasting my time on you!"

"How is it a waste of time if I've been improving?"

"Doing decently in one exam doesn't mean you're improving—you're just too stupid to realise everyone just sucks up to you because they're scared of your parents!"

Heat rises in my cheeks. "Mr Houghton's never sucked up to me. I got those grades because you helped me, and I'm improving, and—"

"If you wanted to improve, you'd be pulling your finger out and actually doing some work for once!"

"I have, though! I've done all the work you set me!" I stare at her, my heart beating so fast I almost have to catch my breath. "I don't get where this is coming from?"

"Oh, you don't?"

She side-steps the desk, standing right in front of me, looking up at me with total disdain twisting her face.

"Could it be coming from the fact that you've been making my life hell all these years? Or could it possibly be because you force me to waste my time tutoring you while you spend all your lessons fucking about? Or, I don't know, could it be because you're a shit person and you cost me my fucking *job*?"

Now it's my turn to sneer at her. "Stop pretending that job was the be-all and end-all of your life, Sutton. You never even gave a shit about that job, I know you were just going there to flirt with that creep."

Sophie's face goes red so fast she looks like I've just slapped her across both cheeks. Her gaze falters. She takes a single step back, enough to tell me I struck true, enough to confirm all my suspicions.

Enough to make me hurt like shit.

"Freddy's not a creep," she says.

Freddy. His name, so common, so stupid, somehow makes him all the more real, like a deformed nightmare monster come to life.

My hatred for him bursts to life like a struck match.

"Hitting on an 18-year-old," I spit out. "That's exactly what I would call creepy."

Her eyes are wide and incredulous as she watches me. For a moment, she's completely speechless. Then her eyes narrow. She tilts her head, and her voice is soft and deadly when she speaks.

"*That*'s why you reported me? Because—what? Because you were *jealous*?"

I swallow hard. My face is hot—my chest is on fire. I'm not even embarrassed—Sophie is saying nothing more than the truth. I *am* fucking jealous, so jealous it hurts. And it almost feels good for her to finally acknowledge it, like scratching an unbearable itch I couldn't reach myself.

I step forward, covering the distance she ceded earlier. I draw closer to her, pulled into the gravitational field of her presence. The smell of her is intoxicating, flooding me with memories of her hot mouth against mine, her pretty pussy against my tongue and around my cock. Desire sears me, scorching my mind, burning away all the things I planned to say.

Instead, words burst out of my mouth, unbidden. "Why would you pick some fucking creep, some complete nobody, when you could have *me*?"

It's not at all what I had intended to say, but I can't even control the flow of words pouring from my mouth. Her eyes are wide with frank shock. I want so badly to touch her I have to clench my fists to stop myself from reaching for her. She's so tantalisingly close—she's always so fucking, so torturously close, and yet always out of reach.

Why? Why can't I just fucking have her?

"I don't *want* you," she snarls, answering both my questions, spoken and unspoken. The shock in her eyes fades, replaced by dark, cruel triumph. "Must be hard to swallow, huh? All the money and abs in the world—and I *still* don't want you."

I surge forward, finally allowing myself to touch her. Grabbing her by her waist, I pull her against me.

"Liar." I take her face roughly in my hand, tilt it back. She stares up at me, unafraid. Something wild and burning is in her eyes. Her lips part wetly, as if she's expecting me to kiss her. "You *dirty* fucking liar."

Instead of kissing her, I tilt her head back further, exposing her neck, and I sink my teeth into the pale flesh. A rasp tears from her lips and her body arches against mine, sending a bolt of brutal arousal through me. Her fingers curl against my arms, digging into my muscles as she holds on tight to me. *Me*.

"You fucking want me," I growl against her neck, pushing her roughly down onto a desk. I grind my hips into hers, my hard cock craving the heat of her. "You can lie until the day you fucking die, but your body doesn't lie. You want me."

She makes no reply. Her eyes are hooded as she stares up at me. Leaning on her elbows, she relaxes back against the desk, as though this is *boring* to her. I wrap my fingers around her throat. I don't even want to hurt her, I just want her to feel something—anything. "Say it, Sutton."

Her lips curl with scorn. "I fucking *despise* you."

My cock hardens painfully at her words. I know she does—I'm beginning to suspect her hate for me might be the only reason she has for fucking me.

So I squeeze her neck, and her smile widens. I shove her skirt back. She's not wearing tights today, just thigh-high black socks, plain as they come, and plain black boxers. But the ribbon of exposed flesh between her boxers and her socks is enough to make me painfully hard.

She doesn't stop me when I slip my hand inside her boxers, and I quickly find out why. My fingers find the silken folds of her pussy; they are slippery with wetness. Savage triumph flares through me. She might hate me all she likes, but her body can't lie the way she can.

I roughly pull her boxers off her. I want to fuck her so desperately I can hardly breathe. More than fucking her, I want to claim her, to pleasure her. I want her to know I'm the only one who could ever make her feel this way.

So I slide my fingers against her wet pussy, caressing her until she's squirming against my hand. I smirk at her. "Do you despise this, too?"

She glares at me as I trace the line of her pussy to where her clit is, rubbing my thumb over the tiny spot. Her hips buck and a tiny gasp of surprise springs from her mouth. She bites down on her lip, but I keep touching her, building a slow, steady rhythm.

Suddenly, she reaches up, covering my face with her hand.

Dark anger and raw pleasure burn through me: she wants to come, but she doesn't want to look at me. Because Sophie loves lying to herself so much, she probably wants to pretend it's not me doing this to her.

"No." I push her hand away and pin her back against the desk with my hand pressed to her chest. She grabs my arm with both hands but she's not strong enough to push me off. I keep the pressure on even while I caress her clit, my gaze fixed on hers. "You can despise me all you like, Sutton, but you're going to fucking *look* at me. You're wet because it's *me* doing this to you. You're going to come because *I'm* the one touching you. Not some fucking random guy, not some nobody you think you like. *Me*."

She must be close to orgasm, because her hips have stopped twitching and she's grown very still, her entire body trembling, her eyes wide and glassy. Lowering myself against her, I pick up her hips, lifting her delicious pussy to my mouth.

"Come on, Sutton. Hate my guts and come for me."

I flatten my tongue against her, tasting her, teasing her. Her hips roll against me, sensual, demanding, irresistible. So I kiss my way up her pussy, and stroke her clit with my tongue, slow at first, just to torment her. Her breath hitches, her thighs quiver around me. I sense how close she is to coming. It's utterly tantalising—the only time I ever have Sophie truly within my power.

This power—the power of keeping her suspended on the edge of an orgasm, the power of making her come so hard she crumbles into a trembling mess—is like a fucking drug. I can't get enough of it. I pick up the pace, stroking faster. It only takes a few laps of my tongue to send her crashing into her orgasm.

A hoarse cry tears from her lips and she bucks against me, her fingers curling in my hair. She grinds herself against my mouth, her trembling thighs squeezing my head. Then she slumps back down limply. She's shaking all over, but she immediately shoves herself off the desk.

Her cheeks are crimson, and her tidy ponytail is dishevelled, dark strands sliding loose. She throws me a look that's a mixture between shame and fury, and immediately begins to straighten his uniform.

"This doesn't mean anything," she says, her voice low and harsh. "We're both old enough to know that sex has nothing to do with emotion."

My heart is beating wildly—the taste of her is still on my tongue, which is blurring the clarity of thought I need right now. In the end, the only thing I can say is the truth. The painful, horrible truth.

"Don't you know how much I like you?" My voice is barely above a whisper. "You're all I fucking think about, all the time. I'd do anything you asked, Sophie, if only you..." I stop to brush my hand back through my hair. It's damp with sweat. "If you were with me, you could have anything you wanted."

"Right, I could have anything I wanted," Sophie rasps, and her voice is much quieter now, and her eyes are sparkling almost like she's about to cry, "up until the point you decide to move on and throw me aside like I'm nothing."

I recoil. "I would never do that!"

"You fucking idiot!" she exclaims. She sounds furious, but tears are hanging like crystal pearls on her eyelashes. "You *did* do that!"

This stops me in my tracks. I drop her gaze because seeing her eyes full of tears again hurts like shit.

"That was different."

"Sure," she sneers, wiping her sleeve angrily across her face. "I'm sure you genuinely believe that."

How can I tell her the truth? That I loved being friends with her, but that I had to choose between our friendship or Spearcrest? That I chose to keep Luca away from her over protecting her? That everything I've done so far has been a misguided attempt to keep her safe from him?

That even when I hated her, I still only ever wanted her?

In the end, between Sophie being happy and having Sophie to myself, I chose the latter. There's no way I can explain any of this to her without sounding pathetic, and she already despises me enough.

She thinks I'm selfish and stupid and a liar—and some of those things are true—but she doesn't need to realise every stupid choice I made was calculated to make her mine. Because ultimately, every choice I've made has only pushed her away.

Even making her come only seems to make her hate me more.

"I'm not going to beg you to be mine," I say finally. "Not when I could have any girl I wanted."

Hearing myself say this is like watching myself jump off a cliff into a shark-infested ocean. I watch myself hurtle to my doom without even being able to stop, knowing full well my pride, and not my brain, has just taken charge.

She smiles. Even before she can grab her stuff off her desk I can tell she's done with the conversation.

"Then do exactly that," she says, quite calmly, her rough voice like nails scratching along my skin, sending shivers down my back. "Have *every* girl you want, Evan. Enjoy yourself. And while you're doing that, I'm going to spend time with someone I actually like, who actually likes me, and doesn't try to hurt me at every chance he gets."

She shoulders her backpack and then tries to barge past me, but I stop her, grabbing her arm.

"He'll never make you feel the way I do," I say in a low growl.

"No, you're right." She shakes her arm free from my grasp. The flush of her orgasm is still colouring her cheeks and neck, but her eyes are cold. "He'll make me feel so much better."

And then she leaves, slamming the study hall door loudly behind her.

## 32

# GREEK TRAGEDY

### Sophie

A STRANGE SENSE OF finality settles over me after my fight with Evan, like something between us is now irremediably broken. I don't quite know why I feel this way, because things are no more broken than they have always been.

The added dimension of sex—or whatever happened in the study hall—might be the reason behind my heightened emotions. Arguing with Evan and making out with him both leave me with the same sense of mingled victory and loss.

Is that what sex always feels like? Like winning pleasure at the cost of losing a part of yourself?

That night, even though I try really hard not to, I cry myself to sleep.

The following day, I finally respond to Freddy's text. I had forgotten about it until my argument with Evan, and guilt overwhelms me after I text him. But he texts back almost immediately, and we arrange to meet for dinner at the weekend.

The implication of meeting him for dinner is not lost on me. Instead of anticipation, all I feel is guilt. Would I have remembered to text Freddy back if I hadn't been reminded of him by Evan's unexpected outburst of jealousy? Would I have agreed to meet him if it wasn't to prove to myself I don't want Evan?

Am I just using Freddy as a weapon in my war against Evan?

I don't want to beat Evan by becoming just like him. Someone selfish and self-serving, who uses others to get what they want and dismiss them as soon as they're done.

Still, as I get ready to meet Freddy, I can't shake the guilt clinging to my skin like a parasite. I wear a plain black dress, boots and red lipstick, but I don't go overboard. The more effort I make, the more it's going to feel like a date, and the more this feels like a date, the more nervous I'll be.

No, this isn't a date. This is me giving myself a chance to experience being with someone who doesn't make me feel like shit, someone who is actually nice to me. Someone who doesn't play games or treat emotions like chess pieces.

The air is icy and crisp when I arrive in Fernwell, and I spot Freddy as soon as I enter the restaurant. True to form, he's on time and waiting for me at the front of the restaurant. He's wearing jeans, a thick jumper and a woolly coat. His dark hair is ruffled by the wind, his cheeks and nose are red from the cold. I rush over to him and he greets me with open arms and a wide smile.

His hug is warm and comforting, and he leads me into the restaurant with a friendly arm around my shoulders. It's lovely—like being with the girls. I shake the thought away.

"How's the Little Garden?" I ask as we sit at our table. I expected to be nervous, but Freddy's presence is so calm and warm I can't help but feel comfortable.

"It's a little chaotic, I must admit." Freddy grins. "With you gone and Jess focusing on her studies, it's pretty much me riding solo at the moment."

"I'm sure the old ladies of Fernwell don't mind."

Freddy laughs. "No, I'm sure they don't. I just don't know that there's enough of me to go around."

"Mm... so many old ladies, so little time."

"Right!" Freddy chuckles then shakes his head. "I mean I'm definitely the consolation prize, because they keep asking about you. Seems you made quite an impression on them."

I'm sure he's saying this to be nice, because those old ladies worship the ground he walks on. And as we sit and eat and chat and laugh together, it's so easy to see why. Freddy is everything one would want in a person: well-spoken, compassionate, friendly. Nothing he ever says feels forced, strategic or calculated.

But the more time passes, the more restless I become.

Because I'm not blind, or deluded, or naive. Freddy is warm and comforting like a warm cup of tea—but a cup of tea has never set my heart racing, or made my blood pump through my veins, and made me so painfully turned on I would have done anything for it.

Everything about Freddy is the opposite of Evan.

Where Freddy is a safe harbour, Evan is a dangerous storm. Where Freddy makes me feel like nothing bad could happen to me, Evan makes me feel like I'm constantly on the verge of having to fight for my life. Where Freddy makes me feel soft and comforted, Evan makes every part of my body pulse with adrenaline, with tension, with anticipation.

Am I broken? Am I so used to the insane pressure and pain of battling Evan Knight I can no longer get excited by kindness and affection? Everything I've done with Evan has been reckless—every time we touch feels perilous, precarious, volatile. Handling him is like cupping gunpowder in your bare hands while you're on fire.

I remember his words the last time I saw him. "He'll never make you feel the way I do." I had been so desperate to prove him wrong.

But meeting with Freddy only did the complete opposite.

After dinner, Freddy walks me all the way to the bus stop. We walk shoulder to shoulder, talking about exams, trading study tips, discussing the books we've read this year, a new exhibition at the National Gallery he wants to check out. When we get to the bus stop, he hugs me again and I swallow nervously, wondering if he expects something more, wondering what I'm going to do if he tries something.

But Freddy breaks the hug and says, "I've had a great evening. I'm honestly so glad I got to see you, Sophe. I was a little worried about you."

I shrug and smile. "Don't worry about me. I'm tough—you know that."

"Mm, yes, that's true." He tilts his head. "But even tough girls deserve to be cared for and looked after sometimes."

Freddy looks past my exterior and sees somebody he wants to protect and care for.

What does Evan see when he looks past my exterior?

Someone he wants to challenge, battle, conquer?

I laugh and give Freddy's arm a little smack. "Whoa, your parents really raised a gentleman, huh?"

He laughs. "What can I say." He hesitates, takes a deep breath, then speaks quickly. "You know, Sophe, I had a great time tonight and I... well, I like you, I'm sure that's not a massively shocking surprise because you're literally gorgeous and must have guys embarrass themselves trying to ask you out all the time, but... well, I like you, so would you like to go on a date, sometime—not just dinner, but a proper date?"

My heart sinks.

Anger and sadness rise inside of me. Anger at myself for being so broken I'm about to turn down the first guy to have properly asked me out. And sadness, sadness for Freddy, but also for myself, for being so caught up in the storm of Evan to even want the safe harbour of Freddy.

"I'm really sorry, Freddy, I don't want to give you false hopes or mess you around." I hesitate, because I *did* mess him around a little. "But I don't think we should go on a date. I..." I don't want to lie to Freddy, but I can't exactly tell him the truth, because I hardly even know what the truth is. "I need to focus on my studies right now, and I'll be leaving Spearcrest soon, so... um..."

He raises a hand and smiles. "You don't have to explain yourself to me, Sophe. A simple no is fair enough. You're too good for me anyway!" He laughs and shoves his hands in his pockets with a tiny shrug. "Well, I'm not going to inflict any more awkwardness on either of us, so I'm going to head home. You're going to be alright?"

I nod, thankful for his understanding, his patience, his compassion. "Yes, my bus should be here soon."

"Good. But also, are you going to be alright, in general?"

It's a complex question. I don't know the answer.

"I hope so," I say.

"Me too," he answers. "I'm always around if you ever want to chat or vent. Take care, Sophe, alright?"

"You too."

He waves, and walks away. I watch him until he disappears around the street corner. I let out a long, shuddering sigh when he does, unsure whether I am devastated or relieved.

Luckily, the weekend is over and there isn't much time for melancholy or introspection. There are exams to prepare for, coursework to complete, and plenty of extracurriculars to keep me busy.

And if I thought tutoring Zachary Blackwood instead of Evan was going to be easier, that only winds up true in the way there isn't any tension between Zachary and me, but only in that way.

On our first session, he's there first, bent over a book. We're meeting in an empty English classroom, and his organisation is enough to rival mine: his notes are filed away in a folder, grouped and tabbed by texts, then characters, themes and context. His notebook is full of notes and essays, the mark schemes stapled to the last pages.

After I've taken my seat next to him I have a look through his stuff, and then I put everything down.

"How on earth do you need tutoring?" I ask. "You seem to be on top of everything."

Zachary shrugs. "Lit is the only subject I'm not getting full marks for."

"I mean..." I raise my eyebrows at him. "Do you *have* to get full marks?"

Zachary observes me in silence for a moment. It's crazy how different from Evan he looks: slim, dark, almost aristocratic. His uniform is impeccable, and his black curls are cropped short, exposing a tall forehead and intelligent honey-brown eyes. Even the way he speaks is different, his posh, clipped British accent a stark contrast to Evan's soft American lilt.

"Do you know Theodora Dorokhova?" he asks.

I nod. "Of course. Head girl."

Theodora is more than just head girl: since I arrived at Spearcrest, she's always topped every grade ranking in every subject. Where I need to work hard to achieve my grades, Theodora doesn't just work hard—she has this insane natural intelligence that's just impressive to witness. Anytime she falls short of being number one for grades in the year or in a specific subject, she doesn't rest until she gets there.

I admire that about her, but could never dream of a friendship with Theodora. Amongst the elite of Spearcrest, she's in the stratosphere, a Young Queen in her own right. Her parents are descended from both British and Russian nobility and probably own more land than the queen of England.

Theodora is the kind of rich and posh even other Spearcrest kids are in awe of.

"What about her?"

Zachary sighs. "She's getting full marks in all her essays in Lit."

"Right?"

I stare at him.

"It's just a point of honour," Zachary says with dignity. "Every class we've ever shared we've tied in. We're tying in Mr Ambrose's programme. But now she's beating me in English."

"Oh."

I stare at him. He seems almost too mature and old-beyond-his-years for this kind of rivalry, but I can tell he's not joking. And I can sort of understand why you'd want to go toe-to-toe with Theodora—Zachary certainly seems like he would enjoy the challenge.

"Alright, " I say, "well, I'll do my best to help you. I've only ever got full marks in one essay, so I'll bring a copy of that next time, but for now, I'd say we should focus on critical theory for the Austen unit. Are you doing *Persuasion* too?"

Zachary picks up his copy of *Persuasion* and hands it to me. I flip through it to see highlighted passages, tabs and exquisitely handwritten notes in the margins.

"Alright, this is a good start. Should we start by swapping notes? I might have some stuff you don't and vice versa."

Zachary nods and we swap copies, both opening our notebooks. We work in silence: like me, Zachary doesn't seem much interested in making conversation and we only talk to clarify points. At the end of the two hours, Zachary is the first to close his books and stand.

"That was helpful," he says solemnly. "Thank you."

"Right, you're welcome. See you Thursday."

He gives a nod, grabs his stuff and leaves. I marvel at his stark professionalism and earnest solemnity. Why can't every student here be like that? It's easy to forget he's one of the so-called Young Kings when his behaviour is so mature and polite.

Instead of following him out of the classroom, I fold my arms on the table and rest my head on my forearms. How did Beatrice get on with Evan? Did he let her teach him, or did he distract her with his big blue eyes and flirty smile? That sounds like something he would do.

And didn't I tell him he was welcome to all the girls he wanted? I'm sure he doesn't need my encouragement to do that.

But instead of thinking about Evan and Beatrice, my mind ventures into muddy, murky territory, straight into the memory of Evan's vivid blue eyes and intense look while he worked me with his fingers. The aggression and hunger in his voice. His face between my legs, his lips gleaming with the wetness from my own orgasm.

His hoarse voice when he said, "*You're all I fucking think about, all the time.*"

After all the lies Evan has spoken over the years, this didn't sound like one. It sounded like the raw, painful truth. Even thinking about it now, it makes my heart beat faster and heat rises in my cheeks and chest.

Would anybody else ever make me feel the way he does? Would anybody else ever turn me on as intensely, as devastatingly as he can? What if my curse is that even though I hate Evan with every fibre of my being, he is also the only person who can make me feel the way he does?

That sounds like the sort of Greek tragedy stuff that would happen to me.

I shake my head vigorously and stand up.

I need to get a grip. To distract myself, I go for a swim. Except that when I get to the pool, it, too, is full of memories of Evan. Evan's crooked grin in the bluish lights, Evan's wicked laughter when he pulled me into the water, Evan pinning me to him by my waist, his hard muscles rippling against me.

I dive into the cold water, trying to shock the memories out of my head. I swim fast laps, hoping I can somehow outswim those stupid memories. My breath burns in my lungs as I force myself to keep going.

By the time I emerge from the pool, my eyes are aching with chlorine, my heart is hammering and my muscles are trembling, but I feel much better. Until I get to the diving board I've left my towel on. Because when I pick up the towel I grabbed randomly from my wardrobe, I spot the letters EAK monogrammed in gold in the corner.

I stare at the towel for a moment and then bury my face in it with a long sigh of despair.

## 33

# PERSUASION

### Evan

Wednesday morning, I track Zachary down in the corner of the library where he tends to spend his free periods nowadays. It's snowing pretty heavily outside, and I stomp my feet at the entrance and brush the snow off my shoulders before going in. Even though I don't spend much time in the Spearcrest library, it is practically hallowed ground here, and I know better than to track snow everywhere.

Inside, everything is warm and brown and gold, the silence undisturbed and the air rich with the smell of paper and leather.

Zachary is in his usual spot at a desk hidden amongst bookshelves, and I pull a chair to sit next to him. He doesn't look up from the essay he's calmly typing into his laptop.

"Well?" I prompt him.

"Well, what?" he asks, raising an eyebrow but not looking away from his essay.

"Well, what happened yesterday?"

Zachary stops typing. "What do you mean?"

"You know what I mean, you jackass. Tutoring. Bea told me that she was tutoring you before she swapped with Sophie."

"Yes," Zachary nods. "It went well, thank you."

I glare at him. He ignores me, so I shove my face against his so that he can see my frown from up close.

"What do you want, exactly?" Zachary says, pushing my face away from his with one hand. "Do you want a minute-by-minute breakdown of everything that happened during our session?"

I nod eagerly. "That would be a great start!"

"Well, we met in E30, I was reading some critical theory essays of Jane Austen, you know, the anthology you've never touched?"

I roll my eyes at him and he continues. "Then Sophie came in, she sat down. I told her about my academic goals in regard to English Literature. We swapped copies of *Persuasion* to share notes, then exchanged our critical theory notes based on the reading we'd done. We did this for two hours. At the end of the two hours, I thanked her and left."

"And then?"

"And then, what? Then I went to eat supper, went back to my room, did some more work and went to sleep. I wore my bespoke blue pyjamas that you always make fun of."

"I don't care about any of that!"

"Then don't ask!"

We glare at each other. But Zachary isn't stupid, he knows what I want to know. He's just choosing to be obtuse, probably because my torment amuses him. My stare turns into a glare.

"What did Sophie say about me?"

Zachary shakes his head. "Nothing at all. She didn't mention you once."

"What! What did *you* say?"

"About you?"

"Yeah!"

"We met so that she could tutor me for English Literature, not to discuss the long and complex history between you two."

I'm almost speechless from the shock of this betrayal. "You didn't mention me?"

"Was I supposed to?"

"You're—argh! Zach! Those tutoring sessions are meant to be *mine*!"

Zachary shrugs. "Is it my fault you made her quit?"

"I didn't—" I start defending myself then stop since it's not entirely wrong that I made Sophie quit. "Alright, I messed up, but now she's tutoring you, I thought you could—why don't you—"

"What is it you want me to do, exactly?"

"I don't know, help me! Be my wingman or whatever."

"How so?"

I throw my hands up in a helpless gesture. "Fuck, I don't know! Just try to explain to her she made a mistake, that I do care about my tutoring and that—and that—"

"Let me make one thing clear: my priority in those sessions is the actual tutoring. Your pitiful love dealings are very much secondary to my goals."

"You don't even need tutoring!" I glare at him. "I swear you're one of the best students in the class."

"I'm not *the* best, though," Zachary says, looking away with a sniff.

My eyes narrow as I draw closer, peering at him. "Is this about Theodora?"

Zachary clears his throat and flushes ever so slightly. On a normal person, it would be barely noticeable, but since Zachary is about as emotionless and unshakeable as a robot made from titanium, it becomes immediately obvious this subject matter is of great embarrassment to him.

"Oh God—so because of your weird obsession with Theodora you get to keep Sophie to yourself and not even help me get her back?"

"Evan," Zachary says, completely deadpan, "she's tutoring me in English, not getting married to me."

"I know." I drop my head into my hands. "But at least it's an excuse to see her. I don't even have that anymore, and we're more than halfway through the year! I'm running out of fucking time."

Zachary hesitates then relents. "Why don't you drop me off at the next session before you go to yours?"

I raise my head. "And then what?"

"And then... I don't know. Just say something nice to her, and then leave. Like this, you get to see her, and she still gets the space she clearly needs from you."

I tap my chin, thinking about his proposal. "It's actually not a bad idea. Maybe I do need to give her space. She did tell me to stay out of her life."

"Oh, she did?"

I groan. "Ugh, she did. And I told her I liked her."

Zachary's eyebrows shoot up. "You did?"

"Yeah."

"She told you to get out of her life and so you decided to tell her you like her?"

"No, the opposite."

"You said you like her and then she told you to get out of her life?" Zachary pulls a face. "That's cold, even for her."

"Well, no. I said I like her, and then I said I could have any girl. Then she said: good, have every girl you want and stay out of my life."

Zachary rubs his face with a long-suffering sigh. "Why are you like this?"

"If you were there, you'd understand! It was so fucking stressful. I basically completely opened myself up to her and put my cards on the table and then she looked down at my cards and tossed them right off the table! She told me she despises me. She didn't even address the fact I like her, as if my feelings don't count because I'm me. What was I going to do, beg?"

"Beg is certainly what you'll end up having to do if you keep fucking things up this spectacularly."

"I'm not going to beg," I snap, glaring at Zachary.

He smirks. "You weren't going to apologise either, remember?"

"Apologising and begging are two completely different things."

"Right. Well, time will tell, won't it?"

I keep glaring at him but he doesn't seem too bothered. He turns back to his laptop with a dismissive flap of his hand. "Now get out of here, Ev. I've got work to do. Be on time tomorrow if you still want to drop me off at my tutoring session."

"Alright, alright. I'll text you."

He gives a curt nod, and I leave. I'm too wound up to go back to my room, and it's snowing too thickly to go for a run, so I end up going to the gym. But even the gym can't distract me from the pressure of tomorrow's meeting, and I end up spending the rest of the evening thinking about what to say to Sophie when I see her.

And that's particularly challenging to do when all I can think about is kissing her and fucking her against a window while it snows outside.

# Sophie

For my next session with Zachary, I turn up fifteen minutes early. Since he arrived first at our last session, it's a point of pride for me to be there first this time.

I settle myself in the empty classroom, a paper cup of coffee nestled in my hands, my copy of *Persuasion* propped against my pencil case. The door opens a few minutes later, and Zach strolls in with long, crisp steps. In his wake, hands in his pockets and hair flopping so low it's a wonder he can see where he's going, is Evan Knight.

I look away immediately, but his presence glows from the corner of my vision like a flare. It's heightened by the memory of our last encounter.

Evan was definitely easier to ignore before I found out how good he is with his stupid mouth.

"Uh, hi, Sutton." His sheepish drawl interrupts my thoughts.

I'm reluctant to appear shaken in front of Zachary. I certainly don't want to give him the satisfaction of witnessing any drama between Evan and me—especially after the embarrassing scene in the rec room.

"Hi, Evan."

"I'm just dropping Zach off," he explains uselessly.

I glance at Zachary, whose expression is completely blank as he unpacks his bag.

"That's very kind of you," I say, trying my best not to sound too sarcastic.

How he thinks we're going to be exchanging pleasantries after what happened during our last meeting is beyond me.

"I wanted to say thanks for all the tutoring so far," he says, his voice both airy and a little strangled. "You were honestly a really good teacher and pretty much the only person to ever make Shakespeare sound interesting."

I stare at him, blinking slowly. His blue eyes are fixed on mine, and there is a dark pink flush smeared all over his cheeks. He's not smiling—he looks totally honest. It's not hard for lies to sprout out of Evan like water from a fountain, but he doesn't sound at all like he's lying.

And he's embarrassing himself in front of another Young Kings, which is probably a risky move.

Maybe this is a clever gambit: he's taking a loss now for a later victory I can't quite see yet. But no matter how little I trust what he's saying, it's still pretty good to hear—and that's the real danger when it comes to Evan.

No matter how much we hate each other, he can always figure out ways of making me feel good.

"No need to thank me," I respond with as much formality as I can muster. "I'm glad I could help."

"Zach is lucky to have you. If anybody can help him beat Theodora, it's definitely you."

Zachary finally reacts, throwing a quick glare Evan's way.

I shrug. "Um, I'll do my best."

I try to keep my answer noncommittal; I don't want to give Zach promises I can't guarantee. He seems the vindictive kind, and I'm not looking to be hearing from the Blackwood lawyers anytime soon.

"Well, I better go to my own session," Evan says, running his hand through his distracting mop of sandy hair. "I'm going to make sure your time wasn't wasted, okay? I'll do everything I can to pass Lit."

He gives me this unnecessarily intense look, like there's fire in his eyes and he's trying to burn me with it. Not sure of what to say, I can only nod.

He sighs, long and deep and tragic, and leaves.

I turn back to Zachary, who is shaking his head with an expression of disbelief on his face. His mouth opens, but words don't come out. He shrugs, straightens his tie, and looks at me.

"Right, shall we do some essay work today?"

Thank god Zachary is so business-like, because this strange interaction with Evan has completely turned my mind upside down, exposing the very raw, very insistent memories of our kisses and my orgasms and our arguments, and I desperately need the distraction.

"So," I explain, "I annotated our exam questions with the suggestions from the mark schemes and examiners' reports. I was thinking you could have a go at planning your responses and then comparing with the exam board suggestions?"

He nods curtly. "That sounds excellent. Let's get to it."

Once more, we settle into a mostly silent session. Zachary writes up his essay plans in meticulous, spidery handwriting while I read. After that, we do some timed essay practice, reducing our time every round to force ourselves to write faster. Near the end of the session, we swap our work to critique it, take notes, and then it's time to go.

Zachary packs away with very little ceremony and then gets up.

"Thank you for today. That was very helpful."

He sounds like he means it and I can't help but feel proud. I nod. "You're welcome."

"Shall we do another Austen session next Tuesday and then switch to poetry on Thursday?" he asks.

"Yes, sounds good. I'll prep some stuff over the weekend."

"Alright. Have a good rest of the week."

"You too."

Zachary strides out exactly as he came in, with long, crisp steps. It's funny how easy it is to forget he is a Young King; he couldn't be more different to the rest of them. He works hard, cares about his grades, and doesn't seem to be all that interested in popularity.

Of course, he could be coming across this way because it's me he's spending this time with, and it's not exactly like I hold the key to popularity at Spearcrest.

But of course, this is me just overthinking things as usual. I have plenty of things to worry about without wasting my time thinking about the Young Kings, especially when the Young Kings are little more than a childish fantasy that's going to fade into thin air the moment we leave Spearcrest.

And soon, there isn't time to worry about anything much at all.

February sets in, brutally cold, depressingly dark. It snows pretty much non-stop, and with the second wave of mock exams rising high as it prepares to crash down upon us, we're all feeling the mounting pressure. The library is always full, even when I end up staying there until late at night, and even the austere study hall is fuller than usual.

"You think this is hard, and it is," our Maths teacher says one afternoon after hitting us with an impromptu pre-mock mock exam. "But half of you here are Oxbridge candidates, and I can guarantee you that no matter how stressed you are right now, it's nothing compared to what you'll go through next year."

It's a chilling reminder, and something that stays with me long after he says it, but it barely helps. I'm so tired I fall asleep every other night without even realising, fully clothed at my desk, and wake up in the morning with a gasp of shock thinking it's still two in the morning. I barely look in the mirror anymore because I know I look like a zombie.

Luckily, almost everyone in our year looks half-undead too.

Almost everyone.

Ever since he dropped Zachary off that time, Evan has been keeping up the strange new routine. Lingering by the doorway to give me long, insistent looks, asking me how I am and bringing me cups of coffee.

It's awkward, and maybe I'm going slightly mad from exhaustion, but after a while, it becomes almost endearing. Until I realise that he doesn't have a hint of a shadow under his eyes, his skin is completely clear and smooth and instead of losing weight like half the students in our year group, he seems to be filling out with new muscles every time I see him.

On the Thursday of the week before the mock exams, Evan is standing in the doorway, as usual, eating an apple as shiny and healthy-looking as he is. I stare at him in baffled shock, not hearing a thing he's saying.

"Do you even know we have mocks next week?" I burst out, more out of sheer bafflement than anger.

He blinks. "Yeah? I have five exams next week, starting Monday. You?"

"Five, too." I narrow my eyes. "You're not worried about your exams?"

He brushes his hand through his hair in that distracted, distracting way and gives a slightly embarrassed smile. "I'm mostly worried about Lit, for obvious reasons." Then he checks his watch and sighs deeply. "Ugh, talking of which. I should probably go to my session."

But he lingers in the doorway, his eyes fixed on mine. His blue eyes send the memory of his face between my legs like a war flashback through my mind.

"I wanted to say..." Evan's voice is soft and low. "I wanted to say that I... that you..." he looks at Zachary, then at me. He gulps, shakes his head and then smiles. "I wanted to say good luck with the exams."

"Oh, um, good luck to you too."

He nods and then leaves, his presence lingering after he's gone like the last caress of heat after the sun goes down.

"He *is* worried."

Zachary's voice surprises me. I turn to look at him. "Pardon?"

"He *is* worried. About exams. Especially Lit, like he said. He's been coming with me to the library every evening to revise."

"I don't understand how anybody at this point of the school year can look like him," I say, completely truthfully. "He looks the exact opposite of how I feel."

"That's just how he is," Zachary says with a sigh. "Must be some strong genetics at play there. But just because he looks like this doesn't mean he's not stressed and worried and sad like the rest of us mere mortals."

I stare at Zachary. He's not looking at me; he's unpacking his books and folders, laying them neatly in front of me.

His words remind me of Evan in his big house during the Christmas holiday, ambling around in his undecorated house, bored and aimless and alone. It sends an uncomfortable twinge of something guilt-like through me.

I drop my gaze to the cover of my notebook and mumble, "I didn't think he cared about Lit."

Zachary laughs, cold and mirthless. "Well, he wants to do well in the exams, but it's not exactly Lit he cares about, is it?"

"What do you mean?"

Zachary looks up at me, raises an eyebrow, and then sits back in his chair, crossing his arms.

"It's you, okay? It's you he cares about, it's you he's stressed and worried and sad about. It's always been you. He's liked you for the longest time, pretty much never stopped. Even when he was dating other girls, it was always you he was thinking and talking about. It was quite irksome, actually."

I'm almost numb with shock and disturbed by hearing this come out of Zachary's mouth, of all people. My words coagulate on my tongue, thick like tar. In the end, I can't say anything other than, "What?"

Zachary shrugs. "I don't even know if he knows it, but he's liked you since you guys were friends."

"He never said anything," I say, my voice so low it's almost a whisper.

"Well, no. You're rather intimidating, as far as girls go, and I'm pretty sure he was too thick back then to realise he liked you. He's worked hard ever since to get over you, as I'm sure you've noticed. But I suppose it was always a matter of time until his obsession won out."

I'm too shocked to say anything, and Zachary gives me a level look and adds, "Still, none of this makes up for the way he treated you, so you're right to reject him. It's just been annoying me that you didn't know. But now you know, and we can move on."

I nod, absent-mindedly taking the essay he hands me.

And even though we spend the next two hours working, when I leave the session it's not Austen and literary analysis my mind is full of.

## 34

# INTERCEPTION

## Sophie

NEAR THE END OF March, Zachary and I agree to cancel our sessions for a couple of weeks since we both have mock exams, so I'm a little surprised when he walks up to me outside the exam hall after our Lit exam.

"Is this your last exam?" he asks.

We've never really had a proper conversation outside the context of our tutoring sessions. I answer with a slight frown. "No, I have Maths tomorrow."

He nods. "No exams Friday, then?"

"No."

"There's a post-exam party on Thursday night in the old building behind the Arboretum. Everyone's going before we break up for half-term. You should come."

I stare at him.

"And bring Audrey and Araminta," he adds.

He's about to walk away when I point out, perhaps a little belatedly, the obvious issue at hand. "I'm a prefect, Zachary."

He smiles courteously. "Then you'll be in good company. All the other prefects are also coming, the head boy and head girl too."

And then he walks away. I stare after him for a few minutes, completely taken aback. This is technically speaking the second time this year I've been invited to a party, by a Young King no less.

I shoulder my backpack and go to my next class, and don't think about the invitation again until the next day. I'm sitting in the common room, eating a slice of buttered toast while rereading my list of equations and formulas for the hundredth time. The sky outside is still dark, and all the lamps are on in the common room, making the morning feel like the evening.

Audrey plops down next to me on the couch, startling me. "So? Are we going to the party tomorrow?"

"What party?" I ask absent-mindedly.

"The post-exam party. Come on, it's right after the mocks, just before our week off, and all the prefects are going, so it's not like you're going to get in trouble. We've never been to a single party together—I wasn't even there for the last one. But you had fun, right? Please come."

I stare at her with a mouth full of toast. I swallow and take a deep sip of coffee. Then I finally admit, "Last party was fun but mistakes were made."

Audrey rolls her eyes and laughs. "That's on you, though. Just come with me and the girls, we'll have a drink and chat and relax and dance a little. Then, when we feel too tired or bored, we'll head back to the dorms. Simple as that. No mistakes need to be made this time."

I nod slowly. "I'll think about it."

Audrey springs forward to hug me with a noise of triumph. "Yes! I'm so excited! Do you have something to wear?"

It's pretty obvious that, as far as she's concerned, I'm going to the party. I give her an unimpressed look, but she responds by widening her delighted smile.

"Do you?"

"...I have a dress."

"Is it cute?"

I shrug. "It's cute enough. I'll ask Araminta to do my make-up."

"Can I curl your hair?"

"You can try, but the curls will never keep."

"Alright, alright, I'll see what I can do. I can't believe we're going to a party together, I'm genuinely so excited. It's like we're going on a first date!"

Her excitement is contagious, and I can't help but laugh. "Are we going to make out and everything?"

She sighs. "I miss Axel so much, I very much might."

"I thought you two met up over Christmas holidays?"

"That was almost three months ago, Sophie!"

I smirk at her. "He must have been pretty good if he's got you in your feelings this soon."

She leans closer, her mouth almost touching my cheek. "Let's just say he's a skilled linguist, and I don't just mean because he can speak several languages."

I shove her face away. "You disgust me."

She stands up and grabs her bag from the side table she left it on. "Good luck not thinking about that during your Maths exam!"

"You perv!" I call after her.

She turns to blow me a kiss and then disappears out of the door. Her shameless words tug at my mind later during the Maths exam. Tragically, the intrusive thoughts don't revolve around Axel and Audrey's amorous adventures. Instead, my mind is stuck remembering how skilled a linguist Evan unfortunately is.

That's definitely not a thought I need to be having right now—not in the middle of a Maths exam. So I throw the thought firmly out of my head and bury myself in the comforting difficulty of trigonometry and kinetics.

## Evan

I GET BACK TO my room after swim practice to find Leo gone and Zachary sitting in the chair by the window, thumbing through my newly-annotated copy of *Persuasion*. He's wearing black jeans and a black turtleneck sweater—his most festive outfit. I unwrap my towel from around my neck and throw it on the back of my desk chair, then glare at Zachary.

"I'm not going to that stupid party."

He doesn't look up from the book. "Why not?"

"Because—because I'm not in the mood. Those exams were stressful as fuck."

"You don't say," he murmurs, peering closer at a page in my book. "You misspelt the word naval."

"Navel?"

"No, *naval*, as in naval officer, as in the navy. Doubt Captain Wentworth made his fortune inspecting belly buttons."

I roll my eyes and grab my book out of his hand to shove it under my pillow. "Shouldn't you be at the party glaring at Theodora from afar or something?"

He smiles. "Shouldn't *you* be at the party, acting excruciatingly awkward towards Sophie?"

My mind flashes an image of the peace garden party, Sophie's hand fisting in my T-shirt, her disdainful gaze, our first kiss. I sigh. "As if Sophie would be caught dead at another party."

"Well," Zachary says, standing with a sigh. "Thought you might prefer to catch her alive, but whatever. If you're not coming then I'll be off."

I grab his arm as he tries to go past me, and shove my face in his. "Are you saying she's going to be there?"

"I can tell you're not interested," Zachary says, shoving my face away from his. "I'll see myself out."

"How is that possible? Sophie probably—Sophie doesn't even like parties."

"Because you've invited her to so many parties, right?"

I glare at Zachary, but he stares back steadily. "As if she'd ever say yes to me."

"I don't blame her, to be honest," Zachary says, glancing down at his nails. "You're annoyingly whiny. Still, I'll tell her you say hi."

He shakes my hand off his arm and walks over to the door.

"Wait!" I shout, yanking off my loose T-shirt.

Zachary leans against the doorway, watching me dispassionately as I stumble around the room, kicking off my shorts, yanking clothes out from the back of my drawers, splashing cologne on. When I'm done dressing I stand to peer into the small square mirror by the door.

"Should I brush my hair?"

"You can, but I'm leaving regardless."

"Alright, fine! I'll leave it. Fuck me, I'm nervous. Do I look good?"

"You look like you committed a crime and you're terrified of getting caught."

"You mean nervous? I look nervous because I am!"

"You're rich and good-looking—what's there to be nervous about?"

I can tell Zachary doesn't mean that, but I still shake my head in melancholy. "If only that was enough."

The party is in the old building behind the Arboretum, an old red brick building with long, narrow windows. It used to be an indoor botanical garden of sorts, but was replaced by the newer, more glamorous Greenhouse.

When we arrive, the party is well underway, music blaring and the room bright with ever-changing colours. Pink and blue, orange and green, purple and yellow. Strings of Christmas lights dangle around the windows, filling my mind with soft flashbacks of Christmas Eve.

Zachary and I walk over to the trestle tables on which the booze is stacked. I grab two beers and hand one to Zachary, but he shakes his head with a grimace.

"Isn't there some good wine somewhere?" he asks snootily, peering at the bottles.

"Uh... champ?"

"Pass me the bottle."

Bottles in hand, we amble around the room, both sweeping the room with our eyes. I can tell the exact moment when Zachary spots Theodora because his stance stiffens and his body language somehow becomes ten times more arrogant and aloof.

"Wanna go say hello?" I call out over the blaring music.

"I won't give her the satisfaction. She can come and say hello first."

"You two are so weird."

I don't hear his reply, because my eyes finally fall on Sophie.

She's standing by a window, framed by rainbow drops of light, talking to Araminta from my Biology class. She looks... well, she looks incredible, of course. She's wearing a black dress with a white lace collar, black fishnet tights and boots. Her hair is tied in a simple ponytail and the only accessory she has is the dark red lipstick she's wearing, making her mouth look the colour of crushed cherries.

There's something edgy about the whole outfit, a sort of grunge-goth glamour that's completely at odds with her usual crisp uniform and collection of big grandpa sweaters. But all I can think about is kissing that crushed cherries mouth, ripping through those fishnets and wrapping that long ponytail around my hand.

I'm walking towards her before I even realise I am. Luckily, Zachary catches me by the arm and pulls me behind the cover of a pillar.

"What's your plan?"

I blink at him. "Plan? What plan?"

"Exactly. Shouldn't you have a plan?"

"What kind of plan?"

"I don't know. What are you going to say to her?"

I stare at Zachary and take a deep sip of beer, thinking hard. "Probably I'm gonna say hi."

"Right. And then?"

"I don't know."

"What do you want from her? What's the intended outcome here?"

I peer around the pillar, at Sophie's soft, heavy hair, at her long legs in the fishnet tights, her crimson mouth. I want her so bad I can barely formulate a coherent thought.

I turn back to Zachary and yell, a little too loud over the music, "I wanna dance with her. I wanna hold her and kiss her. And I wanna touch her legs through her tights. I want to go down on her and make her come."

Zachary's face twists into a grimace. "That's too much information, Ev."

I shrug. "You asked."

"I meant realistically. *Realistically*, what is the intended outcome?"

"Realistically, I'd settle for her not hating me for five seconds."

Zachary nods. "Alright, so you know what you have to do, then."

"Obviously I don't. I never do, with Sophie."

"You could start with the obvious. You know: be nice? Be polite? Don't say or do anything rude or mean?"

"Obviously."

"If it was that obvious then you wouldn't have made her lose her job then humiliated her in front of everyone she hates."

I choke on the sip of beer I'm halfway through swallowing. "Zach!"

He shrugs without so much as a hint of contrition. "I'm not lying, am I?"

"No, you're not, but fuck me, man, you're not exactly filling me with confidence either."

"I'll tell you who doesn't need confidence," Zachary says, glancing around the pillar. "Percival Bainbridge."

"What do you mean?"

I poke my head around the pillar to follow Zachary's gaze.

He's right. Percival Bainbridge doesn't need confidence. He's walked right up to Araminta and Sophie and handed them drinks in blue plastic cups. To my surprise, Sophie takes her cup with a smile. All three of them tap their cups together before drinking.

Percy isn't someone I know well, but he's a decent enough guy. His family are landed gentry in the UK, not filthy rich but not poor by any means. Although Percy isn't the most handsome guy in the year group by far, he makes up for his plain looks with a great track record and some impressive sporting achievements under his belt.

He's the kind of guy who would never harm a fly, but right now he might be a serial baby killer for all I hate him. I watch him, speechless with a mixture of shock and envy, as he talks to Sophie and Araminta with seemingly complete ease.

He says something to Sophie and winks at her, and she laughs. Not a smirk, not a mocking snigger. Actual laughter.

Percy and Sophie are about the same height, and with her dark hair and his short crop of light blond hair, they look like a picture-perfect social media couple.

I glare at Zachary. "How on earth does Percy know Sophie?"

"They're both prefects. Looks like you missed your chance."

More prefects are walking up to Sophie and Araminta and Percy, and the group of them stand there, chatting and drinking.

"Come on," Zachary says, grabbing my arm. "You can try speaking to her later."

He drags me away and we end up joining Iakov and Séverin and some guys from the rugby team. Iakov is drinking straight vodka, which means he's looking to get obliterated. Sev is doing a one-person roast of the outfit Anaïs, his fiancée has chosen to wear at this party, which gives him an excuse to keep staring at her.

We play some drinking games. As I drink, the alcohol makes me both more relaxed and less able to resist the urge to go back to Sophie. I'm stumbling tipsily on my way to get some more drinks when I spot her again. This time, she's standing with Audrey, dancing while they sing along to the song. Audrey's arm is around Sophie's waist, and Sophie's arm is around Audrey's neck. They are dancing cheek-to-cheek, clearly both as tipsy as I feel.

My steps slow to a stop.

The easy intimacy between Sophie and her friends, the shameless affection they openly display, is hypnotic. Araminta dances through the crowd, wraps herself around Audrey and Sophie. They dance together and laugh. Araminta raises her phone for a selfie, her and Audrey sandwiching Sophie's face with kisses as they pose.

They laugh and break apart as the song ends, then they stand to talk. Audrey plays with the silky length of Sophie's ponytail as Araminta shows everyone the pictures she's just taken.

The whole scene, in the pink and purple lights, is surreal, like a waking dream. A terrible sadness falls on me like a weight.

I could have been this close to Sophie.

I could have been dancing with her, holding her by her waist, posing for photos with my cheek against her cheek, lacing my fingers through hers. I could have been receiving her smiles, making her laugh. Her friendship, her affection, her love, is a treasure I once held and tossed carelessly away.

For a social pariah, Sophie never seems to lack company. I can't find a moment to catch her alone. Then I get distracted trying to break up a spat between Theodora and Zachary, who are going for each other's throats like a wealthy couple in a bitter and vicious divorce.

I walk Zachary to an open window so he can catch some fresh air. I'm on my way to go find some water for him when I'm intercepted by Luca.

The last time I saw him was that night in London, but the less time I spend with him the more I realise how much happier I am away from him. He's wearing tailored black pants and a crisp white shirt, his outrageous Rolex shining on his wrist. His bone-pale hair is slicked back, making him look like some storybook villain.

At his side is my ex, Giselle, flushed from too much drink and dressed head to toe in white. I'm surprised to see them together. Luca's already been there with her—he had to, since I dated her first—and it's not like him to spend time with girls he's already had.

"Where are you off to in such a hurry, Evan?" Luca asks in his lazy drawl. "Looking for someone?"

I narrow my eyes at him. Before I can say anything, Giselle jumps in with all the grace of a brick.

"Probably Sophie Sutton, as always. You'd think you'd get over her after finally ticking her off your list." She gives a dramatic sigh and shakes her head at me. "Poor girl sex must be like crack to you."

My stomach churns and my hands clench into fists. Giselle was always a bit annoyed with the special attention I paid Sophie, no matter how cruel and vicious it was. We broke up over it, and I can't believe she's still not over it. No, actually I *can* believe it.

"I suppose poor girls need to put in a lot more effort since they have literally nothing but their cunts to offer," Luca pipes in, his grin shark-like, his eyes cold. "I'm starting to understand this fascination of yours, Evan. Who knows, I might give it a try myself." Bile burns in my throat. I slowly shake my head at Luca, hoping he'll heed my silent warning. But his grin widens. "Isn't Sophie applying to the Ivy Leagues? That's costly business. I bet if I offer to pay for her university tuition, she'd let me do anything to her. Get my father to name a bursary after her and I bet she'd even let me fuck her up the arse."

My vision goes blood-red. My thoughts go dark, the light blown out in my brain. The next thing I know I'm on the floor stradling Luca, smashing my fist over and over again in his smug face.

"You vile, disgusting piece of shit. You're never going to speak about Sophie this way ever again. I don't care how much fucking money your shady fucking father has, I will fucking break every bone in your body if I ever hear her name in your mouth again."

Luca is pretty strong, and far more athletic than he looks. I know for a fact he's a fencing champion. But he's no match for my strength—he doesn't even bother throwing up his arms. He takes my punches and I don't stop until my fist is slick with his blood, until his face is purple mush.

When I'm done, I grab him by his shirt. The snowy fabric is stained with blood. His chest rises and falls quickly. His breathing is a wet wheeze.

Pulling his face to mine, I speak low and clear. "I'm only going to say this once so listen well. Stay the *fuck* away from Sophie."

I throw him away from me and stand. My entire body is shaking. My forehead is slick with sweat. A circle of shocked onlookers have formed around us. I spot the other Young Kings. Zach and Sev's eyes are wide with shock. Iakov's expression is blank, almost bored. He's still sipping his vodka.

Not a single one of them made a move to help Luca while I beat him up.

None of them move to help him as I walk away.

# 35

# FISHNETS

## Sophie

EVAN'S STRIDE IS LONG and quick as he rushes out of the old Botanical Studies building and through the Arboretum. I'm not drunk, I'm a little light-headed as I rush after him. Luckily, the ice-cold air slaps against my face, clearing the fog of alcohol from my mind.

I catch up with him and grab his elbow. He whirls around. His eyes go wide.

Moonlight filters down through the thick canopy of evergreens, dim but pale enough for me to make out his face. His cheeks are flushed, blood splattered across his chin, lips and cheeks. He's breathing hard. His hands are still clenched into fists.

"Are you alright?" he asks, his voice a little hoarse.

I've never seen him like this. Evan always projects this sense that everything washes over him, that everything is just one great joke and he's in on it. But he doesn't look like he's laughing now.

"Are *you*?" I ask.

I grab his arms and lift them to get a better look at his hands. They're caked with blood. His knuckles are a mess of cuts and bruises.

"Look at you." I shake my head at him. "You know the skull is stronger than the bones in your hands, right?"

He rolls his eyes. "Yeah, yeah. Hard on soft, soft on hard." He glances down at his hands with a wince. "It's not my fault I've grown up on action movies and superhero flicks."

"Not Arthurian legends and chivalric romances?"

He frowns. "I don't even know what that is. You know I'm stupid."

I shrug. "Knights in shining armour and damsels in distress."

The moonlight isn't strong enough that I can fully make out the spectrum of emotions on his face. But even in the darkness, I can tell he's not smiling with his usual carefree arrogance.

"I would hardly describe you as a damsel in distress," he murmurs.

"Really? Then why did you beat up Luca's face?"

He's silent for a moment. "Did you hear what he said?"

I shake my head. "No. But everybody heard you yelling at him to—" I put on a fake scream "—*never speak about me like this ever again!*"

"Right." He licks his lips and winces, probably at the taste of Luca's blood. "Well, I wasn't beating up Luca's face to save you. I was beating Luca's face because it was long due a beating."

"Right." I gesture at his hands. "Well, even if you didn't fight for my honour, I suppose I should still help you with this. Put my first aid training to good use."

I lead him away through the trees. He follows me, asking, "Does that make *me* the damsel in distress, then?"

"Maybe. Just try not to swoon into my arms."

"I make no promises."

I take him to the small Spearcrest infirmary. The doors are open even out of hours because the nurse's office and the cabinets are all kept locked, but there's a first aid kit there, and a sink for Evan to wash his hands in. The emergency light is on near the door, a low silver glow, giving the room a ghostly atmosphere.

After forcing him to wash his hands and splashing disinfectant on the cuts, Evan sits on one of the clean white beds and I drag a chair over to sit in front of him. The cuts on his knuckles are disgusting and still seeping blood, but Evan doesn't say anything as I dab disinfecting wipes over them.

His face is a little pale in the low light, and one of his knees bounces up and down, but those are the only indications of his discomfort.

Once I've made sure all the cuts have been properly disinfected, I dress them. Evan winces slightly as I start wrapping the bandages around his hand.

"How did your Lit exam go?" I ask.

"Trust you to be thinking about that right now," he says with a low, scratchy laugh. "Hopefully alright. I answered all the questions. I even filled out the entire answer booklet."

"That's a lot of writing," I say, securing the bandage with some clips.

"Yeah, my hands were killing me by the end."

"Those hands?" I say, taking his wrists and lifting his hands. "You mean those big, strong, manly, athletic hands?"

"Haha, you're so—" His voice catches. He's quiet for a second, then he speaks low and soft. "I've missed you."

My heartbeat stutters, sudden heat pluming in my chest. It's probably the disarming mix of the drinks I had earlier and the intimacy of tending his injuries. I busy myself tidying everything away and say over my shoulder, "Come on, you literally see me all the time."

"But it's not the same." He sighs. "It's not like it was, before, you know... Before everything. Before Christmas. I miss being around you. Spending time with you. In a nice way, not in an angry way."

I put the first aid box away and return to the bed, sitting down next to Evan. "Well, I *was* angry at you."

He turns his head to look at me. There's no smirk on his face, no amused glint in his eyes. Just raw, exposed emotions, bloody and messy as the cuts on his knuckles.

"I was angry at you, too," he says.

We're shoulder-to-shoulder. The heat from his body flows into mine.

"But I didn't do anything wrong," I say softly.

Either Evan is more drunk than he seems, or his system is still pumping with adrenaline. Words come tumbling out of his mouth, seemingly without passing through a single filter on the way out.

"I wasn't angry because you did something wrong. I know you didn't do anything wrong. I was angry because I saw you with that guy from your job and I was jealous because you like him instead of me. And I know that's not fair because of—well, everything—but it made me feel like shit that you like someone else when all I want is for you to like me."

I swallow hard. I don't want to feel sorry for Evan—he doesn't need my pity. But the truth coming from his lips is unexpected and more painful than I anticipated.

I turn away, looking down at my legs, picking at my tights.

"You want everybody to like you," I point out, voice low.

It's half a joke, half the truth—mostly designed to break some of the unbearable tension. Tension that's built between us while I bandaged his hand, tension that's been building since we had sex by the assembly hall, and when we kissed in his house and in the peace garden.

Tension that's been building for years, and started that day he turned his back on me, on our friendship.

Evan lifts his bandaged hand to my cheek. I turn my head to look at him so he doesn't hurt himself, but his fingers trail to my jaw and stay there. His hair, wet with sweat, curls on his forehead, falling over one eye. His gaze is direct and piercing.

"I want *you* to like me," he says, low but firm. "I want *you*."

He pauses. I don't know what to say. I close the space between us, pressing my mouth to his. His lips fall open like flowers unfurling for the sun. A low sound, hunger and want, rumbles in his throat. I brush my tongue against his, letting the heat from his mouth trickle into mine.

This kiss is long and slow and deep, the warmth of our breaths mingling. His fingers are still on my jaw.

I pull away to catch a breath. "Evan."

My voice is so rough it almost breaks. Evan's eyes widen as I speak, a mixture of fear and desire flashing across his face. He stops my mouth with another kiss and I sigh against his lips and kiss him back, incapable of denying him.

My fingers curl into the folds of his shirt while he holds my head gently in his hands, his fingertips tickling the hair at the back of my head. His mouth tastes of alcohol and blood.

I pull away to catch my breath but Evan can't seem to stop. He kisses the corner of my mouth, my burning cheeks, my jaw. I tilt my head back, and shudder as his lips trail burning kisses along the column of my neck, the stretched tendons, the fluttering pulse.

Nestled into the crook of my neck, he speaks quietly. "I like you, Sophie. I like you so fucking much."

I lick my lips nervously and try to push him away. "Evan..."

"No." He shakes his head and touches a finger to my lips. "Don't, Sophie. There's nothing to misunderstand or misinterpret. I like you, I've always liked you, no matter how unforgivably I've acted. I like everything about you. Your frown, your hair, your gorgeous fucking eyes and your voice and your mind. I like your sharp tongue and your mean streak. I fucking like you so much my chest feels like it's going to explode. I even like it when you hurt me, because I'd rather be hurt by you than adored by anybody else."

I stare at him, eyes wide, mouth wordlessly open.

"And I know that I fucked up, Sophie, and you get to hate me if you want to—I understand why you would. I've been a shitty person, I've done shitty things because I was desperate and stupid and didn't grow a backbone when I should have. And you can hate me for all that—I hate me for it too. But you don't get to ignore how I feel or pretend you don't know. You know, now. You don't get to explain away my feelings or analyse me like your Hamlet or Captain Wentworth. I'm a real human being—sometimes not a great one—with real feelings. And I like you, really a fucking lot. I want to take you on dates, I want to go to parties with you and be the one who gets your drinks. I want to kiss you and I want to fuck you face to face, and I want you to say my name when you come. I don't want to be your practice run at having a stupid American boyfriend. I want to *be* your actual stupid American boyfriend."

My cheeks grow hot at his words. Not just my cheeks, my body, too. He leans over and kisses my mouth, a slow, soft kiss, lips closed. Then he lies back on the bed with a sigh of exhaustion. I stretch out next to him and he turns towards me.

We face each other in silence for a moment.

"This evening isn't going at all the way I expected," I say.

He laughs softly. "No, me neither. I had very different plans for tonight."

"Like what? Getting shit-faced and taking bets on who would win in a fight between Theodora and Zachary?"

"Hah! I mean yes. But also plans to do with your tights."

He points at my legs. I frown, glancing down at them. "My tights?"

"Yeah. I'm a little obsessed with them."

"You are?" I roll onto my back and stick up a leg. "So you like my tights, huh?"

"Mm, yeah..." His voice becomes low and rough. "I really fucking like them. I wanna touch your legs through them."

"Yeah?" I turn my head. "What else?"

He moves closer, and leans over me to answer against my ear. "I wanna lick your pretty pussy through them. I wanna rip a hole in them and fuck you nice and slow."

I squeeze my thighs over the trickle of hot wetness pulsing there. I bite my lip and laugh. "Who knew you were so hard for fishnets?"

Evan's mouth moves slowly against my jaw. "It's not the fishnets I'm hard for, Sophie."

Then his mouth is on mine, wet and hot. His uninjured arm traces down my hip and over my leg. His fingers tangle through the fishnet, his nails scratch at the sensitive skin of my thighs. I suppress a shudder and curl my arms around his neck, pulling him closer.

His kisses move from my mouth to my neck. There's no biting this time, only playful nips and lingering kisses. He takes the hem of my skirt and pulls it up. I'm wearing plain black underwear underneath my fishnet tights, but based on his reaction, I might as well have been wearing the most erotic lingerie.

He bunches my dress around my waist and trails kisses over the plain of my stomach. Shudders ripple through me, the muscles of my stomach twitching under his lips. He lets out a low laugh against the skin of my belly. He slides down, kissing my hips and thighs through my tights until I'm gasping and shivering underneath him, until I'm writhing with impatience.

But there's no sense of urgency to anything he does. He closes his mouth on my inner thigh and sucks lightly, sending a shock of arousal through me.

"Come on, Evan," I finally bite out.

He looks up through his golden curls. They're almost silver in the dim emergency light. With a slow smile, he shows me his injured hand, cocking an eyebrow. I take the hint. Scrambling to pull on the waistbands of my tights and boxers, I drag them off me, kicking them away from me.

But he doesn't do anything. He gazes at me, hands slowly tracing up my leg, fingers feather-light. I shift my hips restlessly, troubled by the intensity of his gaze.

"I'm not going to beg," I say finally, glaring at him.

"Are you sure?"

He's grinning, but he settles himself between my legs. I think this might be my favourite sight in the world: that drop-dead gorgeous face framed by my thighs. The muscles in my legs and belly twitch with anticipation, but Evan is unhurried. He kisses my stomach, my hips, my thighs. He nips at the sensitive flesh and soothes it with his tongue. He kisses me until I'm lifting my hips off the bed without realising, my core tight and pulsing.

When he finally lowers his mouth on me I let out a shuddering sigh.

His soft lips and gentle tongue caress me, teasing me open like an unfurling flower. He licks me slowly, intently, as though he's exploring me, tasting me. Every nerve in my body is exposed and alive with electricity. I'm both shaking uncontrollably and holding myself completely still, as if I'm suspended on a tightrope of pleasure.

He pauses, looking up at me.

Meeting his gaze when I'm this vulnerable and exposed, this raw with want, when his lips shine with my wetness, is almost unbearable. I reach down to cover his eyes, to block out his gaze, but he pushes my hand away gently.

"Let me look at you." His voice is low and rough. "You're so fucking hot, Sophie. I could come just looking at you. Fuck."

He closes his mouth on my clit, kissing it, flicking it with his tongue. I gasp and quickly cover my mouth, but Evan reaches for my hand, pulls it away.

"No. I wanna hear you." He speaks against me, his voice vibrating through me. "I wanna hear every moan, every cry."

I'm hot with embarrassment and pleasure. In spite of everything we've done before, it's never felt like this. It's never felt this real, this intimate. Everything he says brings me closer to the edge.

But he's relentless.

He builds a slow, torturous rhythm with his tongue. Then there's a push, and his fingers slide inside me. I tighten around him, a whimper escaping my lips. My senses are overwhelmed—I'm not even trying to stop my hips from writhing, seeking more, wanting more, needing more.

Evan's tongue becomes firmer, faster. The rhythm builds, the pleasure heightened by the sensation of his fingers inside me. My back arches off the bed, the tightrope of pleasure shudders, trembles. I feel myself fall, I open my mouth in a silent scream.

I come so hard my vision goes dark. My hips buck uncontrollably against Evan's mouth as I ride out my orgasm against his tongue. I pulse uncontrollably around his fingers. My thighs are shaking, out of control.

When I slump back onto the bed, I look up to see Evan wiping his mouth with the back of his hand. An expression of feral hunger is in his eyes. He unbuckles his trousers, pulling out his impressive dick—the dick I hate and yet can't seem to get enough of.

He rubs the head of it against me. Coating it in my juices, he rubs it against my oversensitive clit, drawing a hoarse cry out of me. He smiles at the sound, a cruel smirk. "You like that, Sutton? Does it feel good?"

I glare at him. His cock in his fist, he slides it down my wet pussy, pressing against my entrance. "Or is this what you want?"

He waits, tilts his head.

"Answer me."

"Yes," I choke out. "I want it."

He tilts his head. "What do you want?"

"I want you. I want... I want your cock inside me. *Please*."

With a low, hungry growl, he thrusts inside me. My back arches off the bed as I claw the blanket.

He fucks me exactly as he described before: in long, slow, torturous strokes. He watches his cock slowly move in and out of me and bites his lip, stifling a groan of satisfaction. Then he looks up. Our eyes meet, and an unspeakable expression melts on his features. Pleasure, want, and something terrible and beautiful, too close to love for comfort.

I try to turn away, but he growls, "No."

He's so deep inside me I can barely breathe, and just like that, he pulls closer to me, cradling me in his arms. He kisses my cheeks, my jaw, my lips.

"Look at me, Sophie."

I look at him. My face is burning, my mind foggy with pleasure. A distant siren seems to be ringing, alerting me to the danger I'm in. The danger of giving in to Evan, of believing the expression on his face, of letting him completely in.

His eyes are vividly blue when I meet his gaze. I lick my lips nervously.

"Say my name."

I swallow hard. "Evan."

He hardens inside me. He moves his hips, fucking me in long, slow strokes.

"Fuck," he mutters. "Say it again."

"Evan." It's almost a relief to be saying his name. Evan—the boy I've loved, the boy I've hated. Evan, the only person to have ever made me feel this way. Evan, undeniable, irresistible, inevitable. I wrap my arms around his shoulders, tangle my fingers in his hair. "Evan."

"God, fuck." His thrusts grow more frantic, less controlled. "Fuck, Sophie, I l—"

I close his mouth with a kiss, brushing his tongue with mine. I arch against him, taking all of him. Wrapped in the heat of him, the smell of him, my senses are filled with him, overwhelmed. He fills every empty part of me until I'm full—complete.

Emotion wells up inside me—inexplicably, my eyes burn with sudden tears.

Burying my head in the crook of Evan's neck, I pull him closer to me. I whisper his name one more time, my voice muffled by his skin. His arms tighten around me and his hips buck. He comes with a broken cry. For a moment, his thrusts are frantic, desperate.

Then they slow, then he grows still.

We hold each other in the silver light, the rushing sound of our pants mingling in the air. We are holding on to each other so tight our pulses seem to beat as one. We stay like this for a long time, saying nothing at all.

Later, Evan gets up and cleans me up with a towel soaked in warm water. Then he gets back on the bed and pulls me into his arms, and just holds me. His breath flutters strands of hair against my temple, tickling me. Sleep darkens the edges of my consciousness, pulling at me.

A whispered question reaches me through my torpor. "Do you still hate me?"

"Mm. Of course. I hate everything about you."

"Everything? Even my good looks?"

"*Especially* your good looks." I suppress a yawn. "I hate your stupid blue eyes, your stupid smile. I hate how American you are, I hate the way you speak, the way you laugh at everything. I hate your confidence, your stubbornness, your golden boy energy. I hate everything you do."

He lets out a low laugh. "Even the things I do to you?"

"*Especially* the things you do to me."

"Does that mean I need to stop?"

"No." I nestle closer into him. We're going to have to leave the infirmary soon, but I don't want the moment to end just yet. "You have to keep going. Otherwise how am I going to keep hating them?"

# SPRING

"Love is my sin and thy dear virtue hate,
Hate of my sin, grounded on sinful loving."

Sonnet CXLII, William Shakespeare

# 36

# PARALYSIS

## Sophie

My Harvard acceptance letter comes the following morning. I'm barely recovered from everything that happened at the party and after it, I've not even discussed any of it with the girls yet. Then the letter comes. It fills me with such a sickening mixture of elation and anxiety I don't eat for the rest of the day.

That evening, Audrey, Araminta and I meet for a much-needed debrief in Araminta's room.

Every flat surface is covered with bottles of perfume, face mists, skincare products and boxes full of make-up. Her bed is strewn with clothes and books so we settle on the cream carpet flooring, sharing Araminta's impressive collection of decorative cushions.

"Right," Araminta says, clapping her hands together. She's in tiny silk pyjamas and looking radiant. "I know we all want to discuss what happened at the party, but—" She pulls an envelope out from behind her. "Look what I got today!"

Audrey covers her mouth with her hands. "No!"

"Yes!" Araminta hands her the letter with a flourish. "I'm studying Neuroscience at Harvard, baby!"

Audrey lets out a giddy cry. I crawl over to Araminta to wrap my arms around her. Audrey joins in, wrapping herself around us.

"You did it! You actually did it!" Audrey squeals.

"I did it!" Araminta lets out a muffled giggle. "I fucking did it!"

They finally let go and we all stand apart, staring at Araminta, grinning like idiots. Audrey takes the letter and looks at it, shaking her head slowly. "Fuck. It's really starting to feel real, isn't it?"

"Yeah." Araminta sits back down on the bed. "Spearcrest is almost over. It's actually sinking in now."

"Things are going to be so different," Audrey says softly.

"We'll still see each other all the time," I reassure her, hoping it'll be true.

Audrey nods. "I hope so."

"Well, hopefully I get to see Sophie a lot," Araminta says, widening her eyes at me. "Maybe you'll hear from Harvard next week now they're sending out admission letters?"

I bite my lip, trying to suppress a smile. "I got my letter today too."

Araminta's mouth drops open.

"What?" Audrey says, sitting up. "You did? And?"

"And Araminta and I will probably get to see each other a lot, yes."

"Get the fuck out of here!" Araminta screeches, and launches herself at me. "You got accepted?"

I barely get to nod before it's my turn to be swallowed into a multi-layered embrace by the girls.

"Aw," Audrey whispers against my hair. "I'm so jealous of you two! I want to go to Harvard too, for fuck's sake."

After the news of our acceptance letters settle, our conversation turns back to the party. Turns out Evan's fight with

Luca is just one of a few that went down. A lot seems to have happened after I left. By the sounds of it, people were either fighting or hooking up or both.

"Which one were you doing, Minty?" I ask, raising an eyebrow at her.

"Hooking up, of course. With a prefect, no less!"

"A prefect?" I ask. "Check you out! Which one?"

"Percy Bainbridge."

"Percy Bainbridge?" Audrey says. "He's not your usual type."

"No, but..." Araminta smirks. "I came..." She pauses, and then lifts two fingers. "Twice!"

"Well, at least one of us got some action," Audrey says with a pout.

Before I can say anything, Araminta shakes her head. "No. Sophie got some action too, I reckon."

"What?" I blink at her. "How could you possibly know this?"

"You have that good dick glow going on," Araminta says with a wave of her hand.

"Did you and Evan sort your shit out, then?" Audrey asks, raising her eyebrows at me.

"Why would you think it was him?"

She rolls her eyes. "Who else is it going to be? You two are obsessed with each other."

"I wouldn't say obsessed," I say.

"I don't know, *he*'s definitely a bit obsessed," Araminta says.

I nod slowly, and then say, "He told me he likes me."

"He did?" Audrey says with some surprise. "That's very forthright of him. Did he ask you out?"

"He said he wants to be my stupid American boyfriend."

"Stupid is right," Araminta smirks.

"Well, he's always wanted you, let's be honest." Audrey shakes her head. "At least he's realised now—bit fucking late. So what did you say?"

"Nothing."

"Do you want to go out with him? You two have always been so weird about each other. It has to be endgame, no?"

"We've not been weird, we..." I falter to a stop. How do I even begin to explain us? I sigh. "Look, I don't know. I don't even think I could explain how I feel. But it's the least of my problems right now." I say. It's only half a lie. "I don't have time to worry about anything apart from my exams now. And how to tell my parents about Harvard."

"Just tell them," Audrey says, her features softening. "They'll be proud of you, I know it."

I sigh. "They had their hearts set on Oxbridge."

"But you didn't."

I nod slowly. "I guess I'm just..." I swallow. "I guess I'm a little scared."

Audrey walks over to me and takes my hands in hers. "You don't have to be scared, Sophie. Your whole time at Spearcrest, you've never let anyone change you, or scare you out of being the person you're meant to be. Your parents want what's best for you, even if their way of showing it can be misguided. And even if they don't like it, then so what? You have nothing to be afraid of. You're in charge of your own life."

Audrey's words stay with me for a long time after that.

Fear has kept me paralysed for longer than I can remember: fear of getting in trouble, of disappointing my parents, of not living up to their expectations. Fear has haunted me every moment since I arrived at Spearcrest: fear of not fitting in, fear of mockery, fear of not being good enough.

Even now that I've secured an offer from Harvard, fear is still creeping at my heels like a shadow. Fear that this will all go wrong somehow, that everything will come crashing down on me.

But Audrey is right after all—right as always. There's nothing to be afraid of. There's nothing wrong with the truth, with being proud of my achievements and knowing what I want for my future.

I wait until the last day of the half-term to make the call. I'm going to be stuck at school over the holidays, and I don't want that dark cloud hanging over me.

So I do something that always makes my heart drop and my stomach clench: I dial my mum's number.

I don't even get time to brace myself because she picks up almost straight away.

"Sophie! Everything okay?"

"Yes, Mum. I'm just calling to update you on my university applications."

"Oh?"

"I got my first acceptance letter."

"Yes, I checked your application portal and saw. Congratulations, my love. Still, there's plenty of time for other offers to come in. Oxbridge typically send out their admissions letters in early March."

I hesitate. I should have known she'd snoop. I should have known she wouldn't make this easy. Well, time to rip the plaster off.

"Thanks, Mum. But I'll... I'll be going Harvard."

There's a long silence, during which I'm sure Mum is mouthing my revelation to Dad while he frowns at her questioningly.

"I know Harvard is world-class, lovely," she says finally with the careful tact of a politician. "But America is expensive—so expensive. And all the connections you made at Spearcrest..."

My heart is hammering and my palms are sweaty as I grip my phone. "I know, Mum, but some Spearcrest kids have also applied there, and think about all the connections I'll make at Harvard too."

"I know, love, but how will we possibly afford it?"

The lump in my throat makes it hard to speak, but I force my voice out. "Mum, you don't need to worry about it. I'm old enough now, it's my responsibility to worry about that. Even if I don't get any of the scholarships I applied for, I'll get a job over the summer. I'll stay on top of everything."

The silence that follows is so long I check my phone to make sure she hasn't hung up on me. But no, she's still there, quiet.

Then, in a small voice, she says, "It's just... think about everything we've worked for."

"Mum." My heart is beating so fast my pulse slams in my throat. "I know how important you think Spearcrest is. But you wanted me to come here, and I came here. You wanted me to make friends here, and I did. You wanted me to work hard and make the most of my opportunities here—and I did just that. I don't want to spend the rest of my life imitating Spearcrest kids, trying to be one of them. I don't want to be one of them—I want to be *me*. I want to pursue law, and Harvard has one of the best law schools in the world. I..." I swallow back the lump of emotion in my throat. "I appreciate everything you and Dad have ever done for me. I'll never not be grateful for that. But it's time for me to make my own choices now, and this is what I've chosen."

Another long silence follows, but for the first time, it's not filled with lung-crushing anxiety. For the first time in a long time, the weight on my chest is lifted.

I breathe, long and deep, and wait.

"Well, your father and I are proud of you," Mum says. It's a non-committal response. If she's disappointed or angry, she's trying to hide it. "We'll support you no matter what. We've only ever wanted the best for you."

"I know, Mum."

She sighs. "Well, it's late anyway. You should go to sleep, love."

She doesn't want to continue the conversation, which I suppose is fair. "Sure, okay, Mum."

"Goodnight, Sophie."

"Night, Mum."

She hangs up, and I slump down onto my desk, cheek pressed against a pile of Maths workbooks, staring into the blinding white orb of my lamp lightbulb.

I've done it. I can't believe I've done it. I'm going to Harvard. I can finally see the light at the end of the tunnel.

A knock at the door startles me.

I find a Year 12 girl on the other side, wearing a rowing team t-shirt and holding an enormous chocolate bar. She raises an eyebrow.

"Is Sophie here?"

I frown. "Er, I'm Sophie."

"Right. There's a boy outside who wants to talk to you."

"Boys aren't allowed in the girls' building," I remind her severely.

She rolls her eyes. "Yeah, yeah. I told him I'd pass on the message. You go get rid of him. Aren't you a prefect?"

"I'll go sort it out," I sigh.

Since I'm in a t-shirt, shorts and socks, I pull on a baggy jumper and leave my room, half excited, half nervous. In the common room, a couple of Year 12 girls are peering around the curtains, faces pressed to the window as they stare at the boy outside, confirming what I already know about who's waiting there.

I open the door with my most formal expression. "Hi, Evan, it's not allowed for you to be here, so—"

I stop in my tracks

With everything that's happened between us, you'd think I'd be desensitised to his looks, but I guess it's the kind of thing you can't ever get used to.

His hair is slightly wet, brushed back from his forehead, leaving his face and its impeccable bone structure fully exposed for maximum impact. He's wearing black running shorts, white trainers and a baggy grey sweatshirt, his training bag slung over one shoulder.

Behind him, the sun has almost finished its decline across the sky, leaving it the pale shade of violets, and the last sun rays catch the gold of Evan's hair, making it golder still.

"I wouldn't have had to risk your pristine reputation by coming if you ever took calls," he says, waving his phone in my face.

I raise my hands in concession. "Okay, I'm sorry, I was already on a call."

We stare at each other. A slow breeze rustles the ivy leaves that cover part of the building. Evan's gaze is gentle on me, a slight smile playing on his lips. Our last moments together, his words, mine, the pleasure we shared, hangs between us like an invisible, shimmering veil.

I clear my throat. "Well, what did you want anyway?"

"Are you going home for the holiday?"

I shake my head. "No, it's exam season. My parents will be working all week, so I'll be staying here."

He nods and hesitates. He brushes back his wet hair, bites his lips. "I, uh, was wondering if you want to come and stay with me for the holiday?"

I narrow my eyes, frankly shocked he has the audacity to make such a bold and reckless offer, but he raises his hands and hastens to add, "It wouldn't be just the two of us like… I mean, my family is going to be here, and my mum actually went to Harvard, so I thought you might want to chat, or…"

He trails off and stands there, ruffling his hair awkwardly. I watch him with what I hope is ice-cool calm, but in reality, my mind is scrambling around for all the reasons I should say no and finding none. We've just finished a round of mock exams, I don't have a job to go to, I'll be alone in Spearcrest over the holidays which is always really depressing, my parents would encourage this idea so I can't rely on them saying no, and the thought of meeting Evan's Harvard graduate mum is both terrifying and exhilarating all at once.

Not to mention the thought of staying with Evan.

Especially after everything that happened.

Especially now I no longer know where we stand.

Hating him really was much easier than whatever *this* is.

"I'll have to ask my parents," I say eventually.

He nods. "Yeah, of course. I told my parents I'd invite you and they are very excited to meet you. They're impressed that you're a prefect and asked me how on earth I got you to hang out with me." He stops and bites his lip in a gesture of trepidation. "Well, I didn't tell them about... everything, but—but, anyway. So they're very excited to meet you, and my sister is also staying, I think you two might get on."

He stops, staring at me. His eyes are wide and too blue and very earnest. I can tell he's trying to make amends, in his own outrageously bumbling, heavy-handed, American way, and for some reason it makes me smile.

"I'd love to come, alright? This place is depressing this time of year. I just need to let my parents know."

His face breaks into a broad grin. "Alright—great. Let me know. I'm leaving tomorrow, I'll text you all the details. Tell your parents I'll give them the biggest hug if they say yes. Alright, I'm off before the Spearcrest police come to arrest me for indecent behaviour. See ya tomorrow, hopefully."

He leans suddenly forward to press a kiss against my cheek, and then he turns around and disappears into the soft purple and gold of dusk.

# 37

# COMPLICATED

## Evan

"So, you really like this girl, huh?"

My dad's voice comes from behind me, and I jump away from the window, almost giving myself whiplash when I turn around to glare at him.

"Dad! What are you talking about?"

"You've been waiting at this window like a little kid watching out for Santa Claus to bring him his presents," Dad says with a shrug. "Not to mention all the different ways you've told us how perfect this girl is. I might be smart, but I could be stupid and still be able to tell that you like this girl."

I follow Dad into the kitchen as he talks, and absent-mindedly hop onto a seat at the kitchen counter, watching him as he makes a fresh pot of coffee.

"It's complicated, Dad."

"Right," he says. "How?"

"You wouldn't understand."

He looks up from the coffee machine, raising an eyebrow and giving me a piercing look, reminding me that I take after Dad in only one way: we both share the same blue eyes.

"I, the adult who's been married for twenty-five years to the love of his life, wouldn't understand anything about a teenage boy with a crush."

"It's not a crush, Dad."

He gives me a long look, then turns on the coffee machine and comes to take a seat at my side, propping her elbows on the marble top of the kitchen counter and lacing his fingers together. The silent, searching look he gives me makes me realise how much I've missed him, missed talking to him. I wonder if I would have messed up this badly if I'd gotten to talk to him more. After all, he's not wrong: he's actually managed to not only go out with the woman he loved, but marry her and stay married to her for twenty-five years. And Mom doesn't even look unhappy like those married middle-aged women on TV, so you know he must be doing something right.

Dad stays silent, waiting patiently for me to have the courage to tell him the truth.

"I really, really like her, Dad. I might even love her. But she's—" I try to think of a way to explain what the problem is, to summarise, truthfully, *succinctly*, as Sophie would say, why exactly my love is so doomed. "She's too good for me, Dad."

He nods slowly. "Hmm. Why do you think that?"

"Because, Dad..." I take a deep breath. "I really, really messed up."

"Go on."

"I don't even know where to start."

"Start at the beginning."

When I was really young, back in the US, Dad used to help me with my Math homework, and even though I hated Math, I used to love sitting with him at the kitchen island and listening to him explain my homework. He would talk exactly as he is doing now, in a gentle voice, calm but never patronising, and give clear, simple instructions.

"Well. You remember when I was in Year 9?"

"What is that—Freshman year?"

"No—sort of. The year before that."

Dad nods. "Right. No, I can't say I remember. What happened?"

"A new girl started at school."

He raises his eyebrows. "The prefect?"

I sigh deeply. "She wasn't a prefect then, but yes, her. She was, she is... you know. Not like us." I give Dad a significant look, and he tilts his head mutely. "Her parents work for the school, I think she got in on some sort of academic scholarship and because her parents work at Spearcrest. At the time, everyone was saying her parents were cleaners, even though that's not true. Anyway, you know what I mean. So of course, when she started she stuck out like a sore thumb. It was just so obvious she wasn't like everybody else. And some kids were mean to her because of her parents and... well, also, she used to be spotty and have big feet."

"Right," Dad says.

At this point, I'm sure he must be wondering what the hell I'm on about, and honestly I'm half wondering that too. But everything is slowly pouring out of me and I don't feel quite in control of exactly what I'm saying, and Dad doesn't prompt me to hurry up, he just watches me and waits calmly.

"Well, anyway. We started talking and became friends. She was, I don't know... funny. Clever and really funny—sarcastic, like an adult. I liked that about her. And she would always get into fights and arguments when people tried to make fun of her. She was, I don't know, fiery. Like she always stuck-up for herself. I liked all these things about her."

"Sounds like the start of a promising friendship," Dad comments. "So how did it all go wrong?"

I open my mouth to ask him how he knows it went wrong, but I look into his clever blue eyes—the same colour as mine but with far more intelligence in there—and find my answer there. Of course, things went wrong. Otherwise I wouldn't be in the situation I'm in now.

"We stopped being friends."

"Why?"

"It's complicated."

Dad smiles a little. "Hm."

"Okay, alright. You remember Luca?"

"The Novus kid?"

Novus is the name of Luca's father's business, some chem tech company nobody knows about but somehow makes millions. I nod. "Yeah, him."

Dad raises an eyebrow. "The one you got into that brawl with and I had to have a meeting with your headmaster?"

I groan. "Yeah."

"I thought you two sorted your issues? Aren't you friends now?"

"We are—well, we were, but..." I hesitate. "It was a weird friendship, Dad. Do you remember Giselle?"

"The girl you dated for a while last year?"

"Yeah. You know how Luca dated her?"

"I didn't know that. Is that an issue between you two?"

"No—it's not that. I don't think I was a great boyfriend to Giselle and Luca didn't exactly intend on marrying her, it's not like I have a problem with that. But with Luca, being friends with Luca... you have to be ready to share. Luca likes what other people have."

"Hm." Dad nods slowly, his eyes narrowing. "So, what? You didn't want him to take the prefect from you, so you torpedoed your friendship with her?"

I stare at him. I didn't expect him to get it so quickly, and somehow hearing it out of his mouth makes it sound so much worse. It makes it sound stupid, petty, childish. Which, I suppose, is exactly what it is.

"Yeah. And then... Well, I stopped being friends with her, but I was scared Luca would know that I liked her, so I was... uh, pretty horrible to her."

"For how long?"

"Pretty much the last four years."

Now Dad's composure cracks slightly. He sits forward and sighs, rubbing his short beard as he always does when he's working out a problem or thinking over an issue.

"So you're telling me that not only did you end a friendship with this girl, but you then went on to bully her for several years?"

"It's not bullying. More, like... being really mean."

Dad raises his eyebrows, unimpressed. "Yes, son, a very mild explanation of what bullying is."

I drop my head into my hands. "Ugh, I've been a total arsehole, Dad."

Dad pats my shoulder, a reassuring gesture which he follows up with, "It does sound like it, Ev, I won't lie."

I peer at him through my fingers and add, my words half-muffled by my palms. "And also she got a job because she's worried about money because she wants to study in the US, and then I told the school about it because I was jealous she liked some other guy instead of me, and then I called her poor in front of everyone."

Even though I've left out some of the worst stuff, it's still enough to get me a shocked, "Jesus, Ev!" from Dad.

Now he's outright glaring at me.

Then a different voice pipes up. "Why the blasphemy?"

Mom comes into the kitchen, saunters over to Dad, and they kiss as if she's been gone for days, not just been upstairs for a few online meetings in her office.

Dad wastes no time filling her in. "You know the girl Evan has a crush on?"

Mom's face lights up. "Oh, the Harvard girl! Yes, I'm very excited to meet her!"

"Well, our son here apparently got her in trouble with school and has been essentially bullying her for several years."

I stare in horror at Dad, then look quickly back at Mom, whose face has dropped as quickly as it lit up earlier. She covers her mouth with her hands, drawing closer.

"What do you mean? Oh, Evan, what did you do?"

"I didn't bully her, I—" I'm interrupted by Dad's silent frown. "Okay, yes, I was horrible, but I was so scared somebody else would notice her, I thought, I didn't even know what I thought, I guess I thought if I couldn't have her I would rather nobody have her at all."

"*Have?*" Mom exclaims, aghast. "*Have*, Evan Alexander Knight! As if this girl is—what? An object? A toy? A thing?"

I shake my head, raising my hand. In between the disappointed shaking of Dad's head and Mom's expression of horrified anger, I don't even know which is worse, and I don't dare look either in the eyes. "No, I don't mean it like that."

"How else can you *have* someone, Evan?" Mom asks, crossing her arms.

When I arrived home, she was so happy to see me. She gave me a big hug, and we laughed because we were both in the same outfit: black jeans and sky-blue tops—me in the hoodie Sophie gave me, Mom in a big fluffy sweater of the exact same colour. I could tell she'd missed me, and I wouldn't even have been embarrassed to admit that I missed her too.

But now, her affectionate gaze and dimpled smile have both vanished.

"I messed up," I admit miserably. "I really fucked up. I know that. I don't know what to do."

"You could start by apologising. Admitting you've messed up is a good first step, but you have to acknowledge it, too. And apologise when you're in the wrong."

"And do better," Mom says. "Apologies are good, but she'll know you're sorry if you actually show her, through your actions."

I nod. "I know, I'm going to try—I'm trying. Mom and Dad, I—"

Adele interrupts us, whirling into the kitchen with a casual flick of her long hair. Unlike me, she's inherited Dad's dark hair and fair complexion, but we both share his eyes. "Who's the sexy girl outside?"

I turn so fast I almost give myself whiplash. "What sexy girl?"

Adele shrugs and pours herself a cup of fresh coffee. "Smoky voice, bedroom eyes, dark hair."

"That girl," Mom says pointedly, "is Evan's friend we're all going to be exceptionally nice to."

"That girl's your friend?" Adele says with an obnoxious expression of surprise. "She seems well too good for—Dad!"

Dad's just swiped the cup of coffee from under her and she gives him a scandalised look. He shrugs in a perfect imitation of her own shrug earlier. "I made the fresh pot, I get first dibs. Now let's go and welcome that girl we've heard so much about. Best behaviour, everyone, especially *you*."

He gives me a warning look and I sigh, half wishing I hadn't said anything to begin with, half relieved that I finally got it off my chest. As I lead everyone towards the door, I take a deep breath, bracing myself, hoping and praying that introducing Sophie to my family isn't a massive mistake.

I open the door. Whether this week is going to turn out good or bad, it's too early to tell, but there's one thing that's certain: if nothing else, this week is definitely going to be interesting.

## 38

# COMPENSATION

### Evan

OF ALL THE THINGS I definitely should have seen coming, two stand out: my family falling embarrassingly in love with Sophie, and the holiday going far too fast.

On the first day of the holiday, when Sophie arrived with her backpack and her tidy appearance, I could tell that she was very nervous. Mom and Dad, clearly having shouldered the responsibility of making up for my horrible behaviour, were overzealous in their welcoming. They showed Sophie to the guest room, poured her coffee and plied her with food. I barely got to even speak to her that day—Mom and Dad basically spent the rest of the day giving her what I can only describe as a very friendly yet thorough pseudo-job interview.

They asked her about school, her qualifications, her university applications, Harvard. I could tell that they really liked her—how could they not? Adults always love Sophie. She's smart, well-spoken, earnest. Mom especially was excited at the prospect of a potential future fellow Harvard alumnus, and after dinner, she and Sophie stay at the kitchen island for ages, picking at a box of French macarons and chatting endlessly about university.

That evening, I can't concentrate on anything, and I'm peering into the kitchen from around the doorway, wondering when I can finally get Sophie to myself, when Adele's voice pipes up over my shoulder.

"How on earth did you get this girl to be friends with you, Ev? She's far too good for you."

I turn around to glare at her, ready to respond defensively, then I realise that she's totally right. I sigh, my shoulders slumping. "Honestly, I have no idea. She really is."

"Don't be so negative." Dad's voice interrupts. He pops up behind Adele. "You're amazing in many ways, Evan. You're open-minded, optimistic, friendly and kind. You just need to do a better job of showing this girl how amazing you can be, because so far it doesn't sound as though you've made the best impression."

"Well, he's not going to get much of a chance to do that," Adele says, lowering her voice as she peers around the doorway and into the kitchen. "I think Mom might be in love with her—good luck competing with that."

She's not even exaggerating. The next few days, Sophie spends most of her time with Mom and Adele: they go out shopping, for coffee and meals, constantly chatting with her. After dinner, Sophie plays both Mom and Dad at chess—they apparently both used to be in their university chess clubs and get all nostalgic about it. I didn't even know that. It's not until Thursday comes and both Mom and Dad are forced to attend online meetings for work that I finally get a moment completely alone with Sophie.

We're both in the kitchen having a late breakfast. The weather is nicer now, and she's wearing a plain black t-shirt tucked into baggy corduroy pants. Her hair is loose and gleams like polished wood on her shoulders, a plain black elastic band around her wrist. She's wearing tiny flicks of eyeliner at the corner of her eyes, and that's it. It's a simple look, but in the lazy golden sunrays, she looks so pretty it makes my chest hurt.

"Are you having a good time?" I ask, heaping bacon onto her plate before taking a seat across from her at the kitchen island.

She nods. "Your family is really, really nice."

I grin. "I know." My smile falters a little, and I add. "I hope you didn't think they were going to be dicks just because I was. They're just much better than I am."

Sophie tucks her hair behind one ear and bites into a crispy slice of bacon. "Yes... your mom made sure to explain to me how disappointed she was when she heard about some of the things you did and that she raised you better than that and that it isn't reflective of who you can be as a person."

I sit, completely frozen, staring at her in shock. "She said all that?"

"All that." Sophie gazes at me for a second, then her serious face breaks into a grin—a really cute grin, a little goofy. "Honestly, your family is amazing. You're very lucky."

I swallow hard, gathering my courage. "Sophie."

She stiffens a little, her eyes go wide. She looks like a deer in headlights. "What?"

"I'm sorry. I'm really fucking sorry, for... well, for everything, really."

Her cheeks darken, she looks down. "You don't have to do this."

"No, but I do, don't I? I'm so sorry. I never should have stopped being friends with you in Year 9. And I shouldn't have been such an arsehole to you all these years. And I definitely shouldn't have ratted you out about your job."

She stares at me with her wide, dark eyes, and it's hard to tell what she's thinking. The only indication of emotion from her is the dark pink flush in her cheeks, and the way she's worrying her bottom lip with her teeth.

"You don't have to worry about that anyway," she ends up saying with a light smile. "Your mum's offered me a summer job in her company."

I stare at her, shocked even though I really shouldn't be. "She has?"

Sophie nods, a little smugly. "Mm-hm."

I lean forward. "Wait. Which office?"

"She said I can go to her office in London or New York."

My heart feels both really heavy and light enough to float away. I wait for her to say more, but she's simply buttering a slice of toast with small, tidy movements of her knife. "Well? Which one are you thinking?"

She shrugs. "Obviously London."

"Where would you stay?"

"I'm not sure."

I wait a moment, trying to make sure my tone is casual when I speak next. "You know, if you want to work in the New York office, my aunt lives in New Haven..."

She gives me a blank look, biting into her slice of toast. Butter gleams on her lips and she licks it off when she notices me looking. I continue quickly. "Well, New Haven isn't too far from Boston."

Her slice of toast stops halfway between the table and her mouth. She raises her eyebrows. "What are you saying?"

"I'm saying, if you wanted, you could work at my mom's office in New York, and stay at my aunt's house over the summer, and we could go visit Boston. You know. See Harvard before you start there in the fall."

"*We?*" she says, her smoky voice low.

I meet her gaze and don't look away. "Why not?"

She's the first to look away. "How do you know if Harvard even accepted me?"

"How could they not?"

"How could who not what?" Adele says, gliding into the kitchen in a pair of pink pyjamas with her hair in unnecessarily dramatic rollers.

"Nothing," Sophie says quietly, looking down.

"Do you think Sophie should come stay at Aunt Amelia's house this summer? She's going to be working at Mom's office."

"Oh, the New York office?" Adele says brightly, sitting next to Sophie. "I'll actually also be in New York—I'm spending the summer there with Cedric. We could totally show you around. And if you're staying at Aunt Ame's house, we'll come stay there for a bit too. Ugh, Sophie, she has such a good pool, and the summer in New Haven is actually gorgeous, not like a British summer—no offence."

Sophie smiles. "None taken. You're very kind, but I wouldn't want to intrude."

"You really wouldn't'the intruding," Adele says, pouring herself some orange juice. "Her house is massive, and she spends half her time visiting her friends in the Hamptons anyway. You should definitely stay. We can take you to parties! Actual American house parties."

She leans closer to Sophie and lowers her tone conspiratorially. "You know, you'd be so popular with the boys. Your sexy voice and sexy accent combined would be game over."

Sophie's face goes bright pink and I clear my throat loudly. Adele winks at Sophie and whispers loudly. "We'll go without Evan so he can't cockblock you."

I throw the strawberry jelly lid at her and she dodges it with a loud "Ew!"

I do my best to keep Adele away from Sophie for the rest of the week—unsuccessfully. It's not until Saturday that I finally have some more time alone with Sophie. Mom, Dad and Adele have gone out to watch some corny movie, and Sophie and I spend the evening in the living room, playing chess.

"I didn't know you could play," Sophie says, watching me set up the board.

"Mom and Dad taught me, but I never took to it. I suck at thinking long-term and end up making a bunch of mistakes that bite me in the ass later."

Sophie gives me the most comical dead-pan expression. "You do, do you?"

"Oh, ha ha. You're so funny, Sophie. Like, the funniest person I know."

"I probably am, as well," she says. "Do you want to start? You might need the advantage."

"At this point, I'll take whatever advantage I can get."

We're sitting at the little chess table in the reading nook. The sun is just setting outside, lingering rays of pink sunlight fall across the table, shiny particles of dust floating in the slices of light. When Sophie leans forward to move one of her pieces, she crosses the path of one of the sunrays, and it makes her dark hair shine like rubies.

She's very serious and overly competitive, given her clear advantage over me. My mind drifts idly back to the last time we played a game together, the Trivial Pursuit board, Sophie's tipsy encouragements, and of course—

"Don't do it," says Sophie in a low voice.

I turn to give her a surprised look. "Do what?"

"Think about what you're definitely thinking about."

"What? How can you possibly tell?"

She rolls her eyes. "You're gazing out of the window and have an expression on your face like some lovelorn girl in a period drama. It's all very Anne Elliot pining for Captain Wentworth."

I glare at her. "I'm not pi—" I stop, sigh. "Well, how can I not think about it? Don't you think about it?"

"Right now, you should be thinking about my bishop and what that means for your knight."

"My knight?" I glance at the board, realise she's just trying to deflect and look back up at her. "Forget about my knight for a second. My knight hasn't noticed your bishop because he's probably thinking about kissing your queen and having really hot sex with her. Does your queen think about that?"

"My queen has more important things to think about," Sophie says with a serene smile.

I lean forward, narrowing my eyes. "You're telling me you've not been thinking about it?"

She waves a hand, though her cheeks are a little flushed. "It's just sex, Evan."

"*Just sex*? What kind of a life are you secretly living for what we do to be *just sex*?"

Now she leans forward, and her eyes narrow, and her lips curl in a sarcastic smile. "Oh please, Evan. Look me in the eyes and tell me you haven't fucked dozens of girls exactly the same way."

"Definitely not the same way, are you crazy? Besides, it's not like—" Instead of defending myself, I realise she just handed me something to get her with. I tilt my head. "Wait a second. Are you... *jealous*?"

She laughs, a low, scratchy sound that makes the hairs on the back of my neck stand on end. "You have no idea just how jealous."

My heart skips a beat, my throat suddenly feels a little tight. "Really?"

"No," she says, moving her bishop and knocking my knight off the board. "Check."

But I'm too invested in this line of questioning to even acknowledge the chessboard. I watch her face intently, looking for signs of the truth to reveal themselves on her pretty face. "You're lying."

She shakes her head and speaks with a little smirk. "Is it so hard to believe I might want more for myself than hooking up with a rich boy in his dad's expensive cars—or whatever it is you do?"

I sit back in my chair with a shrug "We don't have to hook up in my dad's expensive cars, Sophie. We have options, you know. We can hook up in my dad's expensive jacuzzi."

For a second, Sophie just looks at me. Then she raises an eyebrow. "You have a jacuzzi? You never said that."

"Yeah, we have a jacuzzi." I laugh. "Wait—that actually worked?"

She shrugs. "I'm literally cold all the time. Of course it worked."

I narrow my eyes, trying to work out whether she's being sarcastic, which is always impossible to tell with her. "Really?"

She nods, perfectly earnest. "Really."

# Sophie

AGREEING TO STAY AT Evan's house definitely felt like a mistake at the time. But I've spent so much of my life trying to be careful, trying to do the right thing, that doing something I want somehow always ends up feeling like a mistake.

So I guess, in the end, I make a lot of mistakes while staying at Evan's house. Mistakes like accepting his mum's generous offer to intern at her publishing company, or agreeing to his sister's offer to take me to real American house parties over the summer.

Mistakes like sitting in Evan's jacuzzi with him knowing full well any amount of nudity between us can only end one way. Mistakes like relaxing a little too much under the silvery lights of the jacuzzi, and oversharing about this year and my parents and my hopes and dreams.

Mistakes like noticing the droplets of water tracing the muscles of Evan's arms and chest, and the way his wet hair curls around his temples and neck. Noticing his hooded gaze, the blue of his eyes, bluer in the pretty lights. Letting Evan touch my hand, lace his fingers through mine, pull me closer.

In the blur of steam and bubbles and low music, all the mistakes merge into one mistake.

A slow, dream-like mistake, where Evan draws me gently to him, and whispers in my ear, in a low, broken voice, how much he likes me, how much he wants me. I wrap my arms around his shoulders, and because I'm straddling his lap, I can tell that the sweet, dirty things he's murmuring in my ears are all true.

For someone so blunt and artless, Evan is capable of devastating tenderness.

That tenderness glows in everything he does: the way he sweeps the hair from my face with a slow caress, the way he traces wet, lingering kisses up my neck, the way he wraps his arms around my waist, pulling me to him in an irresistible embrace.

Kissing his open mouth is definitely a mistake, right? But a delicious, delirious mistake, because Evan's kisses are wet and deep, and my body arches against his, beyond my control.

It's a mistake to make out with Evan in his jacuzzi, but I'm saved from my mistake when his family returns home and we both make a hasty, shameful retreat to our respective rooms.

Except I double-down later that night when I sneak into his bedroom and lie on his bed and let him push up my top so he can run his hands up my waist, across my ribcage and over my breasts. His fingers brush over my nipples until they become hard and so sensitive he has to cover my mouth with one hand when he leans down to drag his tongue over them.

Wanting Evan so much definitely is a mistake, but I never want to not feel the way he makes me feel. Like my entire body is hot with pleasure, like he's the sun that sets every inch of my body on fire.

For all the things Evan is terrible at, I always assumed being good at sports was how he compensated, but I was wrong. Evan compensates with his lips and tongue and his gentle, cruel fingers. Evan compensates until I'm suffocating my moans into his pillow and my thighs are trembling uncontrollably and I come against his mouth in deep, shuddering waves of pleasure.

This is a mistake I've made before—why do I keep making it?

Because of him. Because of Evan Knight and the way he looks at me, like I'm the most important thing in the world.

After that, there are a lot of other mistakes. Kissing his wet mouth and listening to him murmur "I love you" over and over against my shoulder while he fucks me long and slow and agonising. He comes with a low, rough sigh, and we lie together, trembling and panting. Later, we tiptoe into his bathroom with embarrassed giggles, and clean up in between giddy kisses.

When I sneak back into the guestroom, I lie in bed still shivering all over. I close my eyes, thinking about how wildly irresponsible I've been when a realisation dawns upon me.

This is the first time this year I've not felt paralysed by fear or worry.

## 39

# WENTWORTH

### Sophie

My final term at Spearcrest begins with a vengeance. In between revision sessions, extra classes, coursework deadlines and looming exams, there's no time to worry about anything else. The tutoring programme ends early in the term, and all of our extracurriculars are suspended for good.

The stress and pressure of the exams throughout our year group have escalated so much that even the students who normally seem unaffected by schoolwork are slowly beginning to cave in. Araminta, the perpetual optimist, has been planning her escape in case she fails her exams. The clouds of girls who normally follow the Young Kings around the school with breathless laughs and silken hair have dissipated. Students who spent their entire time at Spearcrest projecting careless insouciance don't seem so insouciant now.

Even the Young Kings themselves seem to have disbanded, split apart by their different classes and exam schedules. I catch a glimpse of Zachary coming out of his Lit classroom one afternoon with a gaunt face and haunted eyes. Séverin

Montcroix seems to spend an inordinate amount of time in the Art studios even though he's not even studying Art.

One afternoon, I even catch Luca Fletcher-Lowe, his face a map of fading bruises, sitting in the corner of the library with a thunderous frown on his face, bent over textbooks.

After spending my school career feeling like I was in a different world to everybody in Spearcrest, it's as though exams have now brought everybody into *my* world. A world of endless revision, non-stop nail-biting and anxiety dreams.

And now, as well as the crushing workload and the looming exams, I have something else to worry about.

Avoiding the distraction that is Evan has become sort of a full-time job because he seems to be everywhere. In the study hall when I'm working through Maths past papers, in the library when I'm trying to do my background reading on Austen, in the dining hall when Audrey drags me in to forcefully remind me to eat.

Every time I see him, my mind is flooded with memories of our bodies together, his mouth on me, his words. It's the last thing that should be on my mind.

The night before my first exam, I stay in the library so late I lose track of time. My eyes are teary with tiredness, and after wiping tired tears off my revision cards for the third time, I decide to call it a night.

I stand up to return my books to the shelf cart and look around. The top floor, where I've been sitting all night, is empty and plunged in shadows, the only light source the banker's lamp on my desk and the faint bronze glow of the lights rising from the lower floors through the polished wooden railings.

I'm not one to spook easily, but in all my years at Spearcrest, this is the first time I've seen the library empty. The eerie silence seems to follow me through the book aisles and down the stairs as I make a hasty escape from the top floor, my heart beating slightly faster than it should. I emerge into the soft lights of the second floor and breathe a slight sigh of relief, happy to be free from the lurking shadows.

Then I turn the corner towards the next staircase and go crashing into another lurking shadow. I jump back with an embarrassingly high-pitched gasp, and a strong pair of arms grab me to settle me.

"Whoa, Sophie!" I look up to see Evan's wide eyes staring back at me. "You scared the shit out of me!"

I push his arms off me with a glare. "What are you talking about? *You* scared the shit out of *me*! What are you even doing here?"

He gestures at himself: he's wearing a baggy white vest and black running shorts, a blue towel around his neck. His hair is dark and curly with sweat. "I was coming back from a run, I just thought I'd check to see if you were here."

I stare at him. "A run? Why on earth are you running at this time of night?"

He shrugs. "Probably the same reason you're here at this time of night."

"You're on a run to revise for a History exam?"

"I'm on a run because I've got an exam tomorrow and I'm too stressed to sleep."

"Oh."

Then the silence from upstairs, the soft, velvety silence of late night and old wood and dim lights, settles between us. It coils around us, shutting us away from the real world and locking us into each other's presence. I realise this is the first time we've been alone together since that night at his house, and my heart stops beating as if it's just been turned to marble.

Evan swallows, his throat shuddering. His cheeks are flushed, his lips wet. His gaze is dark and glittering, fixed on me. There is an unspeakable expression on his face: something hungry and reckless and a little wild. He steps forward with a sharp intake of breath.

"Evan—" I start.

But he's already crossing the space between us, sweeping me into his arms. Mine curl around his neck of their own volition before I even realise what I'm doing, and then I'm pinned against a wall, pressing him closer. He kisses me hard, hungrily, urgently and I open my mouth to him like a blossoming flower starved for sunlight.

I kiss him back just as hungrily, surprised by my desire, my fingers curled into fists in his hair. He hitches me higher against him, my thighs around his hips, so that my head is tilted down towards him, and for a second I pause to stare down at him, stunned by the naked desire on his face. I take his face in my hands and kiss his open mouth so deep and slow my entire body aches.

His hands reach under my shirt, the glide of his skin on mine so sensual it sends shudders rippling through me. His fingers find the curve of my breasts, the tightening bud of my nipples. He pinches his fingers closed over it with a cruel grin, shocking a small, hoarse cry out of me.

"Is somebody still here?"

The distant voice brings me back to reality as surely as if I'd been tossed into ice-cold water. I shove Evan away from me, almost strangling him with the collar of his own shirt as we spring apart.

A door opens somewhere on the lower floor and footsteps approach. I hastily straighten my jumper and lean over the balustrade to see Mr Eckles, the campus security guard. I look back up, still breathless from Evan's kisses, but Evan hasn't looked away from me for a second. His chest is rising and falling rapidly, his cheeks flushed, his gaze dangerous.

"Just putting my books away, Mr Eckles!" I call out, a hint of desperation sharpening my voice.

Evan's eyes darken and he steps towards me once more. I push him away and make my escape. I run all the way from the library to the girls' dormitories like the final girl in a horror movie and immediately head for the showers.

When I finally climb into bed, my phone lights up.

**Evan**: I want you so fucking much. Just so you know, it's your fault if I fail my exam tomorrow.

I bury my burning face into my pillow and take several deep breaths before picking up my phone.

**Sophie**: I think it's best if we stay away from each other until exams are over. Wouldn't want you to fail every exam. Goodnight x

Then I slip my phone under my pillow and go to sleep, even though I know full well I'll wake up feeling much more tired than I do now.

---

ONCE THE FIRST EXAM is over and done with, I enter into a sort of high-functioning panic mode where everything is sharpened and heightened and intense. Each following exam is a shock to the system. Sleep becomes little more than just an extended period of closing my eyes.

The second English Literature paper is my final exam. By that point, I'm running on pure adrenaline, so when Evan appears from behind a bookshelf and strides towards my desk on the top floor of the library the night before the exam, I look up at him with my most belligerent frown.

"Go away."

He raises a shiny copy of Jane Austen's *Persuasion*, holding it up like a shield as he approaches me with cautious steps.

"Are you revising for Lit?"

"What else would I be doing?"

He lays his book down on the desk and pulls up a chair facing me. "Let me revise with you."

"Absolutely not."

He freezes halfway through sitting down, giving me the worst attempt at puppy eyes. "Oh. Really?"

I let out a deep, pointed sigh. "Fine. Sit down. If you mention even a single thing that's not related to *Persuasion*, I will get you kicked out of the library permanently. Don't think I won't."

"I know better than to not take your threats seriously," he says, hurriedly sitting down and pulling out his battered notebook from his bag.

I avert my eyes, disgusted by the clear mistreatment his book and notes have endured. After a while, we begin swapping questions and revision notes, and tentatively quizzing one another, making notes of areas we both need to revise. We're working quietly when Evan breaks the silence

"What I don't understand," he says, frowning at his copy of *Persuasion*, "is why she doesn't just tell Wentworth how she feels."

I look up from my notes and raise my eyebrows at him. "How could she possibly? Think about it. It was her fault she let him go, her fault she listened to the wrong people, her fault she gave up what she wanted."

"Well, she really is a fucking idiot," Evan mumbles.

Still, he makes a note of what I just told him. I pick up my book, peering at him over the pages and watching him as he writes.

"Why?" I finally ask.

He looks up and gives a rueful sigh, as though he's become the living embodiment of Anne Elliot herself. "Because she wasted all that time for nothing, absolutely nothing. All that time she spends suffering, she could have been with him. But she just ruined everything for herself and then was too paralysed by her own mistake to do anything about it."

I put my book back down. "Aren't you being a little too hard on her? She was young and she fucked up. It happened. So what? Should she pay for this mistake for the rest of her life?"

He looks up suddenly, a frown on his face. "Isn't that what you're making me do?"

I glare at him. "You're not Anne Elliot."

"I know I'm not. She accepts defeat way too easily. I don't know if you've noticed, but I'm willing to fight for what I want, even when the odds are against me."

My heart is beating much too fast for a conversation about a Jane Austen book, which this conversation is rapidly moving away from. I sigh and look back down at my book.

"Don't knock Anne," I tell him, a little more calmly. "She ends up getting what she wants in the end."

Evan seems to relent, too, because he brushes his hand through his hair in that sheepish way of his and mutters, "Only because Wentworth is kind enough to forgive her."

I sneak a glance at him, but his gaze is fixed on the pages of his book. I hesitate, then say, "Yeah, well... I doubt Wentworth would have forgiven her if he wasn't head over heels in love with her the whole time, even while he was angry at her."

Evan looks sharply back up and stares at me. I stare back at him, blinking slowly. His eyes narrow.

"I don't get it," he says quietly. "Are we still talking about the book or are we talking about us?"

"There is no us."

"Right. Right, yes. But there could be. Right?"

"Evan." I cross my arms and lean forward, to make sure I'm looking him dead in the face before explaining this to him. "You're not Anne. You just want something you can't have exactly *because* you don't have it. The moment you do, you'll move on."

"Don't you think that if it was that easy to get over you, I would already have?" There's a desperate edge to Evan's voice. "It's not like I've not tried, Sophie. But even when I'm not thinking about you, you're still there, on the edge of my thoughts. And when I close my eyes I just see you and your hair and eyes and your stupid frown you always have like an angry librarian who disapproves of everything and everyone. I want you so much I feel constantly empty, even when I have everything I want. At Christmas, I wasn't happy because I wasn't alone. I was happy because I was with *you*. Just because I'm not like you, because I don't get excited about university and a job, doesn't mean I live completely aimlessly. It's just that anything I imagine for my future feels worthless if you're not there to share it with me."

I'm so lost for words all I can do is stare mutely at him as he speaks, then he stops and we just stare at each other, my heart in my mouth.

"I don't know what to even say to that," I mumble.

"Then don't say anything. I just wanted you to know. Besides, you said that if I spoke about anything other than Persuasion, you'd have me kicked out of the library."

We fall back into silence, and leave soon after, ushered out by the librarian who tells us the teachers are using the library for a staff twilight session. I sheepishly bid Evan goodbye, but I make sure to text him when I get back to my dorm.

**Sophie**: Good luck with the exam, Anne x

**Evan**: Haha. Thanks, Wentworth. Good luck to you too. Love you x

# 40

# ONE DAY

## Evan

Maybe it's because of my newfound understanding of Anne Elliot, or maybe it's because of Sophie's good luck message, but I come out of the last Lit exam feeling more confident than I've felt after any exam. Maybe that's partly due to the fact that this is also the last exam of the year, it's hard to tell. Either way, I emerge from the hall and into bright sunlight, so full of positivity that I grab Zach as soon as I see him and hug him so tight that he goes slightly purple in the face.

"Let me go, you big oaf!" he hisses.

I release him and he pushes me away, straightening his blazer with as much dignity as he can muster.

"I take it you did well?" he asks, cocking one jet-black eyebrow.

I nod and grin at him. "I mean, I definitely passed."

"Well," he says with a slight smirk. "Let's hope Sophie's good work didn't go to waste, huh?" Zach gives a sudden smile. "Right, Sophie?"

My head turns so fast that my entire body spins with it. Sophie, slinging her backpack over her shoulder, emerges onto the lawn. Her hair is knotted at the back of her head, and she's wearing her summer uniform impeccably. I take in the sight of her like I'm dehydrated and she's a glass of ice-cold water: her long legs, her pretty features and dark eyes, the loose strands of dark hair framing her face. She raises her eyebrows at me as she approaches.

"Well," she says imperiously. "How did you do?"

"I think I did pretty well."

"He told me he thinks he definitely passed," Zach adds.

I throw a kick his way, which he gracefully side-steps, but Sophie laughs and says, "Oh, that good, huh?"

"Couldn't let you down, could I?"

"Can't believe this might be my greatest professional achievement and I've not even started my career yet."

Her tone is aridly dry, but there's a smirk on her face that's so sexy I have to clench my fists to resist the urge to grab her and kiss it off her face.

"How did you do, Sophie?" Zach asks.

"Not too bad," she says. "And you? Full marks?"

He shrugs, hiding a smile. "Mm, we'll see. Are you coming to the lake on Friday?"

On the last Friday of the last year at Spearcrest, it's tradition to have a party by the lake. The lake lies at the northmost end of Spearcrest, past a forest of firs and oaks, and is normally strictly forbidden to students. But on the last day of the year, since everybody is leaving or about to leave, the Year 13s gather by the lake for one last party. I stare at Sophie, ready to get on my knees and beg her to go if I have to.

To my surprise, though, she nods. "Mm-hm. It's tradition, after all."

Gathering my courage and speaking before I can think better of it, I ask, "Wanna go as my date?"

She looks at me, and even though her expression gives nothing away, a faint cloud of pink blossoms at the surface of her cheeks. "I'm going as Audrey's date but... you can get me drinks and I won't be mean to you."

"Oh, really?"

"Yes, really."

"No matter what I do?" I ask, tilting my head.

She meets my gaze boldly and gives me a slow smile. "Mm-hm." And then she turns away with a wave. "See you both there."

---

I SPEND THE FIRST half-hour of the party with my friends, thinking about Sophie the whole time. She's sitting down by the jetty with her friends, and I'm too scared of bothering her and inducing her friends' ire to go over.

As I sit amongst the other Young Kings of Spearcrest, I look at them one-by-one: Luca is sitting a little away from us, staring out absent-mindedly at the lake. We've not spoken much since our fight. Our friendship doesn't feel either alive or dead. It feels like something that never really existed. Séverin and Iakov are reclining in the grass. Iakov is showing Sev something on his phone, but Sev seems distracted, as if he's waiting for someone to turn up.

As for Zachary, he is under the trees having some sort of heated exchange with Theodora—whether they're arguing or flirting, it's always hard to tell with them.

How often will I see them after this week? Probably not all that often. I'll keep in touch with Zachary regardless of where we both end up. Iakov and Sev are headed back to Russia and France respectively, and although I'm sure we'll all text at first, they're equally as bad as I am when it comes to keeping in touch.

As for Luca, I don't think he's someone I want in my life going forward. Somehow, I'm pretty confident he won't want me in his.

Why did I ever worry so much about what these guys would think of me? Looking back, I can't help but feel a mix of wry amusement and regret. I wasted so much time worrying about what they would think, what they would do, but that's all it was: a waste of time. Because this whole time, I could have been making the most of my time at Spearcrest, my time with Sophie.

I spot her, sitting at the end of the jetty with her arm wrapped around a post and her toes caressing the surface of the water. She's wearing high-waisted shorts, a strappy black top and a baggy plaid shirt with the sleeves folded back. Her hair is loose, the sun giving the glossy strands a blood-red sheen, and she's watching with a grin as her friends, Audrey and Araminta, pass a bottle of champagne back and forth, taking deep swigs.

The sun is low in the sky and someone's started a (definitely illegal) bonfire by the time I gather the courage to swim over to her. The water is cold, but the afternoon is warm, the setting sun's final rays turning everything they touch red and gold. I relish the cool waves lapping at me as I wade over to the jetty, where Sophie sits back, her hands propped behind her, her head leaning on one shoulder, watching me with hooded eyes.

Grabbing the edge of the jetty on both sides of her, I pull myself closer. The wood is warm under my fingers, but not as warm as Sophie's skin; I can feel the heat radiating from her thighs inches away from my hands.

"What happened to you getting me my drinks, Knight?" she asks lazily.

I jab my chin in the direction of the multiple empty bottles of champagne crowding at her side, the glass glittering with sunlight. "Looks like you guys had it covered."

She sits up and suddenly leans forward, her face above mine, her hair falling like a dark curtain around me, the feathery strands tickling my shoulders.

"Well, I'm not drunk."

I can't help but laugh. "No?"

"No," she says. "So don't try anything."

"No?" I haul myself up, closer to her so that I can lower my voice. "Not even a kiss?"

She does a hoarse little fake gasp. "What? In front of all your *cool* friends? What would everyone say?"

"I. Don't give. A fuck."

I wrap my arms around her and kiss her, hard and long and slow. I pull away and her lips look pink and wet, glimmering in the pink-gold light of the setting sun.

"See?" I say. "The sun didn't explode. The world didn't tilt on its axis and send us all hurtling through space."

She raises her eyebrows. "I knew that," she said. "I always have. Well done for catching on."

"Well, I've caught on. So why don't you give me a chance?"

She says nothing, so I take her face gently in my hands, draw her to me, whispering in her ear. "Please. Please, Sophie. I like you so fucking much it hurts."

"We only have the summer, Evan." Her voice is low and rough and a little sad.

I swallow hard. "Then give me the summer. Give me a chance to make up for everything."

She hesitates. The wind brushes through her hair, sending it streaming across her cheeks and mouth.

"And then?" she asks finally.

"And then you tell me what you want. Whatever you want—you'll have it. You want me to come with you to New York, I will. Or London, or Massachusetts in the fall. You want me to leave you alone, then that's fine. You want me to become worthy of you, then I'll bust my ass to become the man you deserve to have. Whatever you want, Sophie."

She watches me in silence for a moment, then runs her fingers through my hair, pushing it back, gazing at me thoughtfully.

"Okay," she murmurs. "Let's do the summer."

"Starting now?"

She laughs. "Starting now."

I pull her into the water with me, and she doesn't cry out or tell me off. She laughs and wraps her legs and arms around me and I kiss her, over and over again, until I'm hard and breathless and she's arching against me and loud voices fill the shimmering dusk with jeers.

"Mary mother of god, you two, is this utterly necessary?" Zachary calls out from the shore, where he's probably still fight-flirting with Theodora.

Sophie breaks away from me with a laugh and I throw myself up in the water, punching the air. "She fucking said yes!" I yell out loud to nobody in particular and everybody at the same time.

"For fuck's sake," Araminta says from the jetty, "it's not like you guys are getting married."

"Not yet," I reply, catching Sophie's eyes and holding her gaze. "One day. You'll see. One day."

# THE END

# DEAR READER

Thank you for reading my angsty tale of desire and conflict.

If you enjoyed this book and wish to support me, please consider leaving a review. Without the support of a publishing house behind me, most of my support comes from readers just like you, and the best way you can support me is by posting a review—no matter how short :)

All my love,

**x Aurora**

# FURTHER READING

**If you loved the academia in this book, and were curious about some of the texts mentioned, or wish to channel ♥Sophie vibes♥, here are some books you might want to check out.**

**Othello** – William Shakespeare
(Play – Explores themes of longing, jealousy and prejudice.)

**Hamlet** – William Shakespeare
(Play – Explores themes of power, revenge and sex.)

**Persuasion** – Jane Austen
(Novel – Explores themes of longing, love, class and gender inequality. This book inspired many of the themes of Spearcrest Knight.)

**Jane Eyre** – Charlotte Brontë
(Novel – Explores themes of strength, desire and redemption. Also features a boarding school (not in a good way), a hero who does bad things but is full of want, and a heroine who doesn't let her suffering define her.)

# Annotation & Study Guide

## Themes to annotate

- The Themes of **Desire** and **Longing**
- The Themes of **Class Division** (also known as **Social Stratification**), **Class Inequality** and **Social Mobility**
- The Themes of **Power** and **Control**
- The Themes of **Family** and **Friendship**
- The Themes of **Truth**, **Lies**, **Deception** and **Betrayal**

## Critical Thinking Questions

- **Compare the ways in which friendships are pre-**

sented and explore the importance of friendship in the text.

- Between Sophie and Evan, who holds more power, and how is that power presented?

- How is the motif of chess used to explore the theme of power?

# Acknowledgements

*Thank you Karsyn, for being the first person to read this book back when it was something completely different. Your feedback, support and enthusiasm made me feel like I wasn't just writing into the void, and gave me the motivation I needed to keep going.*

*Thank you Joanna, for your time, insight, advice and suggestions. I can't express how grateful I am for the kindness and support you have shown me.*

*Thank you Raven, for being a muse, a rock, an inspiration and an absolute force of nature. You fill me with awe and admiration. This book wouldn't be what it is without you—*

*nor would I.*

# ALSO BY AURORA REED

**Curious about French playboy Sev Montcroix and the mysterious fiancée he *definitely* doesn't want to be engaged to?**

**I've never met a woman impervious to my charm.**
And they all accept my terms—an evening of fun, a night of pleasure, and then we're done. They leave my bed satisfied, and I keep my heart intact.
Until Anaïs Nishinara comes crashing into my life. Our parents arrange our engagement, and they send Anaïs to my school so "we can get to know each other".
Except she's not interested in doing that. She's a weird loner who prefers her sketchbook to the glamour of my old money lifestyle.
*I don't want Anaïs—I don't even like her. So why can't I seem to keep away from her?*
**Séverin Montcroix is a rude, spoilt, arrogant aristocrat.**

And now I'm engaged with him and attending the prestigious Spearcrest Academy where he rules as one of the Young Kings. But I don't believe in kings—or princes, or fairy tales, or love.

I believe in myself, my art, and my plan to get out of this engagement.

Except that for someone who claims to hate being engaged to me, Séverin just refuses to leave me alone.

Is he playing games, or does he have a plan of his own?

*And why is it getting harder to resist his attempts at seduction?*

## Want to find out exactly *what* is going on between Zachary Blackwood and his academic rival Theodora Dorokhova?

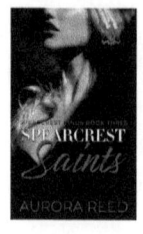

**My life is perfect from the outside.**

But it's all a lie, a perfect illusion crafted to hide the sad truth: my life is a beautiful cage, and my father holds the key. Especially when it comes to my heart.

Dating is strictly forbidden, not that it would matter much to me. If only it wasn't for Zachary Blackwood.

The heir to the centuries-old Blackwood fortune, my academic rival for the past six years... and the only person capable of seeing through the cracks in my facade.

**Theodora Dorokhova is beautiful, intelligent, elusive—and the only student in Spearcrest I can't best.**

No matter how long I try, no matter how hard I work. But this is our final year in Spearcrest, and we've both been selected for an academic excellence programme.

This time, there can only be one victor. And it's going to be me. I won't let anything get in my way—not even my heart.

Because I love Theodora. I love her completely, overwhelmingly, desperately, even though we'll never be together.

*Our love is written in the stars—Theodora is just afraid to look up.*

# About Aurora

Aurora Reed is a coffee-drinking academic who is fascinated by stories of darkness, death and desire. When she's not reading over a cup of black coffee, she can be found roaming the moors or scribbling stories by candlelight.